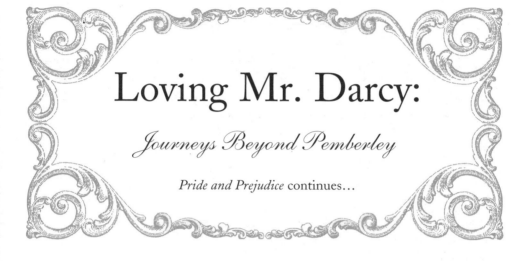

Loving Mr. Darcy:

Journeys Beyond Pemberley

Pride and Prejudice continues…

Sharon Lathan

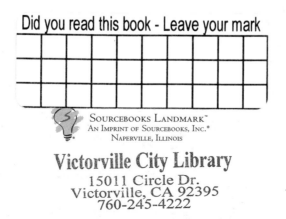
SOURCEBOOKS LANDMARK™
AN IMPRINT OF SOURCEBOOKS, INC.®
NAPERVILLE, ILLINOIS

Published by Sourcebooks Landmark, an imprint of Sourcebooks, Inc.
P.O. Box 4410, Naperville, Illinois 60567-4410
(630) 961-3900
FAX: (630) 961-2168
www.sourcebooks.com

Library of Congress Cataloging-in-Publication Data

Lathan, Sharon.
  Loving Mr. Darcy : journeys beyond Pemberley : Pride and prejudice continues / Sharon Lathan.
      p. cm.
  1. Darcy, Fitzwilliam (Fictitious character)—Fiction. 2. Bennet, Elizabeth (Fictitious character)—Fiction. 3. England—Social life and customs—19th century—Fiction. 4. Domestic fiction. I. Austen, Jane, 1775-1817. Pride and prejudice. II. Title.
  PS3612.A869L68 2009
  813'.6—dc22
                                        2009019075

Printed and bound in the United States of America
VP 10 9 8 7 6 5 4 3

The Darcy Saga

BY SHARON LATHAN

Mr. and Mrs. Fitzwilliam Darcy: Two Shall Become One
Loving Mr. Darcy: Journeys Beyond Pemberley
The Darcys at Year's End

Table of Contents

Cast of Characters

Fitzwilliam Darcy, Master of Pemberley in Derbyshire: 29 years of age, born
   November 10, 1787; parents James and Lady Anne Darcy, both deceased;
   married Elizabeth Bennet on November 28, 1816

Elizabeth Darcy, Mistress of Pemberley: 21 years of age, born May 28, 1795;
   second Bennet daughter

Georgiana Darcy: 17 years of age; sister of Mr. Darcy with guardianship shared
   by her brother and cousin, Col. Fitzwilliam; companion is Mrs. Annesley

Col. Richard Fitzwilliam: 31 years of age; cousin and dear friend to Mr. Darcy;
   second son of Lord and Lady Matlock; regiment stationed in London

Lord Matlock, the Earl of Matlock: Darcy's Uncle Malcolm, brother to Lady
   Anne Darcy; ancestral estate is Rivallain in Matlock, Derbyshire

Lady Matlock, the Countess of Matlock: Darcy's Aunt Madeline, wife to Lord
   Matlock; mother of Jonathan, Annabella, and Richard

Jonathan Fitzwilliam: Heir to the Matlock earldom, eldest Fitzwilliam son; wife
   is *Priscilla*

Charles Bingley: 25 years of age; longtime friend of Mr. Darcy; currently resides
   at Netherfield Hall in Hertfordshire; married Jane Bennet on November
   28, 1816

Jane Bingley: elder sister of Elizabeth and eldest Bennet daughter; wife of Mr. Bingley

Caroline Bingley: unmarried sister of Charles Bingley

Louisa Hurst: married sister of Charles Bingley; husband is *Mr. Arbus Hurst*; residence London

Mr. and Mrs. Bennet: Elizabeth's parents; reside at Longbourn in Hertfordshire with two middle daughters, *Mary* and *Kitty*

Mary Bennet: Elizabeth's sister; middle Bennet daughter

Katherine (Kitty) Bennet: Elizabeth's sister; fourth Bennet daughter

Edward and Violet Gardiner: uncle and aunt of Elizabeth; reside in Cheapside, London

Dr. George Darcy: Mr. Darcy's uncle; brother to James Darcy

Lady Catherine de Bourgh: Mr. Darcy's aunt; sister to Lady Anne Darcy; residence Rosings Park, Kent

Anne de Bourgh: daughter of Lady Catherine; Mr. Darcy's cousin

Stephen Lathrop: Cambridge friend of Mr. Darcy; resides at Stonecrest Hall in Leicestershire; wife is *Amelia*

Henry Vernor: family friend of the Darcys; residence is Sanburl Hall near Lambton, Derbyshire; wife is *Mary*, daughter is *Bertha*

Gerald Vernor: son of Henry Vernor; childhood friend of Mr. Darcy; wife is *Harriet*; resides at Sanburl Hall

Albert Hughes: childhood friend of Mr. Darcy; wife is *Marilyn*

Rory Sitwell: Derbyshire resident and Cambridge friend of Mr. Darcy; wife is *Julia*; residence Reniswahl Hall near Staveley

George and Alison Fitzherbert: Derbyshire residents

Clifton and Chloe Drury: Derbyshire residents and friends; residence Locknell Hall near Derby

Dr. Raul Penaflor Aleman de Vigo: Spanish associate of Dr. George Darcy

Joshua Daniels: son and partner of Mr. Darcy's London solicitor, *Andrew Daniels*

Mrs. Reynolds: Pemberley housekeeper

Mr. Taylor: Pemberley butler

Mr. Keith: Mr. Darcy's steward

Samuel Oliver: Mr. Darcy's valet

Marguerite Charbonneau: Mrs. Darcy's maid

Phillips, Watson, Tillson, Georges, Rothchilde: Pemberley footmen

Mr. Clark: Pemberley head groundskeeper

Mr. Thurber: Pemberley head groomsman

Mrs. Langton: Pemberley cook

Mr. Anders: head coachman

Mrs. Smyth: Darcy House housekeeper

Mr. Travers: Darcy House butler

Reverend Bertram: Rector of Pemberley Chapel

Madame du Loire: Modiste in Lambton

CHAPTER ONE

Hertfordshire

ELIZABETH DARCY STOOD NEXT to Georgiana on the massive portico before the main doors to Pemberley. They were dressed in their traveling clothes and were waiting patiently for the Master of Pemberley, who was currently speaking with his steward, Mr. Keith, while the grandest and plushest of the Darcy carriages waited in the drive.

The warmth of May in Derbyshire had set in full force, making the days radiant with bright sunshine until late into the evening. The vast gardens of Pemberley were responding to the weather as Mr. Clark and his staff diligently engineered the grounds, which were now bursting in nearly eye-piercing splendor with every color of the rainbow. Every species of tree indigenous to England, and many that were not, enhanced the landscape with diverse shades of green and leaves in a multitude of shapes and sizes. Lizzy had regained her strength and mobility by traversing the miles of pathways weaving through the varied gardens. The by-product of her wanderings was a familiarity with and a deepening love for this place that was now her home.

Lizzy dreamily mused at how tremendously she had changed in the nearly five and a half months since she ascended the steps to Pemberley as a nervous bride. Outwardly, her entire appearance was drastically altered; gowns, jewels, and furs beyond her vaguest imaginings six months ago were now typical. Her hair, even in its traveling coif, was superior to anything she had ever fashioned previously. She was largely unaware of it, but there was a serenity and grace to her bearing that had not been present before. She would forever laugh spontaneously and carry a ready quip on her lips, but her character was notably more refined and softened. The minute gestures and vocal intonations associated with the social etiquette of the upper classes had permeated her being unconsciously.

Inwardly, she recognized a happiness and contentment that anchored her soul. Although there remained an enormous amount of Pemberley's management and the Darcy business affairs that she did not understand, her role as Mistress of Pemberley was a comfortable and accepted one. Her place in the household and the community was firm, and her confidence was secure. This massive house, which had frankly frightened her to death initially, was now home. She no longer walked through the endless halls with feelings of paralyzing awe and unworthiness. In five short months, she had grown to love the manor and its surrounds with a devotion transcending anything she had ever felt for Longbourn. Already she missed the library and bedchamber and sitting room and, well, all of it! The approximately six to seven weeks of their planned absence stretched before her as an empty sadness despite her excitement to see her family, and it was necessary to exert every ounce of self will to not rush inside for one last glance.

At that moment her husband strode out the door with the purposeful and powerful gait uniquely his own, mien intense and serious as he imparted a few last minute instructions to his steward. He paused as Mr. Keith commented about something. Lizzy smiled in admiration at the picture he presented. Commanding all to attention as he stood with shoulders back, masculine six-foot-three-inch frame erect, and impeccably dressed, he was elegant and regal, with sonorant voice authoritative. Pure, potent love and incredible pride burst through her as a wave. All that she had become in these past months was due to him. His love for her, his devotion and respect, his loyalty and faith in her capabilities, his steadfastness and latitude, and mostly his intuitive comprehension of her temperament, perceptions, and requirements encouraged her to blossom into the woman she now was.

He nodded in finality, shook the steward's hand, and turned to his sister and wife. Instantly his face lit with a beaming smile, and although no less noble or masterful, his countenance softened considerably.

"My dears, are you ready?"

"Waiting for you, brother."

"Come then," he said, offering an arm to each of his two favorite women in the entire world. He assisted Georgiana into the carriage first, made sure she settled comfortably, and then turned to Lizzy, inquiring with deep concern, "Are you well, beloved?"

"I am fine, William. Do not fuss so." She patted his cheek and took his offered hand.

Leaning close and wholly indifferent to the hovering servants, he kissed her forehead. "I will fuss whether you wish it so or not, Mrs. Darcy. Therefore, you may as well own to any discomfort you have immediately to save me perpetually questioning!"

He assisted her into the carriage, following behind, as she laughed. The truth was that she had been increasingly indisposed for the past five days. She had attempted to hide her infirmity from Darcy, but this was a fruitless endeavor. His eagle-eyed scrutiny and intimacy with all matters regarding his wife penetrated any guile she ventured. The physician had examined her yesterday and confirmed that which they had presumed: She was definitely with child. Despite previously harboring little doubt, the Darcys greeted the valida-tion with jubilance. Although her queasiness and extreme fatigue prevented her from actually jumping for joy, her heart was leaping. Darcy was nearly beside himself with euphoria and only Lizzy pleading with him to enlighten their families first kept him from informing all of Derbyshire.

The doctor had given her a clean bill of health, assuring them both that her symptoms, albeit difficult, were totally standard. He guessed that the worst of her nausea and lethargy would pass in a month or so, at about which time quickening would occur. He had spoken to them both at length and bluntly as to what to expect. As for the trip itself, he saw no reason to postpone or cancel, merely urging them to take it slowly. In light of the occasional mild headaches Lizzy suffered as a lingering effect of her trauma, coupled now with pregnancy, it was wise and essential not to overextend.

With this in mind, Darcy had plotted the normally one-day trip to Netherfield as a two-day journey, departure planned for mid-morning, when Lizzy usually felt better. So here they now were at nearly eleven o'clock and finally pulling out of the long Pemberley drive. The two carriages with their luggage, Samuel, Marguerite, and Mrs. Annesley had left earlier. A courier had been dispatched to London the week prior to prepare Darcy House and another to Hertfordshire for the Bingleys and Bennets.

Lizzy sat close to Darcy, gazing out the open window until Pemberley, with Mr. Keith and Mrs. Reynolds waving their adieus, completely disappeared from view. With a heavy sigh she nestled under his outstretched arm and he hugged her tightly. "I miss it already," she said.

"I always feel that way too," Georgiana replied, "until I get to London. There is so much to entertain! The symphony, the plays, the park across from our townhouse, the little paddle boats on the lake…"

"The shopping," Darcy interrupted with a grin.

Georgiana blushed, "Yes, the shopping as well, although it is you, dear brother, who insist I obtain new gowns and the like. In the end, you buy more for me than I acquire for myself!"

Lizzy laughed. "Somehow that does not surprise me."

Darcy was unfazed. "I shall not apologize in providing for and spoiling the women in my life."

"Elizabeth, you will so enjoy the shopping. We can purchase baby items! Oh, how wonderful it will be." Georgiana glowed and clapped her hands in enthusiasm.

The elder Darcys smiled indulgently, Lizzy too weary and queasy to visualize tromping through the clogged, odiferous streets of London as anything less than horrible. In truth, she was taking this entire excursion one step at a time. Currently, she only focused on seeing her family and proudly being squired about by her handsome husband. As shameful as the emotion was, she experienced fresh surges of vanity at how wonderful he was in every conceivable way—as far as she was concerned—and how amazing that he belonged to her. She glanced up at his face as he exchanged pleasant conversation with his sister, his lush voice vibrating through her body where she pressed against his side. Six months ago she thought her love for him stronger and deeper than her heart could contain, yet it was as a single star in the array of the endless heavens compared to now.

He met her eyes, smiling sweetly as he stroked her cheek and then kissed her briefly. He repositioned his body slightly sideways, long legs stretched completely across the spacious carriage interior, so she could recline onto his chest. She dozed for short spells throughout the journey, snacking sporadically from the generous provisions while Darcy read.

The trip was uneventful, their carriage arriving safely at the inn Darcy had secured near Northampton. From the unrelenting sun and jostling, Lizzy had a moderate headache which she had successfully hid from her husband for the past hour. However, when she exited the carriage, Darcy aiding her, a flash of light reflecting off a glass window of the inn pierced her brain as a bolt. She cried in pain, reflexively released Darcy's hand to press palms to throbbing temples, and crumbled to her knees.

"Elizabeth!" She was in his arms within the span of a heartbeat, Darcy barking orders that sent servants dashing to obey. It was all rather a daze to Elizabeth, her head hammering and stomach churning. In record time she found herself lying on a plush bed with a cold compress over her face, a frantic Darcy at her shivering side.

"Here, my love, drink this. I do not believe you have consumed enough fluids today. An error of mine that I shall not repeat. Marguerite," he said, turning to Lizzy's maid standing nearby, "please retrieve Mrs. Darcy's blue gown and robe." He assisted Lizzy with the glass, unbuttoning her dress as she drank.

"Darling, I will be fine in a moment," she began shakily, but he halted her by pushing the half-empty glass against her lips.

"Hush now, Elizabeth. You need to rest. Drink. That is an order. And then, you must sleep. I will have dinner brought to us later."

"No, William! I will rest here as you wish, but you go and dine with Georgie. Spend the evening with her as we planned. Marguerite will stay with me." He started to protest but she interrupted. "It is merely a headache from the light. My own stupidity for not shutting the shades is to blame. It will fade quickly, these headaches always do. You need to eat a complete meal."

He argued further, but Marguerite assured him she would send for him if needed, and as Lizzy was already slipping into a doze, he reluctantly relented. By the time he returned several hours later she was awake, had eaten a hearty dinner, and the headache had dissipated. She sat on the balcony gazing at the stars when he joined her. She nestled onto his lap, cuddling contentedly, and they talked in hushed tones. She appeared rested and in her usual lively humor, but he remained anxious for her health, internally chastising himself for not lowering the shades.

He kissed the top of her head where it nestled so perfectly under his chin, his arms tightening around her body. "As delightful as it is to stargaze with you,

I insist we retire. You need your rest for the remainder of our journey and I will not risk the health of you or our child."

"You worry unnecessarily, my love. The headache has vanished, I slept, so am well rested, ate an excellent dinner, and am currently blissfully embraced by my handsome husband. What more could a woman possibly want?" She smiled up at his anxious face, wiggled closer, nestled her face into his neck, and bestowed a light kiss. "Actually"—another kiss—"I do have a marvelous idea"—sliding one hand under the hem of his shirt—"for a final activity"—nibbling on an earlobe—"to fully restore my health"—slipping the tip of her tongue into his ear.

"Elizabeth," he sighed, eyes shutting in pleasure, "we should wait until"—he gasped as a nipple was grazed—"settled at Netherfield... please..." Moans interrupted words as she firmly situated his hand on a breast, while lips traveled deliciously along his jaw. "Your headache could return, beloved, listen to me..."

Lizzy stopped his voice by seizing his lower lip and sucking gently. Darcy moaned again, unconsciously rocking a burgeoning arousal into her bottom and rubbing her breast.

"You talk too much, Fitzwilliam."

"No one has ever accused me of that!"

She smiled and began seductively stroking and kissing him. He earnestly struggled to dissuade her but to no avail. Lizzy's obstinacy was manifest in a myriad of ways, and one was when she desired him. Of course, Darcy never strived to avoid romantic activities with his wife so was not well experienced in how to do so!

Lizzy laughed at his stammering opposition and met passion-darkening eyes. "I want to love you, Fitzwilliam, any way you desire. I crave your touch on my skin and your body on mine. I hunger to bring you pleasure and show you how ardent my love for you is." She kissed his eager mouth passionately, overwhelming his senses with her breath and insistence. Pulling away finally, she whispered, "Take me to bed, my lover."

He stared into her eyes for a moment longer, searching carefully for any residual pain or fatigue, but only sheer desire and love shone forth. With a sigh, gripping her securely in strong arms, he stood and entered their bedchamber. The inn's bed was not as large as Pemberley's or as fine, but it was comfortable. Darcy sat on the edge, lying his wife gently back onto the downy comforter while kissing her lovely mouth. Pulling back mere inches, he stroked the hair from her face, twining silky tresses about his fingers as he gazed at her. "Elizabeth, you are incredibly beautiful. With each day your loveliness increases. I do not comprehend how it is possible, yet it is true."

In typical Darcy fashion, he alternately caressed, kissed, and nibbled over each delicate facial feature all the while murmuring endearments and praises for the beauty of his wife. Lizzy's eyes were closed, senses reeling with her husband's words of devotion and heated touch. Darcy paused at her lips, running feathery fingertips over her flesh, observing her rising passion with tremendous satisfaction and indescribable happiness. "Elizabeth," he whispered, "my wife, my lover"—sliding his tongue over her lower lip as she sighed—"mine forever, beloved"—wet tip over the upper lip then slowly sucking between his own—"Mrs. Darcy."

Elizabeth had long succumbed to the amazing reality of her husband. The magnificence of his physique never failed to overwhelm her. His potent masculinity, virility, and stamina continually stunned her. The sensations they roused in each other at the tiniest touch or even at a look staggered her still, yet she embraced it as a heaven gifted expression of the extraordinary bonding love they shared. After nearly six months of marriage, their passion only grew stronger, their lovemaking as necessary as breathing with rarely a day passing without gratifying release and blissful devotion to the other achieved in some manner. They occasionally purposed to experiment with some new technique from the books or an imagined fantasy, yet usually their movements simply evolved naturally at the moment. Opportunities arose spontaneously and were latched onto with zeal, neither of them hesitant to try something new. Trust was unwavering, love unmatched, and desire to please the other first of paramount importance, selfless giving the central goal.

Tonight was different only in Darcy's residual apprehension which induced him to proceed in a reserved manner despite Lizzy's clear desire for a wild interlude. In the end, she did not care, their mutual rapture as blissful and blinding as always.

Slowly, reality and strength returned to them both. Lizzy moved first, turning in his arms that encircled her shuddering, damp skin and bestowed a lingering kiss. "I love you," they spoke concurrently, then chuckled, kissing tenderly.

Smoothing the tangled hair off her forehead, he kissed a perfectly arched brow. "Are you well, my love?"

"I am divine but sleepy. Hold me, William?"

"Forever, Elizabeth. Forever."

The next day dawned as bright and lovely as the previous one. Lizzy felt better than she had in the past week, not even a twinge of morning nausea; however, Darcy insisted on tarrying their departure to be sure. He kept the shades partially drawn and had assured plenty of snacks and liquids packed in the carriage. Lizzy was so continually plied with cups of lemonade and water that frequent stops for physical necessities were required, prolonging the journey. Even so, they arrived at Netherfield by mid-afternoon, greeted enthusiastically by Charles and Jane.

Lizzy's feet barely made contact with solid earth before she was dashing into her sister's embrace. A short curtseyed greeting to Mr. Bingley, and then the two women headed into the manor, arm-in-arm and heads touching as their words spilled over one another.

"Well, Darcy old chap," Mr. Bingley exclaimed by way of greeting, "there you have it. I believe we have been abandoned!"

Darcy smiled indulgently. "Only temporarily, Bingley. Surely they will exhaust their reminiscences and confidences in three or four days and then come crawling back to their mere husbands."

Bingley laughed. "Miss Darcy, I trust you are well? Was the trip too difficult?"

"I am perfect, Mr. Bingley, thank you. And the trip was easy."

They made their way into the house, Bingley asking after Lizzy's health. "She suffered a headache last evening, but today is well. They occur occasionally still but with lessening intensity and frequency. The physician assures us it is to be expected." They had agreed to announce their news once the entire family was together that evening. Darcy privately doubted Lizzy's ability to keep their joy from her sister for even those few hours, but he would not renege on their vow.

"Mr. Bingley, have you prepared the same room for me as before?"

"Yes, Georgiana, we did. Your brother assured me this was your preference."

"Oh, yes! The view is amazing. Thank you. Brother, Mr. Bingley, if you do not mind, I think I would like to rest a bit."

"Of course, dear." Darcy watched her mount the stairs with a smile. "I doubt she is the least bit tired, but male companionship is decidedly boring to a seventeen-year-old girl. I, on the other hand, am in need of a drink. Lead the way, Charles."

Laughing, they made their way into the billiard room, where Bingley poured a whiskey for them both. Sitting onto a comfortably cushioned chair with a sigh of relief, Darcy studied his friend's face. "You look well, Bingley. Marriage agrees with you also, I presume?"

"Very much. I do not require asking you the same question, Darcy. It is evident. By the way, I prepared your room as you requested. The same room you inhabited on your previous visits. A single room." He paused, blushing mildly, the question unasked.

Darcy placidly sipped his drink, gazing at Bingley with amusement, remaining silent.

After a spell, Bingley continued, "Jane was concerned. There is a lovely bedchamber next to yours if…"

"One room will be all that is necessary. I selected that bedchamber when you and I dwelt here last year based on the view and décor. Mrs. Darcy has similar tastes. She will appreciate it with the same enthusiasm, and I am aware of the attached dressing room." He smiled at Bingley's ruddy face. "One bedchamber will be adequate."

Bingley cleared his throat. "So, tell me about the duel. I wish I could have witnessed the encounter." His eyes were bright with a youthful zeal. "I almost pity the fool who would willingly take you on, Darcy."

Darcy smiled grimly, but proceeded to tell the tale.

Down the hall in the parlor, Lizzy and Jane were sharing tea and sisterly conversation. They sat side by side on the sofa chatting companionably, Lizzy sharing her version of the horrific events leading up to and including the duel. Jane shuddered. "How awful, Lizzy. We were so worried. Papa wanted to leave for Pemberley immediately, but Mama was ill with anxiety and begged him to stay." Lizzy made a face but said nothing. Jane continued, "Fortunately, Mr. Darcy sent a second missive soon after informing us of your recovery. Are you wholly restored?"

"Headaches on occasion, that is all. The light, if it is too bright, pains me, but that is lessening. The doctor seems certain that it will resolve in time." Lizzy laughed. "Between my weakness and William's wounds, we have been quite the pair of invalids!"

Jane shuddered once again. "I do not know how you can jest, Lizzy. A duel with swords! I would faint away if Mr. Bingley did something so reckless."

"I did not know until after the fact and I scolded him to be sure. Still, it is rather romantic, do you not think, Jane? Also, Orman received his just reward."

"Has he left Derbyshire?"

"Yes. Apparently, he has an estate in Devonshire. William crippled him. I do not imagine he will hurt any other women."

"I must confess, I cannot picture Mr. Darcy in such a manner. He is so proper and composed. Medieval dueling simply boggles my mind."

Lizzy smiled. "I was not surprised in the least. Remember, during our engagement, how we shared our first kiss experiences, Jane?" Jane blushed and nodded. "I spoke then of William's enthusiasm and you were shocked."

"Please, Lizzy! We should not speak of such things!"

"Oh Jane! You are so silly. We are married women and sisters. If we cannot confide in each other, whom can we talk to?" Lizzy grasped Jane's hands. "I have so missed talking to you! There is no one on earth I can express my joy to as I can to you, dear sister. Are you and Mr. Bingley happy, Jane? You look happy. Please tell me you are as much as William and I!"

"Lizzy, we are extremely happy, but you know it is not my nature to enthuse as you do. You have always yearned for excitement and passion more so than I. There is no doubt you have found both with Mr. Darcy, despite his cool demeanor. Mr. Bingley and I are content and steady in our love, as well as quite joyful."

"How is it living so close to Mama? Tell me truthfully!" Jane attempted to evade but Lizzy laughed at her. "You say more with no words than with paragraphs, Jane! Truly, you and Mr. Bingley should move closer to us. William intends to discuss it with him. Would you not rather have your own home, Jane?"

Jane seemed uncomfortable. "Charles and I have talked about this very matter, Lizzy. He would like to have his own home—our own home. The question is where. We both love it here and Mama would be so distressed if we left. Charles inquired about purchasing Netherfield, but the family does not wish to permanently part with it." Jane shook her head. "I leave these decisions to him. He will do what he believes is best."

Lizzy would have continued the conversation, but the very topics of their discussion entered the parlor at that moment. Darcy went immediately to Jane. "Mrs. Bingley, my wife stole you away forthwith and I did not have the opportunity to greet you properly." He bowed low over her hand. "Thank you, dear sister, for opening your home to us."

Jane blushed prettily.

They all parted then to dress for dinner. Lizzy, as Darcy anticipated, adored the rooms selected for them. They were not as plush or spacious as their chambers at Pemberley, but the décor was the same rustic tones they both preferred. When Lizzy rejoined her husband in the tiny sitting room it was to mutual approbation. Darcy, in blue as usual, wore the pale azure waistcoat Lizzy had gifted him at Christmas; he was incredibly handsome and his eyes sparkled as he gazed in admiration at his wife. Lizzy wore a new but simple gown of lavender and gold chenille with the Darcy strand of pearls around her neck, her lush hair elegantly coiffed by Marguerite, as always.

Darcy kissed his wife's hand and then her cheek. "Are you well, beloved?"

"Do you not ever tire of asking me that, Mr. Darcy?" she teased and he laughed, clasping her arm in his as they exited the room.

It was only fifteen minutes later that the Bennet carriage arrived. Mrs. Bennet was honestly at a loss as to whom to gush over first: her daughter in finery and jewels or her illustrious son-in-law. Darcy had discovered early in his engagement that the best way to deal with Lizzy's mother was to politely and formally greet her then pointedly ignore her. This form of subtle intimidation was a pose Mr. Darcy was expert at, and since Mrs. Bennet truthfully did annoy him profoundly, it was a natural response on his part.

He met the problem head on by purposefully placing his towering body directly in her path, seizing her hand smoothly for a brief kiss, and addressing her with a deep bow and voice lower than normal. "Mrs. Bennet. What an absolute delight it is to see you again. If I may be so bold, you are radiant tonight. Blue becomes you, and I daresay you have shed ten years since last we met."

Without skipping a beat or waiting for a reply—not that one was forthcoming from the stunned Mrs. Bennet—he adroitly stepped to the side and looked at Mr. Bennet. The older man's eyes were twinkling and a cryptic smile, which Darcy had initially found so disconcerting but now delighted in, hovered about his lips. He actually winked at his son-in-law and Darcy solemnly winked back. The two gentlemen bowed and greeted each other formally, barely managing to get the preliminaries out of the way before Lizzy was in her father's arms. Lizzy had jumped at the opportunity provided by her mother's paralysis to greet her father first. Darcy smiled at the obvious joy the two felt at seeing each other after such a long absence. During the engagement, he and Mr. Bennet had developed a relationship bordering on friendship, or at least as close as two men of a nearly thirty-year age gap and vastly differing upbringings could attain. Darcy had been continually amazed at the breadth of the older man's knowledge of literature, science, and politics. Although they argued on some matters, it was in a friendly debating sort of way and they both enjoyed the challenge provided. More and more often, he had found himself secreting away from Mrs. Bennet's boisterous presence to repose in Mr. Bennet's study over brandies and quiet conversation. Lizzy had learned that it was the usual place to find her betrothed when he mysteriously disappeared.

"Lizzy," Mr. Bennet declared with heartfelt relief, "my Lizzy! I have missed you so." Darcy turned away to greet his new sisters and to allow father and daughter a moment. Unfortunately, Mrs. Bennet had recovered her voice and the private interlude was interrupted with her shrill exclamations. Lizzy was captured in a soft embrace and female prattling as both her mother and Kitty descended upon her. Mary, Darcy noted, hung back and was shyly approached by Georgiana, the two young women having formed a tentative friendship prior to the wedding. As the group slowly edged their way into the parlor, Darcy lingered to the rear, as did Mr. Bennet.

"Mr. Darcy, my daughter appears well. Quite well, in fact. I want to thank you for your constant correspondence during her illness. I am sure it must not have been easy for you to take the time."

"You are welcome, sir. Nothing about that episode was easy, but it is behind us now and she has nearly fully recovered." Mr. Bennet detected the note of strain in the younger man's voice and the hint of residual pain in his eyes despite Darcy's careful regulation. He smiled. Any doubts he may have had initially of Darcy's affection toward Lizzy had been dispelled within a week of their betrothal. He further saw the evidence of the deep love that had grown between the two already in the glances shared as they made their way into the parlor.

"She is more beautiful than I remember her," Mr. Bennet continued. "I would not guess her needing to recover any further. She positively glows. Your doing, I am certain." He glanced slyly at Darcy, who looked at him sharply.

"Whatever do you mean, sir?"

"Calm down, my boy. Any secrets you two have are safe with me for the present. I merely was referring to the flush on her cheeks, the radiant happiness she exudes, and the serenity about her. I am familiar with the pose from Jane, but never Lizzy." He clapped Darcy on the back as he moved away, "You have made this old gentleman's heart shine, and I thank you."

Darcy stood there wondering as Mr. Bennet strolled to greet his other son-in-law, catching Lizzy's eyes from across the room. She raised an eyebrow in question with a subtle nod toward her father. He shrugged imperceptibly. Mr. Bennet was far too astute for his own good.

As usual in these family gatherings, Darcy tended to retreat to quiet corners as often as possible. Lizzy and Jane were in the center of a female cluster, all the women seemingly talking at once, Darcy amazed that any of them could distinguish a word the other said. Even his normally bashful sister was caught up in the enthusiasm, which educed a pleased smile.

Dinner was announced; Darcy escorted his wife and sister and was happily ensconced between Lizzy and Mr. Bennet at the table. Conversation flowed in the rather jumbled manner that Darcy associated with the Bennets. Gradually, he had familiarized his sensibilities to what society would universally deem a hideous breach in dining etiquette, seeing beyond the outrageousness of it to recognize the relaxed harmony. It was not comfortable for him, decades of protocol hindering full involvement, but he appreciated it.

He and Lizzy touched clandestinely under the table whenever possible, sparking humorous memories of stolen caresses at this very table during their engagement. Leaning over at one point, Darcy whispered in her ear, "When do you wish to announce our news, beloved?"

She graced him with a beatific smile and a squeeze to his knee. "After dessert, otherwise the entire meal will be delayed."

By the time the dessert course was served, Darcy was ready to erupt with impatience. Standing suddenly and thereby instantly commanding the attention of all at the table without uttering a word, Darcy cleared his throat. Glancing at his beaming wife, he grasped her hand then addressed the staring group. Only Georgiana knew what was to be declared, and she was grinning.

"Pardon me for the interruption. Elizabeth and I have an announcement that we no longer wish to delay in imparting. We have suspected for some weeks now but have just two days ago had it confirmed." He paused dramatically, rather enjoying the varying expressions of curiosity, dawning enlightenment, and frank bafflement that graced the features around the table. Lizzy began to giggle under her breath, knowing her staid husband's flair for the theatric. Smiling, he resumed, "Elizabeth's accident created a scare for us, but we now are certain, so can state with confidence, that we will be, roughly sometime in early December, welcoming our first child."

He kissed her hand as everyone lurched to their feet to converge on the jubilant couple. Darcy's hand was pumped and his back was slapped; Lizzy was hugged and kissed. The party gradually retired to the parlor where Lizzy was plied with questions and baby plans were set in motion. Meanwhile, the gentlemen retreated from the female twittering to celebrate and congratulate the father-to-be with glasses of Bingley's finest port.

As always, Darcy's gaze frequently alit on his wife. Therefore, he readily interpreted her mildly increasing pallor and weakening smile as a sign of fatigue. With alacrity, he weaved his way to her side, smoothly extracting her from the clutches of her family with apologies. Once outside the room, he swept her into his arms, ignoring her protests.

"Darling, I am merely tired not incapacitated!"

"Do not argue with me, Mrs. Darcy. Have you not deduced that I simply create reasons to hold you in my embrace?"

"Oh, is that what you are doing?" she asked, laughing.

"Of course." He kissed her forehead then grinned. "I figure I better take advantage of the opportunities before you are so rotund that I cannot pick you up."

The five days they tarried in Hertfordshire were filled with a vast number of visitations and numerous memories.

Sir William Lucas and his wife, Lady Lucas, hosted a dinner party at Lucas Lodge the second evening after the Darcy's arrival. A generous portion of the four and twenty families of distinction attended. Darcy had met most of them at various events during the time of his previous stays in the region, although the impression he had made on the bulk of them had not been favorable. With the exception of the various young ladies in residence, who had overlooked his reserve in recognition of his wealth and position, many of them had simply abandoned any attempt at ingratiation, finding him aloof and impossible to become acquainted with. During his engagement, Darcy had pointedly striven to rectify the damage done and had largely succeeded, except for the previously mentioned young women who then had no interest in him whatsoever.

Nonetheless, aside from Mr. Bingley and Mr. Bennet, not a single man could claim to know him even moderately. In truth, Darcy could care less. Never a man to make friends with ease or to have an abundance of confidants, Darcy saw no point in endeavoring to form relationships in Hertfordshire. This honest assessment had disturbed him only in that he wished to please his fiancée. He had assumed that she, sociable and popular as she was, would desire him to be the same. He was in error. The agony he had suffered over those initial weeks of forced gregariousness had taken their toll on him, Elizabeth noting his constant tension, increased fidgeting, and loss of appetite. In another one of their forthright conversations, she had bluntly confronted him over his obvious distress. He evaded, fearful of her disappointment, but in the end she drew it out of him. With a multitude of assurances, dangerous kisses, and embraces, she finally convinced him that she loved him as he was and that it mattered naught what the people of Hertfordshire thought.

His relief had been palpable. Now, all these months later, confident in his marriage and the mutual admiration he and Elizabeth shared, not to mention his unrelenting joy, Darcy discovered that there were actually several men he rather liked. Bingley, a walking example of congeniality, had readily made friends with nearly every man his age for miles around. The newly relaxed Mr. Darcy rapidly saw his social calendar filled with shooting, horseback riding, a billiard tournament, a turn at the faro tables, and luncheon twice.

Lizzy was delighted to see her husband busily entertained. Knowing that he was happily enjoying himself with Charles and the rest at the various male pursuits he had neglected over the past months gave her the freedom to devote her time elsewhere. Most afternoons were passed at someone's house for tea, Lizzy utilizing the time to renew old friendships. However, her main purpose in visiting home was to be with her family. In a strange turn of events, Darcy became the social butterfly flittering hither and yon, while Lizzy rarely left Longbourn or Netherfield.

Lizzy's pregnancy symptoms vacillated, but her overall health seemed to be improving. She did not suffer a headache the entire time at Hertfordshire and slept very well, so her fatigue was minimal and her morning nausea was mild. Jane assured Darcy that she would keep a close eye on her sister while he was gone. Lizzy merely smiled indulgently at her husband's solicitude, relieved when he apparently abdicated his self-proscribed guard duty, wholly unaware that Jane and every servant in both households were enlisted to watch her carefully and notify him instantly of any troubles.

The men left each day shortly after breakfast, leaving Jane and Lizzy alone. Georgiana and Mary had taken quite a liking to each other, so Mary had been invited to stay at Netherfield and the two girls quickly became inseparable, to everyone's surprise. Darcy had been concerned that Kitty would resent her exclusion, but the opposite was true. Kitty found her sister and Georgiana dull as posts so was perfectly content to be left out.

Lizzy and Jane, therefore, had an abundant amount of time each day to talk. Walking about the Netherfield gardens the morning after their arrival, Jane inadvertently broached the same topic of conversation so amusing to Darcy when Bingley advanced it.

"Lizzy, did you sleep well last night?"

"Very well, thank you, Jane. I woke refreshed and only slightly queasy. Mrs. Reynolds taught Marguerite a tea recipe that nearly always calms my stomach. The tea along with a few pieces of toast before I rise, and I generally avoid any severe illness."

"That is a relief. I was concerned."

"You need not worry yourself, Jane. Marguerite dotes on me and has the tray at my bedside before I fully awake. William rings for her as soon as I begin to stir. Between the two of them, I am well cared for." She laughed at the understatement.

Jane, however, was looking at her in astonishment. "Mr. Darcy is with you every morning? How early does he arise?"

Lizzy was baffled. "He is an early riser, as am I, if you remember. Lately I have tended to sleep later, prompting him to leave for a ride or business before I wake. We are both hoping the physician is correct in this blasted fatigue being of short duration. I hate being tired all the time! I have no patience… Jane, why are you looking at me like that?"

"He comes to your room every morning?! Is he so demanding, as Mother said?"

Lizzy stared for a moment then burst out laughing. "Oh, Jane! Shall I shock you further by confessing that I am every bit as 'demanding' as he is? William does not 'come to me' in the morning. He never leaves me. Neither of us wishes it otherwise."

Jane was blushing but studying Lizzy's face closely. "He… shares your room with you?"

"In a manner of speaking. We only have one room. Well, technically, there is his mother's bedchamber, but I do not use it. His chambers are now ours. Jane, do not you and Mr. Bingley ever stay together?"

Jane grew even redder and resumed walking briskly. "Lizzy, we should change the subject."

"Oh no, dear sister! You tendered the topic. If you assure me that you are perfectly content with your arrangement then I will desist. However, I saw a curiosity in your eyes. Tell me truthfully." She grasped her sister's arm until she halted.

Jane avoided Lizzy's eyes, but Lizzy could see the tears shimmering. "I do not think Charles wishes to stay with me," she said in a small voice.

"Why would you think that?"

"He… comes to me frequently and it is wonderful. He holds me for a bit, then he… leaves."

Lizzy was frowning. "What does he say when you ask him to stay?"

Jane looked at her with absolute mortification. "Ask him to stay? Lizzy, I could never do that!"

"Why ever not? He is your husband. You should be able to discuss all subjects. Perhaps he believes you want him to leave." Lizzy clasped her sister's arms and intently met her eyes. "Jane, I will not presume to assert that your relationship with Charles should be as mine is with William. However, I will say with confidence that you have listened far too much to Mama's advice. I know several incontrovertible facts. One, sharing a bed with your husband, and sleeping in his arms is heavenly, joyous, blissful, and practical! I was not cold once all winter! Second, the intimacy engendered adds a depth to the relationship beyond comprehension. There is truly not a single matter William and I cannot talk about. We share everything."

She linked Jane's arm in hers and resumed walking. "I know Mr. Bingley fairly well and believe you would be surprised at how deep his love for you. This is my suggestion. Tonight do not wait for him to come to you. Go to him instead and tell him how you feel. Be bold for once, Jane."

"I do not know if I can do that, Lizzy."

"Oh, for heaven's sake, Jane! This is Mr. Bingley and you: the sweetest couple in all of England. He will not bite you!"

That afternoon, after lunch and tea at Longbourn, Lizzy returned to Netherfield for a nap. Darcy and Bingley had been out all day; doing what, she had no idea. She woke to a shadowy room and the pressure of soft lips on her brow. With a happy sigh, she gathered her husband into her arms, pulling him onto the bed.

"Elizabeth, it is time to prepare for dinner. Lucas Lodge, you recall." Despite his words he planted tender kisses along her neck.

"Later, husband. I have sorely missed you. What have you been up to all day?"

"Bingley wanted to show me some property twenty miles north that he is interested in. I found all manner of distasteful proofs as to why the manor and grounds were unacceptable."

"You are a devious man, Mr. Darcy! Has anyone ever enlightened you to that fact?"

He assumed a haughty purse to his lips. "Only employing my business acumen in the service of a friend. I know for a certainty that the Hasberry estate in Derbyshire is far superior to this property."

"And the fact that it sits less than fifteen miles from Pemberley has no bearing whatsoever?"

"Absolutely none. Now kiss me, beloved wife, and then tell me about your day. How are you feeling?"

"Very well. I had a delightful afternoon with my family, a refreshing nap despite the lonely bed, and a most enlightening conversation with Jane this morning." She proceeded to tell him about her discussion with Jane.

"Interesting," he murmured, relating his amusing conversation with Bingley about their room assignments. "Lends an added spin to the questioning. Not certain what I can do about it, though. As close as Charles and I are, we do not speak of such things. I am fairly confident he was as innocent as I was upon marriage. More so probably, as his education was not as inclusive and he is younger, less well traveled. His only journey out of England was when we went to France two years ago. I do not warrant him such a slave to convention that he would not deign to sleep with his wife though, and I know how deep his love for Jane."

"I wish to see them as fulfilled and complete as we are."

He hugged her to his side. "I know you do, beloved. Yet who are we to say they are not? All relationships are different. However, I will observe Charles and exploit any vantage offered."

In the end, it was not necessary for either of them to act. All through the dinner party at Lucas Lodge, Jane seemed pensive, eyeing her husband with a lingering, thoughtful gaze. Darcy and Lizzy noticed, exchanging occasional knowing glances.

It was late when they returned to Netherfield. Lizzy was exhausted, actually having fallen asleep on Darcy's shoulder in the carriage. He assisted her up the stairs, murmuring their goodnights to the Bingleys. A brief backward glance as Darcy opened their door, revealed Jane clutching Charles's hand outside Bingley's bedchamber. The last picture visible was Jane snaking her arms about her husband's neck with clear intent before he had even latched the door. Darcy chuckled softly. Unfortunately, his night did not end as blissfully, his wife already soundly asleep when he reentered their chamber. He nestled close, stroking her face gently, happily gazing at her beauty for a half hour or more before sleep claimed him.

CHAPTER TWO

Billiards

LIZZY WOKE AS THE sun crested the horizon, the merest traces of sunlight entering the darkly curtained room. Darcy lay on his side next to her, one arm lightly draped over her abdomen, his top leg trapping hers. It was rare, even prior to her accident, to wake before him. Consequently, she seldom had the opportunity to simply stare at his sleeping form. She grasped her adventitious good fortune, especially as she diagnosed a state of total wellness for the first morning since early April! Her mind was racing ahead with urges growing as she lovingly admired him. He slept with lips parted, hair in utter disarray, face relaxed and so youthful. His body was akin to an oven in generating heat. It was wonderful in the winter, Lizzy had discovered, as she had not once been cold at night for the first time in the whole of her life. Now that it was summer, it meant that he tended to shove all the covers off, lying mostly exposed. Such was the case now. The thin blanket swathing her body was barely touching him, loosely cloaking hips, lower back, and one leg only. The remainder of his perfect physique was bared for her rapt inspection.

With a delighted smile, she ran dainty fingers through his hair, down to a firm shoulder and chest, edging closer to him incrementally. He slept on.

How many mornings he had roused her in a similar manner were unfeasible to recollect. Therefore, the twinge of guilt felt at disturbing his slumber was overshadowed by her desires and the certitude that he would not be annoyed in the least.

Darcy, she knew, was a deep sleeper. He required little sleep overall, a mere six to seven hours more than adequate, and his body utilized the time proficiently by entering a state nearing hibernation. Therefore, she had the advantage and used it. Without haste and as delicately as possible, she removed the blanket and commenced caressing him. He sighed faintly a few times, stretched once, and rolled toward his back thus exposing more of him to her tender touch. He slept on, breathing regularly for quite some time as Lizzy thoroughly enjoyed herself.

Lizzy never wearied of simply studying her husband. Knowing the delights of his flesh and the perfection to his figure had on several occasions led to her embarrassment. Her decadent musings frequently invaded her during evenings reposing in the parlor. If Darcy glanced up and caught the gleam in her eyes as she stared, he would smile and wink or raise a brow. However, Georgiana had far too often been the one to notice the frankly sexual gazes between her brother and his wife or to interrupt them in an amorous embrace, to their extreme mortification. Yet, they could not seem to stop themselves. Last night, at the Lucas dinner party, Lizzy is almost certain her father saw her run a hand over Darcy's derriere. Earlier in the day, Mr. Bingley had walked into the library mere seconds after they separated from a particularly heated embrace with Darcy massaging one breast and Lizzy brushing the slight bulge emerging in his breeches.

This morning, contemplating the vision before her feasting eyes, Lizzy could raise only the slightest remorse. Honestly, as logical as it was to conclude that they needed to reign in their passion when in public, she had no desire to do so. Let the world know how ardently they loved each other, and if it disapproved, so be it. Lizzy would never regret a single expression of her devotion to Darcy, and she knew he felt the same. Lightly, she trailed her fingertips down the line of hair leading from breastbone to groin, circling then dipping into his navel. He slept on but the unconscious response as her fingers feathered over thighs, groin, and lower abdomen was instinctive.

Steadily, she emboldened her attack, adding kisses to the agenda, finally noting a variance to his respirations and a definite physical consequence to her ministrations. With a mighty sigh of pleasure, he drew her to his lips and kissed enthusiastically before briefly encountering her shining eyes. With a sultry smile he sighed again, closing his eyes and sprawling fully on his back, bestowing unimpaired access.

My lord, he is gorgeous!

Never one to refuse an offered gift, Lizzy besieged his body with relish. Seriously kissing all over his muscular, downy-haired chest, Lizzy stimulated him in all the ways she knew he adored. She knew how sucking his nipples incited him, that lightly tickling down his rib cage and sides thrilled him, nibbling his ears drove him insane, and kissing his neck and the pulsing hollow of his throat made him groan. She did all this and more, delighting in rallying his urgency. Darcy was wholly aroused in minutes, fists clenched together to avoid taking control, breathing heavily, and rumbling deeply in his chest. Nonetheless, Lizzy took her time, glorying in the sight of clenching thighs, rippling abdominal muscles, and thick, wiry hairs… all of him virile and powerful and alluring.

She sat astride him, elbows locked and hands pressed onto his chest, fingertips embedded in hard muscle ridges as she moved, asking throatily, "Reminiscent of the dreams you had when first staying here, Fitzwilliam?"

He merely groaned, grabbing her arms and pulling her onto his body for a voracious kiss.

Down the hall, in the Master of Netherfield's bedchamber, Jane Bingley was being woken up in a similar fashion for the first time since her marriage. It was fortunate that the walls of Netherfield were very thick and that Georgiana, whose room was situated roughly midway between the twin dens of delight, was as deep a sleeper as her brother.

The couples entered the breakfast room much later, Mary and Georgiana already dining. Georgiana glanced up at the glowing countenances of her brother and sister-in-law, youthful innocence nonetheless fully aware of why they beamed and surreptitiously touched while filling their plates. Darcy piled his high, ravenous for good reason, and even Lizzy discovered her appetite tremendously improved. Georgiana never tired of witnessing her brother's uncontrollable happiness; her love for him was so heartfelt that observing the joy he and Elizabeth shared warmed her soul and overcame the occasional embarrassment at witnessed embraces.

Minutes later, the Bingleys breezed in. A rosy-cheeked Jane, arm in arm with her husband, met Lizzy's eyes for the briefest second. Lizzy nearly spit her tea at the supreme smugness visible on her sister's face. Mr. Bingley was frankly grinning like a fool, face ruddy. Darcy and Elizabeth exchanged a meaningful look, vainly struggling not to laugh.

Darcy greeted his sister with a kiss to the cheek then sat across from her and beside his wife. Looking to Mary, who sat next to Georgiana, Darcy inquired, "Miss Mary, I trust you slept well?"

Mary jolted at the sound of Mr. Darcy's voice. Despite the near constant presence of the man at Longbourn during the course of her sister's engagement, Mary had probably exchanged twenty words with him. She was not afraid of him, exactly, merely unsure. He intimidated her, although she conceded that he did nothing to specifically tender the emotion, having been unfailingly polite and almost pleasant. Mary simply had no idea how to converse with him, nor any other man for that matter. She flushed at his serious gaze, briefly encountered his eyes with an expression of perplexity, as if having suddenly been addressed by a frog, and stammered something along the lines of concurrence regarding her night's slumber, then commenced studying her plate as if the answers to the world's problems dwelt therein.

Darcy frowned slightly. Miss Kitty he understood; found her annoying to be sure, but he understood her. Miss Mary baffled him. That she was somewhat shy he acknowledged, yet her shyness was not nearly as profound as Georgiana's or even his own. He had observed her in many lengthy conversations. She avoided men like the plague, universally treating them all as if inferior creatures, or at least so alien as to preclude any possible communion. She seemed to have not the slightest tinge of humor. Of course, many had erringly assumed the same of him, so he was willing to extend latitude. However, try as he might, he could not break through her shell. Frankly, he could not fathom why Georgiana had befriended her or what the two talked about.

His reverie was interrupted by Jane and Bingley taking their seats. Bingley continued to grin. Jane was her usual poised, serene self, although her color was definitely pinker than normal. With a small smile, Darcy spoke purposefully, "Mrs. Bingley, you slept well also, I trust? Refreshed and prepared to meet the day's activities?"

His peripheral vision noted Elizabeth biting her lip, a gesture he well distinguished as one employed to prevent laughing. Bingley coughed, blushed scarlet, and hid behind his napkin. Jane, surprisingly, engaged Darcy's eyes with a calm, albeit mildly teasing smile, replying, "Why, yes indeed, Mr. Darcy. I believe I slept better than I have in months. Thank you for inquiring."

Georgiana noted the strange semblances on all the adult faces at the table, perceived the undercurrent of jesting, but could not divine the cause. Mary decreed them all mad and categorically dismissed them. Breakfast proceeded from there in a predictable and customary fashion. The gentlemen ate heartily, discussing with enthusiasm the planned billiard tournament to commence at mid-morning. The women planned an excursion into Meryton for shopping and lunch at the Raven Inn, Mrs. Bennet and Kitty to accompany them.

They parted shortly thereafter, Darcy sequestering Elizabeth in the library for a private farewell. "Are you over your nausea, dearest?" Lizzy had eaten halfway through her breakfast and then been unexpectedly hit with a severe aversion to eggs, inducing her to hastily rise and exit the room for the nearest chamber pot. Fortunately, she had not been ill, but it had teetered on the edge for a spell. Now, she felt almost completely restored, as long as she did not envision eggs.

"Yes, love, I am fine. If my oddly wavering stomach contortions were not so incredibly bothersome I suppose I would find it comical!"

He laughed and kissed her. "Do not tax yourself, Elizabeth. I will not be here to paddle you if you overdo, so I trust you to care for yourself and our baby."

"I promise to behave. Now," she said, straightening his flawlessly arranged cravat, "you enjoy yourself. I want to hear all the details of how my handsome husband prevailed at billiards, leaving a collection of crushed egos in his wake."

꩜

The gentlemen of Meryton and the surrounding areas, when not gathering for smaller private socializations in their homes, met informally at the two pubs or the lone coffeehouse for gaming and to discuss politics and business. A large, red brick building located on the main street and annexed to the Ox Horn pub was humorously and pretentiously called the Reading Room, due to the cozy parlor in the rear dedicated to gentlemen's intellectual concourse while smoking imported cigars and drinking fine liquors. However, it was the billiard room that drew the largest crowds most days.

The large space housed several billiards tables, along with a few chess and backgammon tables. Darcy and Bingley had visited a few times during Darcy's previous sojourns; however, Darcy, unsurprisingly, had preferred the quiet solitude of Netherfield. Bingley adored socializing and frequently passed afternoons and occasional evenings with the young men of the community.

Last evening, during the dinner party at Lucas Lodge, Darcy had been invited to partake in the billiard tournament scheduled for today. Apparently, his reputation as a skilled player had preceded him; several of the local citizens were familiar with the name *Darcy* being whispered with reverence through the billiard halls of Town. Mr. Darcy was by no means the preeminent player in all of London, but he ranked among the top twenty. As a guest in the area, it certainly was neither expected nor necessary to include him, so he was honored by the inclusion. If it were any other contest, Darcy may have felt obliged to decline the offer or to curb his mastery. Not with billiards, though. After horseback riding, and of course his private activities with his adorable wife, there was no pastime Darcy loved more than billiards.

Mr. Darcy and Mr. Bingley were greeted primarily with enthusiasm. Sir Lucas, Mr. Bennet, and Mr. Phillips were already present as the designated officials for the tournament, busily organizing the equipment and records required for the matches.

"Mr. Darcy! Mr. Bingley!" Sir Lucas exclaimed, beaming at them. "What a delight it is to have you both join us in our meager entertainment."

Bingley bowed. "Thank you, Sir Lucas. However, my occupation shall be that of a spectator. My billiard skills are minimal. For cert not a match for Darcy here, so it would be futile for me to attempt besting him."

Darcy bowed deprecatingly, nonetheless noting several perturbed expressions amongst the gathered men. Apparently, not all the competitors were delighted to have an expert challenger. Those gents who chose to participate in the contest signed the ledger and their names were placed into a hat. The simple expedience of having Sir Lucas, as the highest ranking man in the region, draw the individual names for the first round hailed the commencement of the tournament.

The hall was packed. Chairs and stools were placed along the walls and the game tables removed for extra space. A long side bar was erected with a steady supply of finger foods provided, while beverages of all varieties, alcoholic as well as tea, coffee, cocoa, and juices, were kept flowing in a steady supply from the pub. The atmosphere was jovial and casual, remarkably dissimilar to such events at the billiards rooms in London. Darcy might have been distressed by this, but as a frequent rival of his cousin Richard, who took nothing except his military career seriously, Darcy was immune to constant chatter and distractions.

Darcy was paired with a Mr. Denbigh, a man of some fifty years whom Darcy had met previously. Denbigh, an adequate player offering Darcy a few challenges, was affable and talkative, clearly enjoying himself immensely regardless of the outcome. In the end, Darcy attained the required points with a wide margin, effectively eliminating Denbigh from the match. After a brief respite, Darcy paired with a Mr. Heigt. Heigt was in his early twenties, ruddy faced with flaming red hair, and nearly as tall as Darcy. In appearance, he resembled Bingley, but in temperament was comparable to Darcy. He also left no doubt that he took the match seriously and was not at all pleased to have Darcy partake. With an icy smile, Darcy attacked. No quarter asked and none given, the two men played with careful regulation and intensity. Darcy won with ease, despite Heigt's pose of expertise, and the loser's anger was obvious. Thankfully, he retained his composure and did not make a scene, although he departed shortly thereafter.

His third opponent, Mr. Ravencraw, was a distinguished man in his fifties. Darcy ascertained instantly that here was a first-rate player. In his first true challenge of the match, Darcy called on every skill he possessed. The game was twice as long as the previous two, and Darcy won by a slim margin, thus allowing Ravencraw to remain in the tournament.

Ravencraw bowed. "Excellent game, Mr. Darcy. Your reputation is well reported. I rarely travel to Town; however, even I have heard the name Darcy. I do believe I was fortunate to best your father once or twice at Whites. He was a supreme player as well, although I daresay you surpass him in skill."

Darcy bowed in return, "Thank you, Mr. Ravencraw. My father was a superb player; however, I would merely be reiterating what he himself proclaimed in that my expertise transcended his. Of course, he trounced me substantially in both chess and fencing, so I was forever humbled."

"Perhaps I shall be redeemed in the subsequent games and we shall meet again at the play-off. Just a dream on my part, sadly, as I cannot win over Mr. Dashwell and no one can beat Mr. Simpson."

Darcy smiled. "There are few certainties in this life, Mr. Ravencraw. Chin up!" The name Simpson had been bandied about as the preeminent billiard champion of the county, but Darcy had yet to deduce which man was he. Thus far, Darcy had been too busy with his own games to observe any of the others. As a guest, this was a handicap, as he had no ready knowledge of the strengths, weaknesses, or strategies of anyone. By the same token, they knew none of his, so it balanced out he supposed.

Luncheon was served then, so all the gentlemen repaired to the dining room for a delicious meal served with the finest red wine from France. Darcy was historically not a heavy imbiber, except for a memorable handful of times in his life, and never consumed spirits during a match, so he passed on the wine. The atmosphere remained animated, many of the spectators already partially in their cups. Darcy shared a table with Bingley, Mr. Bennet, Lizzy's uncle Mr. Phillips, and three younger men, friends of Bingley, whom he had met at the Lucas's dinner.

"Mr. Bennet," Darcy inquired, "which man is Mr. Simpson?"

Lizzy's father nodded toward a table by the window. "The fellow to the right of Sir Lucas." Darcy identified the indicated man with staggered surprise.

"Are you certain?" he blurted, setting Mr. Bennet laughing.

"Quite. I have known him all my life. His eldest son was my closest companion, until he passed on some five years ago."

Elliot Simpson was five and eighty if he was a day. He was a stooped, frail man closely resembling a sparrow in his fragility and delicacy. Darcy had noted him earlier in the day but had promptly dismissed the tremulous elderly gent. Frankly, he could not imagine how the same hands which currently experienced difficulty lifting his wine goblet could manage a billiard cue! He was honestly entertaining the notion that a jest was being played on him when Mr. Bennet spoke.

"I fancy the picture before you renders the erroneous conclusion that you have been misinformed. Let me assure you, my boy, place a cue in Simpson's hands and a new creature emerges. In all my days, I have never seen anyone with his mastery. He is a true wizard at billiards." He glanced at Darcy's frowning mien, chuckling softly and smiling inscrutably. "Of course, there are few certainties in life," he said, repeating Darcy's own words to Ravencraw, "so chin up!"

Darcy snorted but smiled faintly, privately anticipating the challenge, as hard as it remained for him to credit. Thankfully, after luncheon Darcy earned a respite for one round so was able to witness Simpson in action. He had sincerely never witnessed the like. The old man shuffled to the table assigned him, wheezing mildly, and took hold of his cue. Instantaneously, twenty years fell from his bearing. He straightened considerably, although still bowed, quivering hands settling around the thin wood steady and confident. He wielded the cue as if it were an attached appendage, his hand-to-eye coordination magical in its accuracy. His opponent, the aforementioned Mr. Dashwell, put up a good fight but lost by a fair margin.

Suddenly, the friendly match took on a note of true challenge for Darcy. In all the years of playing the finest players in London, Darcy had encountered only four men who could honestly be considered supreme masters of the sport. Even Darcy, as excellent as he was, did not fit into that magical realm of the gifted artisan, the virtuoso. That Mr. Simpson was such a man was without dispute. Therefore, it was doubtful that Darcy could defeat him, and he knew it. Nonetheless, like any legitimate lover of billiards or contests of any kind, he intended to try. Win or lose, the test of one's abilities was the paramount trial, not to mention what made it fun!

Now that the tournament was in its final stages—with the poorer players eliminated, leaving only the chief competitors—the excitement level had risen. With each round, as the total number decreased from eight then to six then to four, the atmosphere was feverish. Darcy attacked his next three bouts with all his might. The first two he won handily by wide point spreads. The third, the determinate playoff before the final game, was against Mr. Dashwell. It was Darcy's toughest challenge thus far, Dashwell being on an equal par with Darcy. It was a close game, each scoring readily after the other; however, Darcy won eventually by a mere twenty points.

Enraptured by the charged climate in the room as Sir Lucas solemnly announced the Championship Game between Mr. Elliot Simpson and Mr. Fitzwilliam Darcy, Darcy could not resist smiling inwardly. He experienced the same electricity as all the spectators whenever involved in these sorts of events; nonetheless, it amused him how men became transported by a simple game as if the world's continuance depended on the outcome.

Simpson and Darcy bowed to each other, exchanging pleasantries as the officials prepared the table, cues, balls, and scoreboard. The spectators gathered around, clamoring for the best viewing locations after procuring their preferred beverages.

Darcy won the string, choosing the white ball and earning the first strike, scoring a point easily. Thus, the game began. It ended up, not surprisingly, being the longest game of the entire tournament. Darcy had the time of his life and Simpson did not disappoint. He was one of the finest players Darcy had ever opposed. All his skills were put to the test as the two men fought ferociously for each point. Simpson, to Darcy's amazement, never once fouled, an accomplishment in itself. The scoring was close for a time, but eventually Simpson's mastery ruled and he pulled ahead. Darcy followed on his heels, yet never managed to supplant. Simpson triumphed, as they all expected, the elderly man maintaining his reign as Hertfordshire's billiard champion for practically all of the past fifty years. The end point spread was a slim twelve points, the smallest in recent memory. This exploit alone garnered Mr. Darcy of Pemberley a place in tournament history.

The crowd erupted in jubilant congratulations. Simpson was gracious and Darcy effusive in his praise. The drinks flowed freely, Darcy now happily sharing in a couple of glasses. For another hour or so, he and Bingley conversed and made merry before finally breaking for home.

CHAPTER THREE

Parties and Memories

WHILE THE GENTLEMEN SOCIALIZED, drank, and frolicked, the ladies strolled through Meryton. Elizabeth's queasiness had finally abated and they all had a marvelous afternoon. Mrs. Bennet delighted in reintroducing Elizabeth to every person they encountered—all of whom Lizzy had known since infancy—as Mrs. Darcy of Pemberley.

Meryton is a small village, roughly the same size as Lambton. Fine cuisine or fashionable merchandise was difficult to attain, but Lizzy, despite her newfound status and comfort with opulence, was not too far removed from the country girl of her youth. She had worn her simplest gown, a lightweight muslin frock of forest green, and no jewels other than her wedding rings and dainty diamond drop earrings. As inconspicuous as she deemed herself, the truth was that she stood out in the crowd. However, she remained oblivious to this for the most part, simply enjoying traversing through her old haunts.

Memories assaulted her senses every step of the way. Naturally, the majority concerned exploits of her youth. Although she had only been away for half a year, she discovered bizarrely evocative reminiscences invading her consciousness every step of the way. All the thousands of sites that she had no longer heeded in her day-to-day jaunts suddenly emerged in stunning clarity with vivid images attached. What surprised her further was how many of the visions involved her husband! She could distinctly recall walking with her then fiancé through these dusty streets, pointing to places as she disclosed childhood memories, glancing upward into his stoic face with the glittering eyes that revealed his pleasure in her silly stories. She smiled happily now, filing additional absurd tales to share with him later, knowing he would highly delight in them.

In need of nothing, she purchased little for herself. Her ample purse was put to better use by purchasing various odds and ends for her mother and sisters. By the end of the afternoon, they had each received several new ribbons and clothing items; Mary had also received new sheet music and four books, and Kitty embroidery essentials and perfume. Her mother was lavish in her thanks while expressing equal exuberance to all regarding her daughter's wealth. Lizzy was embarrassed and profoundly grateful that her husband was not present. Fortunately, the shopkeepers and unlucky patrons were rather accustomed to Mrs. Bennet's vocal recitations regarding the matrimonial victories of her eldest daughters.

At the butcher's shop, Lizzy bought a turkey and haunch of beef for that night's dinner to be hosted at Longbourn. The butcher, Mr. Trask, was a jovial man who was a friend to Mr. Bennet and thus well known to Lizzy.

"Miss Elizabeth, how wonderful to see you! Yes, yes, I know it is Mrs. Darcy now," he boomed with a stout laugh, "but you shall forever be little Miss Lizzy to me."

Elizabeth smiled warmly. "For you I will allow it, Mr. Trask. How is your wife, sir? Still putting up with you, or has she finally come to her senses and run away?"

Trask laughed, slapping his knee. "I see married life has not tamed that wit of yours, Miss Elizabeth! Well done! Your poor husband, to be saddled with such a wench!"

Lizzy assumed a mournful face. "Yes, it is a tragic affair. It is merely a matter of time ere a cell at Bedlam will be his home."

The bantering went on for a bit more, interrupted by the entrance of Trask's son, Reynaud, the recipient of eighteen-year-old Lizzy's crush. She smiled inwardly, blushingly remembering her and Darcy's confessions of first loves and the pleasant aftermath in his study. She laughed at the past now, tremendously thankful that Reynaud had ignored her then. He glanced at her briefly and then returned for an open-mouthed stare.

"Son, you remembered Miss Elizabeth Bennet surely. Quit gaping and say hello, only be sure to address her as Mrs. Darcy or she may bite off your head!"

"Mrs. Darcy. It is nice to see you again."

"Thank you, Mr. Trask. Are you well?"

"Quite well, thank you. How do you find… Derbyshire, was it not?"

"Correct. It is beautiful. Colder than here in the winter, with more snow, but so lovely. I understand you married recently to the former Miss Traverston." The pleasantries continued for a bit, Trask the elder interrupting frequently to match wits with Lizzy.

Exiting the shop, Lizzy was in high spirits as they turned to proceed down the lane. It was a beautiful day, warm but not uncomfortably so, a light breeze cooling to the skin. Nonetheless, Lizzy suddenly experienced a rush of heat flow through her. She fanned herself vigorously to no avail, the flush increasing, and she grasped at Jane's arm frantically as her head began to swim alarmingly and her knees to buckle.

"Jane, I must sit down!" Luckily, there was a bench a few feet away, though Lizzy was barely sitting before faintness consumed and her world turned black. Jane efficiently took charge, sending Kitty into the nearest shop, the haberdashery, for water. Georgiana hastily assumed the task of fanning her sister-in-law, while Mary left to call for the carriage. Mrs. Bennet sat next to her daughter, dithering and chattering, but confidently and correctly announcing that the swoon was a classic symptom of pregnancy.

"Oh, yes! My nerves were horrible when I was with child. I fainted dead away more times than I can remember! Why, once I was in church and…"

Georgiana worriedly interrupted, "Perhaps we should alert my brother? He is only down the street a ways."

"No," Lizzy spoke weakly, "I do not wish to disturb his entertainment. This is perfectly normal, as Mama said." Kitty returned with a glass of cool water, and Jane drenched her handkerchief to daub on Lizzy's forehead then insisted she drink the rest.

Georgiana was not convinced. "Elizabeth, he will be angry that we did not inform him. You know how he is!"

Lizzy snorted, "Oh, yes, Georgie. I know how he is! Never you mind, dearest. I will inform him, simply later instead of now, and will accept the wrath as it comes. I can deal with William."

When the slightly tipsy and high-spirited Darcy and Bingley returned to Netherfield, barely in time to change before needing to leave for Longbourn, they discovered Jane, Georgiana, and Mary dressed and reposing in the parlor. Darcy naturally swept the room for his wife, turning his questioning gaze to Jane.

"Is Elizabeth yet upstairs?" he asked. It was an innocent question met with an odd response. Georgiana was guiltily evading his eyes, fingers fidgeting in her lap, as his did when nervous or distressed, and flushing mildly. Jane was composed, as always, yet stammered vaguely in answer.

"She is preparing for dinner, I believe. She rested earlier when we returned."

Darcy frowned. It was nothing he could quite put his finger on, but a shiver of unease ran up his spine nonetheless. "Jane, is she well?" His tone was brisk and without waiting for her reply, he turned to his sister. "Georgiana?"

She started and flushed deeper. "She is fine, William. The fainting is natural, they say, and Mrs. Bennet told us..." But he was gone, long strides echoing down the hall.

Elizabeth was bent over the bed, fully dressed for dinner, carefully wrapping a package when her husband lunged through the door bellowing her name. She jolted in surprise, one hand moving to her heart. "William, you frightened me half to death! What in God's name—"

"Are you well?" he blurted, crossing hastily and clasping her hands as he stared fiercely into her eyes, brows tight and furrowed.

She frowned, honestly having forgotten the minor mishap of earlier. "I am fine."

"They said you fainted! Why did you not call for me?"

"Oh bother! It happens to pregnant women, dearest. What were you going to do? Rush away from your game and carry me all the way back to Netherfield?"

"Perhaps!" he answered stubbornly. "You promised to not tax yourself, Elizabeth. Do I need to follow you everywhere?"

"I hardly think, Mr. Darcy, that walking through the short streets of Meryton qualifies as overly arduous. It could have happened just as easily in the halls of the house. Are you going to next lock me in my room?!"

"If I must, yes!" He glared and she glared back, hands on her hips.

"Try it and I will simply crawl out the window. Ask my father and he will tell you how capable I am at climbing!"

He stared for a moment, then threw up his hands with a growl and paced to the window.

A few moments later: "Here," Elizabeth said as the package was thrust under his nose, "this is for you. A gift I purchased while exhausting myself shopping! Also, there is something adorable on the bed. I, too, think constantly of our child. I will meet you downstairs, hopefully in an improved humor!" And with a toss of her head she walked out of the room.

Darcy sighed, running a hand over his face, torn between frustration and shame. He walked to the bed. Lying there was the tiniest garment he had ever beheld: a gown in pale yellow with miniscule white pearl buttons down the front and a thin ribbon ruffle along the collar. Beside it sat a matching bonnet not much bigger than his palm and a pair of teensy satin booties edged in yellow. He picked up the shoes and plopped onto the edge of the bed, a huge grin spreading over his face while his hands trembled. Darcy was not a complete idiot. Rationally, he understood that newborn babies were small, yet having rarely actually seen one, or even an older baby for that matter, it unexpectedly dawned on him how miraculous it all was. His focus had been so wrapped up with Lizzy's health that he had spared rarely a moment's thought to the future reality. Elizabeth, as a woman, would have thought of nothing else, her symptoms mere inconveniences to endure for the greater joy.

He slipped one large finger into one of the booties, nearly filling it, and picked up the wrapped package she had given him. Inside were petits four pastries filled with lemon custard and topped with meringue. He smiled. Darcy did not generally crave sweets. Except for hot cocoa his only true dessert proclivity was anything lemon flavored. Elizabeth, amazing Elizabeth! Proving once again that she was not only continually conscious of their child but additionally of her love for him.

When he reentered the parlor he crossed the room immediately to where Elizabeth stood talking to Jane. She started at the sensation of his hand on the small of her back, turning her head as he bent to kiss her cheek. Their eyes met and all was forgiven.

Mrs. Langton, Pemberley's cook, was the type of leader who without a doubt was the admiral of her kitchen. Nonetheless, she was also a wise manager in that she recognized that her underlings could, upon occasion, actually teach her something. In fact, in order to please the palates of the Darcys, she searched far and wide for any culinary edification, including the hiring of staff from various nationalities. Therefore, in addition to the standard English cuisines, the kitchen created French, German, Spanish, and even Indian masterpieces. It had taken Lizzy quite some effort to grow accustomed to the varying spices and develop the taste for exotic preparations.

The cook at Longbourn, however, was rooted in conventional English dietary fare. Unoriginal, perhaps, but Darcy had been pleasantly surprised to discover that he was a remarkable cook. The food served at Longbourn may not be colorful, but it was superb. Consequently, no matter how irritating the Bennet craziness had often been for him, he never left the table with his stomach wanting. Happily, nothing had changed.

The usual bustle greeted them when they arrived. Mrs. Bennet flitted about, fawning over Darcy's "fine jacket" and Lizzy's "expensive gown" and nearly fainted at the sight of the Darcy carriage with elaborate crest on the door. They were a bit late so repaired immediately to the dining room. Lizzy was famished again, and a quick survey of the laden table showed no foodstuffs currently incompatible with her stomach. She hesitated a fraction of a second, already biting into a juicy slice of turkey before everyone was seated. Darcy, sitting beside her, smiled but cautioned, "Careful, dearest. You know what happens if you eat too hastily." Luckily, his fears came to naught, Lizzy ingesting without incidence.

"Lizzy," said Mr. Bennet, "we have news of Charlotte. Sir Lucas received a missive this afternoon and sent word. She too is expecting. Her date of confinement is this fall sometime."

"How wonderful!" several voices declared at the same time.

"I am so happy for her," Lizzy finally replied after swallowing. "She deserves some compensation for marrying Mr. Collins."

"Lizzy! Do not be so uncharitable! Mr. Collins is a perfectly respectable man, despite your assessment to the contrary."

"Respectable he surely is, Mrs. Bennet," Darcy smoothly chimed in, covering Lizzy's snort of disgust and forestalling the quip surely to come. "However, I must confess to being profoundly grateful that Elizabeth's opinion was of a negative bent."

"Oh, of course, Mr. Darcy! Naturally it has all worked out for the best for

Lizzy and for Charlotte. How could Charlotte not be content in her situation? Lizzy, you said her home was lovely and they have such a devoted patroness in Lady de Bourgh. How does your aunt fare, Mr. Darcy?"

Darcy's jaw had clenched at the mention of his aunt's name and his tone was cold when he spoke. "I have no recent information, madam. However, familiar with her as I am, I can assert with confidence that she is likely unchanged."

Lizzy rapidly interjected a new subject. "Papa, William tells me that Mr. Simpson has maintained his billiard title?"

This prompted a lively recap of the tournament, the men dramatic in the reenactment. Even Darcy added his theatrical storytelling embellishments a time or two, although he shied away from his own participation. Rather, he blushed as both Mr. Bennet and Mr. Bingley sang the praise of his expertise. Lizzy beamed at her spouse and squeezed his hand. "I was sure he would perform brilliantly," she announced with pride.

After dinner they strolled through the gardens and onto the adjacent paths. Initially all together, the couples eventually diverged, wishing to be alone. Lizzy, from the time she was old enough to wander off on her own, had considered a ramble after the evening meal a necessity. She had been very pleased to discover that it was a habit Darcy eagerly embraced. His tendency through adulthood was to walk along the terrace at Pemberley or the gardens at Darcy House prior to retiring for bed. In both cases, it was the desire for fresh air and star gazing that drew them outside. It was another one of those strange little customs that they had in common. During their engagement the nightly excursions had rapidly become vital, often as the first time in the entire day they were able to secure any alone time, or as alone as they could manage with Jane and Charles within earshot. However, both couples had progressively stretched the ordered proximity requirements until they were often, unbeknownst to the Bennets, on complete opposite sides of the house!

Still, Mr. Darcy had rigidly controlled himself and the private interludes never crossed any permanent boundaries, although it had balanced precariously a multitude of times. Now, they were enthusiastically seizing the opportunities to revisit past places and events without the societal strictures of the pre-matrimonial state. They ambled leisurely in silence, Lizzy holding onto her husband's arm with head on his shoulder, steering toward an oak sheltered clearing at the edge of the lake. When they arrived, Darcy enfolded his wife, pressing her back against his chest.

Kissing her earlobe, he whispered, "Do you know how desperately I yearned to hold you like this during our engagement?"

Lizzy laughed. "Yes, Mr. Darcy, I believe I do! Innocent I may have been, but not imbecilic." She glanced up into his face. "Your eyes reveal your emotions, my love." She patted his cheek and he kissed her.

He tightened his grip, unconsciously rubbing her belly. They gazed dreamily at the cloudless spring sky, a million stars visible. Darcy had studied astronomy at Cambridge so had an adequate knowledge base of the constellations. Lizzy had always enjoyed stargazing but, other than reading a couple books in her father's library, knew little. Darcy happily shared his education with her and taught her how to adjust the telescope located on an upper floor balcony at Pemberley.

"Which constellations are visible, William?"

"There is *Canes Venatici*, the hunting dogs," he indicated. "Over there is *Ursa Minor*, or small bear. Leo is those stars there, with *Leo Minor* faintly seen above the lion's head. Can you see them?"

"I think so, although it is far easier with your telescope." She sighed. "It is a jumble to me, I am afraid. I rather think one could paint all kinds of pictures. For instance," she pointed as she said, "if you connect that star to that one and then down to those three and back up and over, you form a fork!" They laughed.

"My wife the astronomer. We can dub it Elizabeth's Trident." He bestowed soft kisses along her neck, returning to her hair and inhaling deeply. "I love you, Elizabeth, more than I have the words to express. Forgive me for my outburst earlier. I cannot seem to avoid worrying about you and the baby."

She turned in his arms, hugging his waist securely. "All is forgiven. Your job is to worry, I suppose, while I get to enjoy the pleasurable sensations of nausea, raging hunger, and a constantly full bladder!"

She kissed him, but he frowned. "I hate that you must suffer so, Elizabeth. I wish I could ease your burdens."

"I shall remind you of your wish, husband, when I need someone to massage my aching back and feet, provide the strange foods for the bizarre cravings that reportedly occur, and listen to me whine at how plump I have become."

"Very well. I accept the employment."

"Oh! So hasty to concede! Consider the job description cautiously, Mr. Darcy, before you so readily acquiesce. At moments like this, what with moonlight and stars, you tend to get all fuzzy and romantic. You forget to whom you are avowing to placate. I have been known, a time or two, to be difficult." She beamed up at his grinning face.

"I cannot comprehend how you could possibly become any more tiresome and grueling than you already have been, Mrs. Darcy, so I believe I can handle the challenge."

"Ha! I shall show you tiresome and grueling!" And with that, she began tickling him, which was her one advantage over his superior strength.

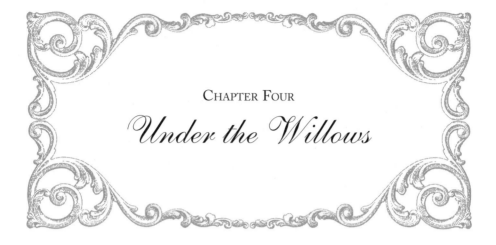

CHAPTER FOUR

Under the Willows

ON THEIR LAST DAY in Hertfordshire, Darcy and Bingley left at the crack of dawn for a last minute hunt with several other men. The weather had consistently remained pleasant, not too hot with a soft breeze blowing frequently. Darcy was busy everyday while Lizzy generally did little. Her fatigue appeared to be increasing, much to her extreme annoyance, despite sleeping each night as if sedated. To her great relief and Darcy's also, she did not faint again nor experience any light-headedness. The nausea randomly occurred and the food aversions varied day by day, offering her no ability to plan ahead. She tried to be jolly but it was a chore. For the most part, she did not feel poorly, and after being inundated by the mothers of the community with story after story of pregnancy woes, she realized that her symptoms were in truth rather minor. Nonetheless, Lizzy did not have the temperament to easily deal with lethargy.

On her third afternoon, while attending a tea party in her honor, Lizzy actually fell asleep in the middle of the parlor! She was mortified, although the ladies were gracious and nodded with sage understanding, using her misfortune to launch into further tales of pregnancy related mishaps.

Once safely returned to Netherfield, Lizzy threw herself onto the chaise with a bark of disgust. "Jane, please recall me to my senses if I ever become the type of old woman who glories in relating all my ailments with relish!"

Jane laughed. "Do not fear, Lizzy. It is not in your nature."

"Neither is this confounded tiredness. My mind desires to walk the fields, yet I know my legs would collapse under me ere I traversed a mile!" Jane smiled indulgently as Lizzy sighed, gazing out the window at the beautiful scenery. "Oh pooh, I am being such a baby. Here I am, married to the best man in the world, carrying our child, and all I can do is grouse." She turned to her sister and laughed. "Poor William! What the man has to look forward to is simply not fair. You see, Jane, I am becoming Mama already!"

"Heaven forbid!" Jane declared with mock horror, and they both laughed. To avoid any further embarrassing incidents, Lizzy opted to stay at Netherfield or Longbourn for the remaining days. She rested frequently and began to feel stronger. Therefore, on the final afternoon, after eating well at lunch and napping briefly, Lizzy decided to take a walk. There was one favorite haunt she wished to visit before she left.

So, with a book and a small basket of edible treats and lemonade, she headed toward a copse of willows she had, when a young girl, christened Willow Bench. On a small rise located at the fenced boundary of Longbourn, where Netherfield abutted, grew a cluster of six willows. A seventh had, at some time in the far past, died and fallen over creating a long wooden settee. Therefore, an eleven-year-old, unoriginal Lizzy had named it Willow Bench. It was one of many secluded spots Lizzy retreated to for respite from her boisterous household.

Approaching from Netherfield, it required climbing over the five foot fence. Lizzy accomplished this easily, tired from the long walk, but exhilarated to be out in the fresh air. She settled onto the log, removed shoes and stockings, drank some lemonade, and bit into an apple. Sighing contentedly, she allowed her mind to wander as she munched. Inevitably, the memory of the first time she had encountered Darcy at this locale entered her thoughts. She smiled.

It had occurred early one morning about a week after Jane and she returned to Longbourn from their sojourn at Netherfield during Jane's illness. She had sat much as she did now, reading, when she noted a flash in her peripheral vision. Glancing up, she recognized a man dashing on a black horse across the field. Almost instantly she realized that it was Mr. Darcy. She had seen him once on his horse at Netherfield, but it was not that fact as much as something in his posture, even from a great distance, that assured her it was him. She frowned with irritation, yet found herself rising to her feet and climbing the fence to better observe him. Even to her relatively untrained eye, there was no doubt he was a superb horseman. He would have to be in order to attain the speed he had raced along at. It was mesmerizing. Grace, power, and oneness with his mount beautifully exhibited as he zoomed along, turning in a wide, flowing arc toward the trees where she stood. He did not see her, nor was she fully cognizant of his directional change until he was nearly beside her. He skidded to a halt, both he and the horse breathing heavily, and rudely stared at her for a very long while, his face a mask of shocked surprise and some other emotion she could not identify. For her part, she was merely embarrassed to have been caught spying on him and annoyed that now her solitude was disturbed and she would be forced to talk to him when he so obviously disliked her.

She raised her chin impudently, noted a flash of confusion cross his visage, and snapped, "Demons chasing you, Mr. Darcy, or do you have a death wish?"

He seemed to have partially recovered his composure and replied seriously in a shaky voice, "Good day to you, Miss Elizabeth. Neither demons nor a death wish inspire me. I assure you I am capable of handling my mount and Parsifal delights in speed. He would be sorely displeased with me if we galloped sedately." His voice warmed slightly as he affectionately patted the horse's sweaty neck.

"Parsifal is it? Can I assume, therefore, that you appreciate the German poem by von Eschenbach, or is it a coincidence?"

Darcy raised his brows, clearly amazed. "I am impressed, Miss Elizabeth. Do you read all German poetry, or is it Arthurian legends which interest you?"

She shrugged. "My father has eclectic tastes, Mr. Darcy. He will read whatever he can get his hands on and then he lends the volume to me. I confess to enjoying medieval literature, although not the romantic varieties as much. As for German poetry, well, I am afraid my knowledge of the modern languages is limited. I am not so accomplished, you see."

Darcy flushed and coughed. "Accomplishment is gauged in a myriad of ways, Miss Elizabeth. Do not take Miss Bingley's words too seriously."

She laughed gaily, eliciting a small smile from him. "Oh, be comforted, sir. I actually have a reputation for frivolity and irreverence. Miss Bingley did not disturb me."

Silence descended, Mr. Darcy staring at her in that strange, undecipherable manner of his. Lizzy, to her utter horror, found her eyes drifting from his face to the open collar of his shirt. She flushed, averting her gaze quickly, mind suddenly revisiting the touch of his bare, warm, and strong hand when he assisted her into the carriage when leaving Netherfield. Anger rose in her chest then, as if it was somehow his fault for the slant of her musings, and she flared. "I imagine you and your sister read von Eschenbach in the original German?" She cringed inwardly at the inanity of her remark as well as the tone but glared challengingly and lifted her chin nonetheless.

Mr. Darcy frowned slightly. "Yes, of course, although Miss Darcy's German is not as fluent as her French. She is improving though." He trailed off lamely.

Concluding that he must be bored silly and annoyed with the conversation, especially with her, Lizzy declared briskly, "Well, Mr. Darcy, if you will excuse me, I need to be returning to Longbourn and I have detained your horse from his race quite long enough."

He seemed to hesitate, struggling internally with something, and then bowed his head. "Of course, Miss Elizabeth. Forgive me for keeping you. I pray your day continues to be a pleasant one." Despite his farewell, he yet hesitated for a moment further then abruptly clenched his jaw and with a curt bow spun Parsifal and cantered off, spurring into a hard run before getting thirty feet away.

Almost a year later, during their engagement, they had met here on two occasions, once by accident and once planned. The accidental encounter had occurred only five days after their betrothal and in roughly the same manner as the first. Lizzy had gone to Willow Bench to read. Darcy was out riding and inadvertently passed by that way, the meadow being flat and lengthy thus perfect to race across. Lizzy had heard the hoof beats and jumped up in hopeful anticipation, heart pounding at the sight of her love whizzing by. She rapidly climbed to the top rung of the fence, waving frantically and quite unladylike, thrilled when he finally saw her.

How altered the confrontation was this time around! Darcy was beaming and relaxed. Lizzy unabashedly admired his windblown attractiveness, although to her chagrin he wore a cravat. He casually directed Parsifal alongside her and without preamble leaned in for a tender kiss. "Miss Elizabeth, what a delightful surprise. Come here often, do you?" Gloved fingertips seared the flesh of her cheek as he caressed tenderly.

They teased and laughed, shared several controlled kisses, as Lizzy told him the history of Willow Bench. The problem of being on opposite sides of the fence was solved by the simple expedience of him galloping full tilt and cleanly jumping over it while Lizzy nearly fainted. She scolded him vehemently and he professed deep contrition, belied by the twinkle in his eyes. Of course, Lizzy had a difficult time maintaining her irritation considering how breathlessly gorgeous he was and the raw excitement rushing through her at the sight of his blatant masculinity.

The planned visit to Willow Bench had transpired on the afternoon before their wedding day. They had walked from Longbourn, initially with Jane and Charles trailing, belatedly discovering their steps haphazardly heading this direction at roughly the same moment they realized that Jane and Charles were nowhere to be found. They shared a knowing glance, nodded and grinned, and by mutual unspoken consent broke into a chase. Lizzy reached the trees first, although it was clear the long-legged Darcy had forfeited. Instead, he grabbed her about the waist, twirling her about while laughing joyously, and then planted a firm kiss to her lips. As had been increasingly ensuing as the day of their nuptials approached, the playful chaste kiss rapidly evolved into a serious breach of all propriety. Within seconds they were fused along every plane of their bodies, hands grasping and seeking, and mouths hungrily tasting. Before long, they were both panting—and not from the sprint.

With tremendous effort they pulled away, withdrawing to opposite trees as they stared at each other with passion imbued eyes. Darcy was totally befuddled, as Lizzy would learn was a typical reaction when his ardor was high. Lizzy was in a similar state, earnestly searching her mind for something to interject into the silence, finally emitting the first words that popped into her head. "I love kissing you!"

Instantly red-cheeked, she stammered, "I suppose you figured that out." He merely smiled broadly and nodded, rigid hands flattened harshly against his thighs and breathing labored. In the shaded alcove, his eyes were glittering and nearly black. Lizzy noted it all and more, flushed further, and looked away.

Spying the fence and field beyond, she asked, "What were you thinking when you encountered me here that day? The day last year before we were engaged?"

She turned back to him, noting the faraway expression in his eyes even as he stared into her face, as he replied, "I thought my dreams had returned to torment me." He spoke softly, voice husky, drawn inward in remembrance.

"What do you mean?"

Darcy jolted, met her eyes, and reddened. "Nothing, Elizabeth. I was just surprised, that is all." He grew stubborn and refused to talk about it.

With all that had transpired since, Lizzy had totally forgotten both instances. Now, she sat on the makeshift bench and wondered afresh what had been racing through his mind. Knowing him as intimately as she now did, she could solve some of the riddles. Obviously he had not disliked her as she assumed but, in fact, was smitten. His confusion, hesitation, and lack of wit she understood now were due to his shyness coupled with the desire to converse with her. What she did not comprehend was the odd emotion on his face when he first saw her and the even odder comment about dreams.

She shook her head, vowed to ask him later, finished her apple, and opened her book.

Back at Netherfield, Darcy and Bingley returned from their hunt, several birds the richer. Georgiana informed her brother as to Elizabeth's whereabouts, and he left with a huge grin.

"Elizabeth… Elizabeth… Mrs. Darcy."

Lizzy slowly opened her eyes, the hazy figure bent over her gradually focusing. "William?"

He smiled. "Miss Elizabeth, what a delightful surprise. Come here often, do you?"

She laughed, accepting his hand to assist her into a sitting position from the slumped pose she currently occupied in her slumber. He brushed off her skirts as he knelt in front of her. She smiled and caressed his face. "Yes, I come here often. However, the best occasions are when handsome gentlemen intrude."

"And how often does that occur, pray tell?"

"A dozen or so, over the course of time, naturally."

"A dozen, you say? That many? Any particular events or gentlemen of special import?"

Her fingers moved to the knots of his cravat as she replied, "Only one gentleman that is burned in my memory. He intruded upon me thrice. On the first occasion I noted he had the loveliest neck and my thoughts were quite wicked."

Darcy was genuinely surprised. "Truly? I did not suspect. I have been under the mistaken impression that you hated me then."

"No. At that time I simply thought you annoying and pompous. Also, I had concluded that you disliked me."

"Foolish girl," he said as he ran his fingers over her lips.

"Yes, to be sure. Of course, mistaken impressions aside, your neck is quite delectable and I was not so completely foolish as to not notice!" She leaned in to his now bared neck for a smattering of delightful kisses. He sighed happily, a hand encompassing each slender ankle. Murmuring against his skin, "Why were you racing so crazily that day, William, and looking at me so strangely?"

"I always looked at you strangely, my dear, because I was enchanted by you and utterly at a loss as to how to proceed. You dazzled me at every turn and rendered me mute and dull. A woman as intelligent as you had no choice but to deduce my moronic behavior unworthy and reproachable!"

Lizzy shook her head and clasped his face with her hands. "Do not say that! I was the fool to not see your worth and love." She kissed him. "You did not answer my question, however. Why on that particular day were you running so dangerously and later spoke of dreams tormenting you?"

"Oh, yes, I remember now." He smiled and laughed. "I had forgotten." He sat back onto the grass, lightly massaging her calves and feet. "You surely remember my confession to you, dearest, of the nature of many of my dreams involving you?" She nodded, blushing slightly. "Later, once we were betrothed, those dreams of making love with you were welcomed. Practice sessions, I deemed them."

"William!" she declared in mock shock, and he laughed.

"However, earlier, during my sojourn at Netherfield and your abiding there, the dreams began and they were not welcomed. Enjoyed certainly, but I was mortified once I awoke. I was dismayed that I, Darcy of Pemberley, a gentleman with superior temperance and constraint, would lose control even in my sleep so as to consider you in such a way. Yet, I could not deny how… pleasant… it was." He chuckled. "It was a torment, Elizabeth. I was madly in love with you, yet successfully fought against it during my waking hours. Then I would dream of you in such a vivid and delightful yet crude and disrespectful manner. Mornings were horrible. I would wake in a sweat, weary, aroused, and ashamed."

He paused, gazing into her beloved eyes. "On retrospection, I was never successful in denying my affection for you. I simply managed to deceive myself, employing my years of discipline to bury my thoughts and urges. That particular morning was one of many in which I woke in a heightened state, unfit for company, and in need of oblivion from my decadent musings. Parsifal offers that. We love running fast, as you are aware. There is a freedom to the exercise. You become one with your horse, and the power and concentration necessary invade your mind and erase all else. It is liberating." He paused again, smiling dreamily and firmly gripping her feet in his lap. "When I encountered you so abruptly, standing on the fence watching me, my first thought was that I was still in a dream. God, Elizabeth, if you only knew how beautiful you were! Your simple dress, the green one it was, no bonnet or fancy gloves, your hair pinned but loose about your lovely face, your feet bare, your eyes shining and cheeks flushed. You took my breath away! Nothing in my dreams compared to the reality of how stunning you were. I wanted to leap off Parsifal and into your arms with an aching desire beyond anything I had ever experienced in all my life, and it was only my embarrassingly acute aroused state that kept me on his back!"

"Hmmm... Perhaps you should have leapt, William. Think how differently things may have gone."

"Do not tease me, Elizabeth. I was a beast, and you would have slapped me or kicked me in a painful location, and rightfully so!"

"Maybe not. I was examining your neckline far too boldly and reliving the touch of your hand. That is why I snapped at you so rudely. You unnerved me."

Darcy kissed her covered knees, laying his cheek on her thigh. "No use contemplating might have beens, my love. We are here now and you are more beautiful and I am yet again breathless and captivated. Now, as then, my mind and heart are consumed by you, dearest wife."

Lizzy beamed, fingering his soft hair as they stared at each other. "I love you, William. Thank you for sharing with me, for persevering in your suit, and for tolerating my fluctuating moods. I do not deserve you but am abundantly grateful that you are mine!"

He rose to his knees, hugging her body with hands on her hips. "I am eternally yours and you are eternally mine." He kissed her slowly and thoroughly, voice husky when he next spoke, "We need to return to the manor for dinner, love. Are you feeling well?"

"Very well," she whispered, seizing his mouth while hands roamed over his chest, unbuttoning the waistcoat. "Love me, Fitzwilliam, as you wanted to before."

"Elizabeth! It is broad daylight. You…" She strengthened the force of her kiss and focused her fondling, eliciting a deep groan from her husband. Finally, struggling for breath and control under the insistence of her attack, he uttered, "Oh sweet Lord, Lizzy! Someone could happen by. We should not…"

"No one passes this way, my lover. No one but you, that is." She pushed his unresisting body backward onto the grass, following with kisses over his now exposed abdomen.

Gasping, he clasped her shoulders. "What… What about those other dozen men?"

She looked up in surprise, "There were never any others, William. Surely you knew I was jesting?"

He grinned. "I had to be certain." Relenting happily, he pulled her up, kissing roughly. "Elizabeth, how I love you! Is there any fantasy or dream you would not fulfill for me?"

She smiled, caressing his face. "Why are you so certain I am fulfilling merely a fantasy of yours, William? Did you not think I ever dreamt of your delectable neck and ardent kisses and arousal as witnessed under these hanging branches?" Nibbling the tender flesh of his earlobe, she whispered, blowing softly into his ear, "I am the clever one, you recall. May I show you what I have imagined?"

"Yes!"

Lizzy sat up, straddling his thighs. With a sensual smile she unclasped the buttons providentially located down the front of her bodice, opening her gown enough to expose her firm, increasingly ample breasts. Many of her gowns were already unable to comfortably contain her bosom now, the purchase of new clothing being a priority once in Town. Darcy loved her shape as it naturally was, never once entertaining the thought of his wife lacking in any way. Nonetheless, he had to admit, internally only, that her newer voluptuous form was enticing. Extending aching hands to caress her, licking dry lips in anticipation of the pleasure she offered, his groin clenching and rising as he avidly watched her movements.

Lizzy smiled, jubilant at the instant reaction evoked. "Remember when we kissed here the day before our wedding? You were aroused then, not for the first time, after holding and kissing me. I had only seen baby boys or marble statues so had no real concept of what you looked like. I tried to visualize." She laughed at his shocked expression. "I told you I was wicked, beloved, and had fantasies of my own. Of course, I pictured it poorly. I am still stunned at how beautiful you are, Fitzwilliam, how potent and… grand. Every portion of you is utter perfection. I suppose I should have been aghast at myself, but even on our wedding night when first I beheld you, I only experienced excitement and pleasure. Never embarrassment or fear. Now I am fully cognizant of how impressive your physique, how rapturous the feel of you inside me. How can I contain my desire for you knowing what you hide under your layers of clothing and how you awaken my lust and satisfy me?" She chuckled, amused at his blush.

She grasped his hands, pulling him to a sitting position. She searched his blue, love saturated eyes, tears suddenly welling in her brown ones. "Fitzwilliam Darcy," she whispered, "What a gift you are in my life! I hope you understand that as much as I yearn for you physically, and I do every moment of every day, it is your heart and soul that have captured me. If we could no longer make love for some reason I would ache for you, but I would still love you as profoundly because you live inside my very essence." She cupped his face fiercely. "Do you know this, my husband?"

Strong, warm hands palmed and stroked her neck and cheeks while he kissed her by way of reply. Passion, devotion, unity, and worship spoke eloquently through the intimate activity. In hoarse, resonant tones he said, "Elizabeth, I know I dwell in your heart and soul because you reside in mine as well. Apart from you I am shattered and fragmented. In your presence I am whole. It shall never be otherwise. I have not the minutest doubt of your love for me, beloved wife. It amazes me yet that you love me, but I do not dispute it."

Words were lost in a rapturous kiss, Lizzy loving him with a rhythmic swaying motion, arms tenaciously over his shoulders and hands weaved in his hair. Oblivious to the outside world, which thankfully remained empty of all but a few birds and one rabbit, they danced and joined in perfect harmony. Pleasures of the flesh merged with the supernatural coalescing of spirits as two souls become one, not exclusively at the pinnacle of carnal glory but for all eternity.

❧

"Why are you standing here and staring into the stable yard?"

Lizzy turned from the window to smile at her spouse as he crossed the empty room to join her with a soft kiss. She reached to caress a cheek, speaking lowly, "This was my chamber when I stayed here nursing Jane all those months ago. Do you remember?"

"Do I remember that you slept in the room three doors away from mine? Precisely twenty-two strides away? Yes, I do."

Lizzy laughed. "You actually counted the steps?"

"Not consciously but, after passing this door numerous times over the course of those five days with an urgent desire to talk to you or at least nod politely, I noted the distance. But why are you in here now?"

"I was recalling a vision of extreme loveliness." She tiptoed to kiss his baffled face and then laughed. She turned to look outside, leaning into his chest and clasping the arms that instantly encircled her. "On my third morning here, I woke early, as I always did, and went first to check on Jane. She was still feverish but asleep, so I returned to my room and sat at this window reading. I do not know how much time passed when I saw you. Down there."

She pointed to the dirt clearing before the main stable doors. "You rode Parsifal, I swear the largest horse I had ever seen, startling me at how you barreled in full bore seeming to stop barely before colliding with the doors, and vaulted off his back in one smooth motion ere he was completely still. I had never witnessed the like. Your face was thunderous and even from this distance I could discern how heavily you were breathing. Fleetingly, I had wondered what in the world could have you so distraught, but mostly I was caught by your appearance."

She gazed up at his face, noting the remote expression in his eyes as he stared sightlessly at the yard. "You wore your typical riding clothes, your hair windblown and shirt open. You spoke to the groom, handing the reins over, and then strode briskly to the water pump. To my mesmerized shock, you grasped the handle, pumping violently, and stuck your whole head and upper torso under the stream of water. Then you stood tall, arched your back, water flying everywhere when you flipped your head backward and ran your hands through your sopping hair. Water cascaded down your body with your shirt clinging and nearly transparent. God, William! You were an Adonis!" She chuckled shakily, squeezing the fingers entwined with hers. "Of course, it all happened so fast, and before I could really assimilate a coherent thought you abruptly swiveled your head toward this window, eyes angry and piercing. I jerked backward and slipped to the floor. I was so embarrassed! I thought you had somehow detected me staring. I can still remember how hot my face was, but am even now unsure if that was due to your catching me gaping, your breathtakingly gorgeous figure, or both! Probably both."

He met her eyes, smiling his sensuous grin and firmly stroking over one hip. "Thank you for the compliment, my love. I did not see you, although I knew this was your room." He bent and kissed her upturned lips reverently, whispering roughly, "That night I had my first erotic dream of you. I woke so angry with myself and with you, as illogical as that was. Not to mention aroused as I never had been in all my life. I could not accept what I was feeling for you, thinking it unacceptable on so many levels. I was an incredible fool, Elizabeth."

"We were both fools, my heart." She pivoted in his embrace, snaking arms over his shoulders and rising on tiptoes to brush plump lips. "So tell me truthfully. Did any of your dreams include sneaking into my room and ravishing me?" His ready flush provided the answer. "Hmmm… I thought so. You know, this room is unoccupied. We could reenact your fantasy tonight if you wish." She finished with a flutter of lashes and arch grin.

Darcy chuckled lowly. "I love you, Elizabeth."

"Yes, I know."

For their last evening at Netherfield, the Bingleys and Darcys hosted a small dinner party of their own with primarily family and a few other couples, the total number around fifty. Elizabeth, deciding it was time for Mrs. Fitzwilliam Darcy of Pemberley to make a formal appearance, wore the ball gown from the Masque. Fully bejeweled and gloved, with hair stupendously arrayed, she was a vision of grace and elegance. Glowing with a radiance borne from within, fueled by a transcendent love and joy, Elizabeth was resplendent. Mr. Darcy was no less magnificent in his finery, with hair freshly trimmed by Samuel, and countenance equally euphoric as a result of his love and bliss and pride in his stunning wife.

Jane Bingley was gorgeous as well. Mr. Bingley, although not as wealthy as Darcy, spared no expense when it came to his wife. Therefore, Jane was gowned brilliantly, jeweled and coiffed and luminous. Only those guests with knowledgeable eyes could discern the finer weave or premiere cut to Elizabeth's outfit. However, every single person, most of them having known the Bennet girls all their lives, could not deny that for the first time Jane did not immediately stand out as the most beautiful of the two.

Darcy and Bingley proudly stood by their wives as they greeted the guests: Jane serene and gracious, Lizzy charming and effervescent, and both men awestruck anew by their good fortune. It was an evening, despite its simplicity, that would be gossiped about for months to come. The women in attendance would ceaselessly discuss the regalia worn; the men spoke of the fine food and spirits. All would comment on the affection displayed between both couples.

Charles and Jane, in the newfound fullness of their relationship, were nearly as giddy and ridiculous as the Darcys. Lizzy, never one to be demure, made no secret of her overwhelming love for her handsome husband. Darcy's musings were already racing ahead to how his Elizabeth would dazzle the ton of London society and his pride was boundless.

The last guest welcomed, Charles offered his arm to Jane, entering the decorated reception hall. Darcy turned to Lizzy. "Are you well, dearest?"

"Perfectly so, Mr. Darcy," she replied, smiling up at his handsome face, straightening his flawless cravat—a sort of ritual for her. "I love you, William."

"I adore you, Mrs. Darcy, more than life. Shall we then?" Arms entwined, they entered the hall.

CHAPTER FIVE

London, 1817

THE LONDON OF 1817 was a city in-between. With a population well over one million souls, London was easily the largest single city in the world. The self-indulgent excesses of the Georgian Period had waned along with the madness of its King. While George III remained locked safely away at Windsor Castle, his son and future King, George the Prince Regent, ushered in an Age of Elegance, embracing the arts and science with all issues devoted to the advancement of beauty, style, and taste. The two wars and crushing defeats by the new United States of America were a memory, and Napoleon Bonaparte had finally been eliminated, thus permanently ending the decades-long unrest in France. This allowed a resurgence of exchange in both goods and culture, inaugurating an influx of technology, industry, and immigrants.

These intervening years, as well as those that would follow, when the Prince Regent became George IV in 1820, were years of tremendous change for Britain. London, as its capital and largest city, would reflect these changes first and to greater degrees than the rest of the country. Embracing the romantic ideals of nature and emotion rather than the serious rationalization of the Enlightenment, theater, art, literature, poetry, and architecture would radically change and flourish. The inundation of technology and science eventually led to an industrial revolution that would burst forth from London to all civilized nations of the world.

Masses of people of all nationalities and classes flooded unceasingly into the city. New suburbs, shopping districts, commerce areas, docks, housing communities, factories, and more seemingly sprung up overnight. The officials, public workers, and law enforcers groaned and strained under the added burdens engendered. Therefore—while such wonders as gas lighting illuminated the streets and houses, agricultural delights from far away places became imported, and structural marvels like new bridges spanned the Thames—pollution, crime, poverty, and the yawning chasms between the classes increased. Whereas the gap separating the richest and the poorest expanded, the middle class rose to fill the chasm. These merchants, bankers, artisans, and tradesmen eventually aided England in becoming an even stronger empire.

London, analogous to most large cities, naturally separated into localities based on class and objective. At the lowest rung were the slums inhabited by those who through choice or misfortune lived a life of poverty or crime, or more often both. These were the areas that the vast majority of London's inhabitants avoided at the risk of life and limb. Other blocks catered to business or government. Bond Street, Covent Gardens, and Cheapside, just to name a few, catered to shopping needs. Fleet Street was world renowned for its publishing. The Guildhall, Houses of Parliament, and Old Bailey at the Newgate Prison complex dealt with governmental and law enforcement aspects.

Scattered throughout London were the residential districts generally surrounding a garden square or park of varying sizes and fulsomeness depending on the affluence of the populace. The Mayfair and Kensington Districts, both bordering Hyde Park and St. James Park where the Royal Palace stood, were unarguably the wealthiest and most fashionable neighborhoods in all of London. Each locality boasted several astounding gardens and splendid houses; however, Grosvenor Square in Mayfair was incomparable. Darcy's great-great-grandfather had been a close companion to Sir Grosvenor and, in fact, had married one of his cousins. Consequently, the Darcy family had acquired one of the initial townhouses built facing the Square itself.

The traffic entering the city was excessively congested, causing the journey from Wembley to the townhouse to take as long as the entire distance from Longbourn! The unrelenting noise and stench of multitudes of horses, fireplaces, sewage, and heaven only knows what else had seriously affected Lizzy, educing a stabbing headache and severe nausea barely held in check. Darcy was extremely disturbed, frantic to reach the house, and mad with frustration as there was no way to speedily do so. Upon finally arriving late in the afternoon, an ill Lizzy insisted on walking into the house despite Darcy's intention to carry her. He opened his mouth to argue, but one glance at her pale yet determined face and he pinched his lips into a thin line, remaining silent. She leaned heavily against his side, steps sluggish, but managing with a reserve of strength truly remarkable under the circumstances. Darcy was nervous but proud of her indomitable spirit. She was quickly reintroduced to Mrs. Smyth, the housekeeper, and Mr. Travers, the butler, then rushed to the master chambers while commands issued forth from a stern Darcy and were hastily discharged. In consequence, the first night was rather chaotic with Lizzy violently ill, Darcy fretful, and Georgiana worried and forgotten.

Lizzy knew that Darcy had a hectic agenda scheduled for the next three days. He had meetings planned with his solicitor as well as several business associates, but had informed her with a mischievous smirk that primarily his affairs involved her birthday. He stubbornly refused to reveal the merest hint regarding his plans, only bidding her to keep the day free of all engagements. When she woke on their first day in Town, Darcy had already risen and was busily writing at the desk in the small sitting room attached, one eye on his slumbering wife. After dashing to the water closet, Lizzy shuffled slowly and shakily to her husband, who nervously stood waiting for her. Instantly he enfolded her into his arms, hugging her tightly then assisting her to the chaise.

"What can I do for you, my love?"

"Nothing, William, thank you. It will pass. Perhaps you could ring Marguerite for some tea?"

"Of course! How thoughtless of me." Once that was accomplished, he sat beside her, stroking her leg gently and raptly staring as if he could will the illness away.

Lizzy smiled through drooping eyes and patted his hand. "Return to your work, dearest. I will be fine and there is no reason for you to hover."

Yet hover he did, repeatedly asking if there was anything she required and not concentrating on the pile of papers on his desk for more than ten minutes at a time. Therefore, although she continued to suffer from a mild headache and

SHARON LATHAN

transient nausea, the combination of foreknowledge regarding her husband's full docket and the fact that his watchfulness was frankly driving her insane motivated Lizzy to bluntly order him to leave. She felt a bit guilty for the necessary rudeness, but once he was finally persuaded to go, she and Georgiana breathed a huge sigh of relief.

The first three days in Town passed quietly and quickly. Georgiana and Elizabeth enjoyed their hours together, since they had spent so little time in solitary communion over the past week. The Bingleys, with Mary and Kitty, would be arriving the day before Lizzy's birthday. As of yet, the appearance of the Darcys to London had sparked no interest, although they both understood that the barrage of invitations and calling cards were inevitable. By day two, Lizzy was almost one hundred percent well with only the usual vague queasiness and food aversions, which were becoming rather normal to her. After two nights of deep sleep in her husband's arms, even her annoying fatigue had vanished. As she had done during her early days at Pemberley, she utilized the time while Darcy was away to wander about the house.

Darcy House was tiny and nondescript compared to the opulence and vastness of Pemberley, but when contrasted with the other manors in and around Grosvenor Square, it was majestic. Constructed of polished white stone, it appeared to glow. Numerous tall, arched, multi-paned windows spaced evenly across the entire front allowed beams of light to illuminate all the rooms. Although possessing far fewer rooms than Pemberley, at two stories high, not counting the basement level, and nearly an entire block wide, Darcy House was spacious and accommodating. The sizable and impressive library was also Darcy's study, the enormous parlor housed the grand pianoforte, and there was only one dining room but it was expansive and lavish. The ballroom was generous, if a fourth of Pemberley's, and the billiard room, a necessity in a Darcy household, included a host of gaming features and was ample. The eight guest chambers were comfortable, luxurious, and modern if relatively modest in size.

The master chambers were located on the first floor and opened onto a walled private garden. These rooms were immense and decorated with Darcy's preferred rustic tones and simplicity. When Elizabeth had toured the house during their engagement, she had been shown every room except for Darcy's. They had not specifically discussed it at the time, but propriety as well as the heightened sensual awareness they both experienced, especially Darcy, during

58

Elizabeth's visit had lent unease to the idea of entering his bedroom. As her husband would confess to her later, having her in his home and so near his bedchamber had nearly broken his will. For the four weeks prior, except for the occasion of their first kiss, Darcy had been the perfect gentleman. His desire for Lizzy had been rigidly controlled and aside from his eyes, which hid nothing, Lizzy had not fully recognized the struggle he daily and hourly fought.

Now, as Lizzy walked through the house she remembered those incidents with a smile. On their first night in Town, Darcy had hosted them all for dinner. With only time for a short tour to the main rooms, they had retired to the dining room for dinner then after to the parlor. Lizzy had delighted in noting Darcy's relaxation and high humor throughout the evening. She well understood how difficult it was for him to spend day after day at Longbourn with the press of visitors and family augmented by her mother's shrill voice and incessant chatter, which is the primary reason she had requested her father chaperone his daughters. Her heart ached at her fiancé's discomfort, and it was with massive relief that she witnessed his contentment now. Therefore, when she observed Darcy's back as he unobtrusively exited the room, she frowned and did not hesitate. With a quick look around, she slipped out the door to follow. She found him on the small terrace, standing perfectly still as he gazed into the sky. With a smile, she paused on the threshold to admire him; the faint porch light glistening on his hair, long legs and broad shoulders so elegantly displayed by the fine clothing and straight posture, and the calmly authoritative stateliness he exuded.

"William?"

He turned to her with a wistful smile on his face. "Elizabeth," he whispered, "I was dreaming about you and here you are, as if conjured."

She laughed softly, taking several steps closer to him. "Not quite that magical I am afraid. I saw you leave the parlor and wanted to make sure you were well and," she hesitated, blushing slightly, "I wished to be alone with you," she finished in a small voice, glancing away.

He closed the gap between them and lightly touched her cheek with his fingertips. "Then it is magic, for I wished the same and here you are." His voice was low and husky. Their eyes met and it *was* magic: the magic of mutual desire and love. Instantly, they were both transported to the day of his proposal and first kiss in Longbourn's garden. Since that day, they had maintained the proper decorum and distance as promised, the kisses and touches shared brief and chaste with nary a hint of their longing that bubbled under the surface. For Lizzy, that morning had taken on a dreamlike quality and she had almost convinced herself that the passion which had flared was not as strong or as real as it had seemed. Darcy, naturally, had relived each touch and sensation unrelentingly, especially in his dreams where the emotions and urgency had taken on a life of their own, and it was only his maturity and inordinate self-mastery that contained him during the daylight hours.

Here, in the feeble moonlight, all regulation faded and he kissed her as he had yearned to do every moment of every day for over a year. He cupped her face and began with tasting her lush lips gently but thoroughly, the tenderness lasting the span of several heartbeats before ardency flared. Elizabeth circled his waist under the open jacket, hands flattening on his back as she pressed into his heated body and the kiss. With a throaty groan, he insistently parted her lips, exploring rapturously, and kissing hungrily. It was only five minutes of blinding ecstasy before they were jerked to reality by Mr. Bennet's voice calling his daughter's name. Darcy recoiled, melting into the shadows by the wall, guiltily forced to abandon Lizzy to salvage her reputation, which she did with surprising aplomb, while he was left shaken and shockingly aroused for quite some time.

The next afternoon, the Bennets and Gardiners had again been invited to Darcy House to dine, arriving earlier as Darcy had specifically requested the time to acquaint Lizzy with one of her future homes. Mr. Bennet had trailed along for most of the tour before becoming waylaid in the library. Darcy and Lizzy had not spoken of the previous night's interlude; in fact, they had not seen each other all day, and now the interwoven wall of embarrassment and seething heat effectively rendered them distracted, mute, and nervous. It was an odd and uncomfortable situation, the two of them having previously reached a place of blooming freedom and communication. As the tour proceeded with Darcy droning on and on about inane topics in a desperate effort to fill the silent void, Lizzy's discomfiture turned to irritation.

Her frustration boiled over quite by accident. They were in his mother's chambers, Mr. Bennet having been forgotten. Darcy fidgeted, fingers flicking unremittingly and white-knuckling the now wrinkled edge of his jacket, as he stammered something about redecorating from his ramrod post by the wash basin. Lizzy wandered inattentively about the room, barely listening to a word he said nor noting a single feature, suddenly catching her foot on the curled up edge of a rug. She stumbled ungracefully and would have fallen, but Darcy was there in an instant, grasping her arm so that she fell against his chest instead.

Time stopped.

She could feel his radiant heat, harsh respirations, and wildly beating heart; his close proximity affected her as greatly. Before she could even contemplate moving, he had buried his face into the curls atop her head, breathing deeply and hoarsely murmuring her name. She tilted her face upwards, and in a flash, he claimed her mouth in a bruising kiss lacking all restraint. She was paralyzed only for a fraction of a second before responding in kind, arms rapidly circling his shoulders and fingers laced through silky hair. They were delirious. Strong, probing hands moved all over her back, down over her hips then up to her waist, halting for a exquisite interval of gentle squeezes, before traveling further to just under her arms. He held her tightly, the kiss absorbing and fierce, concurrently pulling her greedily into his body while tracing thumbs lightly over the swell of her breasts.

Lizzy gasped in enraptured astonishment, sending a bolt of appalled horror through Darcy. He released her so abruptly she nearly fell. Pivoting with a strangled cry, he lunged to the nearest window, leaning onto the sill with hands balled into fists of steel, whole body trembling alarmingly.

Lizzy swayed, her mind in chaos. He spoke suddenly, voice harsh and tremulous, "Elizabeth, you need to leave this room now! Please!"

She stepped to the open door in hypnotic compliance but could not make herself leave. Time stretched and at least ten minutes passed with both of them breathing erratically and emotions in pandemonium. Unexpectedly, Lizzy discovered she was filled with anger. She shut the door firmly and walked to where he stood hunched at the window.

"No, William, I will not leave. Tell me truthfully; am I to conclude that our mutual love and desire are emotions to be disdained and ashamed of? Is this contempt and repugnance to continue after we are wed? Or is it that you honestly reckon you are such an uncontainable beast that you would hurt or defile the woman you love? Or do you have so little faith in my own self-control and decorum that you assume I would willingly allow you to ravage me like a bought woman?"

Her hands were clenched into fists and countenance a mask of monumental rage. She leaned toward him as he stood petrified with mouth hanging open and face pale, utterly shocked and mortified. Add a torrential downpour and it would be Kent all over again.

"Well!" she demanded, stepping even closer and lifting on her toes until only inches from his stunned eyes. "Answer me!"

Darcy was speechless, the pain lancing through his heart unbearable. "No, Elizabeth, I"—he swallowed—"I love you! Please… I have never wanted anything in all my life as I want you. You… are my life… you must know that? Surely…"

Elizabeth interrupted him, voice controlled somewhat, "Fitzwilliam, I do not believe any of the questions I asked are true of you. However, this is what I *do* believe: You are afraid of letting go of your emotions. You are wrapped in an inflexible cocoon of discipline and righteousness and are terrified that if you loosen one single cord you will unravel completely. You love me and desire me, yet resist showing me how much because you fear I will be disgusted or disappointed to discover you are not the towering paragon of virtue and excellence you deem yourself."

She paused for a deep breath, suddenly drained of all energy and anger, cut to the quick by the tears shimmering on Darcy's cheeks and consumed with a fresh rush of irrepressible love.

Placing both hands about his face, sobs catching in her throat, she whispered, "My God, William! Do you not yet comprehend how deeply I love you? You can be free with me and I will *always* love you. I trust you with my life, my virtue, my body, and my heart! You have nothing to fear from me and I fear nothing from you. All I fear is distance between us." She began planting kisses all over his face, his arms now tightly around her waist. "I beg you, my love, do not push me away!"

"Elizabeth," he groaned, responding blissfully to her kiss, relief palpable as a tangible barrier in his soul surrendered. The power of their love crashed over him anew, and for the first time, it wholly dawned on him what it meant to love her and to be loved in return. The veracious definition of *Two Shall Become One*, as she had embroidered on the bookmark for his birthday, was suddenly clear.

The following weeks of their betrothal were a liberating experience for him. Their solitary moments together were brief and stolen but imbued with a heightened communion without the guilt of before. Darcy was always a gentleman, never crossing any permanent lines of propriety, but no longer so rigid or afraid to express his attraction to her. Oddly, the license to exhibit their passion for each other in regulated ways made it easier to control themselves overall. Additionally, the bridled but playful physical indulgences taken enhanced their communication and strengthened their commitment. By the time they were officially declared husband and wife, they were so intertwined and attuned that taking the final step of consummation was effortless and rapturous.

Now, Lizzy sat at Darcy's desk in the combined library and study of Darcy House, lost in pleasant memories as she dazedly peered out the tall window facing the garden, an enormous lilac bush gently swaying in the breeze.

"There you are." Lizzy glanced up at her husband as he entered the room, a ready smile on both their faces. "No one knew where you were hiding. Are you well, dearest?" He stooped for a brief kiss but she grasped his face in her hands, halting him for a consuming exchange.

"I am fantastic, my heart, and even more so now that you are home."

"That is quite the delightful greeting. May I assume, therefore, that you missed me terribly?" He lifted a brow, and she laughed softly.

"I pine for you if you are gone from my presence for more than a minute. All day is tortuous. Now hush and kiss me again, husband."

Some ten heavenly minutes later: "Why were you sitting here in the twilight staring out the window?"

She snuggled closer to him, laying her head on his shoulder. They sat on the sofa, having transferred there for comfortable cuddling and kissing. "I spent the afternoon familiarizing myself with the house and ended here. I believe Mrs. Smyth has decided I am mad."

"Why do you say that?"

Lizzy laughed. "She caught me opening cupboards in one of the guest bedchambers and offered to help me find whatever I had 'lost.' I tried to explain that I was simply acquainting myself with the rooms, but she persisted in questioning me. I finally gave up and left, but every time I turned around that tall footman—Hobbes is it?—was lurking, pretending to not be watching me. So I retreated here."

Darcy was frowning. "This is unacceptable behavior. They have no right to question you or follow you. I will speak to Mrs. Smyth and Mr. Travers straightaway."

"No, William, please. If it becomes an annoyance, I shall deal with it. For now I think they simply do not know what to make of me: ushered in fainting and green, sleeping all hours of the day, hardly showing my face for two days, and then finally appearing only to peak through cupboards! Gracious, even I am beginning to believe I am mad!" She laughed, but he was still frowning.

Lizzy rubbed a finger over the small creases between his brows, smiling impishly. "I know how to cheer you up, Mr. Darcy. Before you arrived I was reminiscing of how you so brazenly took advantage of my innocence in this very study."

Darcy guffawed and coughed. "Really! Perhaps you are going mad, Mrs. Darcy, or becoming feeble minded with advanced age at two and twenty…"

"I am still twenty-one!"

"Not for much longer, and senility may be the root cause of your hideously skewed memory of the events you speak of."

"I daresay, is that very wall not the one you pinned me against while taking shocking liberties along my décolletage?"

"I seem to recall an astonishingly strong armed fiancée forcefully ejecting me from my chair and nearly ripping the lapels off my jacket when she dragged me bodily to the indicated wall, kissing me all the while."

"Hrmph." She pursed her lips and pretended a pout. "Strong armed I may be, and thank you for the backhanded compliment, but you are a stalwart fellow and could have contested had you wished to do so."

"Well, there you have it, my dear. I did not wish to escape, and furthermore, my duty as your future and current husband is to please you in any way I can, so I was caught in the proverbial rock and hard place. I chose the path of least resistance."

He was grinning broadly and Lizzy chuckled. She sat up suddenly, hiking her skirts just enough to free her legs and straddled his lap. "Correct me if my scattered wits are failing me yet again, but did we not end up in this exact pose?"

Darcy smoothed the hair back from her face and kissed gently. "Yes, and I shall confess that ending here was my doing, although it was a result of my knees nearly buckling from the breathless exhilaration of your lips on mine and the creamy lusciousness of your neck. However, I did comport myself as a true gentleman once we were in this compromising position." He kissed her again then smiled smugly. "Therefore, it appears to me that we have reenacted the event and have ascertained that the entire episode was your fault from the outset, and I judge there was no innocence taken advantage of!"

"Very well, I will concede defeat, this time around." She began playing with the knots of his cravat. "Speaking of senility and advanced age," she said as she smirked and fluttered her lashes earning two raised brows, "it probably has yet to occur to you, but we are married now and gentlemanly restriction are a non-issue, so…?"

"I will show you advanced age!" And with a growl he pulled her tight to his chest, kissing as only married couples are freely allowed to do, and euphorically tossing all gentlemanly restriction out the window.

CHAPTER SIX

Dining with the Bingleys

THE BINGLEYS, WITH MARY and Kitty Bennet in tow, arrived from Netherfield in time for luncheon the next day. Darcy was absent, attending to business and birthday concerns, leaving Elizabeth and Georgiana to greet them and host the meal. The rooms assigned to Kitty and Mary were next to Georgiana, and the girls vacated the table immediately after dining to settle in, giggle, and gossip as young girls do, and make plans for the sojourn in Town. Charles and Jane stayed briefly, leaving for the Bingley townhouse to rest and regroup before dinner.

The Bingley townhouse was four streets south of Darcy House, on Hill Street. Although located in the Mayfair District and near Grosvenor Square, the house itself abutted Berkley Square, despite Caroline Bingley's preferred assertions that they lived at Grosvenor Square. Bingley's great-grandfather had purchased the house when acquiring his fortune, moving his wife and baby daughter from Cheapside. Half the size of Darcy House, it nonetheless was plush and beautiful, constructed of red bricks with large windows and an ornately landscaped garden with a small pond nearly equal to the Darcy's garden in size.

As with Lizzy, Jane had viewed her future home during her engagement. Thankfully, the Hursts and Caroline had been vacationing at Bath for that week, so the soon-to-be Mrs. Bingley had been free to become acquainted with the manor and make tentative plans for changes. Charles had previously tolerated his younger sister, within reason, decorating as she wished, with the consequence being rooms overstuffed with furniture, gaudy wall coverings, and a plethora of overly ornate knickknacks. Jane was blessed with the gift of innately excellent taste and instinctively recognized where the alterations needed to be. A battle was fated to ensue between she and Caroline, who would require months of steady and frequently heated reminding by Charles before she finally accepted that she was no longer the Mistress. Jane would display a surprisingly stern backbone belied by her naturally serene and unassuming character. In the end, she would revamp the house as she wished, creating an atmosphere of welcome splendor so perfected that the Bingleys would discover themselves residing there for months out of each year.

Tonight, however, the conflicts were yet to come. Word had been sent ahead, so the staff was awaiting the arrival of Mr. and Mrs. Bingley with instructions to prepare for a small dinner party that night. Caroline had readily transferred from the Hurst townhouse on the fringes of Mayfair at Bedford Square as soon as she knew her brother was expected, the past six months of living with her sister and brother-in-law having been a torture of boredom and exile to her way of thinking.

Caroline's dismay at losing Mr. Darcy had been acute. Until the very moment the actual vows had been recited, Caroline had harbored a frantic hope that the bewitched Darcy would come to his senses. She had so endlessly badgered Charles to talk sense to "the poor man" that even her infectiously amiable brother had snapped impatiently, begging her to desist at threat of strangulation. Mr. Darcy had not been safe from her barbs and embarrassingly forward advances either. The situation had become increasingly awkward, culminating with a horrid episode three weeks after the engagements had been declared.

Within days of the joint Bingley and Darcy betrothals, Caroline had arrived unannounced to Netherfield, ostensibly to congratulate her brother. However, it rapidly became clear that her true intent was to sway Darcy away from his "horrible mistake." The fact that an honorable gentleman could not withdraw an offer of marriage once rendered did not seem to penetrate her consciousness.

Mr. Bingley was distressed and Darcy extremely uncomfortable, but mostly they were both angry at her thinly veiled insults directed to both Bennet women.

Darcy's patience was at its end on the day Caroline accosted him in the library. On the day in question, he stood beside a bookcase picking a volume of poems he conjectured Elizabeth would appreciate, when Caroline entered.

He looked up and frowned slightly but bowed properly. "Miss Bingley." He took a step toward the exit, but she swiftly crossed to block his path, drawing near.

"Mr. Darcy, I was wondering if you could assist me. I was searching for a copy of Shakespeare's *Taming of the Shrew*. Do you know if there is one housed here at Netherfield?"

Darcy strongly suspected she was fabricating an excuse to detain him, as she was not much of a reader, but he indicated the shelf of Shakespeare's works. "I believe there is a copy in the collection." He walked to the case primarily to place distance rather than any desire to serve. He retrieved the book she asked for, turning to hand it to her, only to discover she had trailed and was less than a foot away from his body. He flinched and stepped back, encountering the impenetrable bookcase. "Pardon me, Miss Bingley."

She moved even closer and reached for the proffered volume, fingers firmly caressing over his. Leaning forward until her bosom brushed his hand and gazing upward through her lashes, she said in a throaty voice, "Thank you, Mr. Darcy. You are the soul of kindness. Is there any way I can express my thanks?"

Darcy was furious. He sidestepped so abruptly that Caroline pitched into the case. Drawing stiffly to his considerable height, he gifted Caroline with the full intensity of the Darcy glower and with a brusque bow excused himself, voice cold as ice. By the end of the day, Caroline was bundled off to London to join her sister on their trip to Bath. Jane and Elizabeth were not informed of the truth, as their private relief to have the troublesome Miss Bingley gone overrode any curiosity.

Bingley's sisters had come for the wedding, naturally, but they arrived only the day before, permitting Darcy to ignore Caroline. Now, after all the time which had passed, Darcy no longer fostered any residual anger but instead pitied Caroline. As with many issues these days, his happiness was so profound that his heart simply did not have space for ill feelings.

Darcy was in good humor when they appeared at the Bingley townhouse. Elizabeth was well, the past two days being very good ones for her, and the birthday plans were all set to his satisfaction. The girls, even Mary, were in high spirits at the prospect of shopping and adventures, and their giddiness infected the elder Darcys. None of them knew that Miss Bingley was joining them, but it would not have dampened their spirits.

Caroline stood regally on the staircase landing, having carefully dressed herself in a stunning gown that displayed her fine figure to its full advantage. It was too late to secure Mr. Darcy for herself, but she intended to show him what he had tossed over for the skinny country chit. Imagine her consternation, evidence by a blanched face and visible dropped jaw, when Lizzy breezed in on her husband's arm wearing a divine, fashionable gown of gold crepe, the bodice of which barely contained a far fuller bosom than Caroline recalled. Her hair was stupendous, with a set of fabulous pearl and diamond clips, the strand of Darcy pearls about her neck, and an exquisite shawl of Japanese silk. She positively glowed, as did Mr. Darcy in a way Caroline had never witnessed, and the casual, unconscious way his hands lingered and caressed Elizabeth's bare shoulders as he removed her shawl brought a flush to Caroline's pale cheeks.

None of them noticed her for a time, the greetings proceeding as if it had been months instead of three days. Finally, it was Georgiana who glanced upwards.

"Miss Bingley!"

All eyes immediately raised, a moment of silence descending. Caroline recovered her composure, gliding gracefully down the stairs. She delighted in the sensation of all eyes on her—as it should be, to her way of thinking. Then, with a stab of irritation, she noted that Darcy's gaze touched her for less than a second before moving away to the footman patiently waiting to take Elizabeth's shawl.

Elizabeth was smiling pleasantly. "Miss Bingley, what an unexpected delight. Mr. Darcy and I did not realize you would be joining us. Pray, how have you been?"

"I am quite well, Mrs. Darcy, thank you. You are the same I trust?"

Lizzy laughed. "I believe I am better than well, actually, at least for the moment. Let us pray it continues."

Darcy was studying his wife with a small smile on his lips, a hand lightly resting on the small of her back. Jane laughed softly at Lizzy's words, although

Caroline did not comprehend why. Not exerting the effort to puzzle it out, she turned her attention to Darcy.

"Mr. Darcy, it is a pleasure to see you. Are you 'better than well' also?"

He met her eyes and inclined his head. "Miss Bingley, I am excellent. I daresay the best I have been in my entire life." Before finishing his earnest little speech, his eyes had returned to his wife, ignoring Caroline.

Mr. Bingley chimed in with a call to the parlor until dinner was served. The gentlemen stayed close to their wives, chatting casually. Caroline was reintroduced to Lizzy's sisters. Mary, as typical, stood apart, awed and intimidated by Bingley's sister. Kitty could not stop staring. Ever since the insertion of Bingley and Darcy to the Bennet household, Kitty had been inundated and captivated by finery and grandeur of all sorts. Caroline found herself near Georgiana, surreptitiously observing Darcy nearly as giddy as her ridiculous brother.

"Miss Bingley," Georgiana began shyly, "your gown is lovely. I do not believe I would ever have the courage to wear that shade, but it so becomes you."

"Thank you, Miss Darcy. Proper fashion is a fine art. You are young still and need not yet worry too greatly, although I daresay your debut is rapidly approaching. It is a shame that you have no one to assist with the necessary requirements of society. Men certainly do not apprehend the nuances of stylish dress and feminine exigency."

Georgiana blushed. "Well, there is an amazing French modiste in Lambton, and while we are here, Elizabeth and I will be having new gowns created by Madame Millicent and Frau Braun. My brother insists. Elizabeth needs new gowns, although I surely do not."

"It is fortunate that you have traveled to Town, if Mrs. Darcy needs new gowns. I suppose she has resisted deserting the comfortable and simple clothing she has always been familiar with."

Georgiana frowned. "No, it is not—" but she was interrupted when the footman announced dinner.

"Lizzy," Jane said as they sat, "you must immediately speak if any of the dishes disturb you."

"Thank you, Jane dear. I will be fine. These past two days have been blessedly free of any major discomfort."

"Have you been ill, Mrs. Darcy?" Caroline asked.

"Nothing that will not improve in time, Miss Bingley."

"Bingley," Darcy spoke, "my steward sent me the information I requested on the Hasberry Estate. I brought it with me for you to peruse at your leisure. I do hope you will give it some consideration."

"It is a lovely piece of land, Charles," Lizzy interjected. "William took me to see it before we left. I believe my devious husband was ensuring my 'yea' vote and entrusting me to whisper in Jane's ear."

Darcy smiled. "Do not be ridiculous, Elizabeth. Bingley is a grown man and will make his own decision. We all know that wives have no influence over their husbands."

Lizzy and Mr. Bingley laughed out loud, and Darcy winked at Jane. Caroline could not believe her eyes or ears. Darcy jesting! Unfathomable.

"Yes, yes, of course dear," Lizzy said, patting her husband's hand, "this is why it is fortunate that Charles and Jane will be visiting later in the summer. You can drag Mr. Bingley to Hasberry while we weak minded women stay home and knit."

"Charles, are you seriously contemplating relocating to Derbyshire?" Caroline asked as she smiled winsomely at Mr. Darcy, who was not looking at her, but smiling at his wife. "It is beautiful there. I have always adored the Peak District."

"It is one of many ideas, Caroline. My wife and I are not certain which path we will take, although I know my Jane would like to be close to Lizzy, especially now." Jane smiled sweetly at her husband.

"Jane," Caroline continued, "would you not miss your parents if you moved away?"

"Yes, of course, and that is why we are not wishing to rush into a permanent decision."

"How is your family, Mrs. Darcy? Your mother and father are in good health?"

"They are quite well, thank you."

"And your youngest sister? How are she and her... husband faring in... Newcastle, was it not?" Caroline asked with a smirk and slight emphasis on *husband*.

An uncomfortable silence fell over the table, as Lizzy reached to lightly caress Darcy's hand where it lay on the table. Smiling innocently, she replied, "They are also well, Miss Bingley. Your kindness in inquiring after my family touches my heart. Of course, in an obliquitous way they are also your family, so

I suppose it is natural that their well-being would be of your concern."

Caroline blanched and Jane hid a smile in her napkin. Darcy nudged Lizzy with his knee and took a quick bite of bread to hide his smile. Caroline remained quiet for a time while the conversation varied. She lost count of the number of times Darcy and the upstart shared a tender glance or sly touch. He appeared to observe her every bite with the utmost interest, to Caroline's bafflement. Once, when Elizabeth brought her napkin to her mouth and bowed her head briefly, he rapidly leaned in and whispered something with an expression of deep concern which only cleared when Elizabeth shook her head negatively. Then, to Caroline's shocked irritation, he actually bestowed a brushing kiss to her temple. *Poor man,* she thought, *his hideous bewitchment seems to have overtaken him.*

The rather tragic truth is that Caroline Bingley simply could not fathom the concept of love. It was one thing to see her naïve brother fawn over his pretty but brainless wife; Caroline was accustomed to watching him make a fool of himself over a pretty girl. The fact that he had married this one was embarrassing, but she did not conceive of his emotions as being any different than all the others he had been infatuated with. It was not that Caroline did not care for her brother; she did. Nonetheless, she deemed him shallow and moronic; thus, it would never occur to her to entertain the concept of him truly being in deep anything, let alone love.

Mr. Darcy was an entirely different matter. Frankly, as fortuitous as she had considered it for her future, Caroline could never reason why Mr. Darcy was friendly with her brother. *Charles, God love him, is such a simpleton*, she would think to herself, *so how can an intelligent man like Mr. Darcy be his friend?* Despite the puzzle of the question, Caroline had given it little contemplation. The advantage was all hers, and to her delight, she knew her close proximity over the past several years to one of the most eligible bachelors in England had been the fount of wild envy among three-quarters of the ton. She had seen Mr. Darcy as the perfect catch, and not only because of the size of his pocketbook. Darcy would be flabbergasted, but the fact is that his cool, aloof demeanor as a result of his shyness and disdain for the foolishness and falseness of society had translated to Caroline as superiority of character. Caroline looked down her nose at everyone, was cruel and snide, haughty and arrogant in the extreme. Lizzy was not the first to interpret Mr. Darcy's past behavior in this light. So, Caroline figured they were two of a similar kind.

Even now, witnessing his happiness, devotion, playfulness, and joviality, she did not evaluate it correctly. In her eyes, he was enchanted, which to a degree was true, but she assumed it was in a negative way. In a twisted bit of logic, she reckoned it her duty to point out his error and ridiculousness before he made a bigger fool of himself before all of society. Simply put, Caroline was ragingly jealous and her pride seriously wounded. One would sympathize if there had ever been the slightest hint of love involved in her pursuit of Mr. Darcy, but since it had always been mercenary in nature, sympathy was impossible.

"Mrs. Darcy," she inquired sweetly, "how are you finding Pemberley? I have always regarded it the most splendid manor in all of England, do you not agree?"

"I do not believe I could assert that fact with any confidence, as I have personally seen very few of the vast number of houses in all of England. However, I concur that it is splendid."

"Have you made many changes as Mistress? Redecorated and reorganized? Pemberley has long been without a woman's touch, no offense intended, Mr. Darcy, so I imagine there were numerous areas to address."

"You would be mistaken, Miss Bingley. Pemberley has been excellently managed by my husband and a superb staff. I have seen no need to change anything. Learning where everything is has taken me most of the past six months," she completed with a laugh.

Darcy smiled. "My wife is jesting, of course. Within a month she had mapped the entire estate, out buildings as well. She employs her boundless energy and superior intellect and has assumed most of Mrs. Reynolds's duties. I am quite proud of her." Lizzy blushed prettily and Darcy kissed her hand.

Caroline would not let the subject rest. "Most impressive," she murmured, "I suppose redecorating has consumed much of your time as well?"

"Not really. My private parlor was the only room requiring extensive renovation, having sadly sat vacant for so many years. We did rearrange our private sitting room, but that has been all. William's mother and other ancestors had amazing taste. I see no reason to change a thing."

Caroline was shocked, on several counts. The "our private sitting room" frankly baffled her, as she had never heard of such a thing. "Certainly the esteemed departed Mrs. Darcy did have excellent taste, but styles do change. Surely you must recognize the expectation to modernize and, of course, to compliment your own personality. As Mistress it is essential for you to place your distinctive flavor to your home, Mrs. Darcy. Has no one informed you of this necessity?"

Darcy was scowling and opened his mouth to speak, but Lizzy squeezed his knee and replied with a shrug. "Fashion and trends are fickle, Miss Bingley, whereas elegance, refinement, and graceful aestheticism are timeless. Pemberley boasts the latter in all aspects. Modernizing for the sake of convenience and comfort is legitimate, but to constantly revamp in a vain attempt to chase the whimsy of fads is nonsensical. My ego does not require such superficial blandishments."

Darcy's face had relaxed into its usual serious pose, but inwardly he was jubilant with pride. Caroline was at a loss. She recognized that she had just been insulted but could not readily think how to respond. Fortunately for all, the conversation turned to the planned shopping expeditions for later in the week; Kitty was especially all fluttery at the prospect, having never shopped in Town. A couple of references to baby furniture and clothing were made, but Caroline was so caught up in her own thoughts that she did not note them.

The meal ended without further mishap, everyone in the party retiring to the music room. Georgiana and Mary played a couple of duets they had been practicing, Mary displaying an increased aptitude under Georgiana's gentle instruction. The ladies each sang a couple of songs. Caroline chose a particularly romantic ballad, performed brilliantly as she did possess a stunning alto; however, as her eyes alit on Darcy a great portion of the time, it was uncomfortable for all. Darcy's face was a mask of dark disapproval, fingers warm and tense on the nape of Lizzy's neck. Bingley quickly challenged Darcy to a game of chess, breaking up the musical entertainment session.

Mary, Georgiana, and Kitty continued to play and sing softly in the background while Jane, Lizzy, and Caroline sat on the settees and drank tea.

"Do you have any idea what Mr. Darcy has planned for you tomorrow Lizzy?" Jane asked.

"Not one iota. He has been immeasurably secretive about the affair and rather smug about it all to boot. All I know for certain is that we are dining with Lord and Lady Matlock, but I have no clue as to whether they even know it is my birthday."

"Tomorrow is your birthday? How lovely," Caroline murmured. "Mr. Darcy has planned a surprise, I take it?"

Lizzy laughed. "Oh yes! I joked when I surprised him on his birthday November last that he had six months to plan my surprise and I rather think he took me at my word! He has been scribbling notes and sending couriers hither and yon, asking me all sorts of innocent questions about previous trips to London." Lizzy shook her head and glanced fondly at her spouse, currently scowling in concentration at the chess table before him.

Caroline felt ill. "You have become well acquainted with Lord and Lady Matlock, Mrs. Darcy?"

"Yes. They live quite close to Pemberley, as I am sure you know. They spent Christmas with us, along with Colonel Fitzwilliam, and we dined with them frequently over the winter and spring. Have you been so fortunate as to make their acquaintance, Miss Bingley?" Lizzy did not mention how attentive Lady Matlock had been during her recovery, nor the role Lord Matlock played in the Orman fiasco. These were painful topics and she did not wish to discuss them with Caroline.

"At a few social gatherings, yes. Has the breach been healed with Lady Catherine?"

Jane inhaled sharply and Lizzy's smile froze. After an uncomfortable pause: "This is a private matter, Miss Bingley. It would be best not to pursue."

"Of course, I understand. It is just so sad when families have these little feuds leading to gulfs in the relationship. I know how close Mr. Darcy has been to his aunt over the years so can only imagine how painful it must be for him to suffer this schism." She shook her head mournfully, internally rejoicing at the grim cast to Elizabeth's face. "Sadly, one must live with the consequences of one's choices in life, no matter how regretful they may be."

"I can assure you, Miss Bingley, my husband has no regrets. You presume too much in declaring any knowledge of Mr. Darcy's feelings on this or any matter. I would caution you, as a friend, to remember this." Lizzy smiled sweetly and took a sip of tea, turning then to Jane. "Has Charles made a choice of decorator, Jane? William was mentioning Klaus Breihmer or perhaps Jonathon Worthington. They apparently have fabulous reputations." They then launched into a discussion of redecorating the Bingley townhouse, which gave Caroline something new to complain about.

It was a warm evening, and although the windows were opened, no breeze was forthcoming. Elizabeth fanned herself continuously but began to experience a vague light-headedness and faint headache. Hoping to forestall a more serious affliction, she whispered to Jane that she needed to retreat to the terrace for some fresh air. Caroline had moved to the pianoforte to listen to Georgiana, glancing up as a pale and trembling Elizabeth, after a pointed visual exchange with Mr. Darcy, slipped out the door. Darcy rose quickly and followed his wife, anxiety written all over his face.

Caroline was overcome with curiosity. "Is Mrs. Darcy unwell?"

Georgiana beamed. "Nothing serious. She is actually getting better each day, and the physician says the symptoms should pass soon."

"She has needed a physician? How terrible. She always appeared so healthy and strong. Country stock, they say, usually has greater fortitude. Poor Mr. Darcy! No wondered he appears so dismayed." She tsked.

Kitty flared. "My sister is with child, Miss Bingley, not unhealthy. Mr. Darcy is concerned, not dismayed."

Caroline turned white as a ghost, mouth falling open. "Please excuse me." She exited the room, feeling faint herself. *A baby! An heir to Pemberley!* Of course it was absurd. Her chance with Mr. Darcy had long been an impossibility, and she had already set her gaze elsewhere for a suitable substitute. Nonetheless, she could not stem the flush of anger and melancholy that lanced through her.

She stood in a darkened alcove in the hallway, breathing heavily and unaware of her surroundings for several minutes. Gradually, her misty eyes focused, spying Darcy and Elizabeth on the balcony.

Elizabeth sat on the stone bench, leaning against the wall with eyes closed, Darcy kneeling in front. He was fanning her vigorously and holding her hand.

"Thank you, beloved. That truly helps."

"Do you need something cold to drink, my love?"

She opened her eyes and smiled, softly caressing his cheek. "It is passing. Here, sit next to me." She patted the bench and he complied, leaning first to plant a kiss to her lower abdomen. He sat near, circling an arm about her shoulders and drawing her close. He kissed her forehead, free hand gently rubbing her belly.

Lizzy sighed and shut her eyes. "I think I am just tired. My mistake. I felt so well today that I did not nap and now it is catching up with me." One hand lay on his inner thigh, the other over his caressing one.

"As soon as you wish, we shall extend our apologies and go home. Jane and Charles will understand. Then I can hold you in my arms and ensure you sleep the night through."

"Hmmm. What a delightful thought. I want to be well rested for tomorrow."

He smiled, burying his face in her hair and kissing softly. "I have planned an easy day, my heart. Nothing too strenuous. Just you and me, alone, with plenty of opportunities for me to tell you how deeply I love you."

Elizabeth lifted her face to his with an unabashed glow of love. He cupped her cheek, running a thumb over her lips and chin. "Mrs. Darcy," he whispered, meeting her mouth with a tender but thorough kiss.

Caroline observed and heard it all, a fist at her mouth preventing the choked sob from escaping. With a lurch she retreated to the first room available, the dark library. Never in all her life had she witnessed such a scene. With a stab to her heart she nonetheless recognized it for what it was: love. The elusive emotion spoken of in fairy tales and poems and songs, but rarely seen, at least so openly. Caroline did not quite know what to feel. The anger at losing Mr. Darcy was still there, the resentment at the inferior ranked country chit for becoming Mistress of Pemberley remained, yet she could not deny what she had seen. They truly loved each other. Any interpretations of enchantment or nefarious designs were baseless.

For the first time in her life, Caroline Bingley wondered if such an emotion could be hers. She visualized their countenances as they gazed at each other and her stony, selfish heart melted minutely. Still, she quickly reasoned, what profit is love without status and wealth? With much to ponder, Caroline sought the sanctuary of her bedchamber. Only time would reveal if these epiphanies would usher in a permanent character alteration.

CHAPTER SEVEN

Happy Birthday, Mr. Darcy

G RACEFULLY ESCAPING FROM THE Bingley Townhouse was an easy task, all parties solicitous of Lizzy's needs. No one commented on Caroline's absence; in truth, only Charles noted her omission from the group. Once safely returned to Darcy House, Darcy ordered his wife to their chamber while he bid the girls wishes for pleasant dreams and performed the ritual task of assuring the house was secure. Lizzy sat on the balcony sofa when Darcy rejoined her, patting the waiting space next to her.

"Night dreaming, my love?" he asked with a soft kiss to her temple.

"Speculating on the morrow and recollecting your birthday. I did surprise you greatly, did I not, William?" She turned, draping her legs over his lap. He smiled, beginning his nightly custom of fondling her belly gently.

"You certainly did! I knew on some level that my birthday was approaching, but all my thoughts during those days were on you and November the twenty-eighth, willing time to hurry. As I was departing London the day before, Mrs. Smyth bid me birthday wishes. I covered myself well, I believe, but the truth is she caught me completely unaware. For a moment I had to perform rapid mathematics, as I had not consciously noted the date since jotting it on a correspondence three days prior!"

"Were you never going to tell me? Keep me thinking you were eight and twenty forever?" She tickled him, earning a chuckle.

"Yes, that was the plan," he answered drolly. "Perpetual youth. Actually, I fretted all the way to Hertfordshire. I was stuck, you see. If I mentioned it was my birthday, I feared you would feel guilty for not inquiring. I did not wish this, as I truly do not care about such celebrations, at least as regards me. However, if I did not confess, I feared you being hurt, thinking I was withholding a portion of myself. Never would I want you to think this!" He spoke the last with vehemence, Lizzy lifting to hug him close and bestow a kiss.

"I would never harbor such a thought, beloved. Even then we were nearly one flesh, despite not yet being wed."

He beamed, stroking her downy cheek. "Yes, this is true. In the end you were a step ahead of me and proved, once again, how deeply you love me." He paused, staring intently into her eyes as he caressed. He resumed, his voice low and husky, "What a road we have traveled, Elizabeth. So many delightful memories already, all which testify to our unique love. I will never forget my birthday, my soul, nor not treasure your gift to me. I love you."

"I love you, too," she replied, words then lost to passionate kisses as memories of that special event swirled.

❧

Setting: Evening at Longbourn some three weeks after the engagements of the Bennet sisters.

Dinner had finished, the young couples had taken their evening stroll about the grounds, and now all reposed in the parlor. It had become a sort of routine the past three weeks, although on occasion Mr. Bingley and Mr. Darcy had hosted their fiancées at Netherfield.

Darcy, as always, felt an odd mixture of supreme elation to be with his Elizabeth and annoyance at the presence of the members of her family. Mary was in the other room pounding out a particularly morbid tune on the old pianoforte. Kitty was off somewhere, probably playing with her puppy, Darcy supposed. Jane and Bingley sat on the other sofa in placid companionship. Mr. Bennet sat hunched in the corner chair, alternately reading as he sipped his port and gazing with amused pleasure at his two eldest daughters. Mrs. Bennet bustled about the room, chattering constantly, and being ignored by all.

Darcy sat in one corner of the sofa with a book in his lap propped on a pillow and a tumbler of brandy in his other hand. Elizabeth sat next to him, close enough to feel her warmth and catch an occasional whiff of perfume, yet not actually touching him. She bent diligently over her embroidery, luscious neck arched and oh so very tantalizing.

He shifted uncomfortably, sensuous musings again assaulting his self-control, and forced bedazzled eyes to the page in front of him. He momentarily could not remember his place and, when he did, realized that he had read the same paragraph at least a dozen times and had no idea what it said. In fact, he who could normally devour a book in a handful of days had been attempting to read this one for some two months! To make matters worse, the truth was he had absolutely no clue what the book was even about. He sighed. In point of fact, he had not managed to complete a book since the horrid events at Rosings in April. He kept picking up a different one, telling himself that the book was at fault when he patently knew that was not the root cause of his distraction.

He managed to focus attention enough to finish the current page, but he was again distracted when Elizabeth stretched her neck and brought one delicate hand up to rub her muscles. How he yearned to be the one massaging her aching shoulders! The mental image caused him to grip his glass so tightly that fingers turned white. The all too familiar clench in his groin made him abundantly thankful he had a pillow on his lap. To his increased mortification, he glanced up to see Mr. Bennet staring at him over the top of his book with a wise smile. Darcy flushed and quickly turned his eyes to the book.

He wondered if Elizabeth experienced any of the same discomfort he did. The few chaste kisses they had indulged in had been welcomed by her and—he was convinced—enjoyed. Additionally, he could not erase the passion that had flared between them upon the occasion of their first kiss in Longbourn's garden barely an hour after their engagement. He was confident of her love for him, but remained unsure of its depth. He chided himself for doubting her or for expecting too much too soon. His love, his passionate ardor for her, was of long standing. It often seemed as if he could hardly remember a time when she had not lived in his heart and soul. He understood that her affection for him was more recent and, therefore, perhaps not as profound. He was willing to give her time.

He would have been quite surprised, therefore, to discover the train of her thoughts. His nearness was frankly driving her mad. She was vividly cognizant of every breath he took and every glance sent her direction. His heat radiated and oozed under her skin; his cologne, a mix of cardamom, something vaguely woodsy, and a musky aroma that she rightfully believed was his natural scent, assaulted her senses; and the long-fingered, elegant hands resting on firm thighs elicited graphic images and memories of each time he had touched her. Strange sensations threatened to overwhelm her. Every time he took a sip of brandy she felt a stab of emotion not unlike jealousy! The memory of each and every time his lips had touched hers was etched in her mind and felt deep in her veins. The five weeks remaining of their engagement seemed an eternity.

"Mr. Darcy," she asked abruptly, hoping to dispel the visions and halt the shivers, "the book you are reading, is it an interesting one?"

Darcy jumped slightly when she spoke. He looked up into her amazing eyes and time stopped. He had no idea what she had said. "I beg your pardon, Miss Elizabeth. What did you say?"

She smiled. "I asked if the book you are reading is interesting."

"Oh! Yes. Quite interesting," he answered lamely.

"Do you think it would be of interest to me? You know how I enjoy reading. Improves the mind, you understand."

Darcy laughed softly. "Yes, it does."

"So, then you believe I may glean value from reading your book? When you are finished, naturally."

"If you wish, Miss Elizabeth. I would be delighted to lend it to you."

"I assume it must be a particularly fascinating story. Or possibly it may be too deep for my young mind to comprehend."

He was puzzled. "I am positive your mind is adept enough to comprehend any topic, Miss Elizabeth."

"I was concerned, you see, Mr. Darcy, as it has taken you more than an hour to study this one page. In point of fact, you have been reading this book for the past two weeks and are only on page fifteen. I can only speculate, but considering how intelligent you are, the only feasible conclusion is that the story is so extraordinary that you are rereading each paragraph several times for sheer pleasure, or it is necessary to do so in order to decipher the author's intent." She was smiling impishly and he could not resist laughing.

"You have caught me, my dear." He glanced quickly around the room, relieved to note that no one was paying them any attention. "The truth is, if you must know, I find myself terribly unfocused whenever I am near you and cannot concentrate. I may be on page fifteen; however, I would be unable to render an accounting of the content thus far." He blushed faintly but met her dancing eyes. "Does this shock you, Miss Elizabeth?"

"You see this sampler?" She held up her embroidery.

"Yes, of course," he answered in confusion.

"I have been working on this for a month and should have completed it in a week. These stitches here are all wrong, and I have had to rip this section out three times! And I cannot tell you how many times I have stabbed my fingers. I judge you and I are suffering from the same disease." She, too, was blushing, but she held his penetrating gaze.

He reached down and squeezed her hand, then brought her fingers to his lips for a tender kiss. His eyes captivated her, crystalline blue orbs darkening slightly in what she now recognized was ardor. "I am very pleased to hear you say that, Elizabeth. You have no idea how pleased." His voice was muted and husky, imbued with emotion, and her breath caught in her throat. *Look away from his eyes, Lizzy!* she thought desperately, but could not comply.

In a desperate attempt at levity, she teased, "Pleased, Mr. Darcy, that I have pricked my fingers?"

Darcy, however, was wholly absorbed in her fine chocolate eyes and only smiled. "I am William to you, and my mother used to kiss my wounds to make them better. Should I kiss your aching fingers? Will that relieve your pain?" He proceeded to give the tips of each finger a tiny kiss with full lips soft and warm. Lizzy released a shaky laugh and managed to pull her hand from his grasp, resuming her embroidery with rosy cheeks.

Darcy seemed immeasurably pleased with himself.

"I received a letter from Georgiana today," she said, needing to change the subject.

"Did you? My sister seems to have forgone writing to me these past weeks in favor of writing to you."

Lizzy looked quickly at his face. "I am sorry, William! I have no wish to keep her from writing to you."

Darcy laughed. "I am joking Elizabeth. You know how pleased I am that you and Georgiana are friends." And it was true. Two days after their engagement,

Lizzy had asked him for permission to write to Georgiana. He had lightly scolded, reminding her that Georgiana would soon be her sister. Therefore, he stated emphatically, it was important that they establish a relationship and he, frankly, no longer had any authority over the situation. She had been deeply moved by his assurances, well aware of how dear his sister was to him. It was another of the dozens of ways he daily showed his love for her.

Now he asked, "So what did my sister have to say?"

"Nothing of consequence. Just girl talk." There it was: the two most effective words in the English language to render any man mute. In actuality, Georgiana had imparted information of extreme significance. It was revealed that Mr. Darcy's twenty-ninth birthday was on November the tenth, less than a month away. Elizabeth was unclear on what she would do with this knowledge, but it assuredly was too important to ignore.

Later that night, as she and Jane were readying for bed, Lizzy told her about Mr. Darcy's approaching birthday. "You must help me think of something special, Jane. This is our first celebration together so it must be memorable."

"Of course! We have time to plan, and I am sure Mr. Bingley will assist us. Fret not, Lizzy, we shall make it memorable."

❧

November the tenth, Darcy's birthday and precisely eighteen days before their nuptials, dawned clear but extremely cold with a dusting of snow having fallen in the night. Aware that the weather was unpredictable this time of the year, Lizzy and her cohorts had planned the birthday festivities to take place inside Netherfield. Mr. Bingley had been as giddy as a child at the idea of surprising his friend. In fact, his enthusiasm was so infectious that Lizzy was afraid that he would be unable to keep the secret. Luckily for her, Darcy was so engrossed in his own happiness that he hardly noticed anything Bingley said or did.

Darcy had uttered not a word about his birthday. Although Lizzy was relieved to be able to carry out her plans for surprising him, she did think it odd that he kept silent. She feared that perhaps his normally reticent and shy nature would not welcome being taken unawares. Bingley assured her that he would love it. She worried that he may be wounded as she had not shown interest in establishing when his birthday was. To her chagrin, he had discovered her birthday by boldly asking her mother one evening while at dinner, so maybe he was injured that she had not returned the gesture. She abhorred the very idea of causing him pain, no matter how slight. Thankfully, the day was finally here and soon he would know how special he was to her.

He had returned to Netherfield the previous afternoon, after a short trip of three days to London on business. It was his second such trip since their engagement, and Lizzy missed him terribly when he was gone. His first separation from her had occurred two weeks after their engagement and had only lasted five days. At the time, Lizzy had mentally shrugged, waving adieu with mild sadness but not anticipating how deeply her grief would be by that evening when, for the first time, they did not dine together. It had struck her suddenly and forcibly how utterly his presence had wrapped around her heart. The loneliness she had felt while sitting at the Longbourn dining table with her boisterous family chattering all about was as a knife in her soul. That night she had cried herself to sleep, mortified at her silliness but unable to halt the tears. For the first time in her entire life, she had known what it was to truly mourn and suffer depression. His letters, arriving each day, eased her wretchedness to a degree. Still, her joy upon seeing his staid but oh-so-handsome face had flowed through her in a piercing wave, stunning her in its intensity.

This separation was equally as horrible; however, on this occasion his absence had been fortuitous, as it made carrying out the final plans easier.

It had not been difficult to get Darcy out of Netherfield that morning, since he daily went to Longbourn with Mr. Bingley to meet their fiancées. After the obligatory greetings to Mr. and Mrs. Bennet, Kitty, and Mary, the couples left. Jane had "innocently" suggested that a morning carriage ride to see the freshly fallen snow would be enjoyable. So Mr. Bingley and Jane set out ahead in one phaeton, Darcy and Lizzy following in the other.

It had been almost six weeks since their engagement, and in that time, Lizzy and her betrothed had grown unbelievably close and so very comfortable with each other. They conversed about everything now with an ease that was extraordinarily intimate. The agony of waiting for their wedding day was acutely felt by them both. At times like these, sitting side by side in the carriage with fingers intertwined under the blanket, talking and laughing joyously, their mutual communion and love were overwhelming. Lizzy was hard pressed to remember that they were not already married, such was the level of their unity.

They arrived at Netherfield in time for luncheon. Once they had been relieved of their coats, gloves, and hats, Mr. Bingley took the lead. He offered his arm to Jane and walked toward the dining room. However, he passed by the double doors and continued on down a hall toward a far parlor rarely used. Darcy, who was absorbed in the enchanting appearance of Elizabeth's rosy cheeks and sparkling eyes, did not even notice the detour until they were almost to the door.

"Bingley," Darcy asked, "where in blazes are you leading us?"

"Thought a change of view would be welcome, Darcy. Come along!"

Mr. Bingley swept the door open and nimbly stepped aside so that Darcy was the first to enter the room. He stopped on the threshold thunderstruck. The normally sober room of muted creams and gold was a riot of bright colors. Yards of ribbons in every color of the rainbow were arranged across the windows and along the ceiling, twisted and tied together with some dangling like branches of a bizarre willow tree. A huge banner was draped over one wall with the words *Joyous Birth Day* painted on it. The furnishings were pushed against the walls and in the middle of the room sat two tables. One was set for dining with four chairs. The other was laden with wrapped gifts and a cake. The cake was round, white frosting decorated with tiny flowers and leaves, with one tall lit candle in the middle. Darcy had never seen anything like it.

He came to his senses when Lizzy wrapped her arms around his waist and whispered into his ear, "Are you surprised, my love?" Jane and Bingley were smiling at him.

"I am… speechless," he stammered. He looked at Elizabeth. "Did you plan this? How did you know?"

"Yes I did, with some help obviously, and it was Georgiana who told me," she replied. "Are you pleased?"

"Yes! Yes, I am!" He enfolded her with sturdy arms and kissed tenderly. Jane and Bingley swiftly turned into the room, letting them have a moment without prying eyes.

"I was afraid you were hurt, thinking I did not care when your birthday was," Lizzy whispered with a hint of anxiety in her voice.

Darcy kissed her again, stroking over one cheek with feathering fingertips. "Not at all, dearest Elizabeth. My birthday has passed mostly unnoticed for years now. Georgiana always remembers, as does Mrs. Reynolds. Some years I have completely forgotten it myself until they remind me! I will receive a small gift from my sister and my favorite meal for dinner, but that is all. I have not had a celebration of any significance since I was a child. This is so unexpected!"

Lizzy glowed with pleasure. "Well, then, let the festivities begin! After you, Mr. Darcy."

Luncheon was served first. They were all in high spirits so laughter abounded. After the meal was finished and the servants had cleared the table, a tea service was brought in, but the aroma was definitely not that of tea. It was warm cocoa, a favorite treat of Darcy's. Snow had begun to fall outside, but the room was cozy and the occupants were relaxed.

"So, explain the cake," Darcy asked. "I have never heard of a candle on a cake before."

Bingley spoke up, "Lizzy read of a German tradition of placing a single candle, a 'Light of Life' was it, Lizzy?"

"Yes. The idea is that the candle symbolizes the life of the person being celebrated. It must stay lit all day and be blown out, by you, at dusk. You can make a wish before you blow it out and it will be granted."

Darcy smiled. "I am not one to lend credence to silly superstitions, but this seems harmless fun, so I shall play along. It certainly is pretty."

They spent the afternoon playing several parlor games, charades first. Lizzy and Darcy paired up against Jane and Bingley. They were all astounded to discover that Darcy had a flair for the dramatic and was an exceptional player. Lizzy read his expressions readily now so could guess what he was acting out in short order, and they easily won the most rounds. Next they played Twenty Questions. Lizzy had asked Mr. Bennet, a neutral party, to come up with topics for both games, and he had thoroughly enjoyed conjuring up the oddest things. More than once they were stumped. In the end, Jane and Bingley proved the victors. Lastly, they played blind man's bluff. Darcy always seemed to know exactly where Lizzy was, but she was agile and quick so could easily elude him. Bingley actually proved to be the best player. He had an uncanny ability to outthink another's movements and would catch them every time. Needless to say, whenever a fiancée was caught, a pause would be necessary for a brief interlude of nuzzling and kisses, but no one minded.

Dinner was served late in the evening with the four famished after their activities. Georgiana, upon request, had provided a list of Darcy's favorite foods. Lizzy joked that it was fortunate she had asked Georgiana's advice since she was contemplating serving mutton. Darcy winced and they all laughed. He detested mutton.

After dinner it was time for presents. The table was taken away and a couple of sofas were brought forth. Lizzy sat next to Darcy on one sofa with Jane and Charles on the other. Georgiana had sent her gift: a new riding crop. Charles gave him a pocket watch and Jane a set of handkerchiefs, which she had embroidered with his initials. Darcy was touched that his soon-to-be sister would go to so much trouble for him and he told her so. Jane blushed.

Lizzy handed him her present, wrapped with silk and a blue ribbon the color of his eyes. Darcy opened it gradually, theatrically adding to the tension. Inside was a book: *Paradise Lost* by John Milton.

"It is the first edition volume," Lizzy said. "You said you had been searching for that one."

Darcy was stunned. "Elizabeth, I cannot believe you remember that! I said it in passing when you were at Pemberley, when I showed you the library."

"I vividly remember every moment and every word of that day," she said softly, touching his cheek gently with her fingertips. Neither of them noticed that Jane and Bingley arose and crept silently from the room.

He captured her hand and kissed it, then leaned over and kissed her lips. "You are amazing," he breathed. "I love you so, my Elizabeth. How did you ever find it?"

She laughed. "My father has connections. He is forever adding old books to his collection. He is acquainted with a man at Oxford who specializes in finding unusual volumes. He had three Milton first editions! Open it, there is more."

Darcy was unsure if his heart could take any more, but he complied. Inside was a bookmark of fine silk with a quilted backing. Lizzy had embroidered in her delicate hand a verse from Genesis: "The two shall become one flesh." Below were two hearts intertwined with *Elizabeth* in one and *Fitzwilliam* in the other.

To say that Darcy was overwhelmed would be a gross understatement. Tears welled up in his eyes and he could not speak. He gathered Lizzy into a tight embrace and simply held her, hoping that his wildly beating heart would express his thankfulness. He finally withdrew, gazing into her eyes with bottomless devotion, and then kissed her with reckless abandon. His soul was fiercely touched. She responded in kind, fingers instantly rising to caress the flesh above his cravat and lace into thick hair as their kiss deepened to a dangerous level. Neither of them wanted to stop, and it took a monumental act of strength to do so.

Darcy cupped her face with both large hands, eyes closed and forehead resting on hers as he attempted to regulate his erratic breathing. "God, Elizabeth! How I want you! How desperately I love you!"

"Two weeks," she murmured, "just two more weeks, my heart."

He chuckled harshly and opened his eyes to see her glorious face so near his own. "It feels like an eternity." He met her lips in a tender, controlled kiss. "Elizabeth, my precious love, this has been the very best birthday of my entire life. How can I ever thank you?"

She smiled naughtily. "Well, my birthday will be here in six months. You can start planning now!" They both laughed and the jocularity lightened the mood. After another brief kiss, they recalled Jane and Charles, who had managed to take advantage of their alone time in like pursuits.

More hot cocoa was served, and then it was time to blow out the candle and have some cake. Darcy made his silent wish, glowing eyes locked with his fiancée's, and cut the cake, performing the honored task of serving the others. All too soon it was time to return the ladies to Longbourn.

Some weeks after, Lizzy and Darcy were in their bed at Pemberley lying in each other's arms. They were in the satisfied haze of post lovemaking, Lizzy gently caressing his chest while Darcy played with her hair. Out of the blue Lizzy spoke. "William? What was your wish when you blew out your birthday candle?"

"I wished that I would forever be as happy as I was at that moment."

"Has your wish come true, then?"

"No."

She rose up on her elbow to see his face. "No? Are you not happy?"

He smiled at her troubled face and caressed her cheek. "I wished to be as happy as I was at that moment. Fool that I was, I had no concept of the greater happiness in store for me." He pulled her face to his but paused just before kissing her, whispering softly, "The ecstasy I feel for you now, my heart, is beyond mere happiness."

He would proceed to show her precisely what he meant, then and every day for the rest of his long life. Never would he forget his twenty-ninth birthday even though Elizabeth made a point of having a special celebration each year thereafter, and the plotting wheels had begun turning for her birthday some six months yet away.

CHAPTER EIGHT

Happy Birthday, Mrs. Darcy

NOW IT WAS THE day he had been, on some level, planning for ever since. May 28, 1817, marked the day that Elizabeth Darcy turned two and twenty. By a merry, inadvertent twist of fate, it also was the sixth month anniversary of her marriage to Fitzwilliam Darcy. Neither fact was lost on her husband. In all honesty, it would be a stretch to say he had been plotting birthday events for his beloved wife since she had so delightfully surprised him on his birthday in November, but he most assuredly had devoted a tremendous amount of time and effort in the hopes of this day being one of the best in her life.

Of course all days, no matter the celebrations devised, usually commence with little or no fanfare. Such was the case today. Darcy woke shortly after dawn, nothing atypical in that fact, the filtered sunrise and muted street sounds drifting through the curtained glass windows. Lizzy slept curled on her side in his arms, their fingers entwined under the pillow, thick hair cascading randomly over their tightly pressed together bodies. Darcy's free hand cupped one perfect breast, and again not atypical, he was profoundly aroused.

He shifted somewhat to relieve the mild discomfort, kissed her head, and closed his eyes. Darcy was rarely able to return to sleep, but he did adore these quiet interludes of simply embracing his wife. He lay in extreme contentment while mentally reexamining the day's plans for any possible missteps.

After six blissful months of waking with his adorable wife, Darcy had subconsciously learned the subtle signs of her rousing. The mild change in the cadence of her respirations, the tiny twitches in her muscles, the minute movements to lips and eyelids, and how she instinctively pressed harder into his body and clutched his fingers. How they lay enmeshed in their sleep varied from night to night, but always they reached for the other even further as they roused. So it was that some forty-five minutes after initially opening his eyes, he sensed her stirring. Unable to contain his need any longer, he gently commenced fondling her beautiful bosom while tenderly planting kisses along her neck.

She sighed, smiling sleepily. "Happy birthday, my beloved wife," he whispered while kissing her ear. "Are you feeling well?"

"Hmmmm, quite well."

"Well enough for me, my lover?" He waited no longer, beginning the familiar process of loving his wife. Not even bothering to shift positions, he joined blissfully with his wife as they lay with her luscious curves pressed tightly into his chest. Groaning hoarsely in transcendent pleasure he murmured, "Oh, my adorable wife, how I love you! Your first present for the day shall be your devoted husband bringing you pleasures abounding."

Lizzy immediately reciprocated with a throaty groan, her free arm reaching to lace her fingers through his hair as she arched in intense yearning.

"Fitzwilliam, you feel so amazing. God, how I love you!"

He threw the blanket off, thrilling further at the sight of their bodies joined and swaying together. Burying his face into her fragrant locks, he moaned her name. Oh, to wake and make love with his wife! It was divine.

"Lizzy, I have so ached to love you this way! I have missed our mornings."

They loved each other slowly, delighting in giving in this amazingly special way. Afterwards, they breathlessly held each other, slowly gathering shattered wits enough to caress lovingly as they recovered. Darcy rubbed her flat belly and tenderly kissed behind her ear.

"Are you well, Elizabeth? Nauseated at all?"

She turned slightly to better see his face and clasped the hand adoringly resting on her abdomen. "I feel marvelous, my love," she declared with a smile. "Perhaps the worst is passing. The book and the physician said the middle months are the easiest. I am yet a few weeks from that point, but maybe close enough." She kissed his chin, the only part she could readily access.

"I am relieved. I selfishly wanted you so strongly this morning that I do not think I could have held back."

Lizzy laughed. "There is absolutely nothing selfish in how you love me, William! Although I rather do think if I had lunged to the water closet you would have had little choice but to wait."

He chuckled. "Yes, I suppose this is true." He smoothed the hair from her face, tenderly caressing her features, then returning to her belly. "When will we feel our baby move?"

"Some weeks yet, I am afraid. At times I imagine there are flutters, but I know it is simply my desire to feel something tangible. It is frustrating to only have negative effects." She eyed him saucily. "I do believe you, my lover, have delighted in one aspect of my pregnancy symptoms." He arched a brow in question and she answered by transferring his hand to her notably fuller bosom.

He flushed and she laughed. "Nonsense, Elizabeth. I love your body as it has always been."

"Of course you do, beloved, this is abundantly obvious!" she interrupted, still giggling, "However, if I can confess to rather enjoying being lushly endowed for the first time in my life, even if it is temporary, then you might as well honestly reap the benefits!" She turned in his arms, hugging tightly and kissing him fully. "So, any hints as to what my special day holds? Or must I remain in suspense?"

Darcy smiled. "Is not the dictionary definition of 'surprise' to be unexpected and cause sudden wonder? If I tell you what is to transpire, then the desired consequence is nullified. However, having already embarked on the proscribed day's agenda, the first listed event having blissfully been checked off, I deem I can move on to number two." He kissed her, taking his time, then spoke, "Stay here. I shall return momentarily."

He disappeared into his dressing room. Lizzy stretched, honestly feeling better than she had in weeks. Just to be sure, she rang for Marguerite, who appeared within minutes, and asked for her usual tray of tea and toast. Darcy reentered the room as Marguerite was exiting, carrying a large, wrapped box.

"Are you beginning to feel unwell, Elizabeth?"

"Not at all, but I did not want to take any chances. What do you have there, Mr. Darcy?" She sat up, Darcy assisting her to a position of comfort, pillows plumped behind to recline onto.

He sat next to her, the present nearby, and took her hands. Lizzy giggled. "I sense a well-prepared birthday speech forthcoming."

Darcy raised a brow, pretending to be offended although a small smile danced about his lips. "As you are my captive today, Mrs. Darcy, you have no option but to endure any speeches I decide to give. Considering how well my contrived speeches are delivered and received, this should not be a cause of dismay on your part."

Lizzy laughed and Darcy's smile broadened. Neither of them needed to voice it, but there was a joy to having attained a level of peace in their relationship where they could tease about the past. Dramatically he cleared his throat, closed his eyes, and inhaled deeply while Lizzy bit her lip to prevent further giggles escaping.

"Seriously, Elizabeth, as I was contemplating your day of birth, it occurred to me that there have been twenty-one previous birthdays which I have missed. Naturally, this is normal, and pondering the fact that you were reportedly a rambunctious, unruly, and undoubtedly malodorous child, I am actually grateful at not having known you for many of those years." He grinned.

Lizzy harrumphed. "Well, there is the pot calling the kettle black!"

"That is beside the point. In truth, I do wish I could have seen you as a youth; however, I must content myself with living vicariously through your tales and the antics of our children, whom we have previously ascertained are likely doomed to be recalcitrant and rowdy. As for the here and now, today marks the day you came into this world, my beloved wife, and I am profoundly grateful for the fact. If your mother were present, I would feel obligated to bestow a heartfelt kiss of thanks… stop making faces, Elizabeth," he teased. "I am aware that there will be a multitude of calendar days for us to celebrate as the years unfold, yet for me this particular day is extraordinary."

He paused to caress her face. "My only true regret is that I was such a fool and spoiled the opportunity to celebrate your twenty-first birthday with you."

"William," she whispered, leaning forward to kiss him, "do not think on it." A knock at the door interrupted any further displays of affection, Marguerite entering with a tray for her Mistress. Darcy requested breakfast in their sitting room in one hour and then poured a cup of tea for his wife.

"As I was saying," he eventually resumed, "in honor of this day and all the prior birthdays I have been so unfortunate to evade, you will receive a gift for each year including one other to venerate our six months of blissful matrimony. Here is the first." He placed the enormous box in her lap.

Elizabeth's mouth had fallen open and, for one of the few times in her life, she was speechless. *Twenty-three presents!* It was unfathomable, yet so utterly like Darcy. She sat stunned while he gazed at her expectantly.

Finally, he began to chuckle lowly. "After all this time I have accomplished the goal of rendering Elizabeth Darcy mute. What a day of remembrance this shall be!" He assumed a faraway expression of joyous delight until she shoved him gently with a laugh.

"You tease!" she accused. "William, you spoil me far too much, as I have stated many times before."

He moved closer and fingered several locks of her hair where it tumbled over the pillows. "As I have stated, Mrs. Darcy, I will neither apologize for nor cease spoiling. Open it."

Her first gift for the day was a complete ensemble: a lightweight, airy gown in pale green sprigged muslin with tiny white embroidered flower motifs scattered over the lower half of the skirt, a wide sash in darker green, short capped sleeves, and a scooped neckline with interlaced narrow green ribbon along the edge; a petticoat, also in muslin; short satin gloves with pearl buttons; a bonnet with matching pale green ribbons and soft goose down feathers; a reticule of the same fabric, with variable-colored green beads sewn in a pattern of waves; and lastly, a pair of half boots in white kid.

"Oh, William! It is lovely, all of it! Thank you!" She hugged him tightly, clearly overwhelmed.

"It is for you to wear today on our outing," he informed her. "Also, Madame Millicent says the bodice and skirt are gathered in such a way as to expand with your changing figure, so the gown will be wearable throughout the summer. I do not honestly comprehend how that can be but trust her expertise nonetheless. I chose the fabric, as I have a penchant for you in green. I hope you approve."

Lizzy was laughing. "You are becoming quite well versed in women's accoutrements, my love. It is wonderful, all of it." She moved the box to the side, pulled him toward her while running one hand seductively inside his robe, and kissed him lingeringly. "I did notice that the neckline is quite daring, husband mine. Do you still wish to deny your approval of my burgeoning bust line?"

Darcy blushed slightly but traced one finger over the aforementioned bust line, deigning not to answer with words.

~❧~

Breakfast was taken in the small sitting room. It was a pleasure to resume their custom of privacy in the morning, having necessarily relinquished the habit since leaving Pemberley. As Lizzy rose to retire to her dressing room, Darcy halted her. Handing her a small box hidden in his robe pocket, he stated, "You will need this, darling, to complete dressing. Marguerite will know what to do with it."

Inside was a stunning hair comb with interwoven pearls and emeralds. Lizzy could only shake her head in amazement. "William, how will I possibly find the words to thank you appropriately for such gifts as these?" Tears glazed her eyes.

He cupped her face and brushed away her tears, kissing softly. "Your thanks are in how you love me every day, Elizabeth. Trinkets are easy for me to acquire and pale in comparison to what you have already given me in your life and love and, furthermore, are miniscule measured against the gift you nurture inside you. You and our child are priceless treasures to me and I do not have the words to convey my appreciation, so allow me to shower you with worthless baubles." He kissed her again, and then turned her about, patting her bottom lightly. "Now, go get dressed, Mrs. Darcy. The fun is just beginning."

The gown fit perfectly, Madame du Loire kindly writing Lizzy's measurements down for Darcy. The bodice was an unusual design of gathers and ribbons allowing for adaptation to changing size. Despite the daring cut, a particular fashion trend Lizzy was not overly comfortable with, it was a relief to wear a gown that did not squeeze her blossoming breasts so tightly. Marguerite handily grasped the design, snuggly pulling the gathers under the bosom as Lizzy's abdomen was yet flat. When all the various clothing items and accessories were in place and the hair stylishly primped with the jeweled comb brilliantly displayed, Lizzy was stupendous. She had no idea where they were going, but to her eyes, despite the plain cut of the gown, it could be to see the Prince Regent and she would feel majestic.

Darcy concurred. He was no less aristocratic in his fine clothing: a jacket of forest green, waistcoat with cream and green pinstripes, long trousers of tan nankeen, white shirt, and lacy beige cravat. He wore simple walking shoes rather than his customary boots. As much as Lizzy preferred him in blue, the honest truth is that he was marvelously handsome in any color or style of dress. Once the mutual approbation was completed, Darcy reached up and solemnly removed the earrings she wore.

"No, these are all wrong," he declared in a serious tone. Yet another small box materialized and he opened it to reveal a pair of dainty drop earrings with one round emerald atop a perfect pearl. Adorning each lobe with an earring followed with a kiss, he then stepped back a pace, confirming authoritatively that she was "perfect."

The girls were dressed and anxiously waiting in the parlor when Darcy and Lizzy entered. As delighted as they were to see Lizzy, wish her a happy birthday, and praise the new ensemble, their excitement was due to their own scheduled activities. Darcy had arranged for a carriage to transport them to the Gardiner townhouse where Mrs. Gardiner was awaiting them. She had been delighted at the prospect of entertaining the girls for the day and night, immediately arranging an agenda of local shopping and luncheon out.

Lizzy had been mildly surprised. Heedful of Darcy's extreme protectiveness of his sister, she was fully aware of the trust he was placing in her aunt's hands. The fact that he had instigated this separation spoke volumes of his faith in Mrs. Gardiner and moved Lizzy deeply. Of course, he was taking no chances. The sturdiest of the Darcy carriages would be their conveyance, and two of the brawniest footmen in his employ would be accompanying them everywhere they went.

Once the giggly girls were safely on their way, the Darcys settled into the landau chosen for their transportation. The soft tops were up, providing privacy and filtering any excessive sounds and odors which may disturb Lizzy. A medium-sized, wrapped box sat on the opposite bench. Lizzy pretended to be blind, waiting on her husband's pleasure.

Darcy had ordered the driver on a circuitous route to their destination for a couple of reasons. First, he wished to avoid the crowded and noisome major thoroughfares to save Lizzy any distress, but also because he wished her to sightsee the finer areas of London. He had discovered in his not-so-subtle questioning that Lizzy had only been to Town a handful of times in her life, the last being during their engagement. As sorrowful and inconceivable as this statistic was to the world traveling, part-time city-dwelling Darcy, it allotted him the serendipitous advantage of being the one to expose her to all that the city had to offer. As he had contemplated the various wonders London boasted, two stood out as the ideal inaugural attractions to share with his wife.

Within a block of the house Lizzy was hopelessly lost, so initially, she could not comprehend why the driver kept turning right then left then right again. Was Darcy trying purposely to throw her off track? It did not seem logical since he was well aware that the only portion of the vast city she could claim even meager familiarity with was Cheapside. The mystery of the numerous deviations became clear when Darcy pointed to a lovely townhouse across from a lush oasis only slightly smaller than Grosvenor.

"This is Portman Square and that is the London home of the Vernors. I believe Gerald plans to arrive next week. Is that not what Mrs. Vernor told you, love?"

"Yes, as are the Hugheses and the Lathrops. I am sure the Fitzherberts, Sitwells, and Drurys have already arrived. Needless to say, I have been remiss in informing them of our appearance."

"There is plenty of time for that."

After further driving, they halted before another finely appointed garden plaza. "This is Cavendish Square," Darcy declared. "The house with pinkish stones belongs to the Lathrops. Over there you can see the side of the Sitwell townhouse. It is on Princes Street. We will pass it as we continue."

"Is all this distance we have traveled and all these squares part of Mayfair?"

"Yes. Mayfair proper extends north to Regent Park. We will drive by the park here in a moment. Alas, it is still under construction, so there is not yet much to see. The Fitzherberts and Drurys reside in St. James's Place, as do the Matlocks if you recall, which lies in the opposite direction from where we are headed. I am certain you will have opportunities to see their homes ere our sojourn is ended. The Fitzherberts, especially, have a remarkable townhouse. Do not tell Aunt Madeline I said this or she will box my ears, but it is actually finer than Matlock House, at least from the outside. I have never been a guest there."

He pointed out a few other houses of Derbyshire residents not as well known to Lizzy and a handful of others belonging to people she had yet to meet. Lastly, they passed the home of the Hursts, a modest townhouse of tan bricks across from Bedford Square.

At this point Darcy retrieved the wrapped package, handing it to his wife. "Yes, another one," he teased. "I have a schedule to maintain in order to deliver them all in the course of one day."

"William…"

"Not a word, Elizabeth! Open."

At this point Elizabeth decided that, as three and twenty presents were apparently forthcoming regardless of how extravagant she deemed it, relishing the experience seemed only logical. With an arch smile she furthermore decided to play with her wonderful, silly little boy of a spouse in the process. With that in mind, she studied the box carefully, shook it a bit, put it against her ear, and even smelled it. Out of the corner of her eye she noticed Darcy's crooked, knowing smile as he leaned back, crossing his arms as if they had all day.

With patient deliberation she peeled the ribbons and colored paper away, eventually exposing the box. Inside rested a set of four writing pens in a style she had never seen before. Rather than quills, the handles were of clear hued glass: red, blue, purple, and green. The tips were made of steel.

Darcy leaned forward, eager as a child with a new toy. "These are very new, Elizabeth. Mark my words, some day quills will be obsolete. The steel tips can be cleaned of dried ink, last nearly forever, and write with varying scripts depending on the size. Truly amazing. I have used them a time or two. My solicitor refuses to use a quill. Anyway, these are yours, and I have purchased a set for myself with carved wooden handles. It may take some adjusting to, and if you do not like them, that is fine."

"William, these are fantastic. I have read of the newer steel dip pens but had no idea they were so lovely. Thank you! I look forward to using them." She kissed him with genuine enthusiasm and thanks. With a grin she tilted her head. "I think I now understand why all the presents, my love. Imagine all the kisses you will be receiving today by way of my expressing gratitude, in addition to the undiminished communication of my gratefulness which you will undoubtedly procure tonight in our bed."

"Have I not confessed time and again, beloved, to being hideously selfish. Here is the proof." With a chuckle he clutched her neck and drew her in for another kiss, which she was all too willing to give. Unconcerned with the open window, they blissfully continued until a jolt indicated the landau had stopped.

They alighted on an enormous stone and brick drive before an impressive edifice. The front and rear facades were of seventeen bays, with a slightly projecting three bay center and three bay ends. Extending from each front bay end were protracted one-story wings. The central house was of two main stories, plus basement and a prominent mansard roof with a dome over the center.

Lizzy looked to Darcy in question. "This is Montagu House, home to the British Museum, dearest. During the morning hours, the doors are only opened for private parties. Today that is us, and a few others of course, but it should not be crowded."

Lizzy was speechless with excitement. Of all the places they could have gone, the British Museum was by far the most appreciated. Unable to voice her thankfulness, she instead squeezed his arm tightly, briefly leaning her head onto his shoulder. Darcy smiled and patted her hand, ascending the grand staircase.

They were met by an elegant, elderly gentleman whom Darcy introduced as the curator, Mr. Ellington. "All has been arranged to your specifications, Mr. Darcy. If I may," he turned to Lizzy and bowed, saying, "I do hope your first visit to our humble museum is the highlight of your birthday, Mrs. Darcy."

"Thank you, Mr. Ellington. I cannot express how exciting this is for me. The reputation of the British Museum is stellar and, I am certain, completely warranted."

The three hours they rambled through the museum were unbelievable. To intimately view artifacts only read about was an experience transcending Lizzy's wildest imaginings. For Darcy it was a compounded delight to observe his wife's breathless wonder and to retrace it all, as four years had passed since he last toured. The libraries consisting of rare books, maps and charts, plays and music, and prints and drawings were vast, and they could easily have spent all day exploring the numerous collections. Room upon room housed the myriad of antiquities from the farthest reaches of the globe, spanning centuries of time, and a massive array of artifacts. There were statues, paintings, gems, minerals, coins, relics, clothing, military devices, armaments, and more. It almost became unbearable and futile to attempt assimilating it all.

Darcy worried that Lizzy would overtax herself, especially noting her apparently boundless enthusiasm to see it all. Midway through the morning he insisted they retire to the upper story, where a secluded, windowed alcove had been arranged with comfortable chairs and a table laden with refreshments. The window was open, a gentle breeze blowing, fresh fragrant flowers nearby in tall vases, and an incredible panoramic view of the spectacular gardens gracing the rearward side of Montagu House. Lizzy had resisted leaving the splendors below them, but once she beheld the assorted foods, she realized she was famished, her stomach releasing a loud growl.

Darcy, always amused at how pregnancy had turned his normally dainty and sparsely consuming wife into a ravenous gorger, merely smiled and poured the wine. For a time, Lizzy was far too intent on eating to speak, but gradually she slowed her intake rate and the words fell over each other in their haste. Darcy could not have interjected had he wished to, so effluent was she in her zeal. Not bothered in the least, he happily sat back, nibbling a bit and sipping his wine, but primarily delighting in observing her joy.

"I cannot decide which I adored the most! My father would faint away at the books and manuscripts. Oh, William, we must induce him to come here! I do not think he realizes how amazing the museum is"—she quickly paused for breath and a sip of wine—"the Rosetta Stone! So huge! I had no idea it was that large. The commentaries and sketches certainly do not motivate the proper visualization." Another caesura for a bite of cheese and a drink was taken before she continued. "The Egyptian artifacts... astounding! The mummy and the coffin and all the jewels and statues." She shook her head in awe. "It is nearly too much to endure."

"We have yet to visit the Greek and Roman wings, beloved."

"All this under one roof, albeit a large one. Yet, is not this museum relatively modest compared to the Louvre?" Darcy nodded affirmative. "Well, it boggles the mind. I do not think my heart or mind could digest more. I already feel as if I have forgotten half of what I have recently scrutinized!"

"Prepare yourself, my love. Someday we will travel to the Louvre and all of France, Italy, Spain, wherever you wish. In the mean time..." He purposefully trailed off, reaching under the draped table, and removed two more gifts, one relatively small and the other generous.

Lizzy smiled and clapped her hands, too captivated by the general enthusiasm of it all to pretend embarrassment. The small package revealed a stunning handheld folding fan of ornately carved ash, silk fabric painted with intertwined roses and lilacs, and edged with a narrow strip of lace. She fluttered it before her face, flirting over the top until Darcy dissolved in laughter.

The larger box contained a simple but sturdily constructed backgammon board of wood with polished stone pieces. "William, it is beautiful, but we have boards at Pemberley and Darcy House."

"Not in our sitting room. This is for us to play in the evenings or whenever the mood strikes you to suffer defeat." He grinned.

Lizzy snorted. "I do believe our last overall count was fifteen to ten in my favor, dearest husband. You have the worst luck at dice. Thankfully, you do not gamble or we may be forced to sell some of your clothing to survive." They both laughed, Darcy unable to argue regarding his vast wardrobe—a fact Lizzy delighted in teasing him over—nor about his luck at dice.

Another delightful hour and a half was spent in the halls displaying the Greek and Roman antiquities. There was still much yet to see, but Lizzy reluctantly confessed to beginning fatigue, so they called for the landau. Lizzy reclined gratefully into the plush cushions, again affecting blindness to the two gifts sitting on the opposite seat. Darcy gathered her against his chest, telling her to rest for now. She closed her eyes, settling into a mild doze.

A strong smell of freshly sawn wood coupled with a brisk, moist breeze roused Lizzy moments before Darcy gently kissed her forehead and whispered her name. "Where are we now?" She peaked out the window to catch a glimpse of the Thames passing behind the spacious warehouses lining the avenue they currently drove on. "Are we to go swimming in the Thames?" She turned to him with a laugh.

Darcy smiled. "Hardly. Ah, here we are." The carriage halted in front of an especially enormous building, one of several encompassing an immense courtyard. The noise of hammers, saws, and other tools Lizzy had no name for accompanied the boisterous voices with occasional cursing intermingled of a multitude of men. A sign with scrolling words declared the establishment as *Tillbury's Fine Coaches*. "Stay here Elizabeth," he said, and without another word he leapt out of the landau and strode rapidly across the yard to a door designated "Office."

Roughly ten minutes later, he emerged in the company of two men, one of whom indicated a certain building, as Darcy nodded. He crossed to the landau, leaning in to Lizzy. "Dearest, there is something you must see. I beg your indulgence. This is a working facility and the men are, well, rough. I apologize beforehand for any unpleasantness, but it is necessary. Do you trust me?"

"Do not be ridiculous, William. Naturally I trust you. I also assure you that my ears and eyes are not as delicate as all that. I did grow up in the country, you recall." Darcy laughed, assisting her out of the landau. In the end, his fears were for naught, the men rather in awe at the presence of a lady in their midst. Work halted, and Lizzy only had to contend with stares, which undoubtedly bothered Darcy far more than she.

Entering the specified building, Elizabeth's eyes were instantly drawn to a partially completed curricle off to the right. There were dozens of light craft in various states of construction scattered about the warehouse; however, even before Darcy steered her toward the right, she knew. The curricle was beautiful, to be sure, polished to a lustrous gleam with shiny black steel wheels, the carriage's outer walls painted a deep maroon, and a folding top of thick tan leather. In spite of this, what captured Elizabeth's stunned attention was the Darcy family crest emblazoned on the side. It was the crest as her husband had redesigned it for her seal: daintily feminized with her initials entwined.

Lizzy was flabbergasted, and Darcy gazed at her with undisguised joy while one of the men launched into a detailed inventory of all the intricate parts and mechanisms. Darcy leaned to her ear, whispering, "Happy anniversary, my love. Do you like it?"

Lizzy was truly overcome. Tears filled her eyes and she buried her face into his arm, biting her lip to avoid bursting into sobs. Sudden powerful emotions rushed through her, not unlike the uncontrollable sentiments which had consumed her early in her pregnancy. That he would have her own curricle manufactured when he remained so anxious about her driving one was more than she could bear. She began to tremble, frantically looking around for a place to escape the prying eyes so she could privately fall apart. Spying an open door at the back of the warehouse, the glint of sunlight on water visible, she mumbled something about needing air and bolted.

Darcy stood rooted to the spot in shock for several heartbeats, mumbled his own vague excuse to the coachman, who continued to rattle on about springs and buckboards, and dashed after his wife. She stood by the river, hunched with hands on her knees, gulping air between sobs.

"Elizabeth, my God, what is wrong? Are you ill? What..."

Hands about her face as he peered intently, she interrupted incoherently, "William, I cannot believe... it is too much... I do not deserve... all this... the curricle... gifts and... you are too good... and I... am unworthy... the money spent... and..."

"Shhhh... Hush now, Elizabeth," he cooed as he enfolded her into his arms, pressing her tight to his chest, "cease or you will make yourself ill. You must remember our baby." He rubbed her back gently, swaying slightly as her tears slowly ebbed and shudders lessened. Pulling away finally, he again cupped her face, looking at her sternly but speaking softly, he said, "Listen to me,

Elizabeth Darcy. I do not ever want to hear you utter the belief that you do not deserve anything I chose to give you or that it is my 'goodness' which compels me. First of all, you are worthy of all this and far more for reasons which would take me hours to numerate, yet that is merely one point. I am your husband. I am responsible for your happiness, security, health, wants and needs, pleasures, future, and all else. I take my job *very* seriously and will exhaust myself physically and financially if need be to ensure this. Do you understand?"

She nodded her head, staring raptly into his darkened, intently somber eyes. He continued, "I love you, Elizabeth, more than I have the words to convey. As a result of the depth of my love for you, I delight in surprising you, giving to you, pleasuring you, and all the rest. Yet, the honest truth is that my honor and duty would obligate me to do much the same no matter whom I married. If I had been so unfortunate as to marry Anne or, heaven forbid, Caroline, I would be purchasing gifts, caring for them, providing for them, and," he shuddered involuntarily, "even... being intimate with them." He closed his eyes as if to block the horrid vision and then sighed heavily before again meeting her gaze. "It would be so hollow and empty and emotionless. Can you now comprehend what an uncountable joy it is to me that it is you, precious Elizabeth, to whom I can fulfill my duties as husband? The alternatives are unspeakable. I have not divulged this, but there are times, less now but frequently during our engagement and early weeks of marriage, when I would wake in a sweat, having dreamt a nightmare of Caroline or some other creature in my bed." He shook his head, again embracing her tightly. "Beloved, I can never shower you with jewels or gowns or trinkets or even curricles enough to thank you for sparing me that fate!"

He kissed her tenderly and thoroughly, aware of eyes peering through the windows of the warehouse, but he was indifferent. "Are you better now?" She nodded. "Good, because you are required to select the fabric you wish for the cushions; we still have several events planned, and I am hungry. Shall we, Mrs. Darcy?"

❦

The two gifts patiently waiting in the landau yielded a Kashmir shawl large enough to completely cover her body down to her toes in a typical paisley pattern of yellow, blue, and mauve, and a ladies pocket watch. The watch was gold with an intricate scrollwork design on the case and a blue sapphire embedded in the center of the cover. The landau tops had been folded down per Lizzy's request, so Darcy's kisses of thanks were postponed, settling instead for a firm squeeze to his knee and her hands warmly linked in his.

They drove along the Thames, Darcy pointing to interesting landmarks as they appeared. Slowly they ambled along, the frequently dirty docks and warehouses along the river replaced with fine business establishments and humble residences as the Thames veered to the south, finally disappearing from view. Traffic thickened as they entered an obviously upscale district.

"This is Pall Mall Street," Darcy explained, "and this area is St. James's Place. There is the Royal Academy of Arts, and there is Christie's Auction House. Mr. Anders, take us around the Square, please." He pointed out several of the residences lining the massive and impressive square. "Only titled gentry live here, dearest. Continue, Mr. Anders, to the Palace, please, and then halt." It was only a block or so down Pall Mall to a beautiful building with a well guarded, arched, and iron gated portico. "That is St. James's Palace, Elizabeth, home of the Prince Regent, as you know."

"Have you ever been inside, William?"

He smiled. "Divers times for various fêtes. The first was with my father and Lord and Lady Matlock. I was twenty and had the great fortune to be presented to King George III. It was a highly formal affair, as they all are, and I was nearly petrified with anxiety. Imagine me at Meryton multiplied tenfold, and you may vaguely visualize my unease!" He laughed at the memory.

Lizzy was staring at her husband with fresh awe. Despite his wealth, which she was slowly learning to be comfortable with, and the incredible power he wielded at Pemberley, within society, and at his numerous business enterprises, she had never actually thought of him hobnobbing with royalty. Even the Earl of Matlock, so intimidating to her originally, was now simply his uncle. It was more than she could digest at the moment.

"How was he? The King, I mean," she stammered.

"Gracious and formal. He was an impressive man in appearance, quite tall and broad. His illness was not as apparent then. Most in society were aware of its existence, but certainly not the general public. Of course, I spoke not at all other than the designated greeting then was ushered on. If I had a preference, I would gladly never step foot through those gates or any of the other Royal enclaves. Of course, when one receives an invitation to the palace, one accepts it." He chuckled.

They drove on then, meandering leisurely through the promenade between St. James's Park and Green Park, Darcy again playing tour guide. His knowledge of the area astounded her. They passed through Hyde Park Corner and continued to the west, skirting the edge of Hyde Park itself.

"I planned for us to finish our day relaxing at the Park. We will have lunch by the lake, walk a bit if you feel able, open more gifts, whatever you wish, beloved." He lightly kissed her temple.

The park was immense. Carriages were in abundance along the wide avenue, pedestrians and equestrians wandered over the paths and endless lawn, numerous picnic blankets and the occasional pavilion dotted the landscape. Every imaginable species of tree and bush and flower grew in profusion. Lizzy had heard of the wonders at Hyde and Kensington Parks, and the grandeur of Serpentine Lake, but the reality was stunning. After nearly forty minutes of winding through sights of breathtaking beauty, Mr. Anders finally halted.

They had crossed over the bridge to the north of the Lake, ambled along the edge, and alighted before a generous pavilion erected approximately twenty feet from the water's shore. The white tent was facing the lake, the front flaps tied back to form a sort of doorway and the other three sides of a netted material to allow breezes in. Solid canvas sheets on the netted sides were rolled up, but could be released for added privacy. Two footmen from Darcy House stood at the entrance, apparently having been in charge of guarding and likely arranging the structure. Darcy ordered them to return to the townhouse until evening.

Lizzy entered the pavilion, pausing in amazement. It was as if she had been instantly transported to an Arabian tent in the desert. A thick Persian style carpet covered the ground, a long divan stretched across the back, pillows of all sizes and bright shades and gaudy patterns with tassels dangling were scattered about, and a low table sat in the middle literally digging into the earth it was so encumbered with food. The only incongruous additions to the motif were the stack of traditionally wrapped gifts in the right front corner.

Darcy slipped his arms about her waist, pulling her close as he whispered, "For the remainder of the afternoon, you shall be a Princess lying imperiously on your divan, ordering your slave—a fortunate me—to fulfill your merest whim. I shall fan your beautiful face, rub your delicate feet, kiss your ruby lips, feed you from my hand, anything you desire. Except for singing. I will not sing. Even a slave must draw the line at utter humiliation." They laughed.

"Do not worry yourself, dearest. This day has been thus far too wonderful to ruin by hearing you sing!"

"I cannot be offended at the truth. Relax, my dear, so we can eat. Speaking only for myself, I am ravenous. While I prepare a plate for you, open these. They are part of a set, so to speak." He handed her four gifts individually wrapped but tied together. The set included five handheld tambour embroidery rings, a sewing box filled with an abundant supply of thread and needles and more, several patterns, and an exemplary pair of embroidery shears.

Lunch was delicious, the area where they picnicked secluded with a cooling breeze wafting continuously, and they were together. Lizzy reclined on the divan with Darcy sitting on the ground leaning by her side. They talked and touched, ate until they could barely move, and opened more presents.

As the hours listlessly ticked by, Lizzy unwrapped an array of wonderful surprises. One was an enormous basket of imported rare fruits consisting of peaches, pineapples, Seville oranges, bananas, avocados, and dried currants. Lizzy had never tasted a banana or an avocado, finding both strange but delicious.

"How did you find such curiosities, William?"

"I am a partner in a triune ownership of a shipping company. Have I not informed you of this?"

She shook her head. "Not that I recollect, but there is still much of your interests I am yet learning to comprehend. Frankly, I cannot fathom how you keep it all ordered."

He laughed. "At times I do wonder the same myself. I have been blessed— or cursed, depending on the perspective—with insatiable curiosity, so I am forever enmeshing myself in new ventures. In this case, it is actually my father's fault. Anyway, we own four ships and import mostly wines and liquors and edibles, but will ship whatever pays a profit. An additional advantage is being able to acquire diverse paraphernalia from exotic locales or civilized countries at a substantially lowered cost. Therefore, if you develop a craving for bananas, dearest, I can steadily supply them."

She smiled, leaning to kiss him. "You are a beneficial fellow to have around, Mr. Darcy."

He shrugged. "I am a financial backer primarily. I leave the major decisions to my partners, as I am ignorant of many aspects of the enterprise. My father began the company and he did know a great deal about ships and trade. I inherited the partnership along with everything else. The profits are substantial, and as I devote little effort to it, I cannot complain."

Her next gift consisted of two parts and thrilled Lizzy speechless, again. Nestling on a cushion of green velvet in a polished box of cherry wood sat an exquisite pair of petite opera glasses. The telescopes and handle were of silver, inlaid with mother-of-pearl with *Mrs. Fitzwilliam Darcy* etched onto the crosspiece. While Lizzy attempted to find her voice to stammer her appreciation, Darcy reached into his coat pocket and with a dramatic flourish presented two tickets to the opera, Mozart's *Don Giovanni* to be precise, for the following week at the Royal Theatre in Covent Gardens.

"Oh, William! How wonderful! I love the opera, and to attend with you, well, I can hardly believe my good fortune. Are they good seats?"

Darcy laughed at her delightful innocence. "Dearest, we have our own box lease. It is on the second level, midway to the right of the stage: an excellent position for both visuals and acoustics. Lord and Lady Matlock will be joining us, as will Richard, and I was also hoping the Lathrops and the Gardiners. The Vernors have their own box, three removed from ours, so perhaps they can attend that night as well. I also compiled a list of the various performances scheduled for these next weeks at the theatres in Town. Later we can peruse the list and decide which events pique your interest. You shall have numerous opportunities to employ those new glasses."

He smiled and kissed her. "I know how greatly you enjoy the theatre."

Lizzy said, running fingers through his hair as she spoke, "It will be a tremendous joy to share the experience with you. Also, as I do not speak Italian, you can translate."

"I am afraid my knowledge of Italian is nearly nonexistent, love, but if we attend anything in French or German I will happily translate." He chuckled. "Of course, I do not think it will be necessary. The story is felt in the soul through the music and emotion projected by the actors, as you know. I have watched your eyes when you have related your previous theatre attendances or discussed literature and can readily ascertain how it stirs your spirit." He drew even closer to her face. "It is another of the myriad traits we have in common, my Lizzy, and thus why you are so utterly perfect for me." Thereafter followed a delightful interval of tender kisses and caresses, interrupted by an unstoppable jaw-cracking yawn from Lizzy.

"Oh, darling! Forgive me!"

Darcy chuckled, stroking her lips. "No apology is necessary, my love. Our child is demanding his mother rest and regains strength. I concur. Do you think you can tolerate opening one more?"

Lizzy nodded and gave him an indulgent smile and a loving caress. The next gift was an exquisitely rendered reproduction of Pompeo Batoni's *Madonna and Child* in an oval frame of ethereal and ornate Rococo design with copper gilding and inlays of marbleized enamel.

Lizzy was shocked, sitting up in her surprise. "William! It is… stunning! You incredible, amazing, dear, dear man! Remember my telling you how much I adore Batoni?!"

"You saw an exhibition of his works when you visited your aunt and uncle three years ago. Yes, I remember. Did you view this painting?"

"Yes, it was there. So beautiful. The Madonna's countenance inundated with peace and the babe gently touching his mother's chin as he gazes with love. I adore the colors he uses, the softness to his artistry, and the serene joy of this moment as he captured it. It moved me at eighteen but far more so now, with our baby growing inside." She looked into his shining eyes, hers misty.

"I thought it would adorn the nursery becomingly."

"William, I honestly am devoid of appropriate words to thank you. I love you so very much!"

He kissed her softly, pushing her gently until she was reclining against the plump pillows. "Save the words, my lover. Rather, free your mind and devise stimulating bedroom actions that will convey the depth of your gratitude." He grinned lasciviously, Lizzy playfully slapping his arm.

Darcy read aloud for a spell until Lizzy fell asleep. He continued to read silently for a while, then took a short walk along the lake's edge to stretch his legs. The day was growing warmer, as the afternoon progressed, his pocket watch revealing it to be after three. He stood on the shore, skipping rocks across the surface like a child, smiling with peaceful satisfaction. Aside from Lizzy's emotional upheaval, which he fully attributed to her pregnant state, coupled with a lingering reservation regarding her new station in life, it had thus far been the perfect day. Exactly as he had so carefully planned. Hopefully, the remainder of her day's activities would proceed as flawlessly.

Lizzy woke after a refreshing nap to an empty pavilion. Another two gifts sat beside her divan, but she ignored them for the present, preferring to locate her wayward spouse. She grabbed two bananas, peeling one as she ducked under the tent flap. A quick glance about divulged him to be some fifty feet away, cutting bulrushes. She smiled, chewing as she approached.

"That looks to be strenuous work. I come bearing sustenance."

"Why thank you, kind lady." He took the offered treat, tossing the peel into the lake. "Do you figure ducks or fish eat banana peels?"

Lizzy shrugged, tossing her peel as well. "No idea. At least it is organic. What is the purpose for the bulrushes?"

"I like them is all. They are pretty in vases and last nearly forever; however, the best part is shredding the flower into fluffy bits and watching them float on air." He demonstrated and Lizzy laughed.

"William, you are such a child! Here, give me one." Soon the air was inundated with swirling cottony fragments, many of them lodging in their hair to be plucked later.

Lizzy's seventeenth birthday gift was a finely woven garden basket for gathering flowers, pruning shears with cushioned handles, two pairs of leather gloves, and two protective frocks. It was a gift Lizzy truly needed, as she had nothing like it at Pemberley and had borrowed from the groundsmen when working in the gardens. The other package contained two exquisite perfume bottles. One was of Murano glass in a rainbow of swirling colors and filled with pure lavender perfume. The other was divinely enameled in a night sky with crescent moon and bright stars so finely painted they actually appeared to twinkle. The perfume within was jasmine extract.

They sat on the divan and Darcy nestled his face into her hair and breathed deeply. "I will always associate lavender with you, Elizabeth, as it is your favorite scent. However, I also love jasmine so thought perhaps you would wear it for me on occasion."

"Darling, you could ask anything of me and I would grant it. This is a simple request to fulfill." She stroked his cheeks, gazing intently into his sparkling blue eyes. "I love you passionately, Fitzwilliam," she whispered. "I know you believe it inconsequential, but I am deeply moved by all you have done for me today. Each gift has been selected with incredible forethought and insight, presented in dazzling fashion, and surrounded with exciting events and places. I do hope you realize how grateful I am." She kissed him slowly, teasing his lips in the special way she knew thrilled him.

She then continued, "Yet, it is you, beloved, whom I adore and treasure most. Just as you are spared artificial gestures for someone whom you do not love, I am spared being the recipient of meaningless, duty-bound overtures from some man I had married only for security or to protect my family. We are both so very blessed. I promise I will not forget it." Clutching his head tightly with fingers weaved in his hair, they kissed long and hard.

"Elizabeth," Darcy eventually moaned, "we should take a walk before I throw all caution to the wind and make love to you here on this divan!" Still, he traveled his soft lips to her lovely neck as one hand stimulated a full breast until she breathlessly stayed him.

Eyes glazed, they stared, collecting muddled wits and panting heavily. "Perhaps we can forgo the walk and return to the house?" she asked pleadingly.

He laughed huskily. "Excellent idea, my lover; however, I foolishly desired privacy here and sent the carriages away until five o'clock."

"Well then, I daresay a vigorous walk is the necessary remedy to pent-up passionate energy. My bonnet is over there, if you would not mind?"

Arm in arm, they strolled over the gravel paths meandering through an abundance of blooms and trees. Other pedestrians were encountered occasionally, with cordial greetings exchanged, but the park was vast and the garden pathways mazelike, so generally, they were alone. Despite the aborted passion being their preferential afternoon activity, they thoroughly enjoyed their walk. Lizzy especially, being an avid walker and having curtailed the pastime lately, reveled in her nearly total lack of fatigue and illness.

They returned to the pavilion as the carriages were arriving. Darcy assisted his wife into the landau, another gift inside.

The drive home took thirty minutes. "The strange thing," Darcy told her, "is that our townhouse is two blocks from the Grosvenor Gate entrance to the park. There is a small pond, a splendid garden, and some wooded areas at that edge of the park. Georgiana and Mrs. Annesley walk there frequently. However, we picnicked quite a distance from the Gate and the road travels in a roundabout manner, so we must veer northwest a bit before turning east for home. With this in mind, how about another present?" He grinned.

Another oddity hid inside. It was an intricately detailed picture of a landscape: mountains, tall trees, a lake, and a meadow in the foreground with horses grazing. It was not an exact replica of a Pemberley pasture, but the resemblance was evident. Painted on a thin piece of hard oak, it had been cut into a hundred small, irregular shaped pieces designed to interlock.

Lizzy had no idea what it was and required Darcy to explain. "It is called a dissected puzzle. They have been around for some time as an educational device. We have several at Pemberley, packed away with the schoolroom furniture and supplies. If I recall, they are all of England geography, the countries, the alphabet, and the like. I found this and thought it would be entertaining for us to work on together."

"What an astounding concept," Lizzy declared. "It will be tremendous fun. We should wait until the winter, when it is snowy and I am too enormous to move!"

Darcy smiled. "I cannot conceive of you ever being too enormous to move. I rather believe I will be hiding the ice skates and all your coats to prevent you escaping outside."

The house was quiet when they returned. It was after six o'clock and dinner with the Matlocks was scheduled for seven-thirty, just enough time to clean and dress for dinner. Arms about each other's waist, they entered their sitting room. Lizzy was blissfully happy. Her only shadow of melancholy was that currently she wanted nothing more than to slowly undress her husband and curl up with him in their bed for the entire evening. She adored the elder Fitzwilliams, had grown very close to them both over the long winter and spring, and knew they wished to celebrate her birthday with her. She was touched, and yesterday the idea of dining with them had been a greatly anticipated event. Now, as Darcy hugged her and spoke in his resonant timbre, which always sent rivers of tingles up her spine especially if she were touching him as his voice vibrated lushly in his chest, her desire to continue their marvelous day of solitude nearly overwhelmed her.

She opened her mouth to speak, ready to say or do whatever it would take to persuade him to acquiesce to her preference, when he paused in the middle of the room. Her attention, therefore, was deviated to the table before her on which sat by far the strangest object she had ever beheld. It was of brass, approximately one foot tall, and vaguely resembled a miniature telescope.

"What in the world is it, William?"

Darcy was again giddy as a child. Lizzy was struck suddenly by how many of her gifts had been unusual or rare. She had not previously realized how enamored Darcy was with inventions and marvels. He stood over the bizarre contraption breathless and jittery with fascination.

"It is called a kaleidoscope. Look into the end, Elizabeth, and turn it here."

She did as he instructed, jerking back in startled surprise, then looking again in amazement. "It is beautiful! How... it changes!" She gasped, "This is miraculous. How does it work?"

"You see," he pointed, "the tube is filled with tiny beads and mirrors which reflect the colors in an unlimited medley of patterns. Is it not the most astounding contrivance? It was patented just last year and I have been endeavoring to obtain one since."

"We must keep it in either the game room or the parlor so guests can enjoy it, do you not agree?"

"It is yours, dearest. Keep it wherever you wish."

"This is far too marvelous to horde all to myself." She had yet to remove her eye from it. "One could become bedazzled and never pull away," she mumbled.

Darcy laughed. "As is happening to you. Have you forgotten our dinner engagement, Mrs. Darcy? Also, I have another gift for you, which must be given now to keep to the schedule."

Lizzy reluctantly forced her concentration from the kaleidoscope, riveted next on the rather large box she had not noted on the fireplace hearth. She had frankly lost count of all her gifts. The amount of deliberation applied to flawlessly effectuate the day's happenings was phenomenal, and Lizzy was staggered.

The box hid a cuckoo clock. Lizzy laughed aloud and hugged Darcy in true joy. Longbourn boasted a cuckoo clock that her father had gifted to her mother when they were newly married. It was a family heirloom and all Lizzy's life the sound of the little blue bird announced the hour. It was one of those comforting homely realities which, over time, one no longer consciously recognizes... until it is gone. Lizzy had breezily mentioned a time or two that she missed the unique chime of the cuckoo. Darcy, as with everything, had remembered.

The design was typical: the wooden German chalet with snowy roof, a shepherd boy with three sheep in front, and the trap door above the dial for the blue and yellow cuckoo. The workmanship was superb, and Darcy assured her that it was authentic from the Black Forest region of Germany, not that she would have suspected less from him.

A few more kisses ensued, both reluctantly separating to prepare for dinner.

❧

Lizzy stood before the tall mirror adjusting the snug bodice of her gown for improved comfort. Marguerite was currently retrieving her new Kashmir shawl.

"As always, Mrs. Darcy, you steal the very breath from my lungs with your beauty."

Lizzy did not even turn about, so acclimated to Darcy's presence in her dressing room. "Thank you, Mr. Darcy. I daresay I am gratified that new gowns are top on my list of priorities. I shall soon have naught to wear."

Darcy walked behind her, placing hands lightly on her hips as he whispered in her ear, "Perhaps I should forbid you purchasing new gowns, beloved, then you would be forced to remain bared. I might rather enjoy that."

Marguerite returned at that moment, forestalling Lizzy's retort, and Darcy retreated a pace. "Here you are Mistress. The colors match perfectly with your gown. Mr. Darcy has excellent taste." She bobbed in Darcy's direction.

"Thank you, Marguerite." He bowed, "Are you finished, Elizabeth?"

"I believe so. You may retire, Marguerite. No need to wait up for me. Enjoy your evening." With another curtsey, she departed. Lizzy started to turn towards her husband, but he had rapidly resumed his previous pose, now with hands about her waist and lips nibbling along her neck.

"I rather wish we could stay home," he mumbled. "As lovely as this gown is, I do believe I would prefer you out of it."

"You are echoing the thoughts I was entertaining earlier, my love. However, you have gone to inordinate effort for this day and I would not wish to disrupt the agenda. Hold that vision, beloved, and I will happily allow you to fulfill your fantasy when we return." She pivoted in his arms and pressed into him. "After all, I owe you a plenitude of thanks for all you have done for me today. I have been devising plans as you suggested."

He smiled happily, kissing tenderly in pleasure but also to distract. He reached into his pocket withdrawing the last gift and slipping it about her slender neck. She pulled away with a start, fingers moving to touch the necklace. Darcy was beaming, hands turning her back to face the mirror.

"Alas, this is the final present. Or rather the last present designated for your birthday. I make no promises to desist lavishing you, my wife."

The necklace was dainty, as both Darcy and Lizzy preferred: a single strand of small diamonds and amber linked, the teardrop pendant of translucent amber hanging precisely at the top of her cleavage. It was elegant and flawless, obviously of superior craftsmanship. Additionally, it blended fluidly with her gold-trimmed beige gown.

"Marguerite knew about this, did she not?" Lizzy smiled at her husband's reflection as he nodded. "She suggested this gown. You are a sneak, William." He shrugged, kissing the nape of her neck.

"Amber accents your fine, chocolate eyes, dearest. The dress accents your luscious body. I win on both counts."

"Gifts and excessive flattery. My, my, you surely do deserve abundant expressions of my gratitude, lover."

"I shall wait with bated breath."

The townhouse of Lord and Lady Matlock was located in the heart of St. James's Place, just north of Piccadilly. Lizzy had dined with the Earl and his wife once during her engagement, upon the occasion of her introduction to them. This dinner would naturally be quite different, as Lizzy was now family and Darcy's uncle and aunt were very dear to her. Once they were in the carriage and on their way, Lizzy discovered her previous wish to stay home fading under the anticipated pleasure of seeing the Matlocks again. They had left Derbyshire for London shortly after Elizabeth's recovery and the duel, so Lizzy did miss them.

They were greeted by the butler, who informed them that the Earl and Countess of Matlock were awaiting them in the parlor. He led the way, Lizzy holding the arm of her husband. The butler had spoken the truth. The Fitzwilliams were in the parlor, standing in the exact middle of the room to be precise. Additionally, to Lizzy's stunned astonishment, they were surrounded by a crowd.

Georgiana stood beside them, smiling and nearly hopping in delight, with Colonel Fitzwilliam grinning behind her. Mary and Kitty stood between Edward and Violet Gardiner and Charles and Jane Bingley. Caroline Bingley stood slightly apart with a faint smile gracing her pinched features. Also present were Stephen and Amelia Lathrop, Gerald and Harriet Vernor with his parents Henry and Mary Vernor, George and Alison Fitzherbert, Rory and Julia Sitwell, Clifton and Chloe Drury, as well as Albert and Marilyn Hughes. Even Richard's older brother Jonathan and his wife Priscilla were in attendance.

Virtually in unison they wished Lizzy a happy birthday. Darcy was grinning broadly, remarkably proud for executing the final crescendo to what was undeniably a momentous day of surprises. Lizzy was immediately surrounded, Darcy retreating a safe distance to contentedly observe his wife's glowing face. The press of visitors would prevent them exchanging more than a few words all evening, Lizzy only able to express her gratitude and abounding joy via glancing eye contact.

The evening consisted of a marvelous dinner with lively conversation succeeded by segregated male and female socializing. Amelia was well into her sixth month of pregnancy, with humorous tales to share in her blunt manner. Lizzy was thrilled to be able to officially announce her own expectant state, of which most in the company was ignorant. The female squeals of delight were readily heard down the hall in the game room where the men sipped their drinks, sedately congratulating Darcy with imported cigars and claps on the back.

The cap of the night was combined entertainment reminiscent of the Darcy's Christmas concert. Guests took turns at the pianoforte, while Richard played on the cello, Lady Matlock dazzled them all on the standing harp, voices from every musical range lifted, and Darcy blushingly added his violin talents for five songs. Humor was high and the gathering was carefree; and although it was a late night, Lizzy was rather amazed at her total lack of fatigue. She frequently sensed Darcy's scrutiny and was quick to meet his questioning gaze with a glorious smile.

Neither Lizzy nor Darcy was overly tired when they returned home to Darcy House. Perhaps it was in part a result of the sustained energy from the sprightly amusement of the evening, but in large portion, it was a renewed inclination to make love to each other. The girls were ushered off to their rooms, stumbling with weariness. Without preamble, Lizzy grasped her husband's hand and lead him into their room. Once there, door securely latched, she faced him and, with hands resting lightly on his chest, she kissed him affectionately.

"Fitzwilliam, my beloved, my heart," she purred. "All day I have been blissfully at your mercy, the recipient of your love and caring and adoration. Now, lover mine, you shall be at my mercy as I explicitly communicate my love, adoration, and thankfulness."

Darcy was smiling with breathless anticipation as his wife slowly doffed his jacket and waistcoat, sliding hands over him lingeringly as she went. The cravat easily joined the rest over a chair back, after which she directed him to a comfortable seat. Kneeling, she divested him of his boots and stockings, gently massaging his feet and calves. Darcy was already enjoying himself, the simple touch of his wife's hands on his body enough to arouse him tremendously, yet Lizzy was far from finished.

She stroked along his thighs while positioning herself between his legs, hands traveling with sluggish slowness up his body and eventually to his neck. She leaned close, brushing his parted lips with hers, whispering, "Relax and observe."

She rose, stepped back a pace, and began unpinning her hair. Tress by silky tress tumbled in waves over her shoulders to mid-back. Once unencumbered, she raked her fingers through the curls, shaking her head with seductive swaying causing her hair to swing wildly. Engaging his darkening eyes, she reached dainty fingers to the clasps of her gown, loosening them and peeling the fabric from her shoulders with agonizing patience. Equally as leisurely, the petticoat was untied and joined the gown in a puddle at her feet.

Darcy licked his lips, arousal evident now at the sight of his beautiful wife. She released the laces of her corset, tossing it aside, at last facing her adoring spouse in naught but her short, thin chemise, shoes, and stockings. The soft slippers stripped off with ease. Lizzy paused, standing still as the excitement of Darcy's smoldering gaze raking up and down her body sent shivers of desire racing through her. The powerful and mutual passion they incited with mere glances never ceased to astound.

Taking a step toward the chair, Lizzy lifted a leg, placing her foot on the edge precisely at Darcy's groin. He groaned, shifting against her wiggling toes. Lizzy smiled smugly, leaning over slightly—enough to expose the round top of her bosom—as she delicately and with supreme deliberation untied the ribbons to her stocking.

Darcy was mesmerized, mouth open and nearly drooling. She had never stripped for him in quite this leisurely and seductive a fashion. Both of her precious hands slipped under a silk edge, caressing her velvety skin from thigh to toe as she exposed a shapely leg and pulled the stocking away. Darcy moaned, closing his eyes in intense pleasure and impulsively reaching to caress her thigh. She batted his hand away gently, shifting the other leg to the chair and repeating the entire process.

Remaining within his knees, she finally bared herself completely, the chemise discarded as slowly as the rest, with purposeful caressing over her flesh as he avidly watched, nearly incoherent with the hunger to touch her.

Standing nude, she remained still for several heartbeats, noting his intensity and tense urgency.

"Elizabeth," he whispered. "Lord. You are so beautiful."

Smiling, she grasped his clenched hands, drawing him up. "Do not touch me," she softly commanded, and he whimpered as if in true pain. She started at the top of his head, running unhurried fingers through his hair to scratch lightly along his scalp, to ears, along a chiseled jaw, and onward over each inch of him. Laggardly, tenderly, lovingly, she traveled over his flushed skin, fire trailing in her wake. The shirt was lifted and tossed as her palms and fingertips aroused him to a mania of lust. An inordinate amount of time was spent teasing his chest and abdomen, fondling and squeezing in circles over shoulders and arms to strong hands. Clasped in her own, she brought them to her mouth, devoting minutes to licking, sucking, and kissing each palm and refined finger.

Darcy was faint. His heart raced, breath in punctuated gasps, knees weak and trembling. "Lizzy, please," he begged, his voice rasping and nearly inaudible.

"You wish to touch me, lover?"

"Yes! God, yes."

"You wish to love me?"

Darcy groaned. "Need you ask!"

"Hmmm… I thought you a patient man with extraordinary self control, Mr. Darcy." She teased, but her own desire for him threatened to overwhelm her own careful regulation. Releasing his hands, which he immediately twined through her hair, she attacked the buttons on his breeches.

Darcy did not comprehend how he could keep upright. He trembled with raging desire, dizzy from his rushing, feverish blood and shallow respirations. Yet the sensations she was educing were transcendent. Time had no meaning. He could no longer distinguish her individual motions and caresses, all of her exquisite ministrations melded into one delirious joy. He no longer consciously thought of reciprocating with touches of his own, too lost in furious arousal and animal feeling.

Eventually, he snapped. Grasping her shoulders painfully, he pulled her up, assaulting her mouth with a hoarse cry. Lizzy was more than ready, kissing him ferociously while literally climbing up his body in an urgent need to feel all of him. Haltingly, they stumbled entwined to the bed, never ceasing to frantically touch each other.

Wildly, they made love, weariness nonexistent in the transcendent bliss of indescribable bonding. Rapture and supreme love coursed through every particle of their bodies and souls.

Darcy rolled to the side, his wife embraced firmly within trembling but sturdy arms. They stared at each other, smiling softly as they caught their breath.

He kissed her. "Elizabeth, beloved wife. How immeasurably I love you! Making love with you is…" he closed his eyes in contemplation, "heaven." He kissed her shoulder, stroking over her hip then cupping her abdomen. "Our baby was made in such a way. In joy, rapture, and infinite love. A part of you and a part of me, created by God through our union. Forever I shall gaze upon his or her face and know this. Forever I shall be grateful, and forever, even beyond my life on this earth, I shall love you, Elizabeth Darcy."

Tears swam in Lizzy's eyes and she could not speak. Instead, she hugged him fiercely, letting go only long enough to crawl under the blankets. As they drifted into contented sleep, entangled and touching with her head nestled onto his shoulder, she whispered, "I shall eternally love you, Fitzwilliam Darcy."

CHAPTER NINE

Darcy House Affairs

THE THREE DAYS FOLLOWING Lizzy's birthday extravaganza were a whirlwind of activity. If it were not for Darcy's constant concern and vigilance over Lizzy's and the baby's health, she could well have occupied eighteen out of each twenty-four hours with a myriad of pursuits. In actuality, as Lizzy was entering her fourth month of pregnancy, the symptoms faded dramatically. Her fatigue was blessedly a phenomenon of the past. Lizzy had decided that she would gladly embrace faintness, headaches, and nausea if they replaced weakness; her temperament was quite simply unable to cope with lethargy and inaction. Fortunately, her queasiness, raging hunger, and light-headedness were also passing. Upon occasion, she would briefly experience a fleeting unsettled stomach and her appetite was mildly increased from previously, but it was controlled and in no way caused her distress.

It required another two weeks of convincing before her husband would finally accredit the truth of her state and relent to his oft-frustrating solicitude and anxiety. In the interim, Lizzy did pace herself and managed to rest as much as possible. Of course, since all her friends and family knew of her condition, not to mention Darcy's lack of humor and severity regarding his wife's welfare, Lizzy would not have been allowed to overextend if she had wished it.

Therefore, her new gowns were acquired in easy stages, interspersed with relaxing teas at the houses of her friends or Darcy House. Darcy had encouraged her to plan ahead, purchasing as many outfits as she would need to accommodate her blossoming shape. Madame Millicent, the modiste who had created her birthday gown, was extremely clever. She skillfully designed dresses that were stylish, yet sewn with unique gathers and folds specifically for the pregnant body. By the time they returned to Pemberley in July, Lizzy would have plenty of dresses, undergarments, and nightwear to clothe her well into the fall. For winter wear, when she would primarily be confined indoors, Madame du Loire would provide.

She purchased the occasional baby article, generally clothing, but discovered that she was hesitant to do so. It was fairly odd. Georgiana especially was forever gushing over some tiny item, and if she had it her way, they would require three more carriages simply to haul the items back to Pemberley! Amelia, naturally, was purchasing infant paraphernalia in abundance. At one point, she gently and privately asked Lizzy if her reluctance was due to fear of miscarriage. Lizzy was frankly amazed, not at the question, but at the fact that it had never once occurred to her that she might yet lose her baby. It certainly was not an uncommon event, sadly, yet after her accident and the weeks of subsequent incertitude, Lizzy had not once even entertained the idea.

Amelia's question generated a period of introspection. As Lizzy pondered her qualms, she finally realized that it was not that she did not wish to buy the baby's clothing and other necessaries. Rather, she did not want to buy them in London.

"You see," she told Darcy that evening, "I know it is probably ridiculous, but I want to obtain our baby's needs from Derbyshire. Pemberley is our home and will be our children's home. Somehow it does not feel right or proper to buy things here, so far away." She shook her head, reddening in mild embarrassment. "Anyway, silly as it is, that is how I feel about it and pregnant women are allowed to be nonsensical!"

Darcy was gazing at her quizzically, in that odd enigmatic way he had, with the tiny lilt to his lips. "Elizabeth, come here." He held out his hands and she joined him on the sofa. He kissed her brow. "Beloved, everything you do amazes me and causes my heart to grow fuller with love. Yet, there are those times when you say or do something so astounding that it is nigh on unbearable in how it moves me. This is one of those times. That you would have such strong emotions regarding Pemberley and Derbyshire after so short a span of time is deeply pleasing to me. Your sentiments are not the least bit silly. Or if they are, then I am as silly because I concur. We have plenty of time to provide our child's needs and we will do it together from home."

Despite Darcy's continued attentiveness and desire to remain by Lizzy's side during those first weeks, he nonetheless was forced to attend to an onslaught of business affairs. Prior to his marriage, Darcy had dwelt more than half a year in Town. This year, instead, Mr. Keith had traveled to London for three sojourns over the long winter and spring, and Darcy's solicitor, Mr. Daniels, had power-of-attorney over several interests. Letters and documents arrived at Pemberley's doors and departed with steady frequency, both private couriers and Royal mail reaping financial benefit from Mr. Darcy's choice to sequester himself with his new bride. With this organization, Darcy had delightfully dwelt at Pemberley while the complicated and extensive ventures which generated the Darcy wealth were handled smoothly. Nonetheless, although he had diligently arranged for the longer interval in Derbyshire, there was an abundant array of enterprises and legal issues which now required his personal involvement.

So, while Lizzy shopped and socialized, Darcy worked. He did manage to visit his Club, White's, on several afternoons. To some degree this was a business requirement as a great multitude of deals were transacted, associations were formed, and information was shared over billiards, brandy, and cigars. It was also a necessity for Darcy to engage in frequent strenuous physical activity. Although perfectly content to sit for hours with a book in his hand, Darcy equally craved working up a sweat. Therefore, he patronized Angelo's Fencing Academy and went horseback riding at one of the equine centers as often as possible.

Nevertheless, no matter how engrossed they were in their individual ventures, they reunited by late afternoon and unfailingly spent the entire night together. Nearly every evening they were committed beyond Darcy House at a dinner engagement, the theatre, or soiree; however, they did ensure some solitary time. The calling cards and invitations began in earnest after Lizzy's official appearance on Darcy's arm at the opera. Prior to that event, Lizzy exclusively passed the day with her friends. She was so busy, and naïve regarding the mores of society, that the absence of invitations did not registered in her consciousness. Eventually, it would be brought to her attention, but that part of the story shall be revealed later, as will her presentation at the opera.

For two weeks Lizzy was joyously content. Her only difficulty during those first weeks occurred right at Darcy House.

The fourth day after her birthday, a week after arriving at Darcy House, Lizzy finagled the entire morning to herself. After a romantic morning with her husband and breakfast with the girls, Lizzy retired to the library. Darcy departed for an appointment with a fellow horse breeder, and the girls disappeared to the parlor with Mrs. Annesley.

Immediately, Lizzy asked one of the footmen, Thomason, to send for Mrs. Smyth. Lizzy's initial illness, followed by her bounteous schedule, had precluded the opportunity to candidly chat with the housekeeper of Darcy House as she had with Mrs. Reynolds. An uncomfortable barrier had risen between the two for reasons that frankly evaded Lizzy's understanding. She was polite but cool, avoided eye contact with Lizzy, and when their gazes locked, Mrs. Smyth seemed vaguely disapproving. She granted Lizzy's requests hesitantly and as if burdened, and had resisted Marguerite's inclusion and needs for her Mistress. Darcy had noted it as well and was very angry, but had succumbed to Lizzy's pleading to allow her to deal with it as was appropriate as Mistress.

Her necessary interview with Mrs. Smyth did not begin well, as she took thirty minutes to respond to Lizzy's summons. That alone would have angered Darcy beyond reason, and Lizzy was peeved as well, but she kept her emotions in check, not wishing to start the conversation with a negative bent. She was further challenged to maintain her calm, as when Mrs. Smyth did appear, she knocked perfunctorily on the door as she opened it. Six months ago this may not have even registered, but after living with the extreme propriety and discipline of the Pemberley staff, Lizzy was fully cognizant of the purposeful slight.

"You asked for me, Mrs. Darcy?"

"Yes. Please have a seat, Mrs. Smyth." Lizzy had chosen to sit on the sofa rather than at Darcy's desk, wishing to present an informal pose. She indicated the opposite sofa for the housekeeper.

Mrs. Smyth, however, remained standing. "If it is all the same, Madame, I prefer to stand."

Anger flared, but Lizzy spoke quietly, "It is not what I prefer, Mrs. Smyth. Please sit." She did so reluctantly, folding her hands and gazing vaguely over Lizzy's right shoulder. "Mrs. Smyth, I must first apologize for having not arranged the time in my schedule to introduce myself to you in a proper and private manner. Between my illness and appointments, this has been my first unencumbered morning. Therefore, I wished for us to become better acquainted and for me to discuss several issues of concern with you."

Mrs. Smyth met her eyes with the faint disapproving hint Lizzy had noted frequently. "It is not necessary, Mrs. Darcy. I am an employee of Mr. Darcy's and do not deem it appropriate for us to be friends."

"Nor do I, Mrs. Smyth. I am not referring to friendship, per se, but mutual respect and communication. Also, I must remind you that as Mistress of Darcy House, you are my employee as well." Lizzy had not meant to be curt, but the woman was seriously beginning to annoy her.

Mrs. Smyth reddened slightly, but her lips primly pressed together and eyes flared momentarily. "Of course. Forgive me, Mrs. Darcy."

Lizzy ignored her weakly offered contrition and continued, "Now, I understand you have been housekeeper here for approximately five years? I must praise you for managing so well. The house staff appears to operate suitably and the environment is properly maintained. Nonetheless, there are some areas I wish to address. Obviously, now that Mr. Darcy is no longer a bachelor, the household demands and procedures will alter." She paused, noting the housekeeper's frown. "The first and most essential modification is that I will be handling the household affairs, staffing issues, budget, and the like rather than he."

"But," she blurted in surprise, "Mr. Darcy has always trusted me with these decisions!"

"This has absolutely nothing to do with trust, Mrs. Smyth. Please believe me. Surely you are cognizant from your previous employments that it is the Mistress of the manor who manages the household?"

"Of course!" she declared angrily. "Yet what do you know of managing a household? We have no pigs or cows running about here!"

"Mrs. Smyth!" Lizzy was truly angry now. "You forget yourself most profoundly. If Mr. Darcy were present to hear your insult, I can assure you with absolute certainty you would this instant be unemployed. I, however, am slightly more forgiving. Only slightly, though, and you would be wise to remember that your tenuous position is under my jurisdiction."

Mrs. Smyth was very pale, and, for the first time since Lizzy had entered the house a week ago, was looking at her with some respect. "Please forgive me, Mrs. Darcy. My outburst was uncalled for."

Lizzy inhaled deeply, finally resuming, "Mrs. Smyth, as rude and hideously misplaced as your slur against my character was, I will concur that I do not have years of experience in totally managing all aspects of a household. Be that as it may, I have learned speedily and comprehensively from both Mr. Darcy and Mrs. Reynolds. As at Pemberley, I judge the task as a partnership of sorts. Ultimately, Mr. Darcy and I are in control, but we both trust your expertise as evidenced by five years of stellar execution. I had intended to approach my discussion with you in this vein and attempted to do so, if you recall."

Mrs. Smyth's head was bowed and she seemed truly distressed. Lizzy, however, did not relent. "You have placed a quandary before me. When I reveal what has transpired here with Mr. Darcy, he will be seriously vexed. Your opinion of me and my qualifications may be nominal, but I can assure you his are not. I cannot promise what his reaction will be, as he is already irritated by your manner this past week and only my pleading has prevented his action. How you behave through the remainder of this audience, coupled with your ready acceptance and execution of my wishes, will greatly affect your future here at Darcy House. Do you understand and accept this? If not, then speak now and save us both wasting our time."

Mrs. Smyth struggled to form words, finally expressing penitence. Lizzy tended to believe her sincere, but there remained an edge that she could not quite identify. For now, though, she decided to let it pass.

The conference continued for over an hour. Marguerite was to have free access to all areas of the house and granted instantaneously anything she requested for her Mistress. One of the maids, Helen, was to be brought immediately before Mrs. Darcy, as she specifically had been rude and obstructive to Marguerite, even vilifying her personally with anti-French aspersions. Mrs. Smyth was commanded to uphold any decree rendered by Mrs. Darcy regarding Helen, or anything else for that matter. All menu decisions were to be made by Lizzy, starting with the detailed list for today's picnic luncheon Lizzy planned with her sisters and friends, and for that evening's party with the Bingleys and Lathrops. The housekeeper demurred over some of the mandated edibles, Lizzy simply stating that she had hours to ensure their inclusion.

The library was determined to be far too dusty, only routinely cleaned once a month. Lizzy ordered it to hereafter be thoroughly scoured each week. Mrs. Smyth balked at this, declaring they did not have the manpower. This led to Lizzy's next demand: to review all the staff duties and records. If additional staff was needed, then they would be provided. Mrs. Smyth was definitely not pleased with this, nor was she pleased when Lizzy requested to see the past six months worth of household ledgers. Yet, she did not argue; displeasure was only evident in her eyes and sternly pressed lips.

As she rose to leave, Lizzy spoke, "One more point, Mrs. Smyth. When I summon you, I will expect you to respond in a timely manner and to await my permission before entering."

To suggest that Darcy was vexed would be a monumental understatement! As Lizzy related what had transpired between she and Mrs. Smyth, Darcy's eyes darkened to blue-black, and his jaw clenched so tightly that his lips nearly disappeared. Lizzy had witnessed her husband in an extreme temper on a handful of occasions, and it was a chilling sight to behold. She honestly believed he could freeze boiling water with a glance.

He listened to her without interrupting, rising silently when she finished to pull the servant's bell. A footman responded instantly, and Darcy calmly requested the immediate presence of Mr. Travers and Mrs. Smyth. The footman bowed, but the brief flash in his eyes as he turned left no doubt that even he had sensed the repressed rage in his Master's icy voice.

"William, perhaps we should talk some more—" Lizzy began, but ceased at the sharp gesture from her spouse. Lizzy had learned that Darcy was without a doubt one of the kindest, gentlest, and most gracious and loving men on the planet. She had equally ascertained that he could be ruthless, uncompromising, dictatorial, and domineering. One was a total fool to cross the Master of Pemberley. Lizzy was not a fool. In addition, she recognized clearly and with complete trust that this was a situation he was more than capable of handling and that it was his duty to do so.

When Mr. Travers and Mrs. Smyth entered the room mere seconds later, it was obvious that the former was confused at the abrupt summons, whereas the latter was abundantly aware. Darcy was sitting behind his desk with Lizzy standing to his right.

In a deceptively mild tone, Darcy asked, "Do either of you have any doubts or reservations as to my supreme authority in this house?"

Mr. Travers was shocked. "Of course not, Mr. Darcy!"

Mrs. Smyth was pale as a ghost and trembling. "No, Mr. Darcy."

"Very good. I shall be as intelligible and succinct as I possibly can be. Mrs. Darcy is of near equal stature and authority to me in every single aspect.

Her dictates are law, to be respected and executed as you would for me. She is the Mistress of Pemberley and Darcy House, and is to be honored as this station decrees. Any deviation from this reality, even in the minutest degree, will be grounds for instantaneous dismissal. Is any of this ambiguous?"

His penetrating and fierce gaze bore into Mrs. Smyth throughout the entire speech. Mr. Travers may be ignorant of the specific instigation of his Master's statement, but he was no idiot. That Mrs. Smyth had in some manner foolishly acted on or vocalized her disdain for Mr. Darcy's choice of wife was obvious. Mr. Travers did not concur with the housekeeper's opinion and had grown weary of cautioning her. He hesitated nary a second, loudly and precisely confirming his comprehension and loyalty. Mrs. Smyth readily agreed as well, voice tremulous.

"I shall leave it to each of you to inform the members of your staff as to what has been proclaimed here. Mr. Travers, you may be excused." He bowed and departed. Darcy rose to his feet, eyes never faltering. "Mrs. Smyth, there are two reasons you are not at this second packing your belongings and exiting this house. One is your years of faithful and competent service to Darcy House, of which I am thankful. However, this reason would hold little weight in light of today's events if Mrs. Darcy had not already granted you mercy. She has deemed to bestow her clemency, and I will bow to this. Be warned, this mercy will be withdrawn at the merest hint of you disobeying my orders. Is this understood?"

The relationship between Lizzy and Mrs. Smyth would never be a friendly one, and the housekeeper offered her challenges. There were moments when Lizzy did wonder if it would be easier to fire the woman and start anew, but in the end, she did manage the household excellently, and as the Darcys would not be dwelling in the city often, it was best to maintain the status quo.

Generally speaking, Lizzy needed to make few adjustments to the management of Darcy House. The ledgers were in perfect order and the staff assignments were adequate. An additional gardener was hired to assist the two who managed the grounds. Lizzy spoke at length with them, as there were a number of areas she wanted altered. Specifically, she completely redesigned the private garden and patio located next to the Master's chambers to include a gurgling fountain, potted and hanging flowers, a vine of wisteria along the right edge for further privacy, and extensive trimming of the large elm tree that blocked their view of the nighttime sky. The old brick wall was removed and replaced with one of cobbled river stones to match the patio and a wrought iron gate placed to access the meandering gravel pathways beyond.

Lizzy interviewed each lead staff member. She encouraged open communication, and before her first sojourn would end, each one of them accepted the honesty of her offer, and learned when she was approached with requests, most of which were granted. Mrs. Smyth frowned upon what she deemed a usurping of her power, but Lizzy ignored her. Minor budget issues were addressed. Darcy had tended to allow Mrs. Smyth to spend as she saw fit, generously allotting monies without asking too many questions. This was not a result of mismanagement or laziness on his part, but as the overall budget for Darcy House was substantially less than Pemberley, he simply did not consider it worth worrying about. Lizzy was frugal by nature and due to her upbringing, instinctively noticed dozens of tiny ways that funds could be redistributed. The end product was a savings to the estate while simultaneously leading to a smoother household execution. Even Mrs. Smyth grudgingly admitted the fact. Darcy was further amazed, and his already exalted esteem for his wife grew.

Helen, to Lizzy's dismay, was unrepentant. It seemed that a brother died in the recently triumphant difficulties with France. As sad as this fact was, it certainly was not Marguerite's fault. France may be the country of her birth, but she had lived the past twenty years in England, longer than Helen, in truth, as she was a mere seventeen! In this matter, she appealed to her husband.

"She cannot stay with an attitude such as this," Darcy declared calmly. "I will not allow Marguerite to be treated thus, and one maid is much the same as any other. I will take care of it."

Lizzy squirmed in her seat, finally standing to pace before his desk. "William, I…" She sighed, wringing her hands nervously while he frowned. "I should deal with this myself. Mistress of Pemberley and all that." She waved her hand airily with a tiny giggle.

Darcy smiled, rising to halt her pacing with gentle hands on her shoulders. "Elizabeth, you do not have to handle this sort of problem. Trust me, I have let many employees go over the years. I am quite good at it, in fact." He laughed and kissed her forehead.

Lizzy shook her head with a soft chuckle. "Somehow I doubt that, love. You bluster and pretend, but facing a seventeen year old girl and telling her she is out of a job will not be easy for you." She tiptoed to kiss his cheek and then moved a pace away before continuing. "That is not the point. Household staff is under my jurisdiction and since this directly concerns my personal maid, I need to cope with it. Just teach me how such a matter is properly dealt with, advise me, and I will manage it."

"Very well, Mistress Darcy." He took her hand and pulled her next to him on the sofa. "I will gladly share my brutal techniques, but first let me tell you once again how marvelous you are and how proud you make me." He nuzzled into her neck, Lizzy giggling anew at the ticklish bites.

"This is a brutal technique, Mr. Darcy? I certainly hope not a typical tactic utilized by you when firing maids." Darcy merely laughed, tickling further and saving the Masterly counsel for a later hour.

Lizzy attended to the matter with fortitude and dignity. Only later did she break down with trembles, comforted by her husband who was immeasurably swollen with pride. It was another step taken by the new Mrs. Darcy into the greater world of estate administration.

CHAPTER TEN

A Night at the Opera

DARCY, REGALLY DRESSED IN head-to-toe black except for a pristine white shirt and cravat, stood before the empty fireplace in the parlor with an expansive grin on his face. His sister, with assistance from Kitty, was relating an adventure with the ducks that live on the little pond in Hyde Park. He had never noted it in the past, but his shy baby sister apparently had developed a flair for the dramatic as well. He rather doubted chasing ducks could be as riveting as she was presenting it, but between her and Kitty's gales of laughter and charade-like pantomiming, he was tremendously amused and Richard was actually wiping tears from his eyes. Of course, Richard was easily entertained.

The girls delighted them with their silly exploits while they awaited the appearance of Mary and Elizabeth. Tonight was the opera, and proper preparation was of the utmost importance. The men understood this, and as Marguerite had happily volunteered to style the hair of all four women, well, it could take some time. Georgiana, in a new gown for the occasion and hair pinned elaborately with a diamond clip, was beautiful. With a pang to his heart, Darcy recognized the woman lurking under the girlish exterior of his beloved sister.

Miss Kitty was equally as lovely. Lizzy had purchased several new gowns for both her sisters from her pin money, a fact which had irritated Darcy because he would have willingly and happily provided for them, but Lizzy insisted. They actually had a minor argument over her choice, but she would not budge.

"William, I did not marry you to furnish necessities for my family," she had declared firmly.

"I understand this, Elizabeth. However, when I married you, I voluntarily accepted your family as my own, as did you with Georgiana and the rest."

"Accepted, yes, but not charged to support. You allot me far more money than I can possibly spend on myself, so I desire to do this for my sisters. It is not your place."

"Not my place! This offends me, Elizabeth. They are my sisters now, and therefore, it is my place."

"Technicalities, Mr. Darcy. Are you next going to offer financial support to my father? Buy his wardrobe? Furthermore, imagine the Pandora's box you would be opening if my mother found out you were lavishing the girls, and lavish you would, William. Suddenly the 'needs' would escalate and Pemberley would be bankrupt in a month!"

Darcy certainly could not argue regarding her mother and was aghast at the very idea of insulting his proud, distinguished father-in-law. Nonetheless, he felt slighted somehow and it irritated him. "I will not deny a couple of your points, my dear; however, I still maintain a dress or two is hardly beyond my responsibility."

"Consider it this way, beloved. You are supporting them by guesting them in your house…"

"Our house," he interrupted with a glare.

"Our house," she resumed with a smile, "and the money to purchase clothing and trinkets for them is coming from your coffers, simply via me. So, everyone is happy!"

He hated it when she utilized perfect logic! It continued to annoy him in a vague way he could not quite identify, but any further attempts to change her mind were met with increased stubbornness and an argument, so he finally relented. The gown that Kitty had chosen was remarkable and her hair equally as stunning, accented with one of Elizabeth's ruby hair combs. Kitty was an adorable young girl to Darcy's eyes. She did not look like his wife, but they had the same coloring and hair. She possessed the identical effervescent quality that

Elizabeth did and was very witty. Without Lydia to negatively influence her and with the positive, steady persuasion of Mary and now Georgiana, Kitty had mellowed. Her giddiness was slowly replaced with a pleasant charm and grace. Alas, she still did not boast the intelligence of her three older sisters.

Kitty and Georgiana completed their tale, Richard yet chuckling, when Elizabeth and Mary simultaneously entered the room. Elizabeth, in her ultimate Mrs. Fitzwilliam Darcy regalia, was breathtaking. Normally Darcy's eyes would have been captured as the whole world faded from view. Tonight, however, it was Mary demanding immediate awe. It was not in any way that she was more stunning than Elizabeth; it was the shock of Mary adorned in anything other than a somber gray or black! Her gown was fashionable, with a daring scooped neckline and bared shoulders, a pale pink and sky blue satin with embossed roses over the lower third of the skirt. Her thick, lustrous black hair was pulled up with a half bonnet detailed with matching roses and feathers adorning. Her lips were painted a rosy pink and a faint dash of rouge highlighted her cheekbones. Darcy had never realized how beautiful she was, and Richard's eyes were bulging.

Elizabeth was beaming with pride and Mary was blushing under the intense scrutiny. "Oh, Mary!" Georgiana gushed, dashing to her friend and clasping her hands. "You are stunning! Did I not tell you these colors would be wonderful?"

Elizabeth edged over to her husband, allowing the girls to enthuse. Darcy turned to his radiant wife, freshly rendered awestruck at her sultry elegance. Her gown of scarlet satin was equally as daring, the tops of shapely breasts visible and creamy shoulders bare. The gauzy satin pleated under the bosom with a glittery white ribbon, fell smooth and snug over her abdomen to her toes. The satin gathered into a loose bustle over her buttocks with the same white ribbon sash forming an elaborate bow before diverging into a dozen tails plummeting to the floor. There were no sleeves to speak of: the shimmering ribbon braided with a strip of the scarlet fabric formed a narrow band which edged the top of the bodice and V-shaped back, swept over her upper arms in three individual laces and crossed over the entire back in an intricate pattern. She wore a scarlet and white turban adorned with tiny crystals and a plumed white feather, hair braided, curled, and cascading over her left shoulder. At her throat rested a strand of square cut diamonds with an exquisite round ruby pendant, and rubies graced her ears.

Privately, Darcy never thought his wife more beautiful than when her hair was tumbling down her back and shoulders, a transparent nightgown or chemise clinging to her womanly form, and delicate face flushed with desire. At times, he yearned to see her again in the simple country dresses she had worn at Hertfordshire when her natural luminance and svelte shape had been the focus. Luckily for him, the bulk of her everyday dresses, although of finer quality and style, remained humble and unadorned. Lizzy, like her husband, preferred minimalism and comfort.

Despite the predilection for economy of dress, Lizzy had rapidly embraced the necessity and joy of sophisticated splendor and elegance. She may retain some naïveté regarding the nuances of society, but she did understand the importance of this evening as her first official appearance as Mrs. Darcy in London. Therefore, her attire from top to bottom had been agonized over. The end result was stupendous. As was always the case when Darcy encountered his wife after an absence, no matter how brief, the need to touch and kiss her overwhelmed him. She could have been wearing a canvas sack and he would have experienced the same desire. Add in the resplendency of a gown and jewels, and it was unbearable.

Placing a hand lightly on her elbow, he steered unobtrusively out the side door into the billiard room. Closing the door firmly and leaning against it, he clasped her waist and drew her toward him for a deep kiss. Eventually pulling away, he feathered fingertips over her shoulders and neck. "I beg your forgiveness, my heart. It was early morning since last I avowed my ardent, consuming love for you."

"True, beloved; however, you declared your love so spectacularly that I am yet tingling from the expression. There is no dereliction to pardon unless you fail to comment on my gown. The intention, after all, was to dazzle you. Either I have erred in my choice or you shall be in serious trouble."

Darcy laughed lowly. "Your choice is perfection, my love. You are perfection." He trailed one finger along her bodice. "I will confess to some hesitation and jealousy over any other observing so much of your delightful flesh."

"Yet I belong to you, dearest, and only you shall ever view all of me." She smiled. "Truthfully, William, am I presentable? I wish you to be proud of me."

He cupped her face and kissed tenderly then smiled archly. "You place a dilemma before me, love. If I profess my irrepressible pride in all aspects, internal and external, which attribute to your flawlessness and that you are mine, then you may again accuse me of being arrogant and haughty. However, if I do not extol your exquisite beauty, impeccable character, and sparkling personality, I would be false and—what was it—be in 'serious trouble'?"

She laughed. Pressing into his body with hands traveling over his derriere, she responded with an absorbing kiss. They were interrupted moments later by a rap to the door behind Darcy's head.

"Pardon the intrusion, Mr. and Mrs. Darcy, but we should be leaving now. Unless, of course, you have decided to forego the opera in lieu of alternate pastimes?"

"We shall be there shortly, Richard. Go away."

"As you command, cousin." Lizzy was suppressing her giggles. Darcy tarried for another kiss and then offered an arm to his wife.

The society rumor mill had run full force during the immediate months after the engagement of Mr. Darcy to the penniless country girl of low rank. With some sadness and chagrin, but mostly joy at the fodder for juicy gossip, the topic of Darcy's choice was premier. It had ebbed somewhat after a month or so, only to flame anew at the announcement of the intimate nuptials in Hertfordshire, of all places. Then, with the populace dispersal for the winter and early spring, the chatter had died completely. As the influx of the elite increased in May, the mystery of the Darcy marriage and long absence from Town had resurged as a discussion point. The curiosity of it all was too succulent a morsel to ignore completely; however, after six months, there were dozens of torrid affairs far more interesting to chatter about. Even the crushed unmarried debutantes of the ton had turned their gazes elsewhere. Only in the past week, as the awareness of the Darcys' residence had gradually filtered through the parlors of Mayfair and St. James's Place, did the gossip freshly rage. The question of why the seclusion at Pemberley for six long months and now the week-plus relative isolation was speculated with relish. Those fortunate souls who had been introduced to the new Mrs. Darcy when fortuitously encountering her while shopping were the celebrities of the inner circle.

Therefore, the fervor of interest was high. No one knew when or if she would formally make her entrance, but every last person prayed they would be present when she did. Thus it was with the crowd currently amassing in the grand foyer and reception hall of the Royal Theatre. Would this be the night? Of course, as with all society events, there were always a plenteous number of glittering personages of eminent importance to ogle and fawn over. The appearance of the Prime Minister, the famous boxer John Jackson, and the Russian Ambassador Count von Lieven with his wife, the famous Countess von Lieven, had already fanned the fires of excitement.

When the Darcy carriage finally crept to the front of the line, word had already begun to spread. Naturally, curiosity was high, but the talent involved with sating one's inquisitiveness while not observably appearing to do so was an art form well honed by the elite. Lizzy, ignorant of this skill, was hence spared the blatant stares which she had been expecting, enabling her to relax as she mounted the steps on her proud husband's arm.

A dashing and softly smiling Darcy escorted both his wife and sister. Colonel Fitzwilliam, resplendent in dress uniform, gladly lent his arms to Mary and Kitty. Lord and Lady Matlock stood outside the massive doors under the Corinthian columned portico in conversation with an elegant couple. The Earl noted their approach first, turning with a smile.

"Ah, Mr. and Mrs. Darcy, and Miss Darcy." Lord Matlock bowed, greeting them all with proper hand kisses, Kitty and Mary blushing furiously.

Lady Matlock kissed Lizzy's cheek. "Elizabeth, dear, you are radiant. Please allow me to introduce you to Ambassador von Lieven and his wife Countess von Lieven. Your Grace, Countess, this is my niece, Mrs. Fitzwilliam Darcy."

Lizzy was nearly rendered speechless. She had heard of the Countess, a patroness of Almacks and hostess of one of the most elite salons in London, not to mention notorious as the mistress of Metternich. She was stunningly beautiful, exotic with almond-shaped eyes and raven hair. Her husband was as impressive as she, tall as Darcy but heavily bodied and sporting a full red beard. They greeted Lizzy warmly in their accented voices. Lizzy, thankfully, managed to speak calmly, natural charm and wit rushing to the forefront.

"Mrs. Darcy, the fortunate woman to capture the heart of the elusive Mr. Darcy of Pemberley!" Madame von Lieven proclaimed in a husky intonation, flicking her folded fan on Darcy's arm. "We were worried for you, Mr. Darcy. A man such as you should not remain a bachelor for so many years." Darcy reddened as she tittered musically. "What a delight your surprise marriage has been! I cannot thank you enough, Mr. Darcy, for providing a wealth of titillating gossip for my salon."

Darcy, blushing, bowed regally. "Happy to have been of service to you, Countess."

"No no! The joy is entirely mine, kind sir. I must repay. Mrs. Darcy, you and Mr. Darcy absolutely must grace us with your presence. I shall send an invitation round and refuse to accept your decline!" She giggled again, fluttering her fan before her face as she turned to her silent husband. "There I go yet again, dear, as you incessantly accuse. Selfishly regarding only myself!" She turned back to Lizzy, who frankly did not know what to think of the effervescent and flirty Countess. "You see, Mrs. Darcy, by guesting you at my salon I shall be all the rage! As will you be, too, of course. To receive an invite to my salon is a prized acclamation."

"I shall breathlessly await your kind offer, Countess. We will be delighted to accept."

Conversation flowed along with numerous introductions. Lizzy met so many titled gentry and other members of society that the names eventually melded into a jumble. They slowly weaved their way inside, the mass of people loitering in the massive lobby and staircases talking, laughing, and flirting. Theatre events were valued for the social contact far above the production itself. To be seen in one's finery and conversing with a notable was the prime motive for attendance. The news that Mrs. Darcy had been invited to Countess von Lieven's salon spread like wildfire. Couple this endorsement with her charisma and attractiveness, association with the Matlocks, presentation, favorable reception by a plethora of prominent personages, and Darcy's smiling pose, and her entry into the ton was secured.

The Bingleys and Gardiners were eventually located, chatting amiably with the Lathrops on the second tier balcony. Lizzy delightfully embraced her aunt and uncle. They had been overjoyed and awed by Darcy's invitation to join him in the Darcy box. Lizzy had never seen her aunt fuss so over the proper gown and accoutrements! While the women effused over dresses and jewels, Lord Matlock pulled Darcy to the side.

"Fitzwilliam, I wanted to warn you. Madeline received a letter from your Aunt Catherine today. It was primarily full of her usual nonsense until the last paragraph. She rather nonchalantly mentioned that she had heard of Elizabeth's pregnancy. I was suspect, as you barely announced your blessed news to us, and the manner of her casual remark seemed, well, too casual, if you take my meaning. You know your aunt! Have you written to her?"

Darcy was frowning. "No, Uncle, I have not. The truth is I had given it minimal consideration as yet."

"How do you suppose she discovered it?"

"That I believe I can ascertain. Elizabeth is dear friends with the wife of the vicar at Hunsford if you recall. She wrote to her while we were in Hertfordshire, as we had recently been apprised of Mrs. Collins's expectant state. I did not ask, however, I would imagine Elizabeth told her our joy as well. That husband of hers is a doltish sycophant who would run to Lady Catherine with the news." He smiled dourly. "We have had evidence of his interference in the past."

"Whatever the case, I thought I should give you the heads up."

"Thank you, uncle."

They turned back toward the ladies, Bingley and Lathrop joining them as Lord Matlock spoke, "By the way, William, are you going to accept Duke Grafton's offer?"

"I would be a fool to decline it. The honor in him asking to mix bloodlines is astounding."

Lathrop whistled. "Well done, Darcy! Grafton's thoroughbreds are some of the best in the country. How did you finagle that? Whip him at faro?" They all laughed.

"Hardly. You know me better than that. My luck at cards is nearly as atrocious as at dice."

Richard coughed, pretending to murmur under his breath, "Or darts."

Darcy ignored him. "I will assuredly accept his offer. He has asked me to ride to his estate next week. I have yet to tell Elizabeth, though, so let us speak of it no further. Perhaps, Stephen, you could accompany me? You too, Bingley, then the ladies could freely entertain each other as a soothing balm to their aching hearts in our absence."

"And you will not feel so guilty for deserting your bride, eh cousin?" Richard was grinning.

Darcy scowled at his cousin. "Just wait, Richard. Your day will come and I shall laugh all the way to the altar."

The bell rang, signifying the imminent start of the program. The Darcy box was spacious, comfortably able to seat nine. Elizabeth and Darcy were joined by the three girls, the Gardiners, and the Bingleys. Richard and the Lathrops would be sitting with Lord and Lady Matlock in their box located next to Darcy's. As Elizabeth was entering to sit, a tap on the shoulder caused her to turn, spying the smiling face of Harriet Vernor.

"Harriet, dear! I was beginning to worry. You are coming to Darcy House after?"

"Naturally, dear Elizabeth, we will be there. I shall speak with you at intermission, yet I had to say how amazing your gown." She leaned in to whisper, "Everyone is talking about you, sweetie. You have dazzled the leeches of the upper crust!"

"Harriet! Shame on you!" Lizzy chided with a laugh and slap of her fan, but Harriet merely winked and joined her husband with an airy wave adieu.

Darcy was waiting for his wife behind the curtain, lightly clasping her elbow to lead her to their seats in front. "The Vernors arrived, I see." He brushed her gloved fingers with his lips as she sat, settling himself beside her. He handed over her new opera glasses as Lizzy whispered what Harriet had said. He smiled, stifling a laugh behind a cough, replying, "How could they not be dazzled, beloved? You are the most beautiful woman here."

Lizzy graced him with a brilliant smile. "You, Mr. Darcy, are prejudiced or blind. Yet I shall accept the compliment."

As the lights dimmed, he bent for a quick kiss to her temple. "Thank you for wearing jasmine tonight, my heart. You are ravishing and delectable. How I shall attend to the performance is beyond my comprehension."

In truth, he attended raptly, as did Lizzy. Others may haunt the theatre for the socialization, but the Darcys honestly delighted in the spectacle. The seats were superb, with visualization so perfect that Lizzy had little need for her glasses. Darcy held her gloved hand throughout, absently raising her fingers to his lips for soft caresses, inclining for occasional whispered commentary. Once, Lizzy twisted to meet his eyes for a comment of her own and without thought they briefly kissed, eyes locking for merely a second before returning to the stage. All this was noted by the various curious onlookers, some of who were shocked and abhorred, others who found it sweet and romantic.

The performance was spectacular. Intermissions were abounding with further introductions and invitations. The gentlemen brought refreshments for the ladies, Darcy especially concerned as it was quite balmy inside and he fretted over any residual faintness. Lizzy, however, felt wonderful. It was warm and her new fan was utilized, but no dizziness ensued.

They retired to Darcy House for a light dinner with a group of their closest friends. Lizzy and Darcy played the hosts with tremendous success, the entertainment consisting solely of conversation, but none were left wanting.

It was late when they bid farewell to the last of their guests and ushered the girls to their rooms. Lizzy sat at her dressing table idly brushing her hair while dreamily musing over the evening's events and fought off sleep. Yawning hugely with eyes closed, she was unaware of her spouse's presence until he retrieved the brush from her slack hand.

He commenced brushing after tenderly kissing the top of her head. "Tired, beloved?"

"Exhausted actually. It was a busy day, but so wonderful. Everything was perfect: the music and singing, the company, the greetings." She opened her eyes to gaze at Darcy's reflection. "I believe I was remiss in telling you how handsome you were, beloved. I saw no one to compare." He merely smiled and continued to brush. Lizzy sighed happily and relaxed into his body. "Assist me to bed, Fitzwilliam, I doubt I could manage it alone."

He bent over, pausing for a kiss to her shoulder, and gathered her into his arms, carrying her to their bed. Removing the gauzy robe, he nestled her bare body close to his side and in his embrace, one hand warmly blanketing her belly as they drifted into a satisfied slumber.

The morning following, dawn having peaked hours earlier, Lizzy lazily opened one eye to note a smiling Darcy propped on an elbow, staring at her while tracing one fingertip lightly over her facial features. "Must you do that, Mr. Darcy?" she mumbled sleepily.

"I must, yes, I must. It is a compulsion born from an urgent hunger for you, my wife." He commenced the placement of gentle kisses along her neck, working his way slowly down to below her navel. Lizzy stretched and sighed, playing with his thick hair. His husky voice drifted to her from under the blanket, "Good morning, child mine. Grow quickly and strong so your parents can feel you." He kissed and caressed her belly, murmuring further nonsense while Lizzy roused fully. "Elizabeth, am I simply hopefully wishing, or are you slightly thicker here?" He ran a hand over her hipbones, which did not feel as acute as usual.

"I have noticed the same," she replied with a smile, withdrawing the blanket so she could see his face. "A couple of my favorite chemises are snug now. I frequently discern little flutters inside, like feathers tickling, but I do not know if it is the baby moving or, well, other sensations," she finished with a blush.

Darcy was grinning with joy. "Soon, beloved, we shall feel her regularly." He kissed her pubis again, laying his cheek gently onto her. "She will be tough and kick me firmly, Elizabeth, I know she will. Or he. Sturdy legs to grip a horse."

Lizzy laughed. "Naturally! A true Darcy—on a horse before he walks, gifted with a pony ere he is finished with swaddling cloths, and leaping fences prior to weaning from my breast."

"Foolish girl. I shall wait until he, or she, is weaned at least." With a last kiss, he worked his way back up to her lips. He lay onto the pillow, fingering her hair. "Dearest, I received a tremendous offer yesterday. I apologize for not having the opportunity to share with you until now. Do you recall my mentioning the fabulous racehorses bred by the Duke of Grafton?" She nodded. "I met with him yesterday, per his request, if you can imagine. He has heard of the fine Pemberley thoroughbreds and their reputation for endurance as well as speed. Grafton's horses are bred for speed, and having won the Derby and the Oaks numerous times they have proven their capabilities. Now, though, he wishes to add greater stamina to the mix for the longer races at Newmarket and St. Leger. Therefore, he has come to me and wishes to set up a breeding program."

"Oh, William! This is wonderful!"

"Yes, it is a dream becoming reality for me. A few of our horses have prevailed at the racetrack, but as you know, our main contracts are with the military. The money from the crown is considerable, but nothing compared to what we could earn from racing stock. I have yet to work out the details with Duke Grafton, but the profit from the breeding alone would be substantial, not to mention the reputation gained in the process."

"Dearest, you should be bouncing with joy, so why do I sense hesitancy in you? Is there a negative to the arrangement?"

"Not to the project itself, although I am certain Mr. Daniels will diligently search for any legal mishaps." He smiled and chuckled, caressing the back of his fingers over her cheeks. "The only negative is that the Duke wishes for me to visit his estate in Suffolk to personally inspect his stock, then he would like to visit Pemberley for the same reason. He is adamant and enthusiastic at the prospect, and I do not wish to hedge and possibly have him turn elsewhere. He wants to leave in two days," he finished softly, gazing intently into her eyes.

"Oh! I see. How long would you be away?"

"Five days, perhaps seven. Elizabeth, I do not desire to leave you! A week away is more than I can fathom, yet this is an opportunity of a lifetime, and it would benefit us now and our future…"

"William, stop," Lizzy pressed her fingers against his lips. "You would be an utter fool to not do this. The very thought of being away from you for a week is unbearable, but you have to go."

"I would bring you with me, love, if I could, but he wants to travel on horseback. This will actually be quicker in the end. Elizabeth, it is uncon-scionable for me to desert you here in London at this time, so soon after our arrival, and with the baby. I might miss something important, or you may need me." He exhaled angrily and flopped onto his back, staring at the ceiling as he muttered, "I cannot do it."

Lizzy bit her lip, furiously thinking. A week without him was too horrible to imagine, so she pushed it away, refusing to face it. She drew close, kissing his chest then up to his neck and ear. With fingers to his jaw, she turned his face toward hers and met troubled eyes with a dazzling smile. "You will not be deserting me, beloved, as I will be ordering you to leave. My girls will keep me company and watch over me. Our baby is safe and secure. What you are attempting with Duke Grafton is for our children's benefit." She sighed, lip beginning to tremble. "I will be anxiously awaiting your return with pent up desire and need." She kissed him lightly, running her tongue over his lower lip, speaking huskily, "Imagine how amazing it will be when you come home, my lover."

He groaned and embraced her tightly while rolling to the side, "Elizabeth, I cannot…"

"You can and you will. Now make love to me, Fitzwilliam, before I cry." She grasped him with an iron grip and pulled his body onto hers, claiming his mouth for an ardent kiss.

With a moan, he ran one hand down her side, over her bottom, and clutched her thigh as he pulled the leg over his hip. "I love you, Elizabeth, so tremendously. Are you certain? I could not bear to leave you if I thought you had any misgivings or resentment."

She smiled and stroked his face. "I am certain I shall pine for you every moment of the day and night, but I am also certain you must do this. You would regret it profoundly if you let this opportunity slip through your fingers. I prefer to live without your presence for a week than to live with your unhappiness forever." Traveling a hand to his groin for a gentle fondle, she sucked his lower lip between hers, nibbled lightly, and then whispered, "You reside in my soul, beloved. A week apart will not alter this fact."

Darcy sighed, kissing with abandon as he caressed over her body. He knew she was presenting a brave face, and he loved her for it. He also knew she was correct. He had to pursue this business deal, his duty to Pemberley and the future far too important. Nonetheless, it broke his heart. Already, still two days away and with her currently in his arms loving him, it felt as if his soul was splintering. Logic and duty seemed inconsequential against the thought of separation.

Within minutes they were crazily aroused, Darcy covering his delicate wife with his large frame as they joined. Of all the various ways they made love, each astounding and stimulating in unique ways, there was something expressly intimate in the feel of his body fully over her. Darcy was a tall man with sturdy muscles and broad shoulders. Logically, he should crush her small frame under his bulk, yet using either knees or arms to shift some of his weight off her, he still managed to proficiently excite with masterful hands and a deft mouth. His flesh felt phenomenal pressing onto her. So amazingly powerful, warm, masculine, and protective as her hands were thus freed to massage and tantalize his rough yet soft skin, through his hair, over his chest and abdomen, and on to any other part reachable.

Always facing the other, touching at hundreds of points, sweaty flesh writhing hotly together, Darcy was dominant yet gently responded to her demands, unceasingly cognizant of her pleasure. This was the preferred way they loved each other. Watching the passion rising on their faces, breath mingling as they panted, murmured endearments, vocalized sounds of gratification and lust, hearts beating in time, and then finally climaxing in unity with bodies melded.

The following two days passed quickly—too quickly. They spoke of their separation no further, other than in the abstract. In the end, Darcy decided that Gerald Vernor, as the one friend who knew the most about horses, would accompany him. His solicitor, Mr. Andrew Daniels, would also go for the legal necessities. Col. Fitzwilliam was charged with keeping a close eye on the women and roughly knew Darcy's itinerary in case of an emergency. Darcy assisted Lizzy with planning activities while he was gone, not wishing her to avoid any dinners or theatre events. Between Richard, Lord Matlock, Mr. Gardiner, Mr. Bingley, and Mr. Lathrop, Lizzy would not be without proper chaperones. The ladies all knew how Darcy fretted, so they planned something for each day, even if it was simply luncheon and tea. Most of these careful plans were for Darcy's benefit rather than Lizzy, but she agreed knowing it eased his mind.

In the meantime, they spent nearly every waking moment together. Darcy cancelled all business affairs, other than the ones to do with the trip, and Lizzy postponed her scheduled shopping and afternoon appointments. The logical, sensible portion of their personalities knew they were being ridiculous. It had been inevitable that a separation of extended time would occur, and they recognized that it would likely happen numerous times over the long course of their marriage. In some far corner of their minds, they were embarrassed by and laughed at their panic and dismay, yet they could not halt the emotions. For Darcy it dredged up the terror of her accident, when she was mentally parted from him and he feared her death. Lizzy, strangely, found she relived the moment he had walked out the door of the inn in Lambton and she thought she had lost him forever.

The days were filled with the tension of expectation to the point that both of them actually found themselves privately longing for the day to arrive so that time could then hurry to when he returned. They made love numerous times over the two days with an unreasoning fear of detachment.

On the very morning he had broken the news to her, they made love again in her dressing room after breakfast. Lizzy kissed him and departed to her dressing room, not noting the sensual expression crossing his countenance. Several minutes later, while Marguerite was thankfully in the closet retrieving a gown, Darcy suddenly appeared in the doorway. This was not odd, but the clear suggestive gaze roaming over her body as she stood before her washbasin in only her chemise left no doubt it was not a casual visit. He dismissed Lizzy's maid curtly without turning about, this being unusual, but Marguerite did not flinch. He then rapidly crossed to where she stood, robe falling to the floor and revealing him to be fully aroused—a sight Marguerite would not have been able to ignore if she had taken even three more steps into the room.

"Elizabeth, I need you, please," he said, as his mouth descended in a crushing kiss and he pinned her against the wall, fingers groping. It was sudden and unexpected, but her husband never failed to inflame her.

That evening while hosting a dinner party, their eyes linked from across the room and desire was immediately evident. Darcy nodded imperceptibly and slipped away, Lizzy following a few minutes later. Whether anyone noticed they never knew, nor did they care. Darcy stood in the darkened hall and without a word took her hand, leading her to the library and locking the door. They fell onto the comfortable sofa and wasted no time in their frenetic yearning, moans suppressed. The room was pitch black, but light was unnecessary.

Nighttime and morning liaisons were languid and relaxing, offering a sustaining and consuming rapture, more emotional and spiritual in nature than the chiefly physical trysts afforded. The afternoon of the day before his departure found them in the study, Darcy writing at his desk while Lizzy read on the already several times utilized sofa. Sensing his penetrating gaze, she glanced up into darkened eyes.

"Staring, Mr. Darcy?"

"Admiring, Mrs. Darcy," he answered in a gravelly whisper. "Adoring, loving, wanting, craving." He rose, gliding from the desk toward her. "Worshipping, desiring, cherishing." He knelt and began lifting her skirts, never breaking away from her eyes. "Yearning, esteeming, caressing, tasting…" His mumbled huskiness was lost amid folded yards of fabric and tender flesh.

Lizzy groaned, "William, I so love you!"

Their last night together was spent quietly at home with Georgiana, Mary, and Kitty. Occasional playing of the pianoforte was interspersed with conversation and laughter. Despite the now looming departure, Darcy and Lizzy were in joyful moods, entertained by the silliness of the girls. Darcy contentedly sat beside his wife, who was embroidering a design of bunnies and bluebirds on what was to be a small pillow for the baby's crib. As they finally moved toward their perspective bedchambers, Darcy was stunned to have Mary approach him, Georgiana and Kitty solemnly behind her.

"Mr. Darcy," she said with a small curtsey, "you must not fret over Lizzy. We shall care for her and keep her amused. I know she will miss you, as will we all, but no harm will befall her. We promise."

Darcy was nearly unable to find his voice. Mary had probably spoken ten sentences to him in the past three weeks, and this was by far the longest! "Thank you, Miss Mary. I appreciate your vow and understand it comes from your heart. Thus, you have eased mine." With a stately bow, he kissed her hand, bringing a deep flush to her cheeks, and then repeated the words and action with his sister and Kitty.

Lizzy barely slept, Darcy endlessly embracing and caressing and kissing all throughout the night. They made love again, Lizzy exhausted and sore as she had not been since their honeymoon. Still, it was a monumental effort to not burst into tears when he left. He graced her with a dazzling smile as he waved a final farewell, pretending with all the theatrics at his disposal to not be aching and ripping apart inside. Lizzy retired immediately to their chamber, stretching on the empty bed with his scent-filled pillow clutched to her chest and crying until lack of sleep and heartache overtook her.

She woke refreshed and determined to shake off any depression. Amelia and Jane arrived in the early afternoon, and along with the girls, they retired to the parlor to sew and visit. Harriet was expected to arrive any minute to augment the fun. Lizzy surprisingly discovered her sadness leaving in the delight of lively communion. Her humor was high, health whole, and the tiny flutters far inside a constant reminder of her bliss.

A knock at the door lead to the entry of the footman, Hobbes. He bowed, Lizzy fully anticipating him to announce Mrs. Vernor, when he said, "Madame, there is a visitor asking to see Mr. Darcy..."

Before he could finish, the door flew open with a bang into the wall and, with a flurry of swirling skirts, in breezed Lady Catherine de Bourgh.

CHAPTER ELEVEN

Separation

THE ECHOING THUD FROM the door screamed loudly into the otherwise palpable stunned silence that descended. Hobbes was aghast at the visitor—a Lady, so she had stated—entering unannounced, and he honestly could not fathom how to react. Amelia did not know who the rude woman was, yet it was obvious by the universal expressions of shock and dismay that her company was not particularly welcomed.

Lady Catherine stood imperiously, well aware of the impact her arrival engendered. Her cool gaze swept the room with an utter lack of interest and supreme condescension, alighting lastly on Elizabeth.

Experiencing a rush of anger mingled with frantic consternation, Lizzy nonetheless recovered her wits first, standing and curtsying brusquely. "Lady Catherine. Mr. Darcy is away—"

"Mrs. Darcy," she interrupted, snapping the name as if painful to articulate, "I have been informed that my nephew is unavailable. I wish to see him at once. Tell me where I can locate him."

"My husband," Lizzy emphasized, "is out of Town on business. Perhaps I…"

"Left you alone already, has he? When do you expect him to return?"

Lizzy was only angry now. Drawing up to her full height with a stiff spine, pinched brows, steely gaze, clenched jaw, and lifted chin, a pose of intimidation she had learned from her spouse, Lizzy turned to the paralyzed Hobbes. "Thank you, Hobbes. You may be excused."

He started then bowed properly. "As you wish Madame. Ring if you require assistance." With a piercing look to the "Lady," he exited.

"Lady Catherine, accompany me to the study where we can speak privately." She turned to the ladies. "Excuse me for a moment." Without another word to Lady Catherine or a backward glance, she gracefully departed the room. Walking with stately dignity, Lizzy lead to Darcy's study. Initially unsure whether Lady Catherine was trailing, and unclear as to the proper handling if she refused, Lizzy breathed silent relief upon hearing the tap of heels. Her mind traveled to Darcy with a desperate wish for his commanding presence, but sadly it would be up to her to handle this situation.

Determined to make him proud, she stood behind her husband's immense desk, one hand resting possessively on the polished wood, and turned to face his aunt.

Lizzy opened her mouth to speak, but Lady Catherine burst forth with, "You dare to order me about in my nephew's house! It is fortunate I brought to the fore my breeding and manners—"

"Lady Catherine," Lizzy interjected dispassionately, another Darcy maneuver, "I believe it best we do not discuss manners under the circumstances of your arrival in what is now my house as well as Mr. Darcy's. Mr. Darcy, as I previously informed, is away on business. He will return in a week. Perhaps I can assist you?"

Lady Catherine pursed her lips. "It seems, Mrs. Darcy, that surrounding you are perpetual rumors. Or is it that you delight in persuading my nephew to harbor secrets from his family?"

"I can assure you I do not persuade Mr. Darcy to do anything. He is master of his own life and choices. As for rumors, I regret that I am ignorant as to what you refer."

Lady Catherine flared, gesturing to Elizabeth's midsection. "The rumor that you are with child! The potential Heir to Pemberley, assuming the Bennet stock is even capable of supplying males, and I must receive the news from my parson! This is unconscionable! Why did you feel the necessity to induce Mr. Darcy to confidences?"

Instantly Lizzy realized that she should have suspected this. She had privately wondered when, or if, Darcy planned on informing his aunt, but mentioning her name invariably met with a flash of irritation and stubbornness, so she had not broached the subject. Fighting for serenity, she replied, "Lady Catherine, the confirmation of our blessing has quite recently occurred. We have cautiously shared our news with friends and family. I trust William to decide how he wishes to deal with all matters concerning your relationship. Under the circumstances, it is best this way."

"Those circumstances you so flippantly allude to would not exist if you had listened to reason and kept your proper place rather than grasping for wealth and—"

"Lady Catherine! I will not allow you to insult me in my house! This is a topic that is closed. If you have even the remotest desire to renew a relationship with your nephew and to be granted access to his children, then I beg you to halt your tongue. Continued remonstrations and vitriolic commentary benefit you naught. We are married. You may as well accept this."

Lady Catherine paused, her countenance stony as she appeared to ruminate on the next statement. "Tell me, Mrs. Darcy," always pronounced through gritted teeth, "how many calling cards and invitations and business appointments has Mr. Darcy received? After languishing half the season in Derbyshire rather than attending to his duties in Town, he should be far too busy to absent himself for a week."

Lizzy was unnerved by the sudden altered direction. Aside from the unwitting reference to her prolonged recuperation that had prevented an earlier departure from Pemberley, Lizzy was confused as to where Lady Catherine's inquiry was leading. "Forgive me, Lady Catherine, but I fear I do not apprehend your meaning. Mr. Darcy is—"

"Then allow me to explain," she interrupted, the hint of warmth in her voice bewildering Lizzy further. "A girl with your provincial upbringing would inevitably be ignorant of the requirements for those in the higher levels of society. Mr. Darcy's business ventures and responsibilities are extensive. Normally, he would have arrived in Town by late March, attending to his commitments and social obligations, the flood of solicitations so plentiful as to necessitate declining dozens each day. As Master of Pemberley, his company is sought by the elite members of society, including royalty, all of who are honored by his appearance. As his aunt I am deeply concerned for the ramifications of his... decisions of late. Not only has he eschewed his annual visit to Rosings, thus renouncing his familial obligations forsworn to my late husband prior to his death, his flaunting of conventions could seriously damage the reputation of the Darcy name and financial solvency of Pemberley. Of course, you selfishly considered none of this, did you? You who claim to love my nephew thought of only yourself—"

"Lady Catherine," Lizzy halted her in a barely controlled voice, Darcy's beloved face firm in her mind lending her strength, "I believe our conversation has exhausted itself. I will end this discussion with these words. You have now not only insulted me yet again, a slight your nephew will have difficulty over-looking, but you have outrageously slandered *his* character." In a tightly checked rage, Lizzy stepped nearer the white faced Lady Catherine. "To suggest that he would ever shirk his responsibilities or comport himself in a less than superior manner or hastily engage in activities that he has not thoroughly deliberated is abominable! I wonder if, despite your assertions, you know Mr. Darcy at all, or if you truly care for him."

Lady Catherine's face was pale, expression unreadable, yet she did not reply, merely gazing at Lizzy with a deep intensity. Lizzy calmly reached for the servant's bell, not yet pulling. "Lady Catherine, regardless your opinion of me, I am not pleased with the estrangement between you and William. My heart would desire to see reconciliation, yet I can guarantee this will not occur if you do not reevaluate your judgment of our relationship."

At that moment the door opened, Mr. Travers entering with a formal bow, six female bodies flanking him. "Mrs. Darcy, may I be of any assistance?"

"Yes, Mr. Travers, you can escort Lady Catherine to the door. Madame, I politely request you leave now. I shall inform Mr. Darcy of your visit, you may be assured. Good day."

Lady Catherine hesitated momentarily and Lizzy sensed rising panic at the concept of physically evicting Darcy's aunt. Luckily, with a swirl of skirts and muttered articulations of disgust, Lady Catherine barged past the mass of women and Mr. Travers, her irritated voice echoing down the corridor. Lizzy sank into the comforting bulk of Darcy's leather desk chair, allowing the trembles to race through her. Mary was the first to her side, a glass of sherry pressed into slack hands.

"Drink this, Lizzy. Mama says it calms her nerves." Lizzy sipped the offered beverage, an attack of the giggles bubbling forth as she glanced up at the array of faces above her. Mary and Jane serene and commanding,

Kitty confused, Georgiana anxious and flushed, Harriet and Amelia stern and angry.

Eyes glittering, Lizzy laughingly asked, "Were you all eavesdropping?"

Georgiana flushed further and hung her head, but the others merely nodded. It was Kitty who replied, "Of course we were! We promised Mr. Darcy we would look after you. That harridan should not be allowed to upset you, Lizzy."

"You should order the servants to slam the door in her face if she appears, Elizabeth," Harriet stated firmly, then smiled. "You handled her well, though. I am proud of you."

"Perhaps we should send word to my brother or cousin Richard at least, Elizabeth," Georgiana spoke softly, tension evident in her shaky tone. "William will be so angry. Oh, this is too horrible!"

"Georgie, rest easy, my dear. I am fine, truly. Merely a bit aquiver. There is absolutely no reason to distress or interrupt William. Perhaps I will speak with Colonel Fitzwilliam or Lord Matlock. Honestly, I am fine."

Generally, Lizzy was fine. That night, the first in six months without her husband, she stood in their private garden gazing at the stars, one of Darcy's robes engulfing her, and mused over the day's events. Her friends had comforted her all afternoon by their presence and witty chatter. Lizzy had not spoken of Lady Catherine's words, nor had she shared the event with Richard or the Matlocks at dinner that evening. She planned to speak with them eventually, but a dinner party with some thirty partakers did not offer the proper opportunity. Instead, she buried her turmoil, charming the guests and the hosts, a Lord and Lady Carlyle, passing a pleasant evening, although the ache of Darcy's absence never escaped her heart.

Now, it was quiet. The girls were abed, probably gossiping and giggling in one of their rooms. Between missing her husband and the residual commotion elicited from Lady Catherine's statements, Lizzy dreaded lying on the empty bed and attempting sleep. The majority of Lady Catherine's accusations Lizzy recognized as spiteful and without any foundation. The love Darcy and Lizzy shared was of a depth few could understand. The notion of regrets or faulty decisions on his part was laughable in the extreme.

Nonetheless, Lizzy did wonder. The truth is, she was completely ignorant of the social proprieties of Darcy's world. The idea that his marriage to her may have damaged the Darcy reputation or affected the estate in a tangible way seemed unlikely, yet she suddenly found the words of his first proposal echoing in her head. *My rank, family expectations, your birth and inferior circumstances.* Isolated at Pemberley, deliriously blissful in her husband's arms, Lizzy had given none of it the slightest consideration. Ultimately she trusted Darcy, believed in his love for her and in his competence to manage affairs as brilliantly as always. Yet, his aunt's words stung. How had she known the invitations had been minimal? Until two days ago they had received not a one, other than from their circle of intimates. Additionally, the opportunity with Duke Grafton was nearly refused due to Darcy's reluctance to abandon her. What else had he allowed to slip through his fingers?

Tears slid down her cheeks and the pain of his absence became unbearable. She could not regret marrying him nor could he regret marrying her, and Lizzy recollected his frequent slurs against the fickleness of society with mild encouragement. The influx of calling cards and invitations over the past two days proved how quickly the supposed importance of pedigree and station was overshadowed by wealth and connections. She could hear his voice: "By next year, beloved, not a soul will remember you as other than Mrs. Darcy of Pemberley." The melancholy was not borne of remorse but of causing his life to be troubled in any way, no matter how minute or innocent.

A knock at the bedroom door interrupted her reverie. It was Samuel with an envelope he was charged to deliver to Mrs. Darcy prior to her retiring.

My beloved, precious wife,

I am writing this on the afternoon prior to my departure. You, my love, are sitting across from me on the sofa, your dainty feet tucked under you as you read, absently chewing a stray lock of hair as you always do when you concentrate. My God, you are so beautiful! I have hours remaining to kiss you and embrace you and express my ever-increasing love for you, yet my heart is breaking for missing you. I will charge Samuel to deliver this missive as you retire. I shall present a brave face tomorrow, my dearest, yet I deem there is no point in pretending that either of us will not be miserable on our first night apart. Will I fear attempting sleep in a strange and empty bed, or will I yearn for the oblivion of sleep to erase my pain and lose myself in sweet dreams of your kisses?

Elizabeth, my soul, I wish with all my being that I could promise we will never again be separated! Yet, I cannot. It is inevitable that business will intrude from time to time as our long years as one soul unfold. What I do promise is that I will never desert you unless it is absolutely necessary and that I will carry your love with me as I travel. I will always strive to return to your arms as rapidly as humanly possible. Knowing that you are waiting for me with a love equal to mine for you shall keep me sane. Beloved, you are my life. Be well and cheery, take care of yourself and our child, and doubt not my unwavering devotion to you both. Could I fill innumerable pages with poetic verse declaring my passion for you? Yes. Instead, I believe I shall end this letter so that I may ravish you here in my study. With this decision, and later a delightful memory for you as you nod off in slumber, I will simply say, I love you.

    William

At Euston Hall in Suffolk, some sixty miles from London and Elizabeth, Darcy also stood gazing at the stars. The large window in the roomy and well-appointed chamber assigned him was open, permitting a cooling breeze to waft in and an unencumbered view of the night sky. Darcy fingered the small pouch containing the braided tress of his wife's hair along with the lavender scented handkerchief she had pressed into his hand as he left. He sighed heavily. He did not wonder if she missed him. Any doubts at the depth of her love for him had vanished ere they were wed. His only doubts at the moment were regarding the logic of leaving her. He had lost count after a hundred at the number of times he nearly spun his mount about and raced back to Town. The letter teeming with lavish praises of love and desire written earlier was waiting on the desk for delivery at first light.

A knock at the door broke into his musings and revealed Gerald Vernor, brandy decanter and glasses in hand. "Figured you could use a nightcap."

Darcy smiled. "You have no idea. Come in, my friend."

For Darcy the subsequent three days were busy and surprisingly pleasant for the most part. Gerald was always agreeable company and Duke Grafton possessed a dry wit and a wealth of adventures he enjoyed imparting with a born storyteller's flair. His stables were impressive. Darcy, the consummate horseman that he was, delighted in the endless discussions, ridings, and inspections of the Duke's magnificent animals. The business arrangements monopolized hours and required serious, intense concentration. Evenings were replete with the Duke's tales, fine dining, and manly entertainments. He had an excellently equipped game room, including a beautiful billiard table that Darcy proficiently profited from. Therefore, it was not until the late evenings and horrid nights when Darcy's heartache would overwhelm him. He would wake in the mornings after sleeping fitfully, aroused from vivid dreams of his wife, lonely, and miserable.

He reasoned that arriving at Pemberley on the fourth day after leaving her would ease his heartache somewhat since it was their home, yet he was wrong. He had not fully comprehended how indelibly Elizabeth's presence was etched into every room and corridor. He heard her voice and gentle footfalls constantly, expected to behold her beloved face at every corner, could smell the lingering aroma of her perfume, and his eyes alit on a ceaseless array of her belongings scattered about. Even the stables elicited poignant memories: the curricle she drove, the pairs of thick leather gloves he had purchased for her, and worst of all the now sixth-month-old colt that she had bonded with and named Wolfram after the author of *Parzival*, from which Darcy had chosen his stallion's name. Wolfram scampered up to Darcy the instant he entered the stable yard, nosing behind his body with searching eyes. "Sorry little fellow, she is not here." The colt seemed to understand Darcy's words, or at least the mournful tone, and with a last look about, hung his head and wandered away sadly. Darcy wanted to cry.

The torture was exacerbated when he entered their chambers. The sensory overload of memories associated with her overwhelmed him and for several minutes he could not breathe. He seriously entertained the idea of sleeping in a guest chamber, but in the end, the need to be close to her possessions as a substitute to the flesh and blood reality was too strong. Eventually, he found comfort in the ghost of his heart's survival as Elizabeth's spirit was evident in each corner of the chambers. He lay in their bed that first night with the door to her dressing room open, his gaze resting on her vanity as joyous remembrances of brushing her hair while she smiled at his reflection washed over him, gradually leading to a profusion of rapturous recollections as sleep claimed him.

Prior to departing, Darcy had carefully studied the invitations received, discussing each one with Lizzy, discarding those that were unacceptable for some reason, and encouraging her to affirm those that would be entertaining and appropriate for a woman without her spouse. He further admonished her to confer with Lady Matlock before accepting any other requests. He had so fretted over her boredom or despondency during his absence that he scheduled an activity of some sort for nearly each waking hour over the ensuing seven days. Lizzy had not argued, but it was humorous. First of all, no amount of occupations would prevent gloom residing in her heart. Secondly, he apparently forgot in his ambition to appease her loneliness that Lizzy was a woman who needed solitude in her day. She was a social creature to be sure, yet she equally craved privacy and silence.

Therefore, she had rearranged a few of the planned excursions to allot time to herself. Fortunately, she plotted her first morning without him as one of those times. She woke late, having slept poorly. Despite his beautiful letter, her sleep was plagued with unpleasant dreams of Lady Catherine's disapproving face, William telling her she was unsuitable to be his wife, a sea of faces laughing at her as she entered the opera house in rags, and vague twinges of discomfort emanating from her lower abdomen. Upon waking, the initial thought was of relief. Her husband's letter lay on the bed stand and simply spying it recalled his declarations of love and devotion with sensations of happiness rushing over her. Her heart ached without his body beside her, but her soul was complete.

The familiar deep and feathery flutters that she was almost certain were the baby, abruptly commenced, bursting forth in a frantic minute or so of bustling exercise, and then gradually subsiding. Lizzy chuckled, placing her palm over her lower belly. "Did you not wish to wake yet, little one?" Lying curled on her side, Lizzy rubbed her hand along the flesh of her abdomen, noting the slight bulge and thickening. Bliss shrouded her even in her sadness at Darcy's absence. Sighing, she stretched and yawned, her mind wandering to the day's schedule when a sudden sharp wrenching cramp in her groin area momentarily rendered her breathless. It was not horribly painful and passed as rapidly as it came, yet alarm pierced her heart.

All throughout the morning Lizzy experienced minor pinches and spasms. Amid the mild discomfort, the internal flickers persisted, easily perceived now that Lizzy had identified them. The book was unclear. One paragraph stated that occasional muscle pangs were normal as the body expanded with the growth of the baby. Another firmly expressed the ominous indication of abdominal cramps. To Lizzy, the twitches felt more like muscle aches than cramps, but she fretted nonetheless. Between the unrelenting ache in her heart and the new pregnancy symptoms, thoughts of Lady Catherine had nearly evaporated.

Around noon a footman approached Lizzy in the garden and announced Lady Matlock. Lizzy had not expected Darcy's aunt, but was always delighted to see her. Additionally, she deemed it fortuitous as she could ask her about the recent developments.

"Madeline," she said with true pleasure as they hugged in greeting, "what a wonderful surprise!"

"Elizabeth, dear, forgive me for calling unannounced."

"Do not be ridiculous! You are always welcome. Mr. Travers, lemonade please in the parlor." Lizzy linked arms with Lady Matlock, steering her toward the parlor.

"I was concerned for you, Elizabeth. Despite your charm and brave face last evening, I sensed your sadness."

Lizzy smiled as they sat on the sofa. "I will not deny how empty I am without William. I have grown rather accustomed to his dominating presence."

"Jest all you wish, I know how deeply your mutual affection. I can assure you he is as miserable, if that comforts you." Lady Matlock laughed and Lizzy smiled.

"Horrid as it is to confess, it does. Perhaps his agony will inspire him to conclude his business hastily and return to my side. I truly am so selfish!" A maid entered with their refreshments, suspending conversation for a moment. "Madeline, I am doubly pleased to see you, as I have a concern."

She proceeded to tell her about the faint twinges. Lady Matlock asked several pointed questions, Lizzy blushing but answering candidly. The resulting conclusion was benign muscle stretching. Lady Matlock recalled her own travails, including imparting the woeful information that it would likely intensify as the baby grew.

"Elizabeth, I do have a purpose in my unexpected advent. Lord Matlock and I received a note from Lady Catherine this morning. She is in London with Anne. I am postulating that they arrived yesterday and we are invited to dine this evening. I must beg your forgiveness, dear Elizabeth, as I did receive a letter from her several days ago in which she informed me that she knew of your pregnancy. Malcolm enlightened William of this, although she said nothing of traveling to Town."

Lizzy was torn between confusion and anger. How could he not have shared this with her? She stood abruptly and began pacing, Lady Matlock clearly troubled. "Elizabeth, what...?"

"She confronted me yesterday," Lizzy said in a shaky voice, Madeline gasping. "She burst into this very room, demanded to see William, and then rudely accused me of all manner of terrible things. William too, actually. Madeline, how could he not have warned me? I was so taken by surprise."

"Elizabeth, calm yourself. Sit down and tell me what transpired, exactly. What did she say?" After Lizzy had detailed the entire conversation, Lady Matlock was visibly dismayed. Lizzy was crying, emotions in turmoil. "Listen to me, Elizabeth. William would never leave if he for one second envisioned Lady Catherine assaulting you in this fashion. I shudder to imagine his rage when learning of this. You are correct in Lady Catherine not truly understanding Darcy. I am almost sorry for her." She sighed and shook her head. Taking Lizzy's hands in her own, she resumed, "You, my dear, cannot allow yourself to make the identical mistake. You intimately know your husband. Do you honestly believe he would abandon you to deal with his aunt? If I know William, and I do, he probably wrote to her before he left, unaware as were we all, that she was on her way. Nor would he imagine she would again act so hideously."

"Why ever not? I was not surprised, Madeline. She despises me and my 'inferiority' polluting the halls of Pemberley. She refused to acknowledge our marriage, and now I have the audacity to be carrying a child of low blood. Naturally she would express her outrage. He should have foreseen this!"

"Elizabeth, think clearly. Lady Catherine may never be happy that Anne is not married to Darcy, nor that he chose a wife outside the ton, but much has changed since last September. The entire family has not only accepted you but loves you. William has abundantly clarified his stance on her interference and proven where his loyalties lie. Frankly, we all expected an eventual reconciliation. Malcolm has been quite firm with her and has sensed a softening of her attitude. I am shocked that she spoke to you as she did, especially since she came here seeking conversation with William. I honestly do not comprehend it." She frowned then sighed. "William will be furious, but also his remorse and guilt at not protecting you will devastate him."

Lizzy stared at Lady Matlock, face pale, as shivers consumed and tears sprang to her eyes. In a weak voice she asked, "Madeline, is anything she said true? Has marrying me hurt the Darcy name or Pemberley's prospects, or caused William to be irrational? And now this! You are right, he will be devastated and his pain will be my fault. I love him so completely and never thought..." Sobs broke free and she could not continue.

Madeline embraced her, rocking as one did a child. "Shhh… Elizabeth, you are distraught and not sensible. Pregnancy most likely the culprit, coupled with loneliness. Think, child! *Without you*, William is lost and irrational." She paused, and then inquired softly, "Has he ever shared with you how desolate he was when you refused him?"

Lizzy was stunned. "How did you know about that?"

Lady Matlock smiled. "I am a woman, Elizabeth, and after his dear mother and now you, I know Fitzwilliam Darcy better than any woman alive. It was not until after your engagement that I put it all together, of course. I had sensed a distraction and agitation in him all winter after sojourning in Hertfordshire with Mr. Bingley and I wondered if he had fallen in love. It was merely a guess, but nothing else was logical. Mr. Darcy is *never* distracted. His mother once said to me, when William was only twelve, 'Madeline, my son is serious and reserved but passion lurks in his soul. Watch him ride his horse or play with Georgie and you will know what I mean. When he loves it is with his entire being. Someday he will love a woman, and it will be a fearsome sight.'" She laughed with the memory, and then resumed her narrative.

"Darcy is by far the most focused man I have ever met, yet during that winter he walked in a fog. Abruptly, he seemed to reach a determination and planned his annual trip to Rosings earlier than usual and with an enthusiasm never exhibited before. I learned later, from Richard, that William knew of your presence there from a letter sent by Lady Catherine. Of course, at the time I merely found his rapid transition odd, as did Richard. An offhand remark about a visitor at the parsonage registered not at all to my obtuse son. Instead, he teased Darcy about finally relenting to Lady Catherine's desires regarding Anne, which angered Darcy as it never had previously. When he returned to London from Kent, unexpectedly shortening his intended interval there, he was utterly agonized. Richard said he was ghastly to look at, brusque and rude, and flatly spurned all conversation. He locked himself in his chambers for a month straight, drinking excessively and barely eating. He spoke to no one and denied all socialization, including Richard or us. Georgiana was frantic. Richard was anxious and conveyed the events surrounding their trip, eventually puzzling through it himself. It was immediately clear to me. Miss Elizabeth Bennet of Hertfordshire was visiting Kent, William was in love with her and had proposed or extended some sort of overture, she had shockingly refused and repulsed him, and now he was a shattered shell of the man he had been."

"I never knew," Lizzy whispered. "He said once that he was a wreck after Rosings and that he told Georgiana, but I did not comprehend the depth. Whenever I asked him about that time he would evade. I knew it was a painful period for him so I did not press for information in my shame of how I had treated him. What did you do for him?"

"There was nothing I could do. He refused to see anybody. Frankly, I thought he would pull himself out of his despair, but when that did not seem to be happening, we grew increasingly despondent. It was Georgiana who eventually acted. Her love pulled him out of his desolation—barely, however. He left London at the end of May, pale and ill, at least twenty pounds lighter, and retreated to Pemberley. I was absolutely flabbergasted at his appearance. We saw him from time to time over the late summer, but he remained withdrawn, depressed, and exceedingly edgy. He attended to business, but there was no joy in it. By the end of that horrid summer, he crawled out of the deep mire and began to live again. He laughed even less and smiled rarely, but at least he attended to his work and his sister. He regained his weight and strength, and we rejoiced. Yet, I saw a grief in his eyes that equaled anything I had seen with the death of his parents. I am positive that if you had not reentered his life, William would have remained a bachelor forever, lonely and bitter."

Lizzy was crying silently and Lady Matlock kissed her temple lightly. "Elizabeth, what happened at Rosings is none of my affair and obviously you two have resolved the issues. I tell you this not to further distress you, but to hearten you. As I stated, I know William well, love him almost as much as my own children. His passion for you is frankly beyond my full comprehension. Malcolm and I care for each other, love in our own comfortable way, but I have never experienced what you two have." She laughed softly and brushed a tear from Elizabeth's cheek. "Seeing the misery involved with your love, I think I am relieved! Yet, it is as Anne declared; William loves with his entire being. As you do, Elizabeth. Neither of you would have found happiness apart. Only together are you complete."

She pulled away and intently peered into Lizzy's eyes. "If marrying you had led to the utter ruin of Pemberley or total excommunication from society, William still would have done it. For him there was no choice, and the only pain would be in a separation from you. However, this is not the case. Do you not see, Elizabeth? William is whole as your husband, he is stronger and more capable, his purpose explicit. Certainly there is joy and happiness, but it is more than that. You have filled an empty place in him, just as the sonnets proclaim. Lady Catherine is upside down in her assessment. Bloodlines, upbringing, rank… it is nonsense. Mr. Darcy is supremely more competent and engaged as Master of Pemberley now."

❦

"The impertinence of the girl! To order me about and accuse me of not caring for my own nephew! The situation is intolerable, I tell you, Anne, intolerable. Mark my words, daughter, that woman will turn his head and he will storm and rage, blaming me for her ignoble, vulgar deportment. If he had listened to me and his dear mother's wishes and married you, a properly bred lady, none of this would have occurred."

"William and I never would have married, mother," Anne de Bourgh whispered.

Lady Catherine rounded on her daughter. "I beg your pardon, young lady. You would have married Fitzwilliam had I ordered it!"

Anne flinched but continued, "We did not love each other that way, Mama, and William needs a strong woman. Not a sickly girl as I."

Lady Catherine airily waved her hand. "Love! What nonsense it that, Anne? Marriage for love is acceptable for the common man, the peasants who have no true responsibilities, but not for upper classes. Fitzwilliam appreciates this and would have performed his duty if *she* had not bewitched him. She probably threw herself at him, compromising him, and trapping him into marriage! Women of her class are capable of anything. Anne, why are you giggling as an imbecile?"

"Mother, how could you not recognize it? Mrs. Darcy is correct. You do not understand William at all."

"What are you babbling about?"

"How often had we refused to discuss your wild plan to marry us, Mama? Neither of us wished it, nor would have allowed it. As for Miss Bennet, it was so obvious how he felt about her. I could see it, and so could Mrs. Collins. Even cousin Richard noticed how William stared at her and was flustered when she was about. It was also clear that she did not reciprocate his affections." Anne frowned. "I could never understand that. William is the best of men." She shrugged and looked at her mother, who was staring at her daughter in stunned amazement. "I believe she loves him now, based on what the entire family says, but he pursued her, Mama."

Before Lady Catherine could respond, a footman announced the arrival of Lord and Lady Matlock. Greetings were brief and strained, Lady Matlock smoothly extraditing Anne for a walk in the garden so that her husband could freely talk to his sister.

Lord Matlock wasted no time on pleasantries. "Catherine, you cannot be confused as to why I am here. I am aware of your barbaric violation of Darcy House and the outrageous aggression toward our pregnant niece."

"Malcolm!"

"I am beyond appealing to your intelligence and decency. You have frankly exhausted my patience and stamina. Instead, I am exerting my authority as Patriarch of this family. If love and humanity cannot sway you, then perhaps honor, duty, and protocol shall. I am the Earl of Matlock and as such I far outrank you, Catherine. Therefore, you will hearken to me and obey.

"Your feelings on the subject of Fitzwilliam's marriage are inconsequential. He is the Master of Pemberley, a grown man, and his choice is his. Elizabeth happens to be a delightful woman, perfect for William, and they are devoted to each other. Even so, this too is insignificant." He stepped closer to his sister, voice calm and gaze steely as he spoke, "I expect you to remember who you are, Catherine. The daughter of an Earl does not conduct herself as a crass tormentor of the innocent, nor does she violate her proper authority by endeavoring to dominate a man. I have primarily kept silent, rightfully permitting William to handle this as is his prerogative. However, you have crossed a line, and as William is away, it is my place to protect Elizabeth.

"I am ordering you to hereafter be civil, to formally apologize to Mrs. Darcy, to restrain your acerbic tongue, and to do whatever is required to heal the breach in this family. I cannot promise that William will ever forgive you for what you have done. The blame is entirely on your shoulders, Catherine. Any future relationship you have with the Darcys will solely depend on your attitude and humility. I suggest you prepare to beg. On behalf of the entire Fitzwilliam house, we stand firmly behind William and Elizabeth. If you chose to ignore my demands and persevere in your harassment, then you will be choosing divorcement."

⁓ᴥ⁓

Daily, a letter arrived from Darcy. Amongst the teeming endearments and lyrical phrases of love and yearning were lines recounting his daily activities. In vivid detail he described the environment of Suffolk, the Grafton horses, the business arrangements, the leisure pastimes partook of, the food he ate, and anything else that entered his mind as he wrote. Darcy and Lizzy had grown so accustomed to sharing the specific happenings of their hours apart that it was natural for him to pour the same into a letter. He discovered the action of writing to her each evening to be cathartic, easing his aching heart and permitting him to slip into a relaxing sleep.

In London, Lizzy determined the same. She wrote each morning upon rising when refreshed and alone in their chamber. It gave her strength to face the day's agenda. Aside from the horrible fiasco of Lady Catherine, the week passed swiftly and rather pleasantly. Darcy's well-laid plans to distract his wife from her loneliness partially succeeded. She shopped, attended several teas where her natural gregariousness garnered her new friends, attended the theater twice with Colonel Fitzwilliam as guardian and various friends surrounding her both for added amusement and to offset any inappropriate rumors, and dined at a different house each night. Lizzy could not deny that she was having a marvelous time, but knew that it all would have been exponentially improved with Darcy by her side. Additionally, no matter how delightful the entertainment, she eventually returned to her lonely bed and heartache and fitful slumber.

As the week wound to its anticipatory end, two incidents of import transpired in London. The first was the halting, stilted, surprising, yet seemingly genuine letter of apology from Lady Catherine. Lizzy knew of Lord Matlock's confrontation with his sister, although not the details of what was said. She had decided not to enlighten Darcy, knowing that he would immediately return if she did so, but also because she simply knew not how to convey it all in a letter. Lizzy discussed the apology with Lady Matlock, decided to accept it in the vein it was offered by replying with an equally brief missive, but refused to engage in further discourse until her husband returned and was apprised of the situation.

The second interesting episode involved Mary. One afternoon, Lizzy and her sisters, along with Amelia Lathrop, shared tea and cakes in the Darcy House parlor. Mary, under the gentle persuasion of Georgiana, had taken to wearing lightly patterned dresses which greatly enhanced her fair features. Today she was especially lovely in a stylish yet simple gown of canary yellow with green striping as she sat with Georgiana at the piano learning a new piece by Beethoven. Mr. Travers interrupted to announce a Mr. Joshua Daniels, the son and partner of Darcy's solicitor.

Mr. Daniels the younger was revealed to be young indeed; in his early twenties, sandy-haired with a ruddy complexion, quite handsome with hazel eyes, slender, and just under six feet in height. He bowed politely as Lizzy rose, eyes sweeping the room as he nodded to each occupant, alighting briefly then moving on until he came to Mary. Lizzy had never witnessed such a blatant spark of interest in all her days. Even Darcy's initial jarring contact with her eyes at the Meryton Assembly had been unobtrusive compared to this. Mr. Daniels's head snapped about, his eyes widened and mouth fell open while Mary flushed, yet boldly met his stare for at least fifteen seconds.

Lizzy's brows shot up and she turned to Amelia, who was pressing her lips tightly to avoid laughing. The moment stretched and may have continued indefinitely if Lizzy had not purposely cleared her throat. Mr. Daniels started, reddened, and tore his gaze from Mary's face. All befuddled, he hedged for several seconds as he collected his thoughts, aided primarily by careful study of the envelope in his hands.

"Mrs. Darcy," he finally managed, "I, of course, am aware that Mr. Darcy is out of Town. However, my father instructed me to deliver these documents when they were completed so that Mr. Darcy would have immediate access to them upon his return. I trust you will know the safest place to store them in the interval."

"Thank you, Mr. Daniels. I will ensure he receives them." Throughout the entire short speech, Mr. Daniels's peripheral glances touched on Mary, and Lizzy was amazed he ably articulated. "Mr. Daniels, allow me to introduce you to my family. This is my dear friend Mrs. Lathrop. My sister-in-law, Miss Darcy. Miss Kitty Bennet, my sister, and this is Miss Mary Bennet, also my sister."

Mr. Daniels bowed to all, properly greeting with impeccable manners, lingering in his greeting to Mary. "Miss Bennet," he asked, "do you and Miss Darcy play the pianoforte?"

Of course, the inquiry was ludicrous considering they were both sitting at the pianoforte, but no one chose to mention the fact. To Lizzy's delight and astonishment, Mary smiled shyly and replied, "Yes indeed, Mr. Daniels, although Miss Darcy is far superior to me. I am improving under her kind instruction. Do you play?"

"Poorly, I am afraid. Too many hours passed with a book in my hands to practice, much to my mother's dismay."

"Obviously your study has proven the wiser, as you are now a solicitor. Your mother surely is not overly dismayed."

He smiled brightly. "You are correct, Miss Bennet. She has relinquished her distress in the happy knowledge that I will be residing close to home. Do you live here in Town?"

"I am from Hertfordshire, sir. Merely visiting my sister and Mr. Darcy for a month or so."

"I see," he spoke softly, pausing, and then abruptly remembered the other occupants of the room. Turning to Lizzy, he said, "Pardon me, Mrs. Darcy for disturbing your afternoon." He bowed to all yet again and then, with a last glance to Mary, departed. Mary smiled benignly, and after a tarrying gaze at the empty doorway, attended to the music as if nothing has transpired.

Lizzy was thrilled at what the enchanted moment signified. She wrote a long, descriptive narrative of the flirtation to her husband in what would be her last letter, as he was due home in two days. When Darcy received the communiqué from his wife on the morning of his final day at Pemberley, his heart leapt with joy. The week had been endless and his endurance was depleted. He sat on the terrace reading her humorous, passion-inundated letter with a mixture of intense happiness and profound irritation. The perpetual suffering in his heart had grown to a torment and spread to every cell in his body. The yearning to see her face and brilliant smile, hear her voice and musical laugh, kiss her lips, and touch her soft skin had mutated into a torture of covetous need. He no longer slept for more than a few fitful hours, ate little, found no pleasure in his horses, and for the only time in his life, hated being at Pemberley.

He sighed deeply, reclined his head against the cool stone of the wall, closed his eyes, and readily conjured her face. They had finished their inspection and breeding program technicalities early yesterday and Darcy had urged for departure today, at first light preferably. Duke Grafton, however, was having a delightful vacation, adored Pemberley, and expressed the wish to remain longer. Darcy had grit his teeth, employed the frayed edges of his generally massive self-mastery, and compromised. Relaying a deep concern for his pregnant wife, an emotion the Duke seemed unable to comprehend, Darcy relented to one additional day only. The concession nearly killed him. He was so weary from lack of sleep and misery, the long ride to London was an agonizing contemplation, with only the vision of Elizabeth and the tiny bulge she wrote was now apparent lending him strength. *Tomorrow evening,* he incessantly chanted, *you shall hold her and kiss her, eloquently tell her of your love and make love to her.* He shifted on the bench uncomfortably, the wretchedness of his necessity manifesting physically. With a groan of despondency he lurched to his feet, kissed the scented letter before tucking it into a pocket, and headed toward the stables. As during their engagement, a hard and fast race on Parsifal was required.

He returned to the stable yard an hour later, heartache as acute, but at least his lust had cooled for the interim. Chaos reigned with Duke Grafton, who Darcy had ascertained was not the most proficient rider, despite his vast knowledge of horses, and who was currently desperately clinging to the back of a particularly spirited filly that Darcy had been training yesterday. With a harsh curse, Darcy flew off Parsifal's back and leapt over the fence to assist the frantic groomsmen. He grabbed a dangling rein with his left hand, uttering soothing vocalizations, and pulled with all his strength. The distraught animal began to calm, but Duke Grafton lost his balance and instinctively seized hold of the filly's mane, sending her into renewed fits of rage. She reared up, the precariously perched Duke flying off to land with an explosive grunt flat on his back in the soft sand. Darcy's left arm was jerked wrenchingly upwards, but he held on through the pain, mightily yanking downward. She responded with a wicked lash of her front hooves, sending the two grooms flying for cover. Darcy spun to the side but was not quick enough. One hoof forcefully impacted squarely on his upper left chest just below the clavicle. Instantaneous paralysis to his already injured shoulder ensued, with deadened fingers releasing the rein as he fell to the ground with a cry of agony.

Sharp-witted grooms, now storming the corral in great numbers, dragged Darcy and the Duke to safety while Mr. Thurber managed to finally control the poor beast. The Duke was unharmed except for a few bruises and aching muscles. Darcy was in extreme pain, his arm completely numb and breathing difficult.

The following hours were torture. The physician was called for, determining that miraculously no bones were broken and the obtunded flesh was temporary. He ordered Darcy to rest for several days, but Darcy flatly refused, declaring in a voice that brooked no argument that he intended to depart for Town on the morrow. His only concession was to stage the trip over two days, but even that was for the benefit of the Duke, whose backside was sore, rather than for himself. An express message was dictated and sent by courier to Mrs. Darcy informing her of the delay, after which Darcy demanded solitude. Once alone, he released his anguish of combined physical and spiritual woe with a shuddering sob.

His grief was compounded that afternoon when a letter arrived from his uncle. With a frown and intense stab of fear, Darcy broke the seal and began to read. Lord Matlock's initial sentence of assurance that Elizabeth was well allayed the worst of his anxiety, but it was short lived. A string of foul curses rent the silence as he absorbed his uncle's recounting of Lady Catherine's abuse to his wife and the Earl's confrontation with her. Darcy, as Lady Matlock had predicted, was overwhelmed with crushing guilt. He was proud of Elizabeth's reported handling of his obnoxious aunt, but nearly prostrate with self-condemnation for what he perceived as a failure to safeguard his family.

Lizzy woke on the day she expected her husband's return with an instantly joyous grin. Her heart fluttered rapidly, matching the rhythm set by their tiny passenger in her womb. She did not anticipate his arrival until late, but simply imagining him on his horse and heading her way filled her soul with a rapturous bliss. Her own need for him in all the various ways their love manifested was consuming her. She, too, had slept poorly all week, and the unrelenting empti-ness in her heart was wearing on her. Luckily, the baby's demanding appetite prevented her not eating well and the muscle spasms had ceased, so physically she was strong. All morning she walked about with a ridiculous grin and her feet barely touching the floor. When Darcy's hastily dictated note arrived, Lizzy burst into tears and fled to her room, collapsing in a puddle of dejected misery on their bed. She was inconsolable. The only positive was that her depression precipitated a deep, much needed sleep.

Darcy's journey was tortuous. His pain was severe, a massive bruise spreading over the entire left chest and shoulder, and the decreased sensation to his left arm slow to resolve. Gripping the reins was problematic, and he was incredibly fatigued. By mid-afternoon he was in a haze of suffering, unsure whether it was his physical or emotional pain that vied for supremacy. At the inn, he choked down a hasty dinner then fell into an exhaustive, nearly comatose sleep for close to ten hours.

At four in the morning he woke lying in the exact position, stiff but reju-venated. The pain had dimmed to a dull ache with the feeling predominately restored to his arm. An hour later, the sun a faint smudge of brightness on the horizon, he was washed and dressed. He hurriedly scribbled a note that he slipped under Gerald's door, and roused the stable boy to saddle his horse. Some four hours later he turned onto Grosvenor Square, windblown, dusty, saddle-sore, and aching, yet jubilant. Never in all his life had the shining white bricks of Darcy House filled him with such exultation. He rather prayed his wife was yet abed, but any room would suffice as long as he was embracing her. With a skip to his step, he mounted the front stairs.

CHAPTER TWELVE

Reunion

THE FOYER WAS EMPTY. The soft tinkling of piano keys and laughter sailed on the air from the music room. Wincing slightly, Darcy carefully removed his overcoat and the moist, grimy cravat as a footman rounded the corner, halting in surprise at the sight of his Master.

"Mr. Darcy! We did not expect you until this afternoon."

"No apology is necessary, Peters. Is Mrs. Darcy in our chambers?"

"No sir. She is yet in the garden, I believe."

"Thank you." Thrusting his garments into the servant's hands, he strode rapidly down the hall to the rear of the house with heart pounding and grin spreading. Elizabeth stood amongst a plot of lilacs taller than she was, snipping fragrant blooms with her new shears to join the array of colorful flowers already lying in her new basket. Darcy paused on the threshold, the ache to envelop his wife momentarily offset by the vision she unwittingly presented. She wore a thin, simple-muslin morning gown of pale lavender, hair unbound with only the sides unevenly secured with a loose tie in back. The sun shone brightly, highlighting the multiple hues in her hair and accenting the flush on her cheeks. She was smiling slightly as she smelled the lilacs, and he thought he detected a faint humming.

Smiling even broader, Darcy stepped out of the shadows onto the stone patio. The movement caught Lizzy's attention and she turned. Her eyes widened, the foremost thought being that she was hallucinating. It had required colossal effort on her part and loving persuasion from her sisters to revive her spirits last night. The restful sleep had aided her tremendously as well. Finally, she had attained a state of calm acceptance, willing herself to be strong as she grudgingly bowed to the inevitable wait of one more day. She had no idea where they would stop for the night, since it all apparently depended on the Duke's condition, but had not expected Darcy's homecoming until after luncheon at the soonest.

It was the sound of boot heels striking the stone that convinced her of his reality. With a strangled cry, she tossed the basket and shears onto the turf and raced into his outstretched arms. Darcy felt the impact of her slender frame with a combined grimace and shock through his left side but primarily with a rush of astounding joy and completion. He clutched her tightly, spinning about with a merry laugh while she rained kisses all over his face.

"William! I cannot believe you are here! Oh, how I missed you! How I love you!" Her words tumbled over each other, interspersed with kisses, her fingers moving through his hair and over his exposed neck.

Darcy laughed and was eventually required to grasp her face in his hands to halt her jubilant enthusiasm. "Elizabeth," he whispered with a gentle smile, slowly brushing over her mouth as he caressed her cheeks with his thumbs. Their eyes met, love evident and mingled with profound longing. "I love you," he softly uttered, then his mouth descended, interrupting any reply with a firm, encompassing kiss that deepened rapidly. Bodies pressed harshly together, they kissed as if starved and the only nourishment available was in the breath and taste of the other. Darcy's lingering pain was erased in the rapture of embracing and kissing his delicious wife.

Neither of them had any cognizant awareness of where they were. Their mental states were so enamored with desire and bliss that it was entirely probable they were minutes away from falling to the ground in raging passion. Thankfully, perhaps, they were interrupted.

"William!" Georgiana's delighted squeal jolted them both to reality. Darcy turned to his sister as she rushed through the door, Mary and Kitty trailing. Weakly holding Lizzy with his left arm, he hugged his sister and kissed her cheek.

"Georgie, how are you, dearest? Miss Mary, Miss Kitty," he said as he inclined his head. "It is a pleasure to see you both. I believe I am indebted to you for your excellent care of my wife in my absence. Name your desired reward, and I shall grant it." Kitty giggled and Mary smiled serenely.

Lizzy slipped away from his side and he glanced over with alarm. He observed her slowly returning to the flowers strewn on the dirt. Georgiana was babbling in unrestrained joy, apparently intending to summarize the week's events in the next two minutes. Darcy attempted to listen to his sister and the occasional interjections from Mary and Kitty, responding appropriately while focusing on his wife. Both arms now ached with loss and he sensed a tension in her posture, or more aptly a hesitancy and mild trembling. She bent to retrieve the scattered flowers, hands frequently moving to her face, but he could not determine the cause as her back was to him.

Just as he took a step toward her, she rose and turned, smiling brightly but tears evident on her cheeks. He hastened to her, brushing the moisture away. "Beloved, are you well?"

Lizzy waved his concern away airily. "I am perfect, now, my darling. Simply overemotional these days. I cry at the drop of a hat, so be duly warned." She laughed and smiled, tiptoeing to kiss his cheek while grasping his hand. She frowned, peering at his fingers. "Your hand is so cold and pale." She raised the right to compare. "William, what is wrong with your hand?"

"It is of no moment, love. We shall discuss it later, I promise."

Tears were gathering again. "William..." she whispered, but a footman appeared to announce breakfast. Darcy kissed her lightly and smiled.

"Excuse me, ladies, I must freshen up then shall join you in the dining room." He turned to his wife. "I will not be long," he began, but she was vehemently shaking her head.

"I am not tolerating you out of my sight! I can help you change and clean up."

"The job will likely not be accomplished if you follow me into my dressing room," he declared quietly in her ear with a grin.

Lizzy tossed her head as she clasped his arm and steered toward the door. "I will take my chances. Besides, meals have been known to wait around here without severe deficiency, Mr. Darcy. Martha," she said, addressing a passing maid and ignoring her husband's chuckle, "please place these in the Master Chambers in several vases, and inform Samuel that Mr. Darcy has arrived."

Samuel, however, was waiting for his Master with fresh water and supplies. Lizzy authoritatively sat Darcy on his stool and clinically began unbuttoning his coats. It was a struggle for Darcy to not reciprocate by attacking her garments, the nearness of her body frankly driving him mad and only Samuel's presence forestalling him. A jolt of pain when she unwittingly tugged his coats over his shoulder—eliciting an audible gasp and grimace as he instinctively grabbed her hand and jerked backward—replaced all romantic musings temporarily.

"Elizabeth, love, I have a confession," he hoarsely stated, gingerly rubbing the throbbing shoulder and meeting her anxious eyes.

Never releasing his gaze, Lizzy said, "Samuel, please leave us. I will assist Mr. Darcy." Once the door was closed she caressed his face, speaking softly, "You are hurt. Tell me what happened."

"I did not wish to distress you further, beloved. Please forgive me for not being forthright. It occurred when the Duke was foolishly attempting to ride Athena. You remember which one she is?" Lizzy nodded, working to carefully extradite him from his clothes. "Well, he was thrown, as I wrote, but I did not include the fact that I was in the corral as well trying to control her." He flinched and inhaled with a hiss as the waistcoat was pulled away. Lizzy gently elevated his left arm as she lifted his shirt. He groaned, then continued through grit teeth. "Athena did not appreciate her treatment, so she wrenched my arm and lashed out forcefully, as you can now discern for yourself," he finished in a lame whisper.

A red impression of a horse's hoof in flawless detail graced his upper left chest, surrounded by colorful blotches from sternum to nipple to axilla to shoulder blade. His left arm was noticeably paler and grasp weaker, although the tactility was thankfully normal. Tears were coursing down Lizzy's face as she tenderly palpated the area. Darcy brushed her cheeks. "Do not cry, beloved, it is merely a bruise and muscle strain. Trust me when I say I have suffered much worse. The physician examined me thoroughly. There are no broken bones, the skin intact, and the sensitivity is returning. Please do not fret, Elizabeth."

"You should be resting, not on a horse for two days." She sobbed, leaning in to plant soft kisses along the contused flesh.

Darcy again inhaled sharply, but not from pain. His hands encircled her hips and bottom as he buried his face into her hair-cloaked neck. "I could no longer survive without you, my love," he murmured huskily. "I needed you to heal me, not rest."

She withdrew to gaze into his face, eyes shimmering, smiling sweetly, and touching each feature tenderly. "Sometimes I am yet amazed at how deeply I love you, Fitzwilliam. This week has been torture, but it has been enlightening in revealing to me how profoundly I require you in my life. Not that I doubted our love and unity in any meaningful way, but I do not think I fully realized all the inconsequentials. Hearing your voice, sharing the little moments of my day, reading with you, taking sips of your brandy, stealing food off your plate so I do not appear a glutton, dressing to match your attire, arguing with you over some silly thing. Do you have any notion of how often I would think, 'Wait until I tell William what so-in-so said.' Or, 'How William will laugh when I tell him this'?" They laughed together, Darcy nodding in absolute understanding.

Lizzy smoothed the hair away from his face, cupping his jaw and kissing lavishly before again withdrawing. He moaned lowly, eyes glazed with desire. She removed his right hand from her thigh and kissed each finger before placing his palm over the soft mound on her belly. "Mostly I missed sharing our child with you," she whispered, smiling joyously at the wonder crossing his expression as he gently pressed and explored.

"I cannot believe the difference a week has made." He was grinning foolishly, unaware that Elizabeth had loosened her dress until it fell over his head where he was nestled into her stomach. She laughed as he freed himself from the fabric, grinning up at her as she untied the chemise and exposed her front side.

Bared, the small bulge and thickened waistline were clearly visible, as was the rest of her glorious body, placing a serious dilemma before Darcy. His groin lurched in response to her luscious flesh, but he could not resist reverently touching the evidence of their child. Tears sprang to his eyes, and, kissing her abdomen, he spoke chokingly, "Sweet child of mine, I am home. This is your father and I love you. Oh God, Elizabeth, this is so amazing! Can you feel her often? Will I be able to yet?"

"I feel him frequently. Tiny flickers deep inside only; however, I think we are close to feeling him externally. Maybe another week or two."

Darcy was absently caressing her belly while studying her eyes. "Have you been well? Any further pains? That news deeply concerned me, but I trusted Aunt Madeline's opinion, and you said they ceased."

Lizzy shook her head. "Physically, I am marvelous. My only pains have been in my heart." Fingers laced through his hair, Lizzy continued breathlessly, "Fitzwilliam, my lover and my soul, if you are not too famished or hurting I would prefer to make love. I have longed for your touch on my body and the ecstasy of our joining. I will handle you delicately," she finished with a mischievous smirk.

In truth, Darcy was famished, having not eaten since the previous night. Nonetheless, his hunger for her was far greater. Running hands inside her chemise, he again kissed her belly as he rose slowly, placing moist kisses up her torso to bosom while stroking her shuddering flesh. Lizzy moaned, arching into him and releasing a shaky breath while trailing fingers over his back and shoulders, carefully avoiding the damaged areas, panting with need and delight. He released her breast suddenly with a groan, claiming her mouth in a pervasive kiss as he crushed her body into his, pain seemingly forgotten. He was clearly lost in a haze of desire. The weak hand kneaded one perfect breast as he continued to ravage her mouth, intoxicated by her breath and succulent lips.

Lizzy was no less aroused, but his dressing room was not where she wished to love her husband. Twisting out of his clutches with effort, mildly amused at the expression of glazed confusion flittering over his face, she took his hand and led him into their bedroom. She sat him on the edge of the bed and knelt to remove his boots. Darcy was a man obsessed. The pain of his shoulder was insignificant compared to the raging agony to love his wife. Fleetingly, he wondered how he had ever managed to pass so many years without intimacy when one week was nearly killing him! Of course, he rationally understood that it was not intimacy in the clinical, carnal aspect that he desired, but the consuming demand to bond with his wife. To communicate with her in this profoundly fulfilling way, to give her pleasure, to feel her and taste her, to bury himself into her as they became one body for a time, to possess her as only he ever would, to express his passionate love for her... it was paradise.

He played with her hair as she completed her task, peeling the chemise off each creamy shoulder as he trembled with desire. She looked up at him from her stooped position between his knees, hands traveling over strong thighs to the buttons of his breeches. "You should lie down to avoid hurting your shoulder." She rose to her knees, stroking under the loosened waistband to his bottom while slipping the tip of her tongue into his navel.

Darcy gasped, hands tightening on her shoulders. "God, my Lizzy, do you have any idea how desperately I need you!" She was trailing moist kisses up to his chest with hands probing. Lizzy stood finally, allowing the chemise to fall. Darcy groaned harshly, shaking his head slightly and closing his eyes. "Beloved, I should warn you. My self-control is naught." His voice was rough with urgency. Meeting her eyes with voracious yearning rawly exposed, he stammered, "At the merest touch of you I am certain I will explode in utter rapture."

Lizzy smiled, pulling him to his feet. She kissed him lightly on the lips. "Lay down and fret not." He removed his breeches, joining her on their bed, carefully lying flat with Lizzy to his right, encircled with his strong arm. She kissed his neck, caressing over his firm chest, whispering into his ear, "I can assure you, Fitzwilliam, love of my life, my hunger for you is as tremendous."

With simultaneous sounds of pleasure, they kissed, greedily absorbing each other, drowning in unparalleled love. Always conscious of the injury to his left side, Lizzy loved her husband with abandon, their mutual delight fulfilling and powerful.

Afterwards they lay entwined with Lizzy clutched tightly in Darcy's right arm for several blissful minutes, breathing heavily, and relishing the delightful sensations yet coursing through their bodies as well as the astounding felicity in merely holding the other. Lizzy was crying silently, tears of contentment and relief. With a soft grunt, Darcy turned to the side, hugging her tightly to him while smoothing the tousled tresses of her hair away from her face.

He frowned. "Beloved, why are you crying?"

Lizzy smiled and shook her head. "Happiness, love. I warned you, did I not? I cry frequently, yet now I judge for good reason." She fingered his hair. "I missed you so terribly, William, and am delirious to have you back. I love you, you know."

"Yes, I know." He kissed her, caressing over her body, already sensing reawakening desire, but she pulled away and snatched his hand. Kissing his cool fingers tenderly before sitting up, leaning to bestow a quick kiss to his forehead, she then leapt out of bed. "Where...?"

"You need nourishment of the substantial variety," she declared decisively, wrapping his enormous robe around her.

Darcy smiled. "You stole my robe."

"Borrowed out of necessity," she corrected. "I furthermore liberally splashed your cologne on it, which will likely render it undesirable to you, so I guess it now belongs to me," she concluded smugly, approaching him with two more pillows retrieved from the armoire. "Here, let me help you up. I will prop you up with these pillows and we can have breakfast in bed. Easy, dearest, allow me to... William! Behave!" He had taken advantage of the gaping opening to the voluminous robe and was caressing her skin and amusing himself at her breast. "Mr. Darcy, I am serious! How can I nurse you to health if you are a belligerent patient?" She slapped searching hands and sternly scowled at him, but he unrepentantly seized her head and pulled close for a thorough kiss. Lizzy melted, willingly relenting.

He teased her lips, murmuring his love huskily. "Call for a tray, my Lizzy, but swiftly. Relay our apologies to the girls, for I intend to keep you in our bed all day." He grinned. "The Master has spoken, and I am wounded so must be granted whatever I wish." Lizzy snorted but did not argue.

Couching her phrases carefully, Lizzy explained to Georgiana their need for solitude. Georgiana expressed complete understanding, smiling sweetly and pretending not to notice her brother's robe nor Lizzy tangled hair. The girls had plans to picnic at Hyde Park anyway. The tray was heavily laden and Darcy's stomach released a sustained and booming growl at the sight. Lizzy ate as well, although she had eaten upon rising, having found that her increased appetite would not permit her waiting until breakfast was formally served. She assisted Darcy, claiming his invalid state necessitated feeding him. He did not dispute the assertion, kissing her frequently or stroking her satin skin between bites.

They sat close, legs entwined and talking softly amid the kisses. They both avoided the topic of Lady Catherine. Lizzy was unaware of Lord Matlock's letter and simply refused to spoil their reunion. Darcy felt much the same, augmented by an unrelenting guilt. Instead, she humorously debriefed him on the week's events, the throng of people she had met, and the fascinating conversations. All the while she massaged his enervated arm and shoulder with fragrant oil, forcing life back into it.

Darcy groaned, finally sated, relaxing into the pillows and closing his eyes. "Dearest, that feels marvelous. As always, your every touch enlivens me."

"Provide me clarity on Mr. Joshua Daniels. Is he suitable for Mary?"

Darcy answered sleepily, "I do not know him as well as his father. Mr. Andrew Daniels has been our family's solicitor for years, as was his father before him. It seems to have become a familial business, although that would matter naught if they were not superb financial handlers and lawyers. There is an elder son, Benjamin, who works in the firm as well." He paused to yawn with jaw breaking intensity. "I believe there are two or three younger siblings. Anyway, Joshua is a pleasant young man, intelligent, reserved, and serious. The firm manages numerous accounts besides ours, and keenly aware of the fees charged to me, I can readily conclude their overall income is substantial." He opened one eye to peer at his wife. "Are you requesting I play matchmaker?"

"No. If Mr. Daniels is interested in Mary, it is his place to pursue." She smiled winsomely at her spouse. "Let us pray he is more eloquent at expressing his affection then other gentlemen I could name."

Darcy smiled. "Note: I did not add foolish or moronic to the list of Mr. Daniels's attributes. If the attraction was as immediate as you intimate, I daresay he will proceed with fluent grace and alacrity, unlike other gentlemen I could name." He chuckled, tugging her onto his lap and purposefully untying the sash of his robe.

Lizzy repositioned herself to straddle his thighs, massaging gently along his shoulders. "Your grace was merely gradual in revelation, my love. You have since redeemed your past missteps perfectly adequately, I judge." She was smiling impishly.

"Perfectly adequate is all? This will not do. Let me see if I can further improve your opinion of me." His hands caressed along her thighs and around her bottom, his own smile quite naughty.

"I thought you were about to fall asleep." She sighed, kissing the top of his head as he nestled his face between her breasts.

"Elizabeth," he sighed happily, voice muffled and resonant, "my precious, beloved, beautiful wife. I fully intend to sleep with you enclosed in my arms, but first I absolutely must shower you with kisses and caresses. I covet the warmth of your skin under my hands and lips and body. I yearn to love you slowly, wholly absorbing your essence into my soul as you attain rapture in my embrace. It is essential that I whisper endless words of love and faithfulness and desire and happiness into your dainty ears."

As he spoke he removed the robe, brushing and fondling over her body. With a fluid roll, she was on her back, spread before him in all her naked glory, his right arm supporting him. "William, your arm… we should stay upright." He halted her words with a sensual kiss, left hand traveling with deliberate patience over her abdomen. Lizzy's massaging had done wonders. His arm was warmer and stronger, his amazingly masterful touch not the least bit diminished as was abundantly established in the following minutes.

Darcy watched her face, reveling in her passion and the transcendent beauty of her whole countenance. Lord, she was gorgeous! Observing her joy as accomplished through him was astoundingly erotic and stimulating, his love for her flourishing to a level of near agony in its intensity. As they made love, Darcy could feel the small swell of their child against his abdomen and it excited him tremendously. The blessed creation of their love pressing into him was an aphrodisiac. Their firstborn safe and secure, growing in the womb of his beloved wife thrilled him immeasurably. His release was like a surging tide, rushing over and through every cell of his body as a cleansing, refreshing wave, cries of delight rumbling out of his mouth in a gush of profoundly expressed love.

Darcy collapsed with a prolonged groan and ragged inhalation, barely rolling to Lizzy's side. With one arm and leg heavily draped over her, he grated her name and promptly fell into an exhausted sleep. Lizzy smiled, transferred the dead weight of his arm off her breasts, and then stared at him for very long while. She caressed tenderly, fingering through silky hair, inhaling deeply of his scent, in all ways satisfied and complete. Her husband was home... home not being Darcy House, but next to her and inside her soul. Smiling dreamily, Lizzy too fell asleep.

Lizzy woke refreshed and crushed under the immovable weight of her near comatose husband. Darcy had not budged an inch, respirations deep and regular as he slept. She kissed his shoulder then wiggled from under his limbs, physical necessities demanding haste. Upon reentering the bedchamber, she saw Darcy had yet to move. For another two hours Lizzy sat propped next to his warm, slumbering body, intermittently reading and staring at him. The lunch hour had long since passed when a famished Lizzy decided it was time to wake him, the baby's demand for nourishment coupled with the desire to hear his voice overcoming her sympathy.

She called for a tray of fruit and bread and a bottle of wine, and then returned to his side. Planting gentle kisses over shoulders and back, she whispered his name until he stirred. "Beloved, I am perishing from hunger but wish to eat with you." He groaned, moving sluggishly and grimacing with discomfort. "Easy, love," she whispered, "let me loosen your muscles." She firmly kneaded the tightness across his back, palpating knots in both shoulders.

Applying guarded attention to his left arm, he sighed in relief and it was clear that the rejuvenation was markedly improved.

"I had an interesting dream one night while you were away," she began.

"Only one? I had dozens of interesting dreams every night, lover mine," he said, opening one eye and grinning.

Lizzy laughed and slapped his back. "I am not referring to *those* dreams, Mr. Darcy. This was so vivid, as if a premonition or message. We were at Pemberley, and there was snow falling. I walked through your mother's rooms, now decorated as I have imagined them, on into the nursery. It was warm and cheery, painted a muted blue and yellow. An enormous cradle of oak sat in the corner with pillows of white linen and lace. You sat beside in a rocking chair with a small bundle held in your arms. I knew instantly it was our baby wrapped with blankets, although I could not see the face. You were crying tears of joy, your face resplendent with contentment, your broad hands securely nestling the infant's head and back." Darcy had turned onto his side and was observing his wife's dreamy face, envisioning the scene flawlessly as she described it. "You looked up at me with a luminous smile and amazing pride. Then you said, 'Elizabeth, he is so beautiful. Alexander, as we wished, shall be his name.'"

Lizzy gazed lovingly at her spouse. "It was so real, William. I woke immediately and he was fluttering crazily, so much so that I could almost feel him with my hand. I knew, I do know, as surely as I know my love for you, that this child is a boy. Does this sound insane?"

He sat up, requiring her assistance, and tenderly stroked her cheek. "Alexander is one of my names, as you know, but there are two facts of which you are unaware. Alexander is the name of the boy in the portrait of the first Darcys from the 1400s, the one who so resembles me as a youth. It is a family name that has materialized frequently, both in males and females, over the generations. I was gifted the name after my father's younger brother, who died at the age of twelve. My father had been extremely devoted to that Alexander, and I grew up hearing stories of this namesake whom I had never met. I always liked the name, not simply because of my uncle, but because it is a pleasing name. Strong, the name of a king, and can be shortened if necessary without sounding idiotic, like Fitz, which I abhor, or Will." He kissed her gently. "I do not know if it was a message or a premonition, my love, but I can tell you that I have always desired my son to be named Alexander and we have never discussed this. So, I do not believe you insane." He smiled, kissing her again. "I presume, therefore, that the Christian name has been unanimously decided?"

Lizzy laughed and nodded, hugging cautiously. "By the way, who on earth calls you Fitz?"

"No one more than once, I can assure you. Now, how about some lunch?"

They ate in the sitting room, contentedly snuggled on the sofa, conversing about general topics with laughter and effortless ease. Lizzy excused herself briefly, the need to utilize the water closet frequent. Darcy stood by the window when she returned and she encircled his waist, laying her head between his shoulder blades while he clasped her hands. They stood for a time in silence.

"William, I have something to tell you that I have avoided. Forgive me for evasiveness or concealment, but I feared your anger and disappointment spoiling our reunion. However, I cannot equivocate any longer. Lady Catherine came here on the day you left and… spoke with me. It was… unpleasant."

Darcy turned and embraced her tightly, voice heavy with emotion when he replied, "I am aware of it, dearest. Lord Matlock wrote me, although not until the day of my accident." He cupped her surprised face, eyes mournful. "Elizabeth, can you ever forgive me for not being here? I swear, I never thought she would do this. I thought time would have mellowed her opinion and when I wrote to her about our blessed news I imagined she would be thrilled for me. It is inconceivable that she did this, but more so that I abandoned you. Please, I beg you, forgive me for not protecting you and so foolishly assuming she would behave as a proper lady."

Lizzy was shaking her head, tears springing to her eyes. "Oh William! It is I who should be begging your pardon!" She pulled away and began pacing, Darcy watching her in confusion.

"Elizabeth, I do not understand."

Lizzy sighed. "She said so many things that were simply inane: accusing me of marrying you for your money, intimating that a Bennet could not birth a boy, saying that I was forcing you to harbor secrets from her and encouraging the rift, and other nonsense." Lizzy glanced up at his darkening face then quickly looked away, flushing with shame. "She also talked about the lack of invitations as if she knew and how your social standing and the Darcy name had been hurt by marrying me."

"Elizabeth, surely you lent no credence to that absurdity?"

"Not at first, no. Yet, I wondered. I remembered what you had said when you first proposed, about my rank and circumstances. She was right about the lack of invitations, and I know so little about your world and the requirements. I hated that I may have caused you pain or difficulties, even though I could not have done differently than to marry you. Then, Madeline told me that you knew about Lady Catherine's knowledge of my pregnancy, and I…" she caught her breath with a sob, "was angry and confused and hurt. It made perfect sense that she would attack me, hating me as she does and I thought… you should have…" she covered her face with her hands, collapsing onto the chaise in tears.

Darcy had turned to stare out the window, emotions in turmoil. *Damn you to hell, Aunt Catherine!* he screamed in his mind, yet it was his own guilt as much as anger that raged through him. Elizabeth was crying behind him; and he longed to run to her at the same moment he wanted to yell at her. How could she believe one word of his aunt's vindictiveness? When would she forgive him his past arrogance and misconceptions? How could she think he would purposely desert her? *Of course, that is exactly why you are so riddled with guilt, Darcy.*

He sighed, grasping for control and understanding. He turned, heart instantly melting at the sight of the woman he loved more than his own miserable life crying with heartache. He was across the room and enfolding her into his arms before another beat of his heart. Reclining onto the chaise with her cuddled between his legs, he lifted her chin to meet his eyes.

"Elizabeth Darcy, listen to me carefully. I love you. I absolutely refuse to allow Lady Catherine's spite to separate us, even minutely. We must rationally discuss this. You are correct in that I should have foreseen her actions. Yes, I should have," he confirmed in response to her negative exclamation. "Of course, even if I had suspected that she might still confront you with vicious words, I may not have been available to halt her had I been in Town. I will undoubtedly persist in my self-chastisement because I consider it my duty to shield you from woes, but logically I cannot expect to invariably succeed. Nor can you expect me to, I suppose."

He held her tighter, speaking softly with old remorse, "I have hurt you so in the past, beloved. I wish I could erase my horrid words more than you will ever comprehend, but I cannot. Instead, I want more than anything to make your life perfect, blissful at all moments, full of the love you deserve. I reckon that you feel much the same for me. Naturally, this is ludicrous. Life is not flawless, no matter how close one may obtain excellence. All we can truly promise each other is to love and honor and respect and communicate."

"William, I am so sorry. I feel at times as if I am going crazy, my emotions are in such turmoil. Madeline says it is the pregnancy, and perhaps this is so, yet I cannot place all blame there as if it excuses my stupidity. I had to confess my words and thoughts but I did not truly mean it—only fleetingly in the moment of distress. My faith in you, in your capabilities and choices but primarily in your love for me, is unwavering. I have been distraught all week imagining your anger at Lady Catherine or me—or worse yet, your guilt and disappointment. I never want you to regret marrying me—"

"Elizabeth! I will not listen to you speak those words! Angry I may be from time to time. Guilty for not achieving my set standards, yes, but regret? I could sooner regret breathing than to regret having you as my wife." He embraced her crushingly and actually shuddered, inhaling raggedly.

They held each other for a very long while, reassured by the silence of their hearts beating in tune. Lizzy lazily caressed his chest, the foolish conjectures of the past week fading into the wind as her husband comforted with tender kisses and a sturdy grip. Finally, he asked her to tell him everything that had been said. She did, leaving nothing out except for the revelation of his grief when she refused him. That disclosure was too private and painful to relive, for either of them.

"You are correct, you know, in that my aunt never has understood me. Of course, that is as much my fault as hers. I do not open myself easily to anyone, as you can attest. My aunt and I are not confidantes. My mother and her sister were not overly friendly or intimate. My mother was closest to the middle Fitzwilliam sister, my Aunt Muriel. She passed when I was very young and I barely remember her. Anyway, Catherine was the eldest, and despite her constant assertions, my mother never planned for Anne and me to marry. Oh, I think she probably thought it would be sweet when we were born so closely together, but it was not a serious arrangement. Aunt Catherine always pushed it though, and my mother remained silent, probably out of intimidation from her brazen older sister, but mostly because she knew I am far too stubborn to be forced into anything. The irony is that the compulsory association with each other did lead to a strong affection, but as cousins should.

"My Uncle Lewis passed four years ago, and per Aunt Catherine's request, I assumed the role of advisor to the estate. It was all a ploy, as she had run roughshod over my uncle for years and knew more about the estate's affairs than he did! Still, I found it easier to comply rather than argue. Besides, I like Kent and enjoyed visiting Anne. There was never any agreement with my uncle, or official duty. That is a boldfaced lie."

Darcy paused, peering intently into Lizzy's eyes, piercing her very soul as only he could. "As to the rest, Elizabeth, I honestly do not know where to begin. A part of me wants to shake you until your teeth rattle for being so foolish as to entertain the tiniest notion that I would care one iota what anyone in society thinks. Yet, I recognize your innocence and cannot deny that I planted the seed of doubt by my own words at Kent. I will not lie to you and deny that there are clearly those who will temporarily shun me for my choice of wife. That is the reality of this world I live in. In this my aunt is partly truthful. The invitations have been markedly diminished. What she does not appreciate is that I am utterly indifferent and frankly relieved. In the past, I denied the vast majority of solicitations received because I was not interested. They consisted primarily of families with eligible daughters or business propositions designed to profit by my wealth. I have told you again and again, Elizabeth, how I hated the falseness of the ton. If this is the world and opinion that truly mattered to me, then I would have married a Caroline Bingley years ago!"

He painfully grasped her chin with his thumb and index finger, raptor gaze of darkened blue eyes boring into her. "Elizabeth, we have discussed this ad nauseam during our engagement and I cannot revisit the period during which I lost you, and the torment that caused to my soul. The agony is too extreme. I would lay down my very life for you and our child. That is not merely a poetic phrase; it is the truth. My wealth, Pemberley, my horses, social standings, or family ties—none of it has any meaning without you. If you do not yet comprehend this and my love for you above all else in this world, then there is nothing more I can say or do to convince you."

Elizabeth was crying silently, wanting to hide her face in shame, but he would not slacken his grip. He continued to study her as if reading into her mind through her eyes. She clutched him tightly about the waist, returning his direct stare, pouring all her love and remorse into her teary eyes. At last he nodded, seemingly satisfied with what he gleaned. He smiled slightly and leaned in for a tender kiss. Lizzy released a shuddering sigh of liberation as he kissed her. It was a long kiss, devoid of passion, but replete with love and assurance and peace.

CHAPTER THIRTEEN

Family Matters

"MR. DARCY!"

Darcy turned from the open doorway to view the eager young face of Mr. Joshua Daniels bearing down on him. He was in the process of exiting the building which housed his solicitor's offices, having spent the past hour signing the legal documents pertaining to the arrangement with Duke Grafton, as well as a smattering of other papers. Now, his solicitor's son was approaching, and Darcy did not doubt the purpose although he maintained a neutral expression.

"Mr. Daniels," he replied with a bow.

"Mr. Darcy, I was praying I may speak with you for a moment? Regarding a personal matter, if you have the time?"

"Of course." They entered a small conference room, Mr. Daniels blushing and nervous but determined.

"Sir, I was blessed with the great fortune to deliver the Royston contracts to your house several days ago whereupon I met Mrs. Darcy and four other ladies in her company. Lovely women all; however, I would be perjuring myself if I denied that one of the young ladies in particular captured my attention most profoundly. Your esteemed wife's sister, Miss Mary Bennet, is of whom I speak. We spoke briefly and I sensed a mutual interest. Nonetheless, I deemed it proper to approach you as her guardian ere I pursued the matter."

The entire speech was delivered in a rush, and in practically one breath. Yet Darcy was impressed, as Mr. Daniels boldly met Darcy's eyes throughout, a feat many fail at, and his manners spoke for themselves. Darcy nodded seriously. "Thank you, Mr. Daniels, for your consideration and honesty. Ultimately the decision is Miss Bennet's, and I cannot speak for her feelings on the subject. However, you have my permission to call if she wishes it." Darcy struggled not to laugh at the poor man's visible relief, continuing instead with, "I should enlighten you, though, that Miss Bennet will be in Town only for another three weeks or so, then she is returning to Hertfordshire. At that time, her care will be resumed by her father."

Mr. Daniels lifted his chin bravely, undoubtedly imagining the horrors of dealing with a ferocious father. "Thank you, sir."

Darcy left the offices in high spirits. His affection toward both his new sisters had increased over the past weeks. Mary, although still rather odd to him, had relaxed in his presence and displayed a rare intelligence. She was stoic and did not seem to possess the slightest humor, but she was steady, confident, pretty, loyal, and kind. Georgiana adored her, and this alone recommended her to Darcy. It was far too early to predict where the romance may lead, but Darcy felt it would be a good match.

His spirits waned as he drew nearer to the setting of his next appointment: the townhouse of Lady Catherine de Bourgh. He dreaded meeting his aunt. His anger seethed below the serene exterior, unrelenting since he first heard of her rudeness to his wife. He and Elizabeth, once again, had been forced to revisit the past, dredging up awful memories and emotions that they had successfully resolved. In the end, their indescribable, unbreakable love had triumphed, the only positive in this episode being the proof of how their devotion to each other could and would overcome all odds. Still, Darcy was furious at the interruption to their bliss and communion. He had no clear path, only certain that he must confront his aunt.

She had consented to meet with him, her note impersonal and short, as had been Darcy's to her. As a footman took his coat, Anne appeared to greet him, a sweet smile on her pale face.

"Cousin William! Mother told me you were visiting today, so I have been watching for you."

"Dearest Anne," he replied as he kissed her cheek, "have you been well? Any changes?"

She shrugged. "I am the same, William. Fair days followed by ill. Congratulations on your blessed news. I am so very delighted for you and Mrs. Darcy. Has she been well?"

"Thank you, Anne. She is well now. The early months were moderately difficult, yet nothing unexpected, thankfully."

"I do hope you and mother can resolve your dispute. I so desire to meet your wife now that she is family. I was quite taken with her when she tarried at Kent last year. So lively and witty. It did not surprise me that you were enamored with her as she is perfect for you, Mr. Stuffy."

Darcy laughed through his surprise. "You have not called me that since we were children. I believe I am offended!"

Anne smiled then grew serious. "Mother is in her parlor, practicing a pose of intimidation, most assuredly. Be kind, William, and attempt to check that infamous Darcy temper at the door!" She kissed his cheek, then left him at the threshold.

Darcy knocked and, at his aunt's permission, entered, though with a deep inhale and a silent prayer. Lady Catherine sat imperiously in a massive chair gazing inscrutably at her nephew as he bowed formally before her. "Aunt Catherine" was his only greeting.

"Fitzwilliam," she responded. "Have you come to chasten me as did your uncle?"

"The course this interview runs will wholly depend upon your attitude, Aunt. I do not judge it within my authority to discipline you and have no plans to do so. My only intent is to clarify, again, the facts as they stand. Unless you wish to begin by apologizing for your egregious behavior to my wife?"

"I did extend my apologies to your wife. Was this not sufficient?"

"Unfortunately, no. Your note was brief and vague."

"What, precisely, is it you want from me, Fitzwilliam? To say that I approve of your choice? That I am pleased that Anne is rejected? Is this what you expect from me?"

"It is pointless to discuss Anne and me. All you need do is heed the assertions of your daughter and you would understand that she had no desire to marry me had I wished it. Any proposal on my part would have been repulsed, thus making myself the rejected individual. In regards to Mrs. Darcy, you are correct in that it is my choice, and astoundingly erroneous for you to credit your approval a precondition in any decision of mine. Pardon my bluntness, madam, but you presume an influence on my life that is not your prerogative."

Lady Catherine inhaled with an audible gasp, pursed her lips, and averted her eyes. Darcy remained still for a few moments, struggling to control his temper, and then sat down near his aunt. He leaned forward and took her hands gently, her surprised gaze jerking to his face. Darcy was stern as he spoke.

"Aunt Catherine, hearken to my words. I have had many months to ruminate over your initial interference into my affairs. As misplaced and ill-mannered as it was for you to intercede, I do believe that, to a degree, it was out of affection for me and concern for my welfare. This is a topic I too have some experience with." The last was spoken with a wry twist to his lips. "In hope that this is the case, I appeal to this affection. I am the happiest I have ever been in my entire life, Aunt. My life is complete, and I am whole as I have never been. Even if you cannot comprehend this nor concur with how it has transpired, please, I beg you for the sake of our relationship and peace in our family to trust me and believe."

They stared at each other for several heartbeats. Finally, Catherine asked, "She truly means that much to you, Fitzwilliam?"

"Yes, she does." He paused. "Elizabeth is an amazing individual. If you had given her the opportunity to prove herself, you would have deduced this fact for yourself. I pray you will allow yourself the chance to reach the same conclusion as I—and quite literally all who know her—have."

He released her hands then and stiffened into his full, commanding pose. "Nevertheless, I am obligated to remind you that whether your opinion ever alters, Elizabeth is my wife, and as such she commands respect and honor. This fact is incontrovertible. Secondly, all areas of my life are beyond your purview. We wish for you to be welcomed in our home and to know our child, but you must understand that you have no power or control therein. Thirdly, Mrs. Darcy is owed an honorable and honest apology, as am I. Your actions have been unthinkable, Lady Catherine, and unworthy of the Fitzwilliam name."

He stood, voice softening as he spoke, "Mrs. Darcy and I petition you with heartfelt humility to meditate on these things. If you determine to acquiesce, then we would request yours and Anne's presence at a dinner party we are hosting three days hence. Only family and close friends will be in attendance, and we would very much like to have you there."

Lady Catherine's thoughts or feelings were indecipherable as she sat regally and gazed into space. Darcy concluded, "We shall send a formal invitation on the morrow. Good day, madam." And with an elegant bow, he departed.

Returning to a silent Darcy House, Darcy was emotionally and physically exhausted. His arm and chest ached with a consistent throbbing, and the normally robust Darcy was overcome with fatigue. Elizabeth and the girls, accompanied by the Bennet girls' Aunt Gardiner, Jane, and several others, were out shopping. Darcy retreated to their sitting room and reclined on the chaise to read and consume a light lunch. His next conscious awareness was a tender kiss to his brow and his wife's gentle touch and sweet voice calling his name. Opening bleary eyes and moving his neck, stiff from being in an oddly placed angle as he slumped in the chaise, he spied Lizzy's beautiful face.

"Darling, you will not be able to move if you sleep here. Let me assist you."

Darcy simply stared at her for what seemed an eternity, mind cloudy and thoughts scattered. For a span of time, he had no clear idea where he was. She was speaking soft words but they made no sense. He shook his head, instinctively hauling with his left arm to rise then falling back with a shout of pain, wakefulness instantaneous.

"William! You must be cautious!"

"I am well," he declared through grit teeth, massaging with his right hand.

"No you are not! The pain is intense and your weariness disturbs me. You never nap in the afternoons. We should call a physician. I am very worried about you, my love."

"My body is healing, beloved, hence the fatigue. Observe how much stronger my hand is." He proved his point by grasping her wrist and tugging her onto his lap. "You see how easy that was?" He was smiling bravely, but Lizzy could see the lingering stress in the clenching of his jaw and pallor. "Now, tell me about your day."

"Oh no, Mr. Darcy, you will not distract me that easily and do not even *think* about kissing me!" she firmly declared with a jab to his breastbone and a push backward. "Surely you have a physician in Town? We can send for him right now and—"

"Elizabeth, I will be fine. Trust me, I honestly have suffered worse. It is a bad sprain and a horrific bruise, I will grant you that, and it does pain me, but it is mending." She opened her mouth to argue further, but he cupped her face and interrupted with a kiss. "Tell you what, if I do not feel any improvement tomorrow I will send for the doctor. In the interim, I shall soak in a hot bath and submit to a lengthy massage by my loving wife. Pair that with another blissful night's rest in your arms, and I should be cured. Now, tell me about your day."

Lizzy was frowning and peering at her oft-times devious spouse through narrowed eyes. "Do you promise? To send for the doctor, that is?"

"Cross my heart," he answered solemnly, gesturing over his heart precisely, although the lilt to his lips belied his seriousness. "Now, for the third time. How was your day?"

Lizzy chuckled and shook her head. "It was delightful, thank you for asking. You will be happy to learn that I spent nearly all my money. Satisfied?"

"That depends. Was any of it spent on yourself, Mrs. Darcy?"

Lizzy flushed and avoided his eyes. "A little," she murmured, leaning in toward his exposed neck to be halted by a palm on her forehead.

"Oh no! Distracting with intimate kisses will not be tolerated! Such guile is not to be borne, I tell you."

"Ha!" Lizzy barked, but he ignored her.

"Your giving spirit becomes you, dearest, but you know the consequences of not purchasing worthless items for yourself?" He sighed dramatically. "I shall have to buy them for you, which means tramping through women's establishments and making a fool of myself. Oh, the bother of it all!" And with a heavy sigh, he threw his head back into the cushion.

"You know, if this horse breeding and farming career ever fails you, the theatre would be a logical choice. You could be the next Edmund Kean."

Darcy grinned and drew her in for a satisfying kiss. Unfortunately, they were shortly interrupted by a knock at the door. It was the maid with an express letter addressed to Mr. Darcy, along with the rest of the day's post. Darcy opened the letter and began to read while Lizzy flipped through the stack, happily discovering a letter from her father and another from Charlotte Collins.

"Well, my love, it appears as if your wish will be granted tomorrow after all."

"What wish is that?"

"That I am seen by a physician. This note is from my uncle George. He and an associate are arriving tomorrow and request lodging at Darcy House." Darcy laughed. "As if he need ask."

"How long has it been since you last saw him?"

"Well, let me think. He visited shortly after father died. He was unable to arrive for the funeral, the message announcing father's passing probably not arriving until long after. He is ostensibly stationed in Bombay, but travels throughout the country to remote villages where doctors are not located, so reaching him can be a challenge. It was some three months before he visited. Then he surprised Georgie and me a little over two years ago. He tarried most of the summer at Pemberley. Georgiana adores him, as is only appropriate I suppose since she is named after him. I receive a letter now and again, but he is often beyond any postal center and is very busy. You will like him, beloved. He has always reminded me very much of Richard, although the two are obviously not related, and he has the most astounding stories to tell. He is focused and driven, typical Darcy traits taken to extremes in his case."

"He never married?"

"No. Too focused on his work. No children, as far as we know of. I suppose one can never be sure. He let slip once that he has an Indian mistress, but I did not ask for any further details. It will be delightful to see him. I must tell Georgie. Help me up, love."

Lizzy had been surprised to learn of the extensiveness to the Darcy family. With Darcy and Georgiana orphaned and alone, she had naturally assumed they were the last of the Darcys. She was in error.

The Darcy family was ancient, tracing an extensive heritage back over five hundred years. A multitude of secondary bloodlines from siblings were long since lost, but one could easily presume there were unknown distant Darcy relatives scattered about. The name was not particularly common, but Darcy had told his wife of two occasions where he met someone with his surname. Whether they were an actual relative was impossible to ascertain, but the likelihood was plausible. The main Darcy ancestry was unbroken and included a plethora of noblemen and women on down through the centuries.

The more recent familial history was easier to delineate and also proved the reality of numerous Darcys.

Darcy's grandfather, James Darcy Sr., was the eldest of three sons. His younger brothers each married and settled down to raise their families, begetting a number of Darcy cousins now strewn throughout England, some of whom Darcy had never met. James Sr. and his wife, Darcy's grandmother, produced six children. The eldest, Darcy's aunt Mary, married an Austrian baron and currently lived outside of Linz, Austria, with her brood. Apparently, she and her husband had traveled to England a couple of times when Darcy was younger, and he had journeyed to Austria twice to become acquainted with his Austrian cousins, yet the relationships were distant.

James Jr., the heir to Pemberley, arrived three years later, followed by a sister, Estella; the twins, Alexander and George; and last Phillip.

Estella married a wealthy landowner, Xavier Montrose, and resided near Exeter in Devon with their children and grandchildren. Darcy's father had been quite close to his younger sister, and over the years, she and her family were frequent visitors to Pemberley and vice versa. Their two children, one male and one female, were both married with small children of their own. Despite the distance from Devon, both Darcy's aunt and uncle and his two cousins had attended his wedding, allowing Lizzy to meet them.

The twins were born when James was eight. From the time they could toddle the three had been inseparable—so Darcy told Lizzy—the age difference inconsequential. Estella was a bit of a rowdy girl and had fit right in, whereas Mary was delicate and dainty, finding the four intolerable. Alexander died at the age of twelve from injuries sustained after falling from his horse. The three youngest siblings had been devastated, especially George. The twins were identical and shared the unusual bond seen with twins, leaving George permanently bereft. James always told his son that George changed from that time forward: more serious, his wit caustic, and obsessed with medicine and healing things. He vowed to become a physician at an early age, a choice not pleasing to his father.

James Sr. had balked at the idea of a son of his being a mere doctor, the profession not necessarily considered respectable. Yet George persisted with the inherited Darcy stubbornness brought to the fore. When it became obvious that there was no altering his intention, James Sr. relented, providing George received his education at the Royal College of Physicians in London. George had done so, following his licensure as a physician by also enrolling at the Royal College of Surgeons as well as the Society of Apothecaries. His thirst for understanding medicine in all its aspects seemed inexhaustible. After his apprenticeship he refused to settle down and hang a shingle. Instead, he joined the British East India Company in 1790 and had resided and practiced in India ever since.

The last of the Darcy siblings, Phillip, arrived when James was sixteen and long after his parents expected further children. Due to the great difference in their ages, the Darcy siblings had not been particularly intimate with their youngest brother when he was a child. After Cambridge, James Jr. returned to Pemberley permanently; George was already away to college, and he and Phillip gradually developed a fondness, although the age gap prevented true companionship. At eighteen, Phillip was apprenticed to a banking associate of his father's, the world of high finance being his chosen field of interest, eventually settling in Manchester. James Sr. had been disappointed, wishing his youngest son would also remain at Pemberley and apply his skills to assist in managing the estate. Phillip and his family visited from time to time throughout Darcy's childhood, but only once after his father died. Darcy was not particularly friendly with his uncle, and although invited, they had not come for the wedding, so Lizzy had yet to meet them.

Therefore, Darcy and Georgiana had grown up relatively unassociated on a frequent basis with any of their Darcy relatives. Conversely, the Fitzwilliams all lived within an easy distance to Pemberley and Derbyshire, rendering their relationship effortless to cultivate. James Jr. had fallen madly in love with the lovely Lady Anne Fitzwilliam, daughter to the now deceased Earl of Matlock, when she a mere fifteen and he twenty. The affection had been instantly mutual, and three days past her nineteenth birthday, they were wed. Lady Anne's older sister, Catherine—in fact the eldest of the four Fitzwilliam offspring—was already wed to Sir Lewis de Bourgh and living in Kent. Her dearly loved sister Muriel, only one year her senior, would wed a Derbyshire landowner three years later, only five months after their brother Malcolm married Madeline, settling in Matlock.

Darcy's grandmother passed away long before he was born, some one year after his parent's marriage. James Sr. then chose to follow his dream, a dream Lizzy could easily envision her husband someday fulfilling. He completely relinquished the management of Pemberley into the hands of his vastly competent son and devoted all his efforts to the breeding of Pemberley's horses. James Jr. was Master of Pemberley in all but name, while James Sr. exponentially increased the breeding program and training of their thoroughbreds. Within five years of this arrangement, the wealth of Pemberley had doubled.

Anne embraced her role as Mistress of Pemberley while attempting to produce an heir. After two miscarriages, Anne finally carried and delivered a daughter, Alexandria. The pregnancy and birth were uncomplicated, Anne was robust, and the baby was fat and healthy. Tragically, when the vigorous toddler was just over a year, and Anne was again with child, she suddenly became ill and within a week had died. The doctors diagnosed it as scarlet fever. The family was grief stricken. Luckily, Anne's second successful pregnancy progressed as smoothly as the first and on November 10 of 1787, Fitzwilliam Alexander James Darcy was born, weighing well over nine pounds and screaming loudly.

Almost from the time Darcy could walk, he spent hours in the stables with his grandfather. Anne fretted, fearful of losing another child in the dangerous environment, but the old man was domineering and had not abdicated all authority. James Jr. agreed, his own fears of a similar fate befalling his son offset by the desire for him to be comfortable with horses and an outdoorsman. By the time Darcy was ten, he knew how to shoe a horse, could ride as well as most of the grooms, could muck a stall faster than any of the stable boys, had broken his first pony, and had intently absorbed everything his grandfather could teach him. When he was eleven his grandfather died, plunging Darcy into an abyss of grief. If he had spent the majority his free time in the stable yard before, he now practically dwelt there. His parents barely saw him except for meals, and even his studies suffered. It was the long awaited birth of a sibling which brought him back into the manor and the broader world outside of the barns.

Anne had despaired of ever having another child. After her son, she simply did not conceive. It certainly was not for lack of trying, the love between the two Darcys having multiplied over the years and being frequently expressed in the physical realm. Anne's pregnancy and delivery of Georgiana was complicated from inception to parturition, leaving Anne near death for days and weakened thereafter, but Georgiana was stout and perfect. Darcy immediately fell deeply and wholly in love with his sister. It was this love which would save him on many occasions over the ensuing years, when sorrow and the weight of responsibility threatened to break him. As close as Darcy was to his cousins Richard and Anne, it was his sister who had his heart utterly wrapped around her tiny fingers.

Darcy was a person who required few confidantes, and therefore, he did not exert tremendous effort into cultivating relationships. Those whom he loved, he loved with an entirety that was formidable. Those whom he deemed superfluous would be generally ignored. Hence the minimal energy expended to associate with his disseminated cousins. For this reason, the personal circle of Darcy family members was relatively minute, despite the number reality to the contrary. Lizzy rather doubted she would ever meet the majority of her husband's family, but she was excited about meeting George Darcy. He was a favorite, and the stories she had heard of the adventurous, eccentric doctor piqued her curiosity.

Georgiana was ecstatic. She regaled them all evening with tale upon tale of her favored Darcy uncle. Even Mary expressed a fascination to meet this grand individual. Of course, Mary was in an unusually high humor. Mr. Daniels had wasted no time after speaking with Darcy, formally requesting to call upon Miss Mary Bennet for tea the following day. It perhaps was not the most fortuitous of days, with George Darcy and friend arriving as well at a time unknown, but neither Lizzy nor Darcy would have dreamed of inducing her to decline.

With the excitement of blossoming romance, family visitations, and a dinner party event with Darcy's shipping partners, Lizzy and Darcy had no chance to talk privately until before bed. As typical, he entered her dressing room to assume the task of brushing her hair. Initially, no words were spoken as the two lovers purely delighted in serene companionship. Darcy could never verbalize why it was that he so adored brushing his wife's hair. It was intimate, enlivening, and comforting. Primarily, he simply gloried in her beauty as reflected in the mirror with her luxuriant, silky locks falling about her slender frame and through his hands.

Lizzy smiled and stood, leaning over the vanity bench to kiss her husband. "Shall we sit on the patio for a spell, my love?"

The stars were bright, the air fresh in the warm summer evening, and the fragrance of multiple blooms floated to where they reclined on the patio chaise. Darcy related his conversation with Lady Catherine.

"Do you believe she will cooperate?"

Darcy sighed. "I honestly do not know and am not sure if I care, as horrid as that is to confess. She was silent and inscrutable when I left, so I could not hazard a guess as to her state of mind. If it were not for Anne, I am not certain I would even try." Darcy paused, then resumed with a mournful tone, "Forgive me, Elizabeth. That is an unbecoming sentiment. She is my aunt, my flesh and blood, yet I am still so angry at her for all she has said that I find it an immense struggle to generate leniency."

"I understand, darling. I too have quite mixed feelings on the subject of your aunt. Would you think less of me if I confessed to a desire to never set eyes on the woman again?"

Darcy laughed lowly. "No, as I tend to harbor the identical emotions. I will say this, if she does show up and offers an apology, even a lame one, it will speak volumes as to her repentance."

Lizzy snuggled tighter against his body, Darcy's arms firmly around her with one hand gently stroking her belly. "How is your shoulder?"

"Tolerable. The bath helped tremendously. I probably incited the staff to severe irritation, but the water was so hot I could barely enter it. Nevertheless, when Wentworth clapped me on the shoulder tonight I nearly slugged him in reflexive defense!"

Lizzy stifled a laugh. "That would have made for a lively evening to be sure. Shame you behaved yourself." She turned to better see his face, kissing his smiling lips. "Come, my beloved, infirm husband. A massage was promised and then we shall see what else I can do to improve your overall state of well-being."

CHAPTER FOURTEEN

Visitations

OH! THIS ONE WOULD look wonderful on you, Mary!" Georgiana appeared from the inside of her closet holding a beautiful, deep purple gown with embroidered vines of wisteria cascading from the bodice to the hem.

Kitty clapped her hands in delight but Mary frowned. "I am not so sure, Georgiana. The color is lovely but the flowers are simply not me. Far too ostentatious."

"You must make an impression that he will not forget, Mary," Kitty explained wearily for the hundredth time, while Georgiana rolled her eyes.

"His impression should be of me, not the dress I am wearing," Mary firmly declared. "I do not wish to be courted by a man who is only interested in me for my clothing."

"Well, of course not," Georgiana soothed, "yet there is no shame in presenting an appealing vision. It shows that you care for yourself and desire to please him. Men expect such efforts."

"The expert, are we, Miss Darcy?" Mary said with a soft laugh. "Lizzy never fussed over herself and Mr. Darcy fell in love. This is what I desire. To have a man want me for whom I am." Mary spoke quietly and with embarrassment.

The Mary Bennet sitting sedately on the edge of Georgiana's bed was an altered creature from the antisocial young girl who pounded out morbid tunes and declared how she hated balls. No longer did she look at the world with eyes clouded by misinterpretation and somber disgust. Her character overall had not drastically changed; rather, it was her revelation of the broader world beyond Meryton and Longbourn. The events of the past months and her friendship with the shyly proper but intelligent Georgiana had radically opened her eyes. No longer did she liberally sweep anything remotely frivolous out the door as wholly worthless and unorthodox.

Above all, Mary was amazed at her changed attitude toward the opposite sex. She had grown up with a family of mostly females consisting of a mother who seemingly thought of nothing but marrying her daughters off to the first eligible man who came along, two younger sisters who acted the fool around anything in trousers, and two older sisters who had snapped up the richest men available. Mary was the odd woman who did not swoon over the ridiculous frippery that comprised the standard male population. Mr. Collins had briefly intrigued her in that he was sober and not a dandy. She had thought Lizzy an imbecile for refusing his proposal, totally baffled at the decision until Mr. Darcy's proposal was accepted. Mary was now wholly ashamed for her conclusion, but at the time, it appeared evident to her that Lizzy had succumbed to his wealth, somehow ensnaring the pompous man with her hidden charms and prostituting herself at the altar of riches and prestige. Mary had been horribly disappointed in Lizzy, as she had been the one of all her sisters that she deemed the most sensible and least likely to yield, but there appeared to be no other logical deduction. Not one to study poetry or waste precious time reading romantic novels or gossip with twittery girls about flirtations, Mary simply had no concept of love.

During the two months of her sisters' engagements, Mary had primarily avoided them all in disgust. When she did note the affectionate glance or oblique touch between one of the pairs of couples, she either did not grasp it or chalked it up to men's bestial lusts, those sins of the flesh warned against in scripture and other doctrinal writings. In the following months, she observed the steady affection between Jane and Mr. Bingley, grudgingly deciding that their marriage was not solely about money after all. Her misplaced and low opinion of Lizzy had not altered until this sojourn in London. Mary witnessed a rare emotion between her older sister and husband. She frankly had not comprehended it for a time, been confused at the blatant and occasionally mortifying affection displayed by the two, shocked at the depth of Lizzy's despair when he was absent, but predominately flabbergasted at the metamorphosis in Mr. Darcy. Not unlike Caroline Bingley, although without the accompanying jealousy, Mary gradually came to identify it for what it was: love in the purest form.

It would be inaccurate to state that Mary had a crush on her brother-in-law, but she did recognize his gentleness, intelligence, devotion to Lizzy and Georgiana, maturity, grace, elegance, humor, and many other admirable qualities. She began to wonder if there were other men like him and if even a particle of the love Lizzy and Mr. Darcy shared could be available for her. Her eyes were further opened by Colonel Fitzwilliam and the married men of her recent acquaintance who possessed similar fine qualities. It finally occurred to her, as if a startling epiphany, that men could carry on a conversation with a woman, might even be pleasant to have about, and were not creatures of a divergent species.

Now there was Mr. Joshua Daniels. Mary was mystified by the encounter with him. That Mr. Daniels had immediately been attracted to her was a given fact and Mary was egotistically gratified, although the emotion rather embarrassed her. Her newfound adoption of wearing moderately stylish clothing, limited conversing with the male population, and enjoyment of social activities was pleasurable but still mildly uncomfortable. The few glances and nods her direction while at the opera and dinner parties were flattering, but she also remained confused as to how to interpret the attention. Moreover, no man had ever noticed her in the way Mr. Daniels had nor asked to specifically visit her, and Mary was not sure how she felt about it. Mr. Daniels comported himself with propriety and grace, and impressed her as clever and capable. Still, the idea of actually being courted filled her with anxiety.

"Not all men are as special as my brother, Mary," Georgiana said, interrupting her musings, "and Elizabeth now takes great pains to dress to her station and to please her husband. You do wish to be married, do you not?"

"Naturally she does!" Kitty answered for her, as if the converse concept was unfathomable. "How about the dark blue gown, Georgiana? It is simple, a somber color, yet designed so beautifully."

"Yes! Excellent choice, Kitty!" Georgiana ducked back into her closet, returning moments later with the gown indicated. "This is perfect, Mary. Here, try it on."

Mary scrambled for an excuse, in truth adoring the gown in question. "I do not think one of your dresses will fit me, and what about the—"

"Try it on!" Kitty and Georgiana interjected simultaneously with exasperation, Mary relenting with a sigh.

Down on the first floor, the Darcys sat in quiet company. Darcy read the day's newspaper and drank coffee. His wife finished the last pages of her book while sipping tea and nibbling on a piece of marmalade-smeared toast. Lizzy closed the book with a happy sigh and glanced over at her frowning, intently reading spouse.

"Bad news, William?" He did not answer, wholly absorbed in the words before him. "Dearest? Fitzwilliam? *Mr. Darcy?*"

"Pardon?" He looked up with a start.

"What has so captivated your attention, love?"

He waved his hand airily. "Nothing really. Just a minor riot at the docks last evening. These occurrences happen from time to time. Apparently, a group of Scots took issue with slurs trumpeted by a shipload of Irish and a brawl ensued. I was concerned as one of my ships is currently docked there, but the melee was further upriver thankfully." He nodded toward her hands. "You finished your book?"

"Yes. It was very good, as you professed. Rather deep and meditative, however. I believe I am now in the mood for fluff." She took a bite of toast and stood, walking toward the bookcase, Darcy observing with a smile.

"How about the one Aunt Madeline lent you? *The Mysteries of Udolpho.* Sounds appropriately fluffy to me."

Lizzy glanced over her shoulder. "A perfect woman's book, you mean. All romance, castles, villains, and lovers."

He shrugged and laughed. "You said you wanted fluff. I am merely trying to assist you in not taxing your fragile brain."

"I would argue or tickle you into begging my forgiveness, but at the moment I find I concur with your assessment." She pulled the indicated volume off the shelf, flipping it open as she did. Moments later she felt the delightful sensation of warm, strong hands on her shoulders. Peering up at her smiling husband, she asked, "Riots, world events, and the finance page no longer interest you, my love?"

"Not as greatly as this tiny spot of skin right here," he murmured, leaning in to kiss behind her left ear. She sighed as he proceeded to tenderly suck her earlobe then traveled down the slope of her neck while peeling the robe off her shoulders. Gathering her hair in his right hand to pull the thick mass aside, he attacked the nape of her neck with soft lips, shivers cascading down her spine. His left hand dipped into her bodice to cup one full breast. Lizzy pressed her bottom into him and he responded as would be expected. "I adore you, my Lizzy. Love you so immensely."

"Do you want me, Fitzwilliam?" she asked with a purr. "Desperately?"

He moved to the other breast while simultaneously clutching her hip and pulling harshly against him. "Always I want you, my love. To love you, to be inside you while touching your flesh is my greatest joy." He met her eyes, passion evident in darkened orbs. "I woke this morning with your glorious bared body beside me and I was painfully aroused. I urgently desired you, but you slept peacefully, so instead I contented myself with gazing at your beauty and cupping my palm over our child. Then you woke and expressed immediate hunger, which I certainly cannot in good conscience deny you, as your increased appetite is partially my fault." He laughed, rubbing over her mildly protruding stomach before traveling lower with probing caresses. "Now, however, you have satisfied one pressing hunger and I have satisfied none." He left her bosom to stroke her jaw and cheek, inclining to taste sweet lips.

Leaning fully onto his body, head resting on his right shoulder, Lizzy submitted to the rampant vibrations elicited by skillful fingers and mouth. "Elizabeth, my precious, beautiful wife. I love you forever. The very thought of you excites me tremendously. Your scent, your velvet skin, your breath, your touch…" Endlessly he whispered as he kissed over her neck and shoulder. Darcy was a verbal lover, Lizzy had discovered to her delight. Unless his mouth was otherwise occupied, he generally was expressing words of love and pleasure. It was enormously stimulating, Lizzy found, for both of them. Lizzy tended to principally remain silent and had asked him if this dismayed him in any way. Darcy had smiled and laughed lowly, grasping her cheeks as he replied, "Oh, my lovely Lizzy, you are not the least bit silent when we make love. You moan and sigh and gasp and articulate the most amazingly sensual sounds, all unwittingly in response to me. Then, invariably, you cry my name. You need say nothing else for me to know how profoundly I have moved and gratified you."

Such was the case now, as her incredible husband murmured love while arousing her body with an infinitely perfect touch. For a blissful period of time, they loved as they stood, finding that no place was beyond acceptable for the passion which raced through them. In time, Darcy halted, pulling her hard against his heaving and trembling chest. "My love," he rasped, "come to our bed so I can love you face to face." He inhaled shakily. "I would carry you, but I do not trust my strength."

Lizzy pivoted in his arms with a sigh, capturing his mouth with a hungry urgency and stepping toward the door. Thus entwined and kissing voraciously, they slowly reached their intended destination. Lizzy discarded his encumbering robe, baring all his flushed skin to her seeking strokes. Darcy preferred to keep her gown on, experiencing one of those times when her partially and gauzily draped form whetted his appetite. He sat her on the edge of their bed, kneeling on the floor amid her parted legs.

They allowed a moment to calm and gaze at each other, visually feasting on the beauty to be found in the other's body. Darcy ran light fingertips all over her, admiring and worshipping, but especially thanking God for bringing her into his life. Lizzy kissed sensitively over the colorful contusion to his left chest, palms brushing up and down his back, across derriere and hips.

Lizzy smiled, meeting his intensely blue eyes. "Bruised and beaten, you are still stunningly gorgeous, my husband, my lover. How handsome you are, William! Hard, muscular, skin so soft and fair, your hairs exquisite under my hands," she caressed up his chest to his neck as she said, "straight shoulders and your neck, I love your neck! I do not know why exactly, but I think it my favorite part of you, although that is impossible to pinpoint." She finished with a laugh, pulling him to her lips as she fell onto the bed.

Darcy wasted no time returning to the warmth of her body. They kissed fervidly between pants and gasps of pleasure. Lizzy clutched his shoulders, squeezing mindlessly and causing Darcy to release a muffled cry of pain.

"Oh William, I am so sorry! Are you…?"

He shook his head and smiled, only momentarily faltering in expressing his ardency for her. After a dynamic period of amatory delight, Darcy rose up, smoothing hair from her perspiring, rosy face. "Mrs. Darcy, I adore you," he huskily whispered. "More than my life, I love you and always shall." He kissed her lips, loving totally until both were overcome with flaming sensations.

As he shuddered and fell to rest his head on her chest with unsteady respirations, Lizzy laced fingers through his hair, fighting for oxygen as well, yet contented and trembling with bliss. In time their breathing slowed and Darcy kissed her breasts, lifting to gaze into her glazed brown eyes. She smiled, reaching to feather over his face.

"I love you," she said simply.

"I love you," he answered back, smiling as he kissed her. "Every time with you, my heart, is better than the last. Is this possible?"

"Our love grows, dearest. I suppose it is a reflection of that."

Darcy stood shakily then flopped onto the bed, drawing her into a tight embrace. Lizzy nestled as close as feasible, inhaling deeply of his male aroma that was augmented deliciously by love-induced sweat. She delicately fondled him, reveling in the afterglow of their rapture and so exhilarated to simply be near him. She kissed his chest. "I wish we could stay like this all day. Rest for a spell then make love again, eat a bit then make love more. I think I could happily remain in your embrace for all eternity, endlessly touching and arousing you." She giggled then looked up into his sparkling eyes. "See what you have done to me? Hopelessly wanton and amorous."

"How terrible for me," he grinned. "What shall I do with you?" Twining his fingers through her hair, he drew her in for a lingering kiss.

"You must grant me whatever I wish," she replied saucily once he released her. "Your vows demand it!" He merely chuckled and did not answer except to kiss her forehead and squeeze tighter. Lizzy fingered over his bruised chest. The colors were amazing and Lizzy, no stranger to bruising herself, was impressed. The feeling, circulation, and strength to his arm had been restored completely. It was the shoulder and upper arm that yet pained him. Lizzy speculated it was undoubtedly from the severe wrenching when Athena reared rather than the impact with her hoof. The chest area itself was only mildly painful, as typical with a serious contusion. "You will ask your uncle to examine your injury as soon as possible, will you not, beloved?"

Darcy nodded. "I will. In all honesty, I am anxious to hear his opinion. It does hurt more than I expected it to after so many days, which concerns me somewhat." He studied her anxious eyes, wiping away the tears that readily sprung. "I was not evading when I told you I have suffered worse, love. Once, when I was seventeen, I was thrown and my heel caught in the stirrup. I was dragged only a few feet, but my thigh muscle was strained terribly. I could not bear weight for a whole week, which drove me and every servant in the manor nearly insane." He laughed in memory, softly caressing her face. "I am not a complacent patient, my dear. Your moments of pique during your convalescence were sweet compared to mine."

He turned to his side, caressing over her skin with a heady sigh and penetrating gaze. "You are so beautiful, Elizabeth," he said dreamily.

"We were discussing your body, Mr. Darcy, not mine."

"Yours is profoundly more interesting, my love." He nestled into her neck for gentle nibbles, and speaking lowly, said, "I have been bruised and sprained so many times I have lost count. Not to mention the scrapes, lacerations, and twice broken bones. In the end, I think sprains are the worst in that only time mends them." He met her eyes with a smile. "I told you I had a reckless youth. My uncle may know a different treatment to speed recovery, as he learns varied techniques from the cultures he lives with. He travels all over the Far East—not just in India where he now resides—always learning. The man is insatiable. His thirst for knowledge exceeds mine tenfold, if that gives you any indication of the breadth of his wisdom."

All during his monologue, Darcy had been intermittently kissing his wife and fondling gently, Lizzy trying to attend diligently to his words. He stroked over her abdomen, pausing at the swell of their baby, hoping to feel movement to no avail. Continuing on with titillating manipulation, he lovingly adored his wife, proving yet again his ardent desire for her and astounding potency and masculinity.

"I have rested, my lover, and am perfectly willing to fulfill my vows as you requested," he whispered huskily with a naughty leer.

Lizzy opened her mouth to flash a smart retort, but at that moment the mantle clock chimed nine o'clock. They both glanced over then returned their gazes to the other, Darcy never relenting in his stimulation.

"Breakfast will be served soon, Fitzwilliam. We should rise and dress. I do not think—" She gasped, closing her eyes briefly in pleasure. "Beloved, there is not time…"

"There is always time to love you, my wife," he firmly proclaimed, pulling her body onto his front side, "always time." Then, he halted any further argument with a persuasive kiss—not that Lizzy had any desire to argue.

Mr. Joshua Daniels arrived promptly at two o'clock, adding punctuality to his growing list of virtues. Darcy opted to stay home despite several business needs, both to act as chaperone and to await his uncle's appearance. He worked all morning in his study, listening attentively for the door chime, while the ladies meticulously planned the tea. Mary thought them all slightly mad at the attention to detail, yet was embarrassingly pleased by the fuss.

Mary was beautiful in the gown Georgiana had lent her. It was a solid deep blue with a faint metallic sheen subtly woven in, the cut simple and temperate, although Mary's fuller figure did stretch the bodice beyond true modesty. She resisted Marguerite coifing her hair, insisting on pulling it back into a basic chignon and relenting only in wearing a clip of tiny pearls. Lizzy deliberately rearranged the parlor with a small table and two chairs positioned off to one side, close enough for the other occupants to converse and offer support yet separate enough to allow the young couple to talk quietly together. Darcy had stood insolently leaning against the doorjamb, grinning humorously as Lizzy ordered footmen about like a general planning a military campaign. He extended the occasional quip and droll suggestion but was essentially ignored, Lizzy finally commanding him to "go do something useful."

An array of edible delights had been concocted by the excellent kitchen staff for the tea, and Darcy even joined the group initially, though adding little to the general conversation, his wife being far more adept at orchestrating flowing communication. Correctly assuming that his dominating and severe presence would hamper full relaxation, Darcy shortly excused himself, pleading a pile of work on his desk, which was the truth.

Lizzy was impressed by Mr. Daniels's general ease. He was mildly nervous, but conversed effortlessly on numerous subjects. Following a predetermined agenda, Georgiana and Kitty excused themselves, leaving Lizzy to play chaperone from a chair in the far corner. With head bent diligently over her embroidery, Lizzy surreptitiously observed her sister.

Mary said little during tea, interjecting with the occasional comment, but allowing the others to lead. Despite the fact that Mary was her sister, Lizzy could not well ascertain the thoughts behind Mary's calm demeanor. Now, with just the two of them relatively alone, Mr. Daniels visibly relaxed and Mary slowly opened up as well. Lizzy noted that their dialogue steadily continued with the appropriate amount of smiles, eye contact, and soft laughs.

"How are you enjoying your stay in Town, Miss Bennet?"

"Tremendously. But I will confess that the noise and diminished fresh air is bothersome to me. I have lived all my life in the country, so the environment of the city is odd. However, there is certainly no lack of entertainment."

"Have you never been to London?"

"Infrequently, and not for a number of years. My aunt and uncle dwell in Cheapside, so we visit from time to time; however, my parents are not fond of Town. I must say I have been surprisingly pleased at how enjoyable my sojourn here has thus far been."

"I imagine the Darcys have taken the opportunity to show you many of the sights to be had? The theatre, opera, museum, and the like?"

Mary nodded. "Yes, although it is a vast area with far too many wonders to absorb in three weeks. I have yet to visit the museum, although my sister did and thought it marvelous. Do you appreciate history and ancient cultures, Mr. Daniels?"

"Absolutely. As I pointed out when we met, I am a scholar. Difficult to pull my nose out of a book, to the supreme amusement of my eldest brother, who is the consummate outdoorsman." They both laughed, then he cleared his throat nervously before resuming, "Perhaps, Miss Bennet, providing it is of interest to you and meets with the approval of the Darcys, you would consider accompanying me to the British Museum? Properly chaperoned, naturally. One should not tarry in London without touring the Museum. It would be a sin." He finished with a small smile.

Mary raised her brow, initially unsure if he was serious. With a careful study of his artless countenance, she recognized the jest. "I am not quite certain I agree with it necessarily entering the same realm as sloth and gluttony; however, I will concur that it would be a terrible shame."

"Excellent! By the way, how much longer will you be in Town? After all, there are many other wonders to behold, all of which I would be delighted to show you."

Mary was peering at him intently. "Mr. Daniels, you barely know me. Perhaps you should not be so swift to offer your time and person."

He flushed slightly, startled and discomfited at her bluntness. One look into her eyes though, and he realized it was one of the attributes he liked about her and had sensed immediately. She was honest, forthright, and humble. He leaned forward, meeting her frank gaze. "Miss Bennet, it is precisely because I barely know you that I wish to pass as much time as possible with you. My time is short ere you depart, and I very much desire to utilize the time granted me to improve my knowledge of you."

"Why?" She was frowning mildly, gazing at him intently. With a sudden jolt, he perceived that the question was asked with true perplexity and curiosity.

"Miss Bennet, I shall be completely blunt and honest and beg your pardon if I cross a line in some manner; however, I sense you are requesting a candid response." He paused, awaiting her favor until she nodded. "I feel drawn to you in a way I do not totally understand, yet there it is. I have never felt so inclined toward another. What this connection bodes for the future, I do not know. You are pretty, intelligent, honest, proper, and many other fine qualities I believe I could list without hesitation. I think it entirely probable you and I would be perfect for each other. It is my intention to discover if this is possible. I do not wish to trifle with your emotions, nor do I wish to have my own sensibilities manipulated; therefore, if you cannot imagine even the remotest chance of returning affection, tell me now and I shall abide by your pleasure. On the other hand, if you sense, even vaguely, a returned interest in me, then let us proceed with willing minds and hearts."

Mary remained silent for a bit, studying his guileless face. Her thoughts rushed. Mary was a simple, innocent young woman, unaware of the fact that what was passing between them was highly improper in its frankness. A true society woman would faint away at being addressed so boldly by a gentleman. Mr. Daniels knew this and anticipated her reply with bated breath; fearful of having spoken too candidly and thus frightening the first woman he had ever been truly drawn to. Yet, Miss Bennet appeared not the least bit frightened or shocked, merely intrigued.

With a small smile she said, "Very well, Mr. Daniels. With open minds and hearts, we shall proceed. Now, tell me exactly what a solicitor's duties are." And with a casual sip of tea, she turned the conversation to mundane matters. Mr. Daniels smiled happily, then launched into a detailed accounting of his profession.

Lizzy sat across the room attending with extreme concentration to her needlework, in truth having completed perhaps ten stitches. She could not hear every word spoken between her sister and Mr. Daniels, but enough to glean the context. It was difficult to contain her smile. Approximately ten minutes later, Kitty and Georgiana returned via the arrangement, allowing Lizzy to dash to Darcy's study.

She told him everything, ending by teasing that he should have taken the time to acquaint himself with Mr. Daniels years ago, then perhaps he would have known how to be forthright with a woman. To which he replied that it no longer mattered, for now he had won his maiden's hand and forthright conversation was therefore not essential. Of course, Lizzy took umbrage and assaulted her husband with well-placed tickles, leading to kisses and intimate caresses that quite likely would have lead to further intimate activities, but the door chime interrupted them.

Quickly readjusting clothing, they hurried to the foyer, but rather than Darcy's uncle it was a representative from Tillbury's Carriages. With a broad beam Darcy grasped his wife's hand and followed the man to the street where Lizzy's curricle sat. Completed, it was more beautiful than Lizzy had imagined. Polished to a high sheen, metal and wood glistening in the bright sunlight, the curricle was exquisite. Lizzy had chosen a brocade of forest green with maroon and gold stripes for the cushions, elegantly coordinating with the glossy maroon enameled sides. The Darcy crest blazed in the sun. Again Lizzy was moved to tears, Darcy casually handing her his handkerchief while the man from Tillbury's rendered a full inspection for Mr. Darcy's approval.

Reentering the foyer while the curricle was being properly stowed for later delivery to Pemberley, they encountered Mr. Daniels and the girls approaching.

"Mr. Darcy, Mrs. Darcy," Mr. Daniels said, bowing. "I wish to thank you for allowing me to call upon Miss Bennet and for guesting me in your enchanting home. I have had a delightful afternoon."

Darcy bowed in return, formally welcoming Mr. Daniels to visit whenever he wished, which led to discussions of museums and picnics with Miss Bennet, Mary quietly standing nearby. Kitty giggled, reverting momentarily to her naturally giddy behavior, while Georgiana merely smiled sweetly. A state of moderate chaos reigned while Mr. Travers patiently waited by the open front doors with Mr. Daniels's overcoat and hat. No one was attending to the doorway itself, which is why the booming voice startled all of them into abrupt silence.

"I daresay, William, do you always host festivities in the grand foyer?"

All eyes snapped to the towering gentleman blocking the sunlight from his casual dominance on the threshold. It was Georgiana who first speared the oppressive silence with a squeal as she rushed into the arms of the lanky intruder, declaring with confident delight that it was Uncle George.

"Unhand me, woman!" Dr. Darcy mockingly commanded, with a wink to a broadly smiling Darcy. "It is not proper for a woman of breeding to embrace a strange man!"

"Uncle George! It is me! Georgiana!"

"Impossible! Georgiana is a grubby faced child with pigtails."

"I have never worn pigtails in my life!"

Dr. Darcy peered intently into his niece's face, the corners of his mouth twitching precisely as Darcy's did when attempting not to laugh. "Well, you do resemble her somewhat, although the Georgiana I remember did not have bosoms and curves. William, how could you allow this to transpire? Did I not instruct you to prevent her growing?"

Darcy spread his hands. "Unless you have discovered a potion to stunt aging, Uncle, I have no control over the matter."

George Darcy, a man of some fifty years, so resembled his nephew it was uncanny. They were of an identical height, although Dr. Darcy was far leaner, almost skeletal, with sharp angles at every joint. His eyes were the same brilliant blue, hair the same brown, though with streaks of gray at the temples and wavy where Darcy's was straight. His handsome face was a thinner, lined mirror image of Darcy's, with skin tanned bronze by the harsh desert sun. Instead of traditional English garb, he wore an impeccably tailored Indian Punjabi suit, consisting of churidar trousers and kameez tunic in bright turquoise with red trim and a tan sherwani richly embroidered with a rainbow of hues across the hem and over the long sleeves. The effect was exotic and beautiful.

Georgiana was beaming, far too ecstatic to be embarrassed by references to "bosoms and curves," tenderly gripped by her uncle's right arm as he surveyed the stunned occupants of the foyer. "Well, as my nephew appears to have lost his wits and well-honed English manners, I shall guess." He looked straight into Elizabeth's face with a friendly but piercing gaze all too familiar to her and stated assuredly with a proper bow, "Mrs. Darcy, I am certain. The combination of intelligence, long-suffering, and humor, all of which are of necessity to endure marriage to the man-child behind you, as well as the fact that you are obviously with child, mathematically compute. Congratulations, Mrs. Darcy, on your nuptials, and blessed tidings."

He bowed yet again, brushing her slack fingers with his lips, and then laughed a resonant chuckle identical to her spouse's. "Do not be so shocked, my dear. I am a physician. Your state is clearly written upon you." Still laughing, he glanced up at Darcy. "Congratulations to you as well, nephew. Despite the paralysis of your beautiful spouse, I am confident of my original assessment and am therefore relieved that you have chosen wisely."

Darcy laughed and bowed dramatically. "Thank you, Uncle George, on both counts." He stepped forward, clasping hands with his uncle who then enveloped him in a hug, Darcy wincing slightly but returning the embrace with enthusiasm. "Allow me. This is my wife, Elizabeth Darcy. Dearest, my uncle, Dr. George Darcy."

"Please, 'George' is what I prefer. I am on vacation, so the *doctor* has been left in India, although I will take a gander at that arm of yours, William, if you wish it."

"How did you…?" Lizzy blurted in surprise.

George smiled. "He flinched, grunted faintly, and did not grip as tight as he normally would have. Let me guess. A horse, William? Or have you taken up pugilism as well as dueling? Ah, there you are, Raja!"

All eyes now focused on the new arrival: a man in his mid-thirties of average height, stocky build, and swarthy, with coal black eyes and thick, curly hair as black as a starless midnight sky. He smiled, teeth gleaming ivory as he bowed. He too wore an outfit of traditional Indian style, although far more sedate and unadorned than George Darcy's. So dark was he that Lizzy thought he *was* Indian, but then he spoke. "Saludo. Greetings."

"Allow me to introduce my colleague Dr. Raul Penaflor Aleman de Vigo. His full name is far longer and I frankly cannot remember it all. A Spaniard, but do not let that influence your opinion! He is a good man and excellent physician—nearly as skilled as me! Is not that so, Raja?"

Dr. Penaflor flashed another dazzling smile. "As you say, George." His voice was rich with a heavy accent, his enunciation of "George" so altered as to be nearly indistinguishable.

Darcy stepped forward, exerting his authority as the Master of the manor to extend all the proper introductions. Mr. Daniels, with a last glance and nod to Mary, finally escaped. The rest retreated to the parlor, Dr. Darcy's robust timbre frequently ringing out with a witticism or comment. Lizzy understood why Darcy said his uncle reminded him of Richard Fitzwilliam. The two did have a similar easy humor and irreverence about them at odds with the seriousness of their professions. The comparable traits between Darcy and his uncle were as striking as their contradictory characteristics. Despite the aforementioned minor physical differences, there was no doubt to Lizzy she was catching an arcane vision of her husband in twenty years. Like his nephew, George Darcy missed nothing. His hawk-eyed gaze was piercing and showed his supreme intelligence, and his brows arched intensely, as did Darcy's, but with a profound softness at the edges, undoubtedly a result of ultimate empathy and daily dealing with suffering. Both men were quick witted, but George Darcy seemed utterly indifferent to the nuances of propriety and clever phrasing. He spoke eloquently but bluntly, not purposely offensive yet unconcerned with coddling one's sensibilities. Lizzy found it refreshing and liked him immensely.

Dr. Penaflor, in contrast, was reticent. When he spoke it was meaningful and succinct. Nonetheless, he sat in gentle repose with an amused lilt to his mouth, obviously highly entertained by his friend's banter and family felicity. When Darcy eventually submitted to an examination by his uncle, Lizzy hovering in nervous interest, Dr. Penaflor trailed along with clear professional curiosity.

Darcy related the event while Lizzy assisted the removal of his jackets and shirt. All traces of humor disappeared as Dr. Darcy and Dr. Penaflor bent over Darcy's left side. No words were spoken as George carefully palpated the chest and rib cage. He asked a few brief questions as he prodded, glancing frequently into Darcy's face.

"The bones are intact, although there is internal bruising of the cartilage over the print itself. I am surprised your breathing has not been affected. The bruising is as expected. Did you bring any leeches with you, Raul?"

"Leeches!" Lizzy exclaimed in horror.

Dr. Penaflor answered them both, "Unfortunately, no, George. Leeches reduce the bleeding and swelling, Mrs. Darcy, and inject substances that coagulate the blood and aid absorption. We do not know why, yet it works."

George had moved on to the left hand, testing each finger and Darcy's grip strength before feeling the pulses and then probing along each ligament and muscle as he traveled upward. Darcy displayed no ill effect until the upper arm and shoulder were touched. He winced and recoiled instinctively. George pursed his lips, gingerly proceeding with his inspection in miniscule increments, not overlooking an inch. He gently but purposefully rotated and lifted the arm in all directions, gauging the injury's intensity by the expressions of discomfort crossing Darcy's face as sweat beaded. Lizzy sat at his side and clutched his right hand, dabbing at teary eyes with his handkerchief still in her possession, bravely enduring his crushing grip.

Finally, Dr. Darcy ceased his examination. Lizzy wiped Darcy's perspiring, pale forehead while he offered the diagnosis. "As you figured, William, the muscles were torn a bit. Also, you have developed a nasty inflammation to the bursae. That, Mrs. Darcy, is not as horrid as it sounds."

Dr. Penaflor was already rummaging through his trunk of medical supplies, extracting several glass jars while George continued. "The bursae are the fluid pouches found in the joints and ends of muscles. With a serious tearing as you have suffered, William, those areas are damaged and become inflamed. Anyway, enough medical gibberish. Your treatment is twofold. We have several ointments which will decrease the inflammation and swelling, menthol and camphor primarily, so the odor will not be pleasant. Mrs. Darcy, you will need to massage a generous amount in each night, deeply into the tissue, as firmly as William can handle it. Keep the area wrapped and immobilized. Raul is very good at constructing comfortable straps if you have any extra fabric about, my dear, and will demonstrate how it must be. William, you are required to be a complacent patient and do all I say. Once the swelling is reduced adequately—as I deem it, not you—then I will show you some exercises to strengthen the muscles."

"How long?" Darcy asked.

"A week, perhaps two. If you comply, the recovery will be swift. Loving care is the key, and I think you have that in abundance," he finished with an affectionate smile to Lizzy, who had yet to relinquish Darcy's hand.

Lizzy accepted her nursing responsibilities seriously. Dr. Penaflor mixed the foul-smelling unguent and concocted several cushiony arm slings, instructing an avidly absorbed Lizzy in their use. Darcy, now recovered from his uncle's exploration, observed his wife's anxious study with a fond smile. Fortunately, his adoration was immense, because Lizzy so intensely enforced her duties she burst in on the gentlemen's revelry much later that evening, declaring with a firm voice and tapping foot that it was time for her husband to retire for his medicine. The three of them were more than slightly intoxicated, George winking broadly at Lizzy as he sent Darcy on his way with several observations about henpecked spouses.

Darcy submitted blearily to the massage, essentially feeling little pain. This mild anesthesia was to Lizzy's advantage, since she pressed harshly with strong hands, kneading deeply as instructed, the only deterrent to her treatment being the need to constantly slap her husband's seeking right hand. However, by the time she had him slathered and wrapped as a mummy, he gratefully sank onto the pillows and fell immediately asleep.

Lizzy lovingly observed his restful face for a time, eventually curling up alone on the far side of the bed. The combination of his pungent aroma and rumbling snores, activated, as always, when he imbibed excessively, precluded any snuggling—for this night at least.

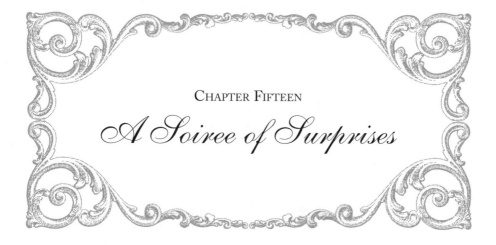

CHAPTER FIFTEEN

A Soiree of Surprises

DARCY WOKE LATE, CONFUSED and with heart pounding from a troublesome dream: He was bound to a post with thick ropes, unable to control any of his limbs, and having extreme difficulty inhaling deeply, with spasms pounding through his head and entire left side blazing. Meanwhile, his luscious wife performed an erotic, disrobing dance far across the room. His dream self was obscenely aroused, throbbing in agony with the need to join with her, yet he could not move and any effort to do so caused her to slip further away. The mingled torments of frustration, desire, and physical pain jolted him awake.

He was alone in their bed, sunlight streaming through the crack in the curtained window, marked physical arousal evident while his bound shoulder and arm weighed him down. "Elizabeth?" His voice cracked oddly with a note of hysteria, the unsettling dream still lingering about the edges of his consciousness and the combined pains a reality. "Elizabeth!" he called again, attempting awkwardly to rise without success. During the night, the carefully wrapped bandage had constricted further, preventing even the slightest mobility.

"Beloved, I am here," she replied, her voice floating through the sitting room door mere moments before she entered bearing a coffee-laden tray. "Stay still, love. I will help you up." Then she laughed at his appearance. "Apparently I was mistaken. You obviously need no assistance from me as you appear fairly 'up' already."

"Most amusing, Mrs. Darcy. Suffering from grievous injuries and hideous nightmares, yet she teases me. What happened to the doctor's prescribed tender loving care?"

"If nightmares elicit this response, I cannot fathom what sensual dreams inspire." She threw his robe off her shoulders, exposing her nakedness to greedy eyes with bed sheets fluttering from the response.

"Elizabeth, please do not toy with me! I need you, now!" Forcefully hurling the blanket aside so she could access his body, Lizzy straddled his thighs and attacked.

"Oh God!" he cried with an arch, moaning blissfully as his perfect wife worked magic. Quite adept after their months of experimenting with all aspects of lovemaking, Lizzy knew precisely how to stimulate her fabulous spouse. Her own passion escalated at the taste, aroma, sight, and sound of him. Even his fabric-swathed body with its lingering medicinal scent was insufficient to quench her excitement. It was crazy morning loving, their fiery passion rising to indescribable levels as Darcy's hurting miraculously dissolved.

All medicinal treatments unified over the following days, with Darcy healing rapidly as a young man vigorously in the bloom of health can do. He argued the prescribed trammeling of his arm fruitlessly but with minimal cogency, as the truth was it did help the pain.

The atmosphere inundating the house escalated dramatically with the arrival of George Darcy. His naturally extroverted and loquacious personality was on full display, heightened by the parade of visitors suddenly flooding the place in a desire to see him. Darcy attempted to concentrate on estate business, but rapidly gave up. He happily relinquished the endeavor for the time being in order to delight in his uncle's company.

The dinner party planned by the Darcys for the following evening was greatly anticipated. Darcy had sent a formal invitation to his Aunt Catherine and Anne, but had not received a reply. He and Lizzy had mixed emotions on their possible attendance, although primarily they discovered, to their mutual surprise, that they hoped for an appearance. Their desire was to place the rift in the past. Perhaps aspiring for a close relationship was misguided; however, they could seek relative peace.

Nonetheless, with the sudden addition of a gregarious and eccentric Uncle George, further speculation or worry over the de Bourgh situation was forgotten. Darcy hired an orchestra for an informal ball and ordered the polishing of the long disused ballroom until it gleamed from the hundreds of lights gracing the three chandeliers. Lizzy planned an exotic menu of unusual cuisines, augmented with enthusiasm by George and Dr. Penaflor, both of whom marched into the kitchen amid cries of dismay from the cook to whip up a couple Indian and Spanish dishes.

The guest list was small, or at least small compared to most London society soirees. Naturally, the Bingleys, Miss Bingley, the Gardiners, Colonel Fitzwilliam, and Lord and Lady Matlock attended. Also invited were the Drurys, both Vernor couples, Miss Bertha Vernor, the Lathrops, Fitzherberts, Sitwells, and Hugheses. Darcy had added a few of his other close friends from Town, along with Mr. and Mrs. Andrew Daniels and Mr. Joshua Daniels.

The general reception was held in the ballroom, the foyer far too humble in size, with the orchestra playing softly in the background. Dr. Darcy and Dr. Penaflor stood next to Lizzy, Darcy, and Georgiana for easy introductions. Lord and Lady Matlock, as well as Richard, were delighted to see George again, it having been years. Lord Matlock and George had known each other all their lives and were rapidly engaged in reminiscences and storytelling, to the amusement of all.

Darcy was seriously annoyed at the insistence of his wife and uncle that his arm remain bound. This required, in his opinion, not only the ludicrous exhibition of his coat sleeve dangling emptily and the handicap of managing one-handed, but also the wearying certainty of repeating the tale of his injury endlessly. He argued to no avail, the two only relenting in loosening the bindings enough so that he had limited use of his hand.

His vexation was mitigated by the overall festive atmosphere, the beauty and vivaciousness of his wife, and his excitement at the surprise planned for his beloved Elizabeth. He gazed at her, dressed exquisitely in a new white and silver gown, face radiantly glowing with mirth and health as she greeted the Vernors. For Darcy, these events have always been painful. The need to create idle conversation compounded by the pressure of the spotlight on him as host had prevented him from organizing anything grander than intimate family gatherings since becoming Master. Now, with the unequaled perfection that was Elizabeth Darcy as Mistress, his joy and enthusiasm for parties and social activities of all kinds had drastically altered. The truly amazing aspect of it all was that many other women would have made delightful hostesses but none with the innocent honesty, true grace, and artless pleasure of Elizabeth. Darcy was so overwhelmingly proud that he felt near to bursting.

He stood quietly by her side, greeting friends and family in his usual reserved manner, but a soft smile danced over his lips, widening appreciable every time Elizabeth laughed, which was often, or met his eyes. They remained close to each other, frequently touching in sweet communion. Over her shoulder, as she spoke softly with Harriet Vernor, Darcy noticed the Gardiners entering. His grin spread and he lightly caressed the small of her back.

"Dearest, your aunt and uncle have arrived."

Lizzy turned with a ready smile on her face, a smile that was instantly replaced by a dropped jaw and widened eyes. Darcy was laughing at her pleased astonishment, Lizzy pivoting for a quick embrace and kiss and whispered *I love you* before twirling about to dash into the arms of her father.

"Papa! I cannot believe it… Mama!" The wonderment multiplied by the sight of her mother's stupefied countenance as she peered about the ornate room from behind her husband. Lizzy embraced her goggle-eyed mother. Mrs. Bennet had not yet seen any of the Darcy homes and was clearly speechlessly impressed. Mr. Bennet had visited Darcy House during his daughter's engagement, remembering the library with special fondness, yet was amazed anew at the glittering opulence of the ballroom and surrounds. His amazement was increased by the casual elegance of his second daughter and the improved appearances of both Kitty and Mary, who were now approaching for hugs and kisses.

He gazed over his daughters, Jane and Mr. Bingley crossing the room as well, and addressed Lizzy, "Your husband bribed me with unfettered access to his library and port, so how could I refuse." He winked at Darcy. "Your mother needed only to hear the word 'shopping' and she was compliant. Quite the shindig, Lizzy. I am duly impressed."

"Perhaps, Papa, I can induce you to dance with me? As you can see, my usual dancing partner is crippled and you appear dressed for the occasion," Lizzy teased with a tug on his jacket.

Mr. Bennet, in fact, was dandified in a new suit tailored in the latest fashion, although he had refused long trousers clinging stubbornly to the familiarity of knee breeches. Lizzy had never in her life seen him dressed so finely. "I shall consider the matter, Lizzy. If I dance with you, I will likely be required to extend the courtesy to Jane, Kitty, your mother, and Mary, the last of which will probably make this young man irritated."

His amused eyes lit on Mr. Daniels, who was trailing Mary about as if physically tied to her. Of course, it was understandable to some degree, as Mary was stunning. Kitty and Georgiana had sufficiently nagged until Mary exhaustedly relented and agreed to wear the purple gown with woven wisteria. Mr. Daniels's eyes had literally bulged when he saw her, and the two were since inseparable. If Mary was in any way disturbed by his attention, it did not show. In fact, she was radiant, blushing prettily at her father's reference.

Introductions were extended all around, the flamboyant Dr. George Darcy joining the fray. Mr. Daniels boldly enforced his acquaintance on both Bennet parents, snatching at the fortuitous circumstance. The hubbub around the doorway was convivial and rowdy; therefore, it was several minutes before anyone noticed the newest arrivals.

"Lady Catherine de Bourgh! What a delightful surprise." Dr. Darcy's booming voice ruptured the tumult, silence descending suddenly as nearly every eye jerked to George and then the door. Lady Catherine stood placidly under the glare, Anne meekly at her side with head slightly drooping. Darcy immediately placed a hand onto the small of Lizzy's back, jointly stepped forward without hesitation to sequester the new arrivals near the elaborate lintel. He bowed regally before his aunt and cousin, Elizabeth at his side with an elegant curtsey.

"Lady Catherine, Miss de Bourgh. Welcome to Darcy House. Mrs. Darcy and I are pleased you have come." Darcy paused, waiting patiently for her acknowledgement.

"Fitzwilliam, thank you for the invitation. Darcy House is lovely. Reminiscent of the days when your dear mother was Mistress." She turned toward Lizzy, inclining her head. "I esteem the manor responds positively to having a woman in residence. Mrs. Darcy, I am willing to accept that my prior opinions were hastily reached, and perhaps I should apportion the time to amend this oversight now."

"'Perhaps,' Aunt Catherine?" Darcy said with a cold inflection and scowl, his free hand possessively about Elizabeth's waist.

"Fitzwilliam, you stated as much yourself, accusing me of not allotting the former Miss Bennet the opportunity to prove herself to me. In this you are correct and I confess to this being a fault on my part. Mrs. Darcy she may now be, and I do recognize this as an unalterable fact, yet should I not be given the chance to form my own opinion of your wife? Even if it is arrived at late and after extreme errors in my conduct?"

Darcy was glowering, not at all certain he wished to be reasonable when it came to any action remotely demeaning or judgmental on his wife. Lizzy sensed his rising irritation and spoke first. "Lady Catherine, Mr. Darcy and I wish to end this dispute and heal the rift. We are willing to bend to a degree. This invitation to our home was in an effort to accomplish this, and we are pleased you are here. If you feel you need to observe me to ease your heart, then do so with my blessing. However, I pray you do fully understand that your opinion ultimately matters naught to either of us."

"Furthermore, Aunt, your assaults on Elizabeth demand an apology which should be rendered, regardless of what your estimation of her may be. In addition, although I cannot fathom an opinion of my wife less than enthusiastically favorable, I will not tolerate a negative word uttered in this house. In that incomprehensible event, you will be escorted out and never welcomed again. Are we clear?"

"Perfectly, Fitzwilliam. Mrs. Darcy, I do apologize for my behavior both recently and in the past. I will not attempt to offer excuses and only pray you will forgive me."

Lizzy nodded. "Very well, Lady Catherine. Let us start fresh. Welcome to Darcy House." She glanced past her to Anne and curtseyed politely. "Miss de Bourgh, it is wonderful to see you again. William speaks so fondly of you, and I am overjoyed to have the opportunity to enhance our relationship."

"Thank you, Mrs. Darcy." Anne smiled shyly, glancing timidly at the array of bodies in the room. At the initial greetings, most in the ballroom had moved away, busily diverting their attention from the drama unfolding at the door. Lord Matlock and Colonel Fitzwilliam stood nearby, as did Dr. Darcy and Mr. Bennet. Lord Matlock smoothly apprehended his sister, with Colonel Fitzwilliam offering an arm to Anne, both men steering them away and performing the task of introductions.

"Interesting family intrigue," George stated with a chuckle. "One of the disadvantages of living a continent away is all the fun interpersonal dynamics one misses. Lady Catherine has always been fodder for a laugh or two." He breathed deeply and patted his chest with both hands, smiling broadly. "All I need now is food and dancing with a beautiful woman or two and life will be complete! Come, Mr. Bennet, let us see what we can scare up." Laughing, the gentlemen moved away, leaving Lizzy and Darcy in relative solitude.

Darcy was gazing intently into his wife's face, tenderly cupping her cheek while running his thumb over her smiling lips. "You were brilliant, my love. Are you well?"

Lizzy's smile widened. "I am perfect." She kissed his palm, encircling his neck with both hands and rising on tiptoes to brush his lips. "I have you. How could I be anything else? Now come, we have other guests to attend to. I am rather enjoying being Mistress!"

Darcy laughed, leaning for a kiss to her temple. "You should enjoy it since you are quite adept, as I knew you would be. I love you, you know?"

"I love you too, William."

Arm in arm, they rejoined their guests. Gerald and Harriet Vernor were talking with Stephen and Amelia Lathrop. Amelia was fast approaching the final two months of her pregnancy and planned to return to Leicestershire on the morrow for the remainder of her confinement. Lizzy was already saddened, especially knowing that with her own condition advancing, it would likely be months before they saw each other.

"Ah, Darcy! Excellent timing," Gerald Vernor said. "The ladies insist on discussing birth and infancy related topics. Lathrop and I are turning green over here, so rescue us before they move on to the riveting issue of swaddling cloths."

"Yes, by all means," Lizzy replied with an impish smile and wave of her hand, "move away, feeble men, and discuss something delicate such as hunting or boxing." Darcy and Lathrop blushed but Vernor winked, guiding the two toward another knot of men seemingly centered on an effervescent George Darcy.

The orchestra struck up a lively dance tune, the floor taken by several couples. Mary and Mr. Daniels, not surprisingly, were accompanied by the Hugheses, Colonel Fitzwilliam and Miss Bertha, several others, and, to Lizzy's amazed curiosity, Anne de Bourgh and Dr. Raul Penaflor. Lady Catherine sat beside Lord and Lady Matlock, scowlingly observing her daughter.

The mystery of Anne de Bourgh had, in all honesty, not overly interested Lizzy. Her stay in Kent had offered her few opportunities to talk to Anne, only enough to arrive at the conclusion that the sickly young woman was polite but rather timid. Darcy spoke fondly of his cousin, mostly regarding their childhood antics. Lizzy gathered that Anne had been healthy as a youth, or at least Darcy intimated so. Lizzy had no idea what the illness was that rendered Anne pale and listless. Suddenly, Lizzy felt shame for not having taken the initiative to inquire as to the history involving Darcy's cousin, but any mention of the name "de Bourgh" educed the infamous Darcy glower.

She observed her now with inquisitiveness. Anne wore a dark green gown of an older style that completely covered every inch of her skin, only her blood-less, pinched face visible. She was pretty, with a slim figure, lovely brown eyes, and curly black hair. Her pallor was a sharp contrast to the dusky-hued Dr. Penaflor. Little in the way of words was exchanged as they danced. Surprisingly, the frail Anne managed the dance easily and with a natural grace. A faint flush rose on her cheeks, although whether from the exertion or touch of her partner Lizzy could not ascertain. When the dance ended, Dr. Penaflor escorted Anne to her mother's side, bowing with cultured finesse and brushing her fingers with his lips. Lady Catherine glared, though the physician remained unperturbed as evidenced by the dazzling smile sent her way before he retreated.

Lizzy hid a laugh as she meandered through the room, engaging her guests in easy conversation, eventually reaching Darcy's side. He stood with his Uncle George, Richard, and Lizzy's parents. Dr. Penaflor was now dancing with Kitty.

Lizzy linked arms with her spouse but addressed the doctor. "Your friend is apparently intent on squiring each young maiden in the room, Dr. Darcy."

George laughed. "Yes, that would be Raja. Raised with courtly manners, he would deem it his duty. Although I judge his interest in Miss de Bourgh is primarily professional."

"What do you mean, Uncle?"

He waved his hand dismissively. "One of the side effects of being a diag-nostician. We never can fully push our instincts aside. We were both curiously discussing what treatment she is on for her anemia. Do you know, William?"

Darcy, however, was staring at him in total bafflement. "I fear, Uncle, I do not understand. The physician my aunt employs has determined it to be a heart condition."

Dr. Darcy raised a brow, apparently an inherited Darcy gesture when perplexed. "A heart condition? That seems unlikely. Of course, I would need to examine her fully to be certain, but she is pale, not cyanotic or breathless, nor is there obvious evidence of edema." He was frowning as he muttered, studying Anne as she sat across the room, fingers twitching over his lips.

Lizzy found the whole episode intriguing, not only Dr. Darcy's unconscious gesticulations so akin to her husband's, but also the references to Anne's affliction. Darcy was watching his uncle with interest and a glimmer of hope.

"I have long encouraged Aunt Catherine to seek an alternate opinion. Do you think you could help her, Uncle George?"

Dr. Darcy shrugged. "I know of several tonics as well as natural remedies for anemia, if that is her ailment. Heart diseases are difficult. Far too many variables. I have seen some success with the distillation of digitalis. Hmmm… The question is your Aunt Catherine. She never cared for me. I am too outrageous and improper," he declared in Lizzy's direction with a grin. "You are not the first to earn her disfavor, my dear."

"How comforting," Lizzy murmured sarcastically.

"Dr. Darcy, pardon me, but what did you mean by Dr. Penaflor raised with courtly manners?" Mrs. Bennet asked, a keen glint in her eyes.

"Raul Penaflor, Mrs. Bennet, is the third son of a Spanish Duke, and his mother is one of many royal sisters to King Ferdinand. It is all rather a jumble of intermarriage intrigue that exhausts me, frankly."

Mrs. Bennet's eyes had opened widely, and she was peering at Kitty and Dr. Penaflor as they completed their dance with unveiled calculation. Lizzy coughed a laugh, turning slightly to hide her face into Darcy's sleeve as Mrs. Bennet continued. "How very interesting! Has he a grand inheritance then? Or perhaps a family income?"

Dr. Darcy smiled innocently at Mrs. Bennet. "They have not disowned him, Mrs. Bennet, if that information profits you. Raja, however, is apathetic regarding his lineage and rank. I tease and call him 'raja,' which is *prince* in Hindi, yet he is indifferent. Healing is all that truly matters to him."

Mrs. Bennet was obviously saddened at the news and chose to ignore Dr. Penaflor thereafter. The evening progressed with all in attendance enjoying themselves immensely. Lizzy danced twice, once with Colonel Fitzwilliam and then with George Darcy. Primarily, she stood happily by her husband, the two randomly conversing with all guests equally. Occasionally, she sensed Aunt Catherine's eyes boring into her, but essentially, she ignored the woman, far too delighted in the evening's gaiety to be irritated. Darcy was in a felicitous mood, smiling incessantly and laughing often. Even his trifling annoyance at his bound arm was insufficient to dampen his spirits.

Dinner was a success, Aunt Catherine and a couple others the only members to express repugnance at the exotic cuisines. Lizzy sat to Darcy's right, ready to assist him if necessary, but he managed proficiently without moving his left arm beyond the proscribed degrees. Lizzy had quickly rearranged the seating assignment so that Anne de Bourgh sat next to Dr. Raul Penaflor and quite far from her mother. She also rapidly ensured that her parents sat close to Mary and the Daniels family. Lady Catherine sat on the far side of Lord and Lady Matlock, near Darcy and Elizabeth. This, too, was on purpose. If Lady Catherine wished to "observe" Lizzy, then she would encourage the action.

All in all, it was a lively gathering. Food and wine flowed in abundance, the entire meal lasting several hours. Lizzy was amused to note Lady Catherine ingesting a vast quantity of red wine, becoming cheerful and borderline animated as the meal progressed. The Darcys shared many an entertaining glance and whispered comment, not to mention the typical loving touches that were now so natural and essential to their existence that they hardly noticed them any longer.

The largest shock of the evening came as they said their farewells to their guests. Lady Catherine approached with a shyly smiling Anne. She was a bit unsteady on her feet, yet appeared in control of her faculties when she grasped Elizabeth's hands. Peering intently into Lizzy's eyes, she spoke clearly, "Mrs. Darcy. I regret my prior actions. I may not fully approve of how Fitzwilliam went about choosing his bride, but I can no longer deny his... affection for you and yours for him. He is happy. Any fool can see that. Tonight's event has proven to me conclusively not only this fact, but also your excellence as Mistress. Thank you for the invitation. Understand that you are always welcome at Rosings Park."

Finally alone, weary yet jubilant, Lizzy sat astride Darcy's lap as she firmly massaged the medicinal ointment into his shoulder. They talked quietly, comparing notes and laughing in remembrance. Darcy endured the massage, expressing clearly how he intended for the evening to end.

"How am I ever to manage fulfilling my nursing duties each night if you distract me so, Mr. Darcy?"

"Am I distracting you, beloved? So very sorry. Perhaps you should give me what I want so I shall no longer disturb you so." His muffled voice rose from the vicinity of her bosom.

"Fitzwilliam," she began hoarsely, grip faltering yet again.

He pulled her into his chest, kissing lustily as he rolled to the side with her pinned beneath his body. "Such an excellent Mistress as you, Mrs. Darcy, deserves to be rewarded in a most satisfying way. I believe I know exactly what you shall find most satisfying."

Lizzy gasped in pleasure, yet attempted one last time to forestall his raging amorousness, "William, we should at least bind your arm..."

"Damn my arm! I love you, Elizabeth, and I have wanted you all evening. No longer shall I wait to love you, my wife, my heart and soul. Kiss me, my Lizzy!"

She did, wholeheartedly. They loved blissfully and, indeed, most satisfyingly.

CHAPTER SIXTEEN

Return to Pemberley

THE DAY IN MID July when the Darcys were to return to Pemberley dawned fair with the promise of extreme heat. Darcy woke even earlier than usual, the sun barely cresting the tops of the buildings surrounding Grosvenor Square. The bedchamber remained sunken in deep shadows, the drawn curtains effectively blocking the faint rays of light. Darcy lay comfortably in that hazy realm between sleep and full wakefulness. Elizabeth lay with her head nestled perfectly in the bend of his shoulder and chest, the remainder of her lovely body pressed firmly into his with one leg draped over him. Her steady respirations indicated her sleeping state.

Darcy smiled drowsily and pulled her closer, softly stroking her hip. The prospect of being home filled him with bliss and peace. This sojourn in London, although of less duration than usual, had without any doubt been his most satisfying in recent memory. The reason was all wrapped up with the woman he held in his arms… his wife. Each event attended, soiree or ball danced at, and conversation engaged in had transcended all past ones. In addition, he had managed to conclude all pressing business, paving the way for another long tarriance in Derbyshire.

His happiness was almost frightening in its intensity. That small pessimistic part of his subconscious occasionally reared up, invading his joy with a stab of fear. His heart would clench, breathing increase, and skin cool for brief moments, all evaporating the second she looked into his eyes or laughed her sparkling laugh. He simply could not harbor anxiety in a soul so utterly invaded with love. Is that not what the Scriptures taught? Light drives out all darkness? She was his light, his lover, his breath and heartbeat, his soul.

He yawned and stretched slightly, not wishing to wake her. It was very early and, once again, they had entered their bed late. His greatest concern lately had been her health. While his arm healed and strength increased, Elizabeth had grown paler, with tiny lines of weariness appearing about her fine eyes. It was the endless agenda of visitations and parties in which she insisted they partake. Despite his assurances to the contrary, she yet fretted over his societal responsibilities and continued to foster a residual need to prove herself to both him and the ton. It angered him and they had argued over it, but she could not be swayed.

Recognizing that his irritation and attempts at logic merely wore on her already fragile emotions, he turned in frustration to his Aunt Madeline. She encouraged him to surrender and allow Elizabeth to follow through on what she perceived as her responsibility to him.

"Elizabeth is far stronger than you give her credit, William. She is well, and the child is well. She needs to do this to feel wholly competent as Mistress and Mrs. Darcy. Soon you shall be in Pemberley without the demands on your wife. In the end, this time to dazzle society and win their approval will benefit her heart and mind. Quit playing the mothering hen, and leave her be. Do not attempt to comprehend her emotions because she is a female and you will not succeed. Instead, trust me and trust her. Your wife loves you, William, and does this for you, however misplaced you deem it. Show your appreciation and quit harping!"

Thus, he had done so, as difficult as it was. His relief at the prospect of being surrounded by the solitude of Pemberley was a tangible thing; however, he could not deny that Elizabeth *had* dazzled the ton, far beyond what he had expected. His pride in her had grown profoundly. She was amazing in all ways and he loved her deeply for the extents she had gone to for him. Once he figuratively stepped back and allowed her free rein, it further stunned him at the breadth of her nearly inexhaustible stamina and shrewd assimilation of society's mores. She was always perfectly groomed, always witty and lively, remembered all names and gossipy facts gleaned, was suitably serious or humorous depending on the situation, never remotely overstepped the boundaries of propriety, and never once forgot that she was Mrs. Darcy of Pemberley. In all situations she shone, yet in a way that placed the spotlight equally on both of them.

If all that was not enough, she heightened his love and respect by always supremely placing his needs and desires first. She met his hungry passion with equal fervor, devoted time to be with him, and proved daily, in the minutest details, just how boundless her love, adoration, and appreciation. The unique methods she devised to demonstrate her love amazed him. For instance, each meal taken at home included at least one of his favorite dishes. In fact, lemon-flavored desserts in dozens of varieties had so frequently been served that he was nearly to the point of desiring to never see a lemon for the remainder of his life. Not that he would dream of revealing this to her.

There were the little gifts she purchased for him whenever she wandered near a shopping district; the fresh cut flowers daily placed by her hand in his dressing room; the household duties she flawlessly assumed that, in turn, freed his time; the spontaneous massages to his feet or neck, shoulders or back; the tea or cocoa or brandy she brought to his study while he worked; and the notes she secreted in one of his pockets whenever he left the house. The first time she had done this, the third day after arriving in London, he had discovered the folded piece of parchment while in a meeting with Mr. Andrew Daniels. The note was brief, but contained an explicit reference to a particular part of his anatomy, raising a brisk flush to his cheeks and causing Mr. Daniels to inquire after his health! Some of the notes simply said "I love you" or something equally romantic, some were humorous or contained a short sonnet, others were extremely intimate or downright erotic. He never knew what to expect. His favorite was the one which merely had an imprint of her perfectly pursed and luscious lips. All of them now resided in his third box of Elizabeth-related mementos.

Darcy smiled into the fading light, turning to plant a tender kiss to her head as he sighed. *God, how I love her!* He captured a clump of her scattered hair, running it through his fingers and bringing it to his nose to inhale her scent. Lavender, as usual, and soft as silk. Seven months plus they had now been wed. Such a short amount of time, really, in the larger span of one's entire life. Yet, for both of them, it was as an eternity while also seeming like a mere day. They knew each other so intimately, their faults and virtues revealed in total, and they were connected on a visceral level; nevertheless, they still were daily stunned at how tremendously they desired to understand even more of each other. Not merely physically, although their ardor certainly was intense, but in even the tiniest ways. Simply to be in the same room was bliss.

Darcy turned slightly, gently drawing her even closer. He could feel the firm swell of their child pressing against his hip. Three times now in the past week Lizzy had felt the baby push into her hand. Each time she had dashed to wherever he was; the last time had occurred just the day before while he was in his bath. Samuel had started, almost dropping the bucket of water onto Darcy's head, but recovered quickly. He was quite used to these sorts of interruptions now and exited hastily, neither of them noticing. Darcy had intently and patiently waited, but the baby did not cooperate. His disappointment was acute. He would never admit it, but he had moments of serious pique thinking it monumentally unfair that Elizabeth was the only recipient of these marvelous sensations when he was equally responsible for the child's existence!

He sighed again and closed his eyes, attempting to recapture sleep, although he knew it was fruitless. He ached to be home with an urgency only once matched, and that was when they were first married. The reasons were similar: He wanted to be alone with his wife. Darcy jested about being a selfish man, yet it was banter based partially on fact. He selfishly wanted her all to himself without the endless demands of work or society. Before they knew it, the baby would be born, and as anxious and excited as they were, the reality is that life would drastically change. These next few months, to his reckoning, must be treasured.

Sadly, their complete solitude would not commence quite yet. Charles and Jane would be traveling with them and planned to stay for at least two weeks, possibly more. The Bingleys wished to examine the Hasberry Estate, and Elizabeth expressed the desire to spend quality sister time, the two having had few occasions over the past weeks to be alone. If all went according to the Darcys' hopes, the Bingleys would be settled in Derbyshire by winter. Caroline Bingley had somehow insinuated herself into the invitation. Darcy was not at all pleased, but, as Charles was his dearest friend, he had grit his teeth and succumbed.

Mary was to stay with the Gardiners for a spell, the courtship with Mr. Daniels progressing at a steady pace, but Kitty would be joining the Darcys for a few weeks. Georgiana was in tears at leaving Mary behind, but the friendship with Kitty had finally blossomed, and allowing her to join the entourage traveling to Pemberley eased Georgiana's unhappiness.

Dr. Penaflor and Uncle George planned to stay in London for an additional week or so before traveling to Pemberley in time for the Summer Festival. How long they intended to stay in England was a mystery. George was taking his "vacation" quite seriously, refusing to discuss timetables or pinpoint agendas with any degree of accuracy. Darcy smiled and chuckled lowly. In truth, he was delighted with his uncle and Raul Penaflor, both men welcome to stay forever if they wished it. The combined persuasion of every member of the family, aided by the insistence of Anne herself, had finally worn on Lady Catherine and she had allowed both doctors to examine Anne. The collaborating diagnosis was chronic anemia, to the near apoplectic rage of Anne's aged physician, who had screamingly abused both men with accusations ranging from quackery to witchcraft and more. Surprisingly, it was Anne herself who commanded a servant to physically remove the man, with Lady Catherine frozen in shock and at a rare loss for words. The remedies prescribed were primarily dietary in nature, with a regimen of herbal extract teas and a special tonic. How she would respond to the treatment remained to be seen, but Darcy was hopeful. He and Elizabeth formally invited Anne to Pemberley for the Festival, but definitive plans were yet to be made. Lord and Lady Matlock had taken the entire, "Anne Situation"—as they jokingly referred to it—under their jurisdiction.

Darcy began to sense the early tendrils of sleep retaking him, his wife's warm body and steady breathing lulling him into an extreme place of content-ment and relaxation. However, just as his mind clouded, a sudden, prolonged prod into the flesh of his hip jolted him into full wakefulness. His eyes flew open as paralysis consumed him so utterly that he ceased breathing and his heart abstained from pumping. The insistent poking continued with amazing strength, considering how small the extremity utilized. His son, as they had unconsciously began referring to the baby, apparently was displeased with being squeezed. Darcy realized he was grinning rather foolishly, and now his heart was palpitating. He slid his left hand carefully along Elizabeth's abdomen, until between his hip and the bulge, and pressed lightly. Evidently, his son was engaged in a bout of extended exercise, as he proceeded to punch, poke, and roll about inside his warm cocoon, all felt by a teary-eyed father.

It was some minutes of incredible soul-shattering joy before Darcy became aware that Elizabeth had woken and was staring into his face, smile brilliant and eyes watery. They simply stared for the longest time, no words necessary, not that Darcy would have been able to speak.

Finally, the baby tired and his movements ceased. The Darcys gazed with love and some other emotion too intense to name. Darcy left the swell of her belly, encircling her, hip to buttocks, as he inclined to her lips. "Elizabeth," he whispered, kissing slowly with indescribable tenderness, wet cheeks brushing over hers with tears mingling. Wordlessly, he traveled over her face, tasting their salty tears as he lingered over each precious feature, returning to her mouth only after adoring her face thoroughly. Still gently, he probingly penetrated her mouth, absorbing her essence as he gave of his own.

Eventually—no haste involved—he withdrew and met her eyes. Fingers feathered over her face as they studied each other, passion evident yet primarily veneration and happiness. "I love you, Elizabeth Darcy, with all my being," he said, his voice a husky whisper. "I cannot express how precious you are to me. The mother of our children. The wonder of the miracle inside of you moves me so profoundly." He kissed softly. "I never imagined…" his voice caught and he swallowed before resuming, "how blessed I am to have found you, my Elizabeth."

He kissed deeply then, rolling her slowly to her back while lightly caressing over her warm skin. With a beaming smile he left her mouth, traveling leisurely down her neck with moist kisses and nibbles. Lizzy yawned and stretched deliciously under his strong body, twining her fingers through his thick hair as he attended to her bosom with gentle caresses and kisses. Weaving idly down her torso, he eventually nestled between her legs with mouth pressing delicate pecks over her belly.

Lying flat, the small mound of their child nearly disappeared, with only a palm-sized hardness palpable below her navel. Darcy murmured nonsense over this evidence of their love, tickling Lizzy's skin so that she giggled and squirmed.

"What are you saying to him, love?"

"I am informing him that he has been gifted to the very best mother in the entire world. Also, I am reintroducing myself and thanking him for finally allowing me to feel him. If need be, I shall squeeze him several times a day. He can kick me whenever the whim takes him!" He glanced up into her mirth-filled face. "He is strong, beloved, as I knew he would be. No wonder you have been able to feel him for so long." He kissed her belly, then laid his cheek on top.

"How strange to love someone so small and yet unseen. You carry him, my heart, thus your love is undoubtedly stronger yet. It is such an amazing experience!" He began to turn his head but a sharp stab halted him.

As if in response to Darcy's voice and expressed devotion, the baby commenced a series of lazy pushes into his father's cheek. Darcy gasped, reaching quickly for Lizzy's hand to lie next to his cheek. Together they waited in silence as the tiny life exerted his individuality and vitality. In all the years and pregnancies that would follow—each of which were a miracle and cause for intense celebration, with Darcy and Lizzy never tiring of the simple wonder to be found in these internal movements—this first experience would eternally hold a special place in their hearts. Darcy wept silently without shame, so overcome that it was several minutes before he could think clearly. Lizzy rose slightly, grasping him in her arms and pulling upward until nestled snuggly in her embrace.

Tenderly and slowly they made love, passion cresting at a leisurely pace, yet intense and fulfilling as always. Afterwards, tingling and satiated, Darcy's body draped partially over Lizzy's while they dreamily caressed each other, they kissed softly and drowsily. "I love you, William," Lizzy whispered as sleep claimed her, Darcy mumbling the same as he too drifted into a blissful slumber.

❧

"I see it! Pemberley at last. Look, William!" Lizzy was bouncing on the seat as a child in her enthusiasm, Darcy laughing as he stroked her back.

"Yes, dearest love, I see it. Finally we are home."

The carriage proceeded slowly up the lengthy drive leading to the Manor, tall trees shading the gravel avenue and interspersed so as to offer glimpses of the River Derwent to the left. Lizzy had been literally on the edge of her seat for the past hour as familiar Derbyshire then Pemberley terrain came into view. The trip of two days had passed uneventfully. The Darcys led the small caravan in their carriage, followed by Georgiana, Kitty, and Mrs. Annesley in a second, the Bingleys and Caroline in the third, and last the servants. The massive quantity of luggage, far more than when they left Pemberley two months ago, was distributed between all four conveyances.

Lizzy sighed and turned to her husband with a bright smile. "You understand that I do adore Darcy House, but nothing can compare to Pemberley." She leaned into his chest, playing with the knots of his cravat and smiling sweetly. Brushing against parted lips, she whispered, "Tonight, my beloved husband, we shall stand on our balcony gazing at the stars over the valley. Then we shall make love in our bed in our chamber in our home and it will be fantastic, amazing, and beautiful. The perfect homecoming."

Darcy spoke hoarsely, "My love, you should cease or we will not be waiting until tonight, I can assure you!"

"Tsk tsk. What an impatient man you are, Mr. Darcy! No self control whatsoever."

"Who was it, Mrs. Darcy," he spoke breathlessly, "that lowered the shades on this trip because she wanted what only I can give? Hmm?"

"You certainly did not argue the treatment, my dear. Very well then, we both lack the most basic virtues of bodily control and discipline. What a pity. We must work on that."

"No, we shall *not* 'work on that,' my lover. When it comes to my desire for you, and vice versa, I never wish to rein in our impulses." He kissed her tenderly, smoothing a few loose strands of hair and retucking them into her coiffure.

"Thank you, dear. Am I presentable?"

He chuckled. "Oh yes, love, you are presentable. Beautiful. Perfect. Delicious." The carriage bumped over the cobblestones, drawing their attention away from each other. Moments later they halted before the grandly carved stone steps leading to the massive portico and front doors of Pemberley Manor. Mrs. Reynolds, Mr. Taylor, and Mr. Keith stood on the top steps, several footmen on the drive springing into action the second the carriage stopped.

Darcy assisted his wife from the carriage, glancing over to see the others exiting their carriages. Linking his wife's arm, they mounted the short stairs toward the smiling trio.

Mrs. Reynolds spoke first. "Mr. and Mrs. Darcy, we are so delighted to have you home. I have a light repast and tea waiting in the parlor, and all is prepared for the guests, sir. I took the liberty of preparing a couple's chamber for Mr. and Mrs. Bingley."

"Thank you, Mrs. Reynolds. That completely slipped my mind. Did you place Miss Bennet next to Miss Darcy?"

"Yes, sir. Miss Bingley I placed in her usual room, seeing no call to alter that. Is this sufficient?"

"Perfectly, thank you."

"Mrs. Reynolds, are the plans proceeding for the Festival as we had outlined?"

"Yes, Mistress. I have a detailed report on your desk. We can meet and discuss the particulars whenever you wish."

"Excellent. Tomorrow will be soon enough."

The others had alit and were climbing the stairs. Kitty's jaw had dropped, eyes sweeping the facade of the house rather than attending to her steps. Luckily, Georgiana was guiding with arms linked. Jane, naturally, was controlled in her surprise, yet Lizzy could tell she was impressed. With a broad smile, Lizzy grasped both her sister's hands, leaning in for kisses to their cheeks.

"Welcome to Pemberley! I am so happy to have you both here. Come inside and let me show you our home." Darcy smiled at Elizabeth's zeal, also noting Caroline Bingley's sour expression. Lizzy, thankfully, did not notice, already steering her sisters through the doors. Inside the grand foyer, Lizzy introduced them to Mrs. Reynolds and Mr. Taylor, assuring that they could be called upon for any needs. Then she proceeded to tour them about the enormous room, pointing to various objects and offering history and insight with a thoroughness that surprised them all, even Darcy, who had not realized the depth of her knowledge regarding the house. They followed Lizzy as she ascended the grand staircase, chattering as she unerringly led to the main parlor, settling with relief onto comfortable sofas and chairs.

"It is as you claimed, Mrs. Darcy; you have changed nothing."

"A few alterations here and there, Miss Bingley, but as I said, Pemberley is lovely as it is." She glanced up at Darcy, who was talking to Bingley as he poured a brandy from the sidebar. "I did redecorate my parlor, which I shall show you all later. I suppose next I must tackle the nursery and bedchamber, but that chore shall be a delight."

"Oh, I wish I did not have to leave!" Kitty moaned. "I want to help with the nursery."

Lizzy patted her hand. "There there dear. Perhaps we can do some shopping before you return to Hertfordshire. Also, you can offer any opinion you may have on furnishings. After all, I am a novice and could use all the advice available!" She laughed, smiling up at her husband who had rejoined the group.

Miss Bingley spoke, "Surely you intend to hire a professional for this, do you not, Mrs. Darcy? Infant requirements are so specific, I would imagine. Would it not be wise to allow the nanny and others to arrange the needs?"

"Thank you for your concern, Miss Bingley," Darcy replied in his firm voice, "however, Mrs. Darcy and I intend to educate ourselves fully. We will be proactive and wholly in charge of all aspects of our child's necessities. Jane, my steward informed me that the Hasberry Estate is still available, although there have been two seriously interested parties. He took the liberty of arranging an inspection for the morrow."

"Jane, dear," Bingley addressed his wife, "Darcy thought it wisest for us to meet alone with Mr. Greystone this initial time, man to man, so to speak. We can return the following day with you and Lizzy if the manor is acceptable."

"Whatever you think best, Charles," Jane replied calmly, but Elizabeth was frowning faintly.

"Excellent! Darcy and I will ride out there early then and perhaps..."

"Ride!" Elizabeth interrupted with a raised brow and harsh glance to her husband. "Your *physician*, Mr. Darcy, has ordered you not to ride as of yet."

"Pardon me, Lizzy," Bingley spoke quickly, "Poor choice of words. We shall take a phaeton and," hastily finishing at the look on her face, "I shall drive."

Jane smiled at her sister's concern. "How well do you know this Mr. Greystone, Mr. Darcy?"

"Somewhat. My father was more familiar as they were close in age. Tragically, Mr. Greystone never sired any children and his wife passed last year. I heard he plans to dwell with a sister who lives near London once he sells the estate. It is a lovely piece of property, Jane. I do believe you will find it more than adequate."

Lizzy clasped her hand in excitement. "Then, Jane dearest, you shall be nearby. I can reach you in my new curricle in no time at all!" She grinned up at Darcy.

"How is your injury mending, Mr. Darcy? It must be extremely disturbing to not be able to ride your horse. I know how very much you enjoy the activity," Caroline asked with a familiar smile.

"Nearly one hundred percent. I rather believe my personal physician is being overly cautious." He patted Elizabeth's shoulder and smiled into her eyes. "Nonetheless, I promised to obey the professionals, including my nurse. I have the remainder of my life to ride my horse, although it is undoubtedly sensible to avoid Parsifal just yet. He will not understand."

After dinner entertainment was blessedly brief, all individuals in varying states of weariness due to the long trip. Darcy and Lizzy entered their sitting room hand in hand and eager to be alone. The servants diligently managed to unpack the luggage and properly distribute most of the packages. However, they had been flummoxed as to what to do with the contents of the massive trunk which sat forlornly in the middle of the floor. Lizzy laughed, kneeling on the carpet to open the crammed trunk. Within were the presents that George Darcy had brought from India and further abroad.

Darcy sat on the chaise and began removing his boots while Lizzy rummaged inside. Mostly he had brought a stunning array of fabrics of a quality and color nearly impossible to find in England.

"Indian women," George had said, "are a bold people. The peasants even wear bright colors, but the wealthier wear elaborate weaves of silk." As he spoke he pulled yards upon yards of vibrantly patterned cottons and silks from the trunk, tossing them randomly at Lizzy and the girls. Then he proceeded to use a grinning and compliant Dr. Penaflor to demonstrate the numerous methods of draping a sari. Raul had posed and pranced while they all dissolved into hysterics.

Lizzy retrieved a particularly colorful silk, and with a flutter of her lashes toward her smiling spouse, draped it over her head. Apparently George had accumulated the odd assortment of gifts over a long period of time, some purchased and others given as payment for medical services. The trunk held a collection of exotic spices and teas; jewelry in an endless array of styles for fingers, toes, upper and lower arms, necks, ears and more in designs simple and intricate made from gold, silver, glass, ivory and copper; incense; engraved glassware; pottery; musky perfumes; hand-woven carpets and wall hangings; an exquisitely crafted silver tea set engraved with roaring tigers; pictures of Indian peoples and scenes both painted or created with tiny pieces of wood or glass or beads; and for Darcy, an English saddle constructed of camel skin with a superbly carved pattern of racing horses over sand dunes.

"We could redecorate an entire chamber as an Indian harem or some such. Perhaps one of the bedchambers, then we could charge for travelers to stay in Pemberley's exotic Far East Chamber of Passion!"

Darcy laughed, tossing his stockings toward the pile of shoes and wiggling toes as he stretched long legs. "Precisely the reputation I have been seeking. Excellent suggestion, Mistress Darcy."

Lizzy crawled on all fours over to the chaise, gaudy silk trailing over her back onto the floor in her wake. Spreading his legs, she rose to her knees and began untying the knots of his cravat. "Do you know what sounds delightful, my love?"

"I think I can hazard a guess," he murmured from the top of her head.

Lizzy smiled up at him. "A walk in the moonlight in our favorite garden. Remove your coats and I shall return in a moment." After a quick kiss she left, but did return within a few minutes with her hair loose and petticoat, stockings, and shoes discarded.

Barefooted and holding hands, they ducked behind a hanging tapestry several feet down the hall from their sitting room door, behind which was a servant's staircase. This hidden door and staircase was one of many throughout the manor that allowed the servants to ascend and descend unobtrusively and speedily from the kitchen and other basement chambers without disturbing the residents. Darcy had revealed this little fact of life causing his wife surprise a month or so after her arrival to Pemberley, when she had innocently commented on how she never saw the servants in the hallways, and how the footmen, especially, seemed to disappear as if by magic. To her amazed curiosity, this apparently was a typical design of large manors, and so common a fact that Darcy was stunned she had no knowledge of it.

This particular stairway led to the basement, naturally, but also to a small side door on the ground level that opened onto a private garden on the east side of the house. Darcy frequently utilized this route not only for the evening moonlit strolls, which for years have been a habitual relaxing pre-bedtime activity, but also as a way to sneak into or out of his study and thus the lower level rooms without encountering visitors.

One particular visitor whom Darcy had discovered an increased necessity to use the hidden stair and corridors around was Caroline Bingley. On five different occasions over the years, Miss Bingley had joined her brother, at Darcy's invitation, for a stay at Pemberley. Darcy's prior feelings toward Caroline were mixed. He had not disliked her in any great way, found her rather amusing at times in her arrogance and attempts to display her lacking intelligence, dull wits, and poor humor, and did honestly admire and appreciate her frivolous but inclusive knowledge of gossip and feminine trivialities, which did liven conversation. Of course, it had been readily apparent to him, despite his often retarded awareness of the machinations of the opposite sex, that Caroline had "set her cap" for him, as they say. Sadly for poor Miss Bingley, she was one woman he never remotely entertained the idea of courting. As time passed and her maneuvering became frantic, Darcy began to avoid her in any way possible. Naturally, this was problematical considering his close relationship with Bingley, and Darcy had attained a point of desperation in his annoyance. It was nearly brought to an eruption during his sojourn at Netherfield when he met Elizabeth.

Darcy had agreed to accompany Bingley to Hertfordshire, partially as a friend offering his business acumen, Bingley even then considering purchasing a country estate, but also as a way to avoid Caroline and her ilk in Town for a spell. He had no great desire for or interest in Hertfordshire personally, agreeing to the excursion only to please his friend. Imagine his anger when Caroline insinuated herself into the invitation, a fact he had not discovered until the very day they departed! Of course, there was nothing he could do at that point. Needless to say, between his vexation with her attitude and improperly blatant advances, growing affection and turmoil over Miss Elizabeth Bennet, and concern over his dearest friend falling in love again, the Netherfield trip was an agony on numerous levels. Darcy had never been so emotionally confused upon departing a place in his entire life.

The subsequent winter and early spring encounters with Caroline were distressing and blessedly few. Darcy was an emotional ruin and Caroline's mannerisms were no longer even mildly amusing. In a sad way, it was fortunate that Bingley's own state was a distraught one over the Jane affair, as the two men saw each other rarely in the months succeeding the autumn in Hertfordshire. Otherwise, Darcy was positive he would have exploded in a rage that likely would have severed their relationship permanently. By the time the Bingleys visited Pemberley for the summer, Darcy, grief ridden but at least restored to a state of semi-equilibrium, found that as long as he evaded Caroline as much as feasible without being shamelessly rude he managed well enough. Thus, the hidden stairway was utilized so extensively that the servants often forgot to even acknowledge their Master as he passed them by.

Caroline knew abstractedly of the existence of servant's passageways, but aside from having no intimate knowledge of Pemberley despite her bold assertions to the contrary, it also never would have occurred to her that a resident would employ them. Therefore, she could not fathom how it was that she consistently missed Mr. Darcy day after day considering her carefully arranged location at the second floor landing.

Upon Caroline's first ever stay at Pemberley, she requested the guest chamber located directly across from the top floor staircase. Mrs. Reynolds had prepared a chamber at the far end of the wing, a much larger room with a stunning view of the Peaks at sunrise and the River Derwent. The housekeeper was baffled when Miss Bingley instead requested the smaller room which faced the inner courtyard. She was not a fool, however, and it soon became obvious why Miss Bingley desired the room as she "inadvertently" accosted Mr. Darcy each morning when he descended for breakfast, and numerous other times throughout the day. Darcy was a bit sluggish on the uptake, and it actually required three visits before he figured out her manipulation and began regularly servicing the hidden passageway.

Now, Caroline was yet again residing in the first floor chamber. It was comfortable and spacious, as all Pemberley chambers were, simply not as grand as many of the others and allotted nothing in the way of a landscaped view. Caroline actually rather liked the room, having grown accustomed to it, but the irritation of being so ensconced, without the benefit of engaging Mr. Darcy in private albeit brief conversation and flirtation, was galling. Her aggravation prevented sleep so she quietly snuck down the hall to an east-facing chamber, thankfully empty, to sit on the wide window seat and gaze at the moonlight glimmering on the rippling waters of the Cascade Falls and family gardens.

With a sigh she rested her head against the cool stone, the window open with a gentle breeze blowing, and wondered for the hundredth time why she had asked Charles for an invitation. Yes, the season in London was over and anyone of any importance had escaped the oppressive heat of the city for their country abodes; nonetheless, there were always a few who remained for various reasons. Also, she had received a number of solicitations by her friends, including the sister of Sir Wallace Dandridge of Essex, a gentleman of moderate wealth and prestige who had shown a steady interest in Caroline for the past three seasons.

So, why was she here? Merely to torture herself? The truth is that Caroline could not say. For the past nearly two months she had frequently socialized with the Darcys, either in their home or the Bingley townhouse or at other venues, always avidly drawn to observing their interactions. Her stunned shock upon realizing the true nature of the love between the two had evolved into an intense curiosity vacillating between jealousy and covetousness. At times she hated Elizabeth for what she had with Mr. Darcy, yearning for it herself and persisting in a ludicrous sense of believing it stolen from her. Then she would smile internally at the happiness she witnessed on their countenances, especially the perpetually somber Mr. Darcy, with a gladness that bespoke of affection toward him that she had not realized she possessed. The concept of her being the fount of such joy in a man was a novel and appealing idea.

As these musings rambled through her brain, Caroline's attention was caught by movement on the grounds below. Illumination in the garden was cast by the nearly full moon and infinitude of stars, bathing the scene in relative brightness. Therefore, Caroline could clearly distinguish Mr. and Mrs. Darcy as the hand-holding strollers. In shock she noted that Darcy wore only his linen shirt and breeches, casual attire she had never seen him in, and that Elizabeth apparently wore no undergarments, as the outline of her legs was visible in the moonlight through her thin dress. A faint murmur reached her ears through the cracked window, but they were far enough below for the words to have no clarity.

Darcy and Lizzy wove leisurely via the flowering bushes to the bronze statue of Hercules fighting the Nemean Lion. Lizzy stepped upon the dais, placing her at eye level with Darcy. He paused, watching as she balanced on the narrow edge and with careful concentration walked heel-to-toe around the circumference of the platform, returning to her softly applauding spouse with a graceful curtsey.

"Well done yet again, my dear. Excellent balance."

"I must keep in practice," she said with a laugh, "then perhaps I shall be able to accomplish the task when grossly distended with *your* child, Mr. Darcy." She kissed his nose. "Show me the stars out tonight, William."

He turned, Lizzy encircling his waist with chin resting on a shoulder as he pointed to the various constellations visible in the July skies. She loosened his shirt to enable her to massage the warm skin of his chest as he spoke. They stood in serene contemplation of the heavens, both supremely content to be home as the breeze lifted their hair and carried pleasant fragrances from the masses of blooms, clean water and air, and fresh tilled earth.

Lizzy sighed happily. "It is so wonderful to be home. The city has its charms, but nothing that compares to the raw beauty of natural landscapes and the extensive gardens of Pemberley. I do so love it here and wish we would never have to leave."

"Not even to see the ocean?"

"What do you mean?

He turned, embracing her waist. "I was thinking that later, perhaps in

September when it will yet be easy for you to travel, that we could vacation on the coast. You and I only. You have never seen the sea, beloved, and I am thrilled to be the one to aid your discovery. In addition, I would have you all to myself. Does this sound appealing?"

Lizzy was smiling broadly and bouncing on her toes in excitement. "William, it sounds wonderful! Oh, to be utterly alone with you for a time! How blissful that would be." She met his mouth with a deep sigh. They kissed for a while, slowly and teasingly, Darcy nibbling and suckling her lips while caressing over her back and hips.

Abruptly Lizzy pulled away, grasped his hand, and positioned it squarely over their child. They beamed as the baby flipped about, gazing with love and joy into eyes mere inches apart.

"I shall never weary of feeling him move, never!" Darcy declared with awe, voice husky. "I order you, dearest, to find me if I am anywhere nearby whenever he expresses the urge to exercise." He knelt and nuzzled his face onto her belly, kissing firmly, then rising and returning to the delight of her mouth.

He kissed her deeply, probingly and absorbingly, desire rising rapidly as it always did when they touched. Lizzy untucked the remainder of his shirt, hands roving all over his back and under the waistband of his breeches as she pressed her body tightly against his. Darcy's strong hands were everywhere, caressing and squeezing. He encompassed a plump breast while lips traveled down her neck.

Lizzy arched and moaned softly, "Fitzwilliam, I want you so. Please, take me to our room."

Darcy smoothed the hair from her face, cupping her cheeks as he kissed with sensual intoxication. "I love you, my Elizabeth," he murmured, "so beautiful you are in the moonlight." In tandem he rubbed his palms over her neck to shoulders, onto both breasts for gentle fondling, downward with tender strokes as he whispered words of adoration mingled with seductive kisses. "Tonight, my beloved wife, I shall love you in our bed until you are screaming in uncontrollable ecstasy. Tomorrow we shall steal away to the copse amongst the willows and there we shall make love with the moonlight and stars shimmering over your skin. All day I shall envision you there, under my body, entwined and joined with me. Will you too imagine us there, precious love, so that your ardor will equal mine?"

"Yes," she replied breathlessly with a nod, meeting his crystal eyes. Darcy ran one hand under her skirt to her bottom, the other tangled in her flowing hair as he teased her with the tip of his tongue softly flickering over her ear and elsewhere, returning to her mouth for further plundering.

"My love. My eternal love. How I need you," he groaned as he circled her body, powerful arms lifting her off her feet and onto the hard planes of his chest. Darcy buried his face into the satin flesh of her neck, inhaling vigorously. "Yes, I must take you to our room immediately before I ravish you right here! God, how you arouse me Elizabeth!" He stood her onto her feet, yet holding tightly in shaking arms with forehead resting on hers as he fought for control.

Suddenly he chuckled. "If any of the servants see me on the way upstairs, I shall never have the nerve to face them."

Lizzy laughed too, reaching down to stroke the indication of his passion, eliciting a throaty groan. "Do you honestly believe your prowess and our frequent bedroom activities are not already a topic amongst the staff?"

Darcy looked at her in surprise. "Whatever do you mean?" He started to add something ludicrous about the fine staff of Pemberley never gossiping about their Master, but her laughter halted him.

"Truly, William, at times I think you more naïve than I! Servants are simple folk and do not possess the vaunted and rigid moral proprieties of the elite. Trust me, I can recall more than a few overheard conversations between the maids at Longbourn, not to mention the field workers. Samuel and Marguerite are the only two who see the vivid evidence of our love, and I trust them implicitly, but the others are not imbeciles and can do elementary deductions."

Darcy was actually blushing furiously, peering into the darkened windows as if he expected to see an audience of eyes staring back. Lizzy was laughing harder by the second as she took his hand and led him toward the door.

Caroline watched them move slowly toward the door, pausing several times for fresh kisses and extremely intimate caresses, finally disappearing from view. Her breath was shallow, cheeks flushed, and body trembling with strange sensations. She had distinctly seen it all and did not need to hear their words to know that she had witnessed a scene of indescribable intimacy and raging passion. Caroline Bingley, like most well-bred young ladies, was largely ignorant of the finer details of marital relations. The occasionally borderline naughty twittering among her friends, maidens all, was vague and steeped in misinformation anyway. Caroline did not have a mother or close female relative with which to discuss such things, her sister Louisa far too prudish to even consider, aside from the fact that she had never remotely been curious. Caroline was mercenary and narcissistic by nature, passion for anything other than clothing or jewels not of interest to her. Marriage was a necessity to fulfill those desires and if intimacy entered into the proposition, so be it. The idea of marital relations being pleasurable had never crossed her mind or entered her awareness.

However, there was absolutely no denying that what she had beheld in the garden were two people deeply in love and also obtaining tremendous pleasure from each other's touch. It was also astoundingly clear, and the blush to her face increased at the remembrance, that there was far more to come. Yes, she had seen it all and despite the lingering mystery of the love act, Caroline was not a total idiot and could form deductions of her own!

Quite unexpectedly, the vision of Sir Wallace Dandridge entered her mind. He was a fairly handsome man in his mid-thirties, of medium height with blonde hair and a lovely smile. Caroline had been so focused on Mr. Darcy for the past several years that she had given little thought to any other. Sir Dandridge had barely entered her consciousness, despite her friendship with his youngest sister. This season, Mr. Darcy no longer a possibility, Caroline had seriously cast about for the logical replacement, successfully working her magic on a number of eligible bachelors. Of all the hopefuls, Sir Dandridge was the most persistent, if not as wealthy as she may prefer.

Caroline smiled and closed her eyes as the image of his kind face appeared. Dreamily she conjured the fantasy of him kissing her as Mr. Darcy had kissed Elizabeth. With tingles of a strange variety fluttering through her, Caroline eventually returned to her room where dreams of a unique nature would invade.

Meanwhile, the Darcys ascended the flights of narrow stairs, halting a dozen times for breathless kisses and cuddles. Only once were they required to quickly duck behind a corner to avoid a maid heading toward the basement. Darcy covered Lizzy's mouth to prevent escaping giggles, but utilized the interruption to press into her soft body. Once safely behind the latched door of their chambers, Darcy grabbed his wife and pulled her roughly against his body for a passionate kiss. His fingers nimbly attacked the buttons to her gown as they stepped toward the bedchamber. Clothes fell randomly as they were discarded until, naked, they tumbled onto their bed in a tangle of limbs.

Laughing, they panted and kissed and groped and squeezed all while attempting to navigate to the middle of the enormous bed. Lying on their sides as they faced each other to caress and kiss, the tactile enhancement continuing for some time. Few words were uttered, even Darcy caught up in a state of rapturous delirium inducing voiceless hunger. They loved slowly then with increased intensity, Darcy mesmerized by his wife. She was so beautifully sensuous and he experienced a fresh rush of amazement that she was his and, most profoundly, that she loved him as she did. In all his years of hoping and dreaming for a marriage based on love, and as self-awareness of his sexual desires matured, he refused to allow himself to imagine that he would actually find someone who would fulfill both cravings. Astoundingly, Elizabeth was such a woman. The fact that she was his for the entirety of his life was frequently a phenomenon that quite literally staggered him.

Darcy's own excitement was nearly unbearable in its intensity, but he held himself in check, preferring to further heighten his arousal by observing the fervor and gratification of his wife. Darcy enfolded her in his arms with overwhelming joy. She was trembling and inhaling raggedly yet ceaselessly planting kisses over his shoulders and neck. Darcy smoothed her tousled hair from a perfect, dewy brow as he kissed her, murmuring soft words of adulation. She rose, eyes glazed with satisfaction as she looked at him and tenderly touched his face.

"William," she whispered, "I could not wait. You excite me so! What you do to me is indescribable." She closed her eyes, shuddering still. Releasing a prolonged gush of air as she nuzzled her lips over his. "My love, my own. Ask anything of me and it is yours. How can I please you, best beloved?"

Darcy smiled and laughed lowly. "Lizzy, my Lizzy, do you not yet understand that my greatest pleasure is in bringing you joy? The fact that you love me so awesomely as to attain such dynamic rapture is a joy transcending my own. Merely holding you and feeling your trembling is heaven."

His words were truth; nonetheless, the ache of his need could not be denied. He sat up with her encased in his arms, hands all over her body. He devoted a period of time to her constantly changing breasts, far fuller and heavier than when they married as they prepared for their baby. All the changes of her maturing body—some related to pregnancy, but others a result of a natural blossoming from their intimacy—incited him. It was not at all an exaggeration or opinion based on blind adoration to note that Elizabeth Darcy was luminous and gorgeous beyond what she had been seven months ago.

Darcy loved his wife with growing enthusiasm. If the maids did discuss the Master's prowess, Lizzy thought with a smile, they would undoubtedly be astonishingly inaccurate. Lizzy rather doubted anyone could match her husband's stamina or mastery. Of course, she had no frame of reference, but anything beyond Darcy's virility would likely incapacitate a woman! In fact, there was many a time when she believed she would faint from the experience and was often left sore and raw, not that it mattered one iota or inhibited her ardor.

Together they rose, passion growing to incomprehensible levels. Finally falling over a cliff of mindless, spiritual jubilance, they merged and were transported to a place of replete fulfillment. Darcy buckled in exhausted satiation, crushing her into the mattress, but Lizzy did not mind. Their son, however, was not as forgiving and began a series of furious punches, causing Lizzy to giggle. "Dearest, your son does not appreciate all this activity," she declared with a nudge to his inert side.

Darcy grunted, rolling lazily off his wife but drawing her close and placing a hand over the swell. "Get used to it, my son, as I do not intend to halt loving your mother." He kissed Lizzy's ear, nestling into the bend of her neck with a sigh. "I love you, Elizabeth, with all my soul." He kissed her yet again. "Are you still certain this is a male child? I would hate to damage her fragile mind by referring to her as 'my son' or 'he' all the time."

Lizzy laughed. "My heart says it is a boy." She turned and cupped his face, blue eyes piercing hers. "Our son, Fitzwilliam. I only pray he has your eyes." She kissed each brilliant orb, then chuckled. "Of course, if he is very fortunate he will possess all your marvelous attributes and, therefore, make some woman as deliriously happy as you have made me." Darcy blushed but smiled with mild egocentric satisfaction. "Anyway, we cannot call the baby 'it,' so a sex designation of some sort is apropos." She paused, tracing each feature on his face lightly, lingering on his lips, and then resting a fingertip into the cleft on his chin, speaking dazedly. "You are majestic, Fitzwilliam Darcy. I could stare at you all day and never tire of the simple perfection and beauty of your face. I am fortunate on more levels than countable. I love you so, William!"

They embraced fiercely, silent in their mutual adoration. Contentment bathed them as sleep drifted in. Darcy released her briefly to retrieve the crumpled covers, and then gathered her near, sleeping with her body tightly woven over his all through their first night home.

CHAPTER SEVENTEEN

Hasberry Hall

THE ENGLISH COUNTRY HOUSE named Hasberry Hall rested in a narrow valley approximately seven miles southwest from Lambton near Winster. The property, as most of Derbyshire besides the Peaks, was pastoral with gently rolling hills and a narrow brook. A small portion of the acreage was set aside as a walnut orchard, but primarily Hasberry was known for the raising of prime sheep. The parcel was a fifth the size of Pemberley, but more than sufficient for the sheep to roam as they grazed and for the manor itself to be surrounded by lovely gardens and private lawns. The mansion was two stories constructed of grey brick, generous and comfortable. Several out-buildings and stables were clustered nearby; the sheds for the shearing, housing, and breeding of the sheep were a distance away.

Bingley and Darcy met with Mr. Greystone, receiving a thorough tour of the entire grounds as well as a detailed summation as to the business aspect of the estate. Darcy, as the one far wiser in both the financial and livestock realms, led the discussion, asking pointed questions. A prepared sheath of papers was given to Mr. Bingley for later study. On the way back to Pemberley, taking a circuitous route so they could talk, Bingley was childlike in his zeal. He had fallen in love with the spacious but humble country house, never one who was entirely at ease with the grandeur and opulence of Netherfield, or Pemberley for that matter. Additionally, he was ecstatic at the idea of actually managing a working farm.

Bingley had inherited his fortune. His great-grandfather was the Bingley who first amassed the greatest portion of the family's wealth as a spice and fur trader. By the time of his death, a huge percentage of the accumulated funds had been invested. So substantial were the various investment revenues that Bingley's grandfather sold the trading company, at an enormous profit, and devoted his efforts to advancing their capital via further diversification. Bingley's father, therefore, had not worked an honest day in his life, more than content to live comfortably on the earnings that poured in. He had been perfectly willing to dwell in Town, enjoying all the entertainments offered to a gentleman of means. Charles Bingley had been raised to follow his father's example and was quite agreeable to do so.

Until he met Fitzwilliam Darcy.

Bingley was a mere nineteen, fresh-faced and naïve, a student at Oxford where his studies consisted primarily of men's pursuits, with the occasional business or literature or science class thrown in for good measure. Darcy was three and twenty, and it was his debut season as Master of Pemberley. Why the two had cultivated a friendship when so divergent in character and maturity will forever be one of life's unsolvable mysteries. Essentially, each young man offered the other something he desperately needed.

Darcy was a man grief ridden and overwhelmed with the sudden weight of tremendous responsibilities, all of which compounded his natural severity and reticence. Bingley was a man without a focus or purpose to his existence. Effervescent and extroverted by nature, he began to recognize an emptiness to the life his father led and yearned for more. Bingley brought laughter and simplicity to the somber and complicated Darcy. Conversely, Darcy brought ambition and stability to the wayward and capricious Bingley. By the time Bingley graduated from Oxford, he had learned more of finance and commerce from Darcy than in any class. During those years, he slowly grew more enamored with the country from his stays at Pemberley, and the deep conversations with Darcy over the management of his vast estate birthed a gnawing desire in Bingley to own his own estate. The respect Bingley witnessed directed toward a man of Darcy's stature and intelligence strikingly contrasted to the disdain engendered by his father. Bingley loved his father and was heartbroken when he died nearly three years ago, yet the opportunity to boldly accept his inheritance and use it for something real was a joyous challenge that he grasped with both hands. First, he took control of the family enterprises, to the lament of the solicitors and agents who were earning a hefty wage and, with Darcy's advice and gentle persuasion, was performing admirably.

Emboldened by his success, he was ready for phase two. Hence his wish to obtain a piece of property that he could not only call his home, and now with his dear Jane begin a family, but to also prove to himself that he was capable. For the past two years he had searched for a country manor. To his dismay, Bingley discovered that uncovering a functional farm with a decent house within his price range was extremely difficult. Families tend to dwell perpetually over the generations on their ancestral estates. In addition, Bingley's wealth, although considerable, was insufficient for the grander land holdings or to establish an estate from the beginning. He had searched far afield to no avail. His hope for Netherfield was waning, as the family refused to sell and there were no other acceptable options in Hertfordshire.

His despondency notwithstanding, Bingley honestly was pleased with the Hasberry ranch. The price was reasonable, the house wonderful, and sheep and walnuts were as good as anything else. Darcy raised sheep and grew a number of crops on his estate, so Bingley knew he could count on his friend for guidance.

Bingley's only concern at this point was with Jane. That she would adore the house and grounds he did not doubt; however, he knew that leaving her parents, hometown, and the shire she had known all her life would be distressing. Living close to Lizzy would certainly soften the heartache.

"What troubles me," Bingley said to Darcy as he drove toward Pemberley, "is whether my Jane will honestly reveal her thoughts and feelings to me." He noted Darcy's frown and continued quickly, "I do not mean to imply that she would purposely mislead or lie! It's just that... Jane does not easily share her feelings, even to me. She will consent to whatever course I choose and deem it her duty to submit." He sighed. "I love her placid nature, Darcy. We compliment each other so well, yet at times I do wish she would speak her mind more forcefully. Do you know what I mean?"

Darcy shrugged and smiled wryly. "Not completely, Bingley, to be truthful. Elizabeth has no problem whatsoever in clearly expressing her mind to me. She never has," he finished quietly in memory.

"Jane knows how deeply I want our own home; she does as well of course, but probably not to the same degree as I. For me, moving to Derbyshire is coming home, yet for Jane it is leaving her home. I shall be frank, Darcy," he glanced over at his friend with a blush on his cheeks as he finished, "I need distance from Mrs. Bennet."

He clamped his lips in shame, but Darcy laughed aloud and clapped him on the shoulder. "You need explain no further, my friend! You are a far braver man than I and have the patience of a saint."

"I believe Jane experiences some of the same irritation, although she would never dream of verbalizing dishonor toward a parent. This, I judge, is partially the problem. She too wishes for independence and solitude, but the price is guilt. Furthermore, I fear she will express enthusiasm for the Hasberry Estate to please me even if she is not delighted with it." He shook his head in confusion and melancholy. "I cannot proceed unless Jane is fully committed and content."

"Listen, Charles. Elizabeth, let us be factual here, undoubtedly understands Jane superior to even you. Women, especially sisters, share intuitively. She will divine the truth if you do not. I will speak with her on the subject. It may seem a roundabout, rather juvenile way to go about it, but Elizabeth can discover the honest feelings of Jane."

Much later that evening, as Darcy and Lizzy walked along the moonlit path to their isolated rendezvous, Darcy relayed his conversation with Charles. Jane had remained quiet during the dinner discussions regarding Hasberry Hall, interjecting rarely with a question or ambiguous comment. Darcy had learned long ago that he was utterly incompetent in reading his sister-in-law's composed visage, so he did not try.

Lizzy seemed unperturbed by Bingley's disquiet. "Charles frets where he should not," she declared firmly to her husband. "Jane is not attached to Netherfield and wants a home of their own. Any remorse she may experience at departing Hertfordshire will be overwhelmed by her joy. How about here for the blanket?" She looked at him expectantly.

"Are you certain?"

"Well, it is flat here and the grass is soft…"

"No, I mean about Jane," he said in exasperation.

Lizzy laughed, taking the blanket out of his arms and kissing him tenderly. "Yes, I am certain. You are sweet to worry so, beloved, but trust me.

Charles is anxious for naught." She smiled slyly. "Want to know a secret?" He nodded. "Jane would deny it if you asked, but she is as annoyed at Mama's interference as Charles. She told me that every time Charles broaches buying Netherfield, she cringes internally and prays the family refuses. Then she blushed and bit her lip, swearing me to not repeat her 'uncharitableness and wickedness' to another living soul. You do not count, of course, as you are my soul. However, I will tickle you mercilessly if you tell her I told you. Now, assist me with this blanket and kiss me as you promised."

The following day the four of them drove to the estate, Mr. Greystone once again conducting a thorough tour. The housekeeper escorted Jane and Lizzy through the kitchen areas, discussing household management minutia while the men departed to further discuss business. In this instance, it was Lizzy's experience that aided. She asked pointed questions about the staff and various duties, budget, merchandise and foodstuff ordering procedures, and much more. Jane was amazed.

The house itself was easily three times the size of Longbourn, but architecturally constructed in the same simplistic country style. Vaguely Tudor in design, the two-hundred-year-old structure of grey stone included all the rooms essential for a true country manor, but with an understated elegance that lacked the opulence of a grandly prodigious mansion such as Pemberley. Gardens and pathways were naturalistic, flowing gracefully amid the babbling creek and small lake. Trees, shrubs, and flowers grew wild with minimal cultivation; the extensive main patio with granite sculptures and one fountain was the only area of formality.

The manifestation of Jane Bingley's endorsement of the Hasberry Estate was eloquently reflected by the radiant smile gracing her features. None of them, even Darcy, were unsure of her positive impression. The relief washing over Bingley's face was laughable in its intensity. Mr. Greystone was unequivocal in his delight and liberation. The readiness of Bingley to seal the purchase as soon as feasible, combined with his anxiousness to retire and pleasure at bestowing his beloved ancestral home to a young couple with a bright future, encouraged Mr. Greystone to accept Bingley over the other two hesitant parties. Before the week ended, the initial documents were signed and a down payment conferred.

Jane's only request was to forestall alerting anyone outside the immediate persons at Pemberley until they had the opportunity to speak with Mr. and Mrs. Bennet. Bingley agreed. The tentative plan was to stay until after the Summer Festival with occupation of Hasberry Hall roughly three months hence. The Darcys were jubilant. Kitty assured Jane that Papa and Mama would understand. Georgiana, who had grown fond of Jane and adored Mr. Bingley, was delighted. Even Caroline displayed a charming smile at the news and asked for a tour of the Hall, kindly offering Jane dozens of decorating tips, a few of which were actually heeded.

For the following several days, the company at Pemberley basically did absolutely nothing.

Darcy spent approximately an hour with Mr. Keith discussing estate affairs, hastily and randomly shuffled through the stack of papers on his desk, sighed and ran a hand over his face, and then walked out of the room without a backward glance. He would not even enter his study for another week. Mr. Keith had smoothly handled all pressing concerns, of which there had been few; the crops were on their own as they grew and ripened, and the various livestock were not a pressing issue as they fattened up, so not much human interference was called for. What work was mandated was efficiently managed by the tenant farmers and livestock handlers.

Therefore, Darcy was freed to attend to the onerous task of relaxing! This he embraced with a ready heart… for a time. Day after day he lounged about reading, playing billiards or chess with Bingley while they discussed sheep, entertaining the women, taking strolls with his wife, and avoiding the stables. Therein lay the down side. Darcy had not been on a horse since his brief stay at Pemberley with the Duke, and he missed the activity profoundly.

It was more than the desire to ride itself that disturbed him and wore on his nerves. It was the raging need for strenuous physical activity. Darcy was a man who required a balance in his life: tranquil pursuits entailing minimal energy or concentration, enterprises offering a challenge to his intellect or that advanced his education, and labor of a concrete variety where his muscles were exercised and a healthy sweat attained. The first he was surrounded by in limitless quantities, and the second he was happy to eschew, his mind quite overdue for a caesura. To the frustration of all, the latter was impossible due to his uncle's proscription.

Lizzy, on the other hand, experienced a sort of exhaustive collapse. She slept late each day and was yawning by early evening. It was not exactly the same as the crushing fatigue encountered during the first months of her pregnancy, but reminiscent. She simply could not muster the emotional or physical energy to do anything beyond strolling about the gardens and visiting with her sisters. She did visit the stables once, the women in tow, to bring gifts to Wolfram. He capered in jubilant happiness, pausing between leaps to munch the treats she brought him. Parsifal studied Lizzy with great intensity, Lizzy actually discovering herself blushing guiltily at a horse! She did not leave Pemberley at all, the closest excursion abroad being to visit the children at the orphanage. They capered about their patroness as happily as Wolfram had, delighted with the toys and sweets she brought.

Mrs. Reynolds had proceeded efficiently with the plans for the Summer Festival as outlined before Elizabeth departed for London, so there was naught to do but wait for the day to arrive. She luxuriated in having zero demands on her person while her husband grew increasingly edgy and irritable. Twice he disappeared for several hours on long, strenuous hikes through the rough wooded areas of Pemberley, rationalizing that his legs were not injured so Dr. Darcy could not scowl at him for walking! He returned sweaty, filthy, with torn clothing, scraped hands, and brambles caught in his hair, indicating to his frowning wife that at least some rock climbing had ensued. However, the obvious pleasure and release attained from his exercise, without noticeable strain to his shoulder, prevented Lizzy from scolding.

Nevertheless, they all breathed huge sighs of relief when it was announced that a carriage and three men on horseback were approaching the manor. It was late afternoon and the occupants of Pemberley were scattered about in various pursuits. Darcy was currently in the attic storage rooms with several men assisting in the retrieval of nursery furniture from amongst the unorganized piles of boxes and ancient furnishings. Bingley had ridden over to the Hasberry property, as he had nearly every day, to learn first hand from Mr. Greystone. The older gentleman had taken quite a shine to Charles and was delightedly giving him a crash course in sheep rearing and walnut harvesting. The women sat in Lizzy's homey parlor, the windows open to the flowering garden beyond, actively discussing baby decorations.

Lizzy could not erase her vivid dream, so decided that subtle shades of blue and yellow would grace the walls. Harriet Vernor had recommended the decorator who had assisted her with their nursery, so an appointment was made for the following week. In the meantime, the women gladly offered inspired advice, more for the enjoyment of doing so than out of any real knowledge or expectation. Even Caroline chimed in now and again, apparently caught up in the enthusiasm, and was actually quilting a baby blanket. They were all shocked at the effort, and doubly at the skill she employed, as none of them would have imagined Caroline Bingley capable of wielding a sewing needle.

Thus, the footman announcing impending visitors found the ladies all bent over a baby project of some sort when he entered the room. Collectively, the fabrics and yarns were stowed as the occupants hastened from the room. Lizzy instructed Phillips to inform Mr. Darcy as she rushed to the foyer.

Entering the long, curved promenade were Dr. Darcy, Dr. Penaflor, and Colonel Fitzwilliam mounted on horseback trailed by a carriage with the Matlock crest. The females clustered on the porch as the men dismounted, Richard waving in greeting as he turned toward his parent's carriage. Dr. Darcy bounded up the steps first, sweeping Georgiana into an embrace and leaning for a kiss to Lizzy's cheek before either was fully aware of his intent. Lizzy blushed and Georgiana giggled, while Dr. Darcy's eyes swept over the house.

"Ah, Pemberley," he said in a tone of deep affection. "How beautiful she is." He sighed and smiled brightly. "It is good to be home!" He kissed Georgiana's forehead and turned toward Dr. Penaflor. "Did I not tell you it was the most excellent home in all of England, Raja?"

Dr. Penaflor merely nodded, busy bowing elegantly to each lady in succession. Darcy marched over the threshold at that moment, pulling his jacket over a dusty shirt in an attempt to make himself presentable, unaware of the cobwebs clinging to his hair.

"Uncle! How wonderful you have arrived. Welcome to Pemberley, Dr. Penaflor. I see you have brought the Matlocks in your wake." Darcy shook hands with his uncle, both men grinning identically.

"Are you not too old to play adventurer in the attic William?" George asked with a brush to his nephew's hair.

Darcy swept frantically through his hair, making it worse in the process, finally laughing as he shrugged and gave up. "I was retrieving nursery furniture actually. Attics are not designed for frames such as mine."

"Besides," chimed in Colonel Fitzwilliam, "the game was 'explorer' and Darcy cannot be Marco Polo if I am not present to be Kublai Khan." Richard mounted the last few steps, smiling broadly with a shyly smiling Anne de Bourgh on his arm, Lord and Lady Matlock following.

"Anne! How delightful." Darcy kissed his cousin's hand. "We were so hopeful that you would visit."

Joyful and heartfelt greetings proceeded all around as the group slowly wend their way into the house. Anne had not visited Pemberley in over five years and was thrilled to be here—and to be away from her mother. The Matlocks had cajoled, pleaded, threatened, and bribed, finally eroding Lady Catherine's will. The fact that Anne was twenty-seven and more than capable of deciding her own plans had very little bearing as far as Lady Catherine was concerned. Anne, however, was manifestly improving each day. She felt stronger and her cheeks were pink. Her daily-increasing exuberance, supplemented by her aunt and uncle's involvement, had bolstered Anne's usually timid nature and weak backbone. She had kindly but forcefully exerted herself, stating with a tremulous voice, yet unequivocally, that she *was* traveling to Pemberley. Lady Catherine had countered with the imperious declaration that she, therefore, would also be coming. Anne had blanched and hung her head in disappointment. Lord Matlock rapidly annihilated that threat by firmly reminding her that the Darcys had not invited her. One could almost raise a smattering of sympathy for poor Lady Catherine, who lately seemed to be receiving a lashing from nearly everyone!

Anne was immediately accosted by Georgiana, who reintroduced her to Miss Kitty, and the two were soon chatting giddily as they led Anne into the house.

"Dr. Darcy," Lizzy began.

"It is George, Elizabeth. GEORGE." He spoke slowly, shaking his head in mock exasperation, "Why can she not remember my name, William?"

Darcy smiled, squeezing his blushing wife's arm. "She is exhibiting proper manners, Uncle. You recall manners and propriety, I assume?"

"Ah yes. Manners: the bane of the English existence. Very well then, how may I help you, Mrs. Darcy?"

"Forgive me, George, I was hoping you could allot the time, as soon as feasible, to examine William's arm. He is frankly vexing us all with his moping glances toward the stables." She smiled winsomely at her husband, who mumbled something about never moping.

Dr. Darcy, however, was gazing at him with raised brow and a slight lilt to his lips, "Does your arm yet pain you, William?"

"Not in the least, Uncle."

"Even when you raise it above your head?"

"No."

He shrugged. "Then why are you not riding your horse?"

Darcy stopped abruptly with a glare. "Because you, *Doctor* Darcy, ordered me not to until you examined me and gave the approval."

George arched both brows in surprise. "Did I really say that?"

"Yes, you did," Darcy said through gritted teeth.

"Hmmm, how odd." George was stroking his chin in perplexity. "Although it does sound like something I *would* say, is that not so, Raja?"

"Yes, it does sound like you, George," Dr. Penaflor was grinning, sparkling teeth flashing.

"If you declare it so, William, then I believe you. What I *should* have said is that you may resume all normal activities once no further pain is felt." He clapped Darcy on the shoulder, the left one, with a brilliant smile. "How is that? Happy now?"

Darcy was staring at him open mouthed. With a final glare and shake of his head, he pivoted and stomped into the parlor. George met Lizzy's glittering eyes, winking broadly and grinning as he gallantly offered an arm. Once in the parlor, Lizzy approached her husband who was brooding by a far window. As humorous as George Darcy was—and a part of Lizzy did want to burst into laughter at his teasing of Darcy—she nonetheless sympathized with Darcy's frustration. She gently placed her hand on his arm and he turned to her.

"Are you alright, beloved? Your uncle was merely teasing you, so do not be too angry. I, for one, am glad you have given your shoulder the additional time to fully heal. I rather like you perfectly intact and functional." She tiptoed to kiss his cheek, caressing briefly over his chest.

Darcy sighed and smiled sheepishly. "You are right, of course. Am I pathetic if I admit that the truth is I miss my stallion?"

Lizzy chuckled. "Not in the least. If I must share your affections, I can endure it being for a horse. Promise me that you will rise early tomorrow and go for a long ride?"

Darcy hugged her and kissed her forehead. "Thank you, my dearest. I love you."

"Yes, I know." She brushed through his hair, removing the last of the cobwebs and smoothing it flat. With a final check to his cravat she declared him perfect.

They rejoined the group lounging about on the numerous sofas and chairs of the spacious parlor. George had helped himself to Darcy's whiskey, sipping with delight. "Wonderful blend, William. For some reason I have never ascertained, whiskey is nearly impossible to acquire in India. You should try some, Raja."

"Thank you, but I prefer a nice red wine. Spirits do not agree with me. Mr. Darcy," Dr. Penaflor addressed from his perch behind Anne, "is not your cousin, Miss de Bourgh, the very picture of health?"

The phrase was perhaps a bit overzealous, but Anne certainly was flourishing, especially with the bright blush currently spreading over her fuller cheeks. Darcy smiled fondly at his cousin. "She is radiant and beautiful. What exactly did you two prescribe?"

"Primarily foods rich in iron. Green vegetables, beans, red meat and organ meat, grains and nuts, and strawberries. Also, an herbal tea brewed of ingredients found to strengthen the blood. The taste is bitter, but Miss de Bourgh is brave and an excellent patient." Dr. Penaflor was clearly pleased with the improvement to his patient.

"Miss de Bourgh," Lizzy said, "you are radiant as Mr. Darcy stated. How are you feeling?"

Anne answered in her quiet voice, "You are too kind, Mrs. Darcy. I must confess that I am feeling so much stronger. I do not sleep as much as I did, I breathe easier, have more energy, and my appetite is improved. William, you remember the ruins a half mile or so from the manor that we used to play in?" He nodded. "I visited them the other day for the first time in probably twelve years! I could never walk so far." She smiled brightly and giggled. "It brought back so many memories." She turned to Lizzy. "Your husband, Richard, and I would play hide-and-seek amongst the fallen stones. I always won!" She declared with childish pride.

Darcy chuckled in remembrance. Richard spoke up with a grin, "You won, dearest cousin, because you were far smaller and could squeeze between and under the stones."

"Remember how dirty you would get, Anne?" Darcy chimed in with an evil laugh. "Aunt Catherine would grab your ear and march you off for a bath, declaring all boys the spawn of Satan for messing up proper ladies. How many times did she forbid us to play outside?"

"Hundreds, I am sure," Richard answered, suddenly bursting into a deep laugh. "Remember the one time when Anne had that big, black spider caught in her hair? Aunt Catherine shrieked so loudly we thought the rafters would cave. Maids and footman were running about trying to kill the poor arachnid while Aunt perched precariously on the arm of a chair. It was the funniest thing I ever saw."

Lord Matlock spoke, "She wrote me a scathing letter demanding I thrash you. I know she wrote the same to James."

"What ever happened to the spider?" Kitty asked.

"Smart fellow crawled away. Probably still resides in some unused room of the manor, begetting hundreds of little black children," Darcy replied. The women shuddered but laughed nonetheless. The afternoon passed with remembrances and laughter, while the Pemberley staff efficiently readied guest chambers. The Matlocks would journey on to Rivallain after dining, but Richard would stay at Pemberley.

"I promised Lady Catherine I would be Anne's official chaperone," he shared with Lizzy and Darcy, rolling his eyes. Then he glanced pointedly to Dr. Penaflor, who was relating a story about King Ferdinand of Spain to the avidly listening group. "I think she is afraid of the scary, swarthy-skinned fellow! He is a foreigner, after all, and you know you cannot trust them foreigners," he whispered in a perfect imitation of his Aunt.

Dr. Darcy approached Darcy and Lizzy as the party broke up to prepare for dinner. "Elizabeth dear, I have something for you." He handed her a large jar filled with tallow-colored cream. "It is a mixture of oils and wool fat. Indian women massage this over their bellies and breasts when pregnant to prevent the skin unduly stretching."

Both of the Darcys peered at him with absolute incomprehension. George looked from one to the other with a raised brow. "You know, the splitting of the skin that can occur as the child grows?"

Lizzy frowned but Darcy paled in horror, clutching his wife to his side and speaking with a weak squeak, "The skin… splits! This is… abominable! How is it the book says nothing of this? What other grisly realities should we know of, Uncle?" He was trembling, grasping Lizzy so tightly that she could barely breathe.

George laughed and patted his shoulder. "No no, nephew. It is not as you imagine. Forgive me for frightening you. I sometimes forget how repressed this culture is, not sharing private details." He shook his head. "Let me explain: the skin can tear, very superficially, as the baby grows. Usually the scars disappear, but at times they remain and can be unsightly, although in no way damaging. Keeping the skin well lubricated aids in the natural process. That is all. I was merely attempting to help. Please pardon me for frightening you both or crossing any lines of that proper English behavior that I persist in forgetting!"

Darcy was so visibly relieved that he nearly collapsed. "No, Uncle, please, share your knowledge with us by all means. Elizabeth and I want to be prepared for this experience."

George smiled and nodded. Lizzy thanked him for the cream, her own relief intense. George bowed and turned away, pivoting back a second later. "By the way, William. Some find that having the spouse be the administer of the cream and massage leads to other enjoyable activities." He grinned as the Darcys' blushed. "Of course, I am a single man so have no idea what they are talking about." With a final wink, he strode briskly down the hallway, whistling cheerily.

The next morning, three days now until the Festival, Lizzy woke to a room of blazing sunlight and already stifling heat. It was nearly nine and she was alone in their huge bed, the warmth of her husband's body long since dissipated. She had no memory of his leaving, assumed it was probably in the wee hours after dawn, not even an imprint remaining partly because she was clutching his pillow into her chest. She yawned and stretched, the baby flipping about in wakefulness, as her eyes alit on Darcy's hastily scratched note. She retrieved it from where it was propped against the lamp on the bed stand, laughing as she read the four words he had scrawled: *Gone riding. Love you.*

"How romantic," she murmured with a smile, rising and pulling on her gauzy robe, moving briskly toward the water closet as the baby painfully danced on her bladder.

Darcy entered the room moments later, a rapid scan concluding that she must be in her dressing room. He rather doubted she had risen and was already downstairs. The oppressive heat in the closed room struck him as a physical blow, so he crossed to the balcony doors, opening them wide and then moved to the other windows. One of the advantages of being on the top floor, surely one of the reasons that the Master chambers were located here and facing the valley with the lake and river, were the crisp breezes consistently flowing. He stood for a moment at the far window, allowing the cooling current to brush over his sweaty brow and damp linen of his shirt.

He was aware of the fact that he was grinning happily. Parsifal had greeted his Master with unmistakable enthusiasm. Darcy saddled his stallion himself, softly scolding him to stand still, Parsifal leaping forward before Darcy was fully mounted. They had run for hours. The sad result of Darcy's injury was that the horse had not been run for close to a month. There was not a groom in Darcy's employ, not even Mr. Thurber, who would brave taking Parsifal out, even if Darcy had ordered it. It was not that the animal was particularly reckless or unmanageable; it was the reality that he belonged to Mr. Darcy, the only person who had ever ridden him, and the thought of another on his back was quite simply unfathomable.

Darcy ended their race with an exhilaration not felt in weeks. He was renewed, with a sensation of health and vigor coursing through his body and making him feel a teenager again. His eyes had lifted from the stable yard to the corner of the manor where he knew his beautiful wife lay in slumber, and he had grinned slowly. Tossing the reins to a groom and nuzzling Parsifal one last time, Darcy rushed with long strides to a side door. In an odd twist from the last ride with Parsifal necessary to cool his passionate lust, this ride had heightened it. Taking the steps several at a time, nearly bowling over a towel-encumbered maid in his haste, Darcy lurched through their chamber's door with frankly only one thought on his mind.

Now he stood by the window, aroused, and impatiently allowing her about another minute to appear before he barged into her dressing room. She entered seconds later, yawning and rubbing her face. Darcy watched secretly from the corner as she arched her back in a sinuous stretch with arms over her head, the growing bulge of their child peeking through the diaphanous folds of her untied robe. He could easily see her pert breasts and the outline of all her luscious curves through the gossamer fabric. A sudden gust of air from the balcony stirred her hair and caused the silk of her robe to swirl away from her legs. Lizzy pivoted toward the window in fright, finally cognizant of the now open windows, when Darcy spoke.

"Elizabeth."

She twirled about, a hand rising to her heart. "William! You frightened me! When did you return?"

"Only a moment ago," he answered huskily as he slowly and gracefully moved around the bed and toward his wife, a sensual smile playing over his lips as darkened eyes scoured over her body. Lizzy was staring with undisguised appreciation. It had been two months since beholding him after a ride, and she swiftly recalled why it was she became so incredibly aroused when he returned. Darcy's handsome virility never failed to stun her, but the appearance of him in only a thin shirt and tailored pants damply clinging to tight muscles, unshaven face flushed from the wind and sun with hair disheveled, and his natural musky scent mingled with horse and sweat, buckled her knees.

Without a further word, he snaked one arm about her waist while tangling the other through her hair, pulling her into his body for a pervading kiss. Lizzy clutched his upper arms, moaning hoarsely and wilting weakly into his embrace. He swept her into his arms, kissing ardently without cessation, and carried her to the unlit fireplace. Laying her onto the bearskin rug, carefully ensuring her comfort without leaving her lips, he positioned his body fully over hers. Legs parting naturally, Lizzy encircled his waist and squeezed.

Darcy groaned with desperate need, kissing vigorously as he rapidly joined with his wife. Darcy rumbled in his chest but spoke no words, mad with desire and passionate fire. Lizzy gripped his head with steely fingers twined in his hair, returning his bruising kiss with equal fervor. On they loved with raging heat, gasping and growling, hearts racing frantically, and sweat soaking both of them.

Darcy's moans turned to whimpers as the torrents focused with a knot of indescribably pleasure before exploding outward to all points of his sizable body, releasing with an unleashed cry of rapture. Lizzy grazed her nails over his shoulders, so overcome with passion that she bit his lower lip hard enough to draw a drop of blood.

As the mutual tremors waned, their eyes opened sluggishly and met. Far too breathless to vocalize, they merely stared in profound rhapsody. Lizzy gently suckled his slightly swollen lip then tenderly kissed over his face. "My precious love," she whispered as he finally dropped his head to her chest, inhaling with a shudder and not yet attempting to move off her.

Lizzy blissfully held him, stroking over his back as they recovered. Darcy rose enough to kiss each breast, only then rolling to her side. Propping on an elbow, he caressed her chest lazily for a time before traveling leisurely down her abdomen. Palming the firm rise above her pubis, Darcy pressed gently.

"Apparently, he is growing accustomed to being jostled about," he smiled, and Lizzy laughed.

She feathered fingertips over his face while he resumed caressing. "How was your ride?"

"Invigorating, stupendous, refreshing, intoxicating, and heavenly." He kissed her softly. "The horse ride was nice, too," he finished, burying his face into her neck and nibbling while Lizzy giggled.

"Silly man!" she said as she sighed contentedly, absently running the back of her hand over his abdomen. "I was about to call for a tray when you so pleasantly startled me. Are you hungry, beloved?"

"Starved," he mumbled into her ear, lips and tongue exploring along her neck, journeying from shoulder to bosom, one hand stroking her inner thigh. Unhurriedly, he roused her with the magic of his hands and mouth, worshipping all of her body as he drove her insane.

Lizzy's need for food was forgotten as her husband artfully restimulated her ardor. Skillfully, he brought her to the pinnacle of perfect desire, her release sending ripples of frenzy washing head to toe. Rapidly he was there, enfolding her trembling body against his sturdy chest with arms and legs wrapped about her. Murmuring endearments incessantly, he kissed her forehead and smoothed her hair until she was breathing easier. He cupped one cheek, loitering over her mouth with his, sighing happily. "Mine, sweet wife only mine, forever. I love you so tremendously, Elizabeth, my soul."

Lizzy smiled. "Fitzwilliam Darcy, you are truly amazing. I think I should order you out of bed every morning for a long ride!" She kissed him, nestling tightly into his embrace with a contented sigh.

Later that day, after a boisterous luncheon with the entire Pemberley household, Darcy retreated to the solitude of his study to catch up on a stack of neglected papers. All were fairly straightforward, more along the lines of reports and inventories with an occasional document requiring his signature. Midway through the pile, a gentle knock at the door revealed his lovely wife. She smiled sweetly at his beaming face, crossing the room with a flowing grace until near enough to bestow a tender kiss to his brow.

"What do you need of me, dearest?"

"I need you, only you, my love," he answered, reaching to clasp her head and pull in for a kiss.

Lizzy caressed his face, love clearly evident in their eyes. "You are silly, William, but I do so love you. You called me in here merely for a kiss?"

Darcy raised a brow in surprise. "I did not call for you, love. Not that I am complaining mind you."

Lizzy frowned. "Mrs. Reynolds said you asked for me."

At that moment, there was a knock at the door. Leaving the mystery aside for the present, Darcy granted entrance. To the shock of both Darcys, it was Samuel and Marguerite. Samuel approached hesitantly, clearly nervous, with Marguerite a pace behind.

Samuel was the quintessential valet: utterly proper and seriously devoted to his Master. He had been Darcy's manservant since Darcy was twenty, Samuel now in his early forties. Yet, despite the long association and obvious intimacy with Darcy's personal preferences and requirements, Darcy had revealed to Lizzy that Samuel was intensely private. Any attempts on Darcy's part to converse or familiarize himself with Samuel as an individual was met with stony silence and disapproval. Therefore, Darcy had given up years ago. That Samuel was incredibly shy was evident. Lizzy had probably heard him speak a handful of times and he rarely addressed her.

Marguerite was nearly as decorous. She took her job very seriously and had endeavored to learn all personal information with a steadfast vigor. However, she did laugh upon occasion with her Mistress and shared the sporadic story or anecdote, albeit with reserve and caution. Lizzy knew little about her private life or intimate thoughts, but there was warmth between the two women and her dry humor frequently shone forth, even with Mr. Darcy.

Both Master and Mistress had not the least doubt they could trust their personal servant implicitly and although not friendly, they cared deeply for them and would grant nearly any wish requested. Seeing them enter the study together was astonishing. That Samuel and Marguerite spoke was manifest by how Lizzy and Darcy's clothing inevitably matched whenever dressing for a formal event, the frequent messages passed, and the perfection in timing between the two dressing rooms. However, neither had ever actually witnessed them speaking or in the same room, for that matter.

Samuel bowed toward his Master and then toward Lizzy, Marguerite dropping flawless curtseys. "Mr. Darcy. Mrs. Darcy. Pardon the deception. Miss Charbonneau and I implored Mrs. Reynolds's assistance, as we wished to speak with you together in a formal setting." He paused, glancing to Marguerite, who smiled faintly and nodded. Samuel cleared his throat, cheeks pink as he met Darcy's confused eyes. Lizzy was looking from one to the other with a dawning suspicion.

Samuel continued, "Sir, Miss Charbonneau and I have, naturally, increased our acquaintance since she joined the staff. Our friendship has grown to an affection and," he paused and took a deep breath, Marguerite stepping closer until beside him, arms brushing lightly. "Sir, Madame, we humbly request your permission for us to be wed." He finished in a rush, visage scarlet. Marguerite was smiling lovingly, delicate face radiant as she possessively laid her hand on his arm.

Darcy was stunned speechless. Lizzy was equally as surprised but collected her wits before her husband, rounding the desk to clasp Marguerite's hands. "Oh! This is marvelous! We are so delighted for you both. Surprised, certainly, but extremely thrilled." She leaned in to kiss Marguerite's flushed cheek, squeezing Samuel's hand briefly.

Darcy stood, senses slowly restored, as he too rounded the desk. Clasping Samuel's hand, to the valet's intense embarrassment, Darcy congratulated him as well, adding, "You do not need my permission, Samuel, but you do have my complete blessing. This is remarkable news. Mrs. Darcy and I are delighted and will grant whatever you wish for your nuptials."

Samuel's face was a shade of red truly magnificent to behold. Lizzy wanted to laugh but maintained her composure. "Thank you, sir," he stammered, "Miss Charbonneau and I do not want a fuss nor to disrupt the household or abandon our duties. We can marry quietly in the village without causing any disturbance or lack of service to you or Mrs. Darcy."

Darcy waved his hand airily. "Nonsense, Samuel! Weddings are special events and a marriage should not begin in haste or with anyone besides the couple unduly considered. It is your day and we, Mrs. Darcy and I, intend to make it as unforgettable as possible. Many staff members have been married in the Pemberley Chapel and, naturally, you two would need time alone afterwards. We can arrange this for whatever date you wish."

"Definitely!" Lizzy chimed in with enthusiasm, "There are available rooms in the couple's apartments both downstairs and at the Staff Domicile. In fact, one of the cottages is vacant since Morrison's wife passed. Mrs. Reynolds will happily show you the options, and you can choose whichever one suits your taste."

Lizzy and Darcy continued to verbalize plans and offerings, Samuel and Marguerite nearly forgotten in their excitement. Their personal servants were overwhelmed by the outpouring, rarely interjecting into the conversation. In the end, it was decided that the two would be wed in the Pemberley Chapel one month hence. Marguerite was to be dressed in a new gown purchased as a gift from Mrs. Darcy, and then the newlyweds would embark on a two-week honeymoon to the Lake District arranged and paid for by Mr. Darcy.

Samuel's mien had rapidly transmuted from its impressive shade of maroon to bloodless ivory at the concept of his Master without Samuel's service for two whole weeks, stuttering and stammering in embarrassed shock. Darcy, however, waved his concerns aside, clapped him on the back, and assured the devoted valet that his absence was in fact fortuitous.

"I will be vacationing with Mrs. Darcy at the seacoast during that time and was not planning on taking you with me anyway, so now you will have a far more pleasant diversion to occupy your time than fretting about me."

"But, sir," Samuel spluttered, the redness creeping over his cheeks once again, "Who will shave you or assist you dressing or draw your bath or—"

"Have no fear, Samuel. I *can* take care of myself in a pinch, and there will be staff available. None as efficient as you, but I will survive." Darcy smiled at his servant, touched at his devotion, and terribly amused, wisely choosing not to remind the man that he had managed capably before Samuel's procurement and on several occasions over the years. Marguerite was smiling serenely but with a hint of adoring humor, noticeably not offering the same arguments regarding her Mistress.

Eventually it was settled; Samuel's bashfulness was so acute at moments that Lizzy honestly feared the man would faint. She offered to learn how to shave her husband, thinking the idea would ease his disquiet, but he had looked at her with such horror at the concept that she hastily demurred. Marguerite's dulcet tones of French accented English calmed him while she skillfully and lovingly steered the wedding discussions along their proper course, all matters eventually established as Lizzy strongly suspected she had intended it all along.

When the betrothed couple finally exited, the Darcys collapsed onto the sofa in hysterical laughter. "After an hour of discussion, I am yet flabbergasted at what has been revealed here! Have you ever seen the two of them together?" Darcy asked his wife.

"Rarely, and never speaking to each other," she answered, wiping at wet eyes and still laughing.

Darcy shook his head. "She must be the most tenacious woman on the planet to crack Samuel's shell. I have noted maids gazing speculatively at my valet in the past, but I am quite certain he has remained oblivious." He laughed afresh. "Heavens! The man's shyness is unparalleled. I am convivial compared to him! I never thought I would see the day. Must be the rumored allurement of the French. The sensual mystique they purportedly have," he mused with a small smile.

Lizzy glanced at him. "You have been to France. Did you observe this French mystique and allurement? Did any French maidens attempt their magic on you, Mr. Darcy?"

He looked at her sharply and noted the teasing lift to her beautiful mouth. He snorted, "You know me, dearest, blessedly inconscient to the machinations of the opposite sex. I was far too busy exploring museums, ruins, and old chalets to notice the ladies. Bingley was nigh on ready to strangle me for dragging him to such places. I think that is why he tricked me into dancing the waltz. As payback for avoiding the numerous fêtes and cotillions we were invited to. What magic ventured was nullified by my ignorance or imbecilic behavior."

Lizzy laughed at the vision educed, hugging her husband's arm. "Oh, William! You are a priceless treasure! I love you so."

He grinned, kissing the tip of her nose. "Excellent news that is! Now, I must talk to Mrs. Reynolds. My curiosity is raging." He rose and rang for the housekeeper, who arrived moments later with eyes downcast and a mild flush to her dear cheeks.

"Sir," she began, "please forgive the deception with Mrs. Darcy…"

"Do not be ridiculous, Mrs. Reynolds, it is of no moment. Tell me what you know of this romance. How long has it been in the works?"

Lizzy sat on the sofa, listening to the tale and observing Darcy's avid face with a rising humor. *What an old gossip monger he is!* she realized, though, that it was not so much a desire for juicy gossip as it was an honest affection for his servant and interest in his well-being. Quite touching, actually.

According to Mrs. Reynolds, Marguerite had set her sights on a fortunate but utterly unsuspecting Samuel immediately upon entering the house. With careful and circumspect deliberation, she stalked her prey and snared her prize. None of the staff had any notion of the budding romance, the two cautious in the extreme and intensely private. Samuel's only true friends amongst the staff are the footmen Phillips and Watson. Marguerite's only confidante has been Miss Jameson, the still-maid, the two having developed a close bond. Mrs. Reynolds herself was completely unaware of the two personal servants being more than casual acquaintances until four days ago! Now the entire staff knew, the engagement having officially been proposed and accepted a week ago, and all were delighted if tremendously shocked.

Darcy had vacationed at the Lake District of County Cumbria twice in his life, so he was acquainted with the area somewhat. He and Mr. Keith sat down that afternoon and set the plans in motion for both the honeymoon of Samuel and Marguerite and the vacation of the Darcys. Lizzy left the men to their plotting, rejoining the ladies in her parlor for tea. Some three hours later the group of chattering females, accompanied by Colonel Fitzwilliam and Dr. Penaflor, returned to the manor having taken a leisurely and entertaining stroll about the grounds. They were greeted on the southern terrace by a reclining Dr. Darcy, attired today in an Indian kurta of deepest blue with swirls of fuchsia, book in hand. Lizzy had readily discovered that Darcy's uncle boasted an identical love of books as his nephew, happily ensconced in the Darcy House and Pemberley libraries for hours unending as he thoroughly examined the shelves for anything new.

"New books can be very difficult to attain while rambling through the far reaches of the Indian countryside," he had told Lizzy, "I think I visit home as much to obtain fresh reading material as to see family and friends!"

"How was the walk?" he inquired now, peering at Miss de Bourgh with a smile. "Why Miss Anne, you have rosy cheeks and are perspiring so delight-fully! How wonderful."

Anne blushed further, but met his direct gaze. "Dr. Darcy, we walked all the way to the stone arch and around the lily pond. It was invigorating and I feel marvelous, thanks to you and Dr. Penaflor." She glanced to the beaming Spaniard with an easy smile. "However, I must say I am vaguely fatigued and thirsty."

Lizzy started to speak but George jumped up from his chair with a lurch, bony frame towering over all of them, and offered his arm to Miss Anne. "This can be arranged! Lemonade all around," he declared, ushering them into the hall by sheer force of presence.

There they encounter further evidence of the power emanating naturally from the Darcy men by the appearance of the Master of Pemberley. Walking sedately, yet with a coiled energy and dominating deportment, Darcy approached with a wide smile and barely contained vibrancy, eyes sweeping the crowd but alighting on Elizabeth.

"Ladies, gentlemen," he said as he bowed, "How was your walk?" He spoke calmly, but Lizzy could detect the scantily regulated ebullience to his tone. Praise burst forth on the plethora of virtues to be found on the landscape of Pemberley, Darcy nodding and offering his thanks as expected. Nevertheless, his impatient gaze repeatedly returned to his wife, Lizzy clearly deducing he wished to share some news of import but having no clue as to the direction. Finally, the proper pleasantries completed, Darcy extended his hand to Lizzy. "If I may be so bold as to claim my wife for a brief interval, thus divesting her enchanting company from the assemblage. I promise to return her forthwith to further charm you all with her witty conversation."

Once out of earshot and ascending the stairs, Lizzy said, "Quite the charming speech, beloved. Where are we going? Or is that a redundant question?" She grinned impishly and Darcy laughed.

"Later, my lover, later. You quite exhausted and satisfied me this morning. I shall likely not be up to the task for several days."

"Ha! Unlikely that! You, Mr. Darcy, are insatiable."

"Not insatiable, my Elizabeth, merely in passionate love with the most beautiful creature in the entire world." He paused on the stairs to kiss her chastely, resuming their climb. "Actually, at this particular moment my thoughts are on the end product of our love. I am escorting you to the nursery."

Crossing into the chamber that Lizzy still persisted in thinking of as Darcy's mother's, they entered the nursery. Darcy was grinning with undisguised excitement. Several boxes marked "baby items" were scattered about the room among large sheet draped pieces of furniture. In the middle of the floor, resting on a canvas tarp spotted with drips of paint and varnish, sat a cradle of hard English oak. The cradle was big, elaborately scrolled with etchings of trailing ivy along the side railing and an incredible carving of a horse, naturally, gracing the head panel and the Darcy family crest on the footboard. The entire cradle had been freshly stained, varnished, and polished to a high gloss. It was exquisite, the workmanship unparalleled.

"It is still wet, my love, so you cannot touch it, but what do you think? Do you like it?" He was staring into her face with puzzlement, Lizzy displaying a mingled expression of appreciative awe and faint fright. "It has been in the family for generations, carved and constructed by a distant grandfather from an oak cut down in Pemberley's forest. However, if you do not like it we can purchase a new one."

"No, no, William! I love it, truly. It is astoundingly beautiful and I am overwhelmed. It is just," she paused and swallowed, looking into Darcy's anxious eyes with her own teary ones, continuing in a whisper, "in my dream of you with our son, this cradle was there! I remember the horse and beveled rails, although it was lighter in color. I know I told you how real the dream, like a premonition or message, and I do feel certain in my soul we are having a boy, yet this…"

Darcy smiled and laughed, enfolding her into his arms and kissing the top of her head. "I assured you before that I did not warrant you insane and I still do not. Nor do I reckon you are suddenly a soothsayer." He cupped her face. "Undoubtedly your unconscious mind recalled the cradle, as it has appeared in several portraits in the Hall. Particular heirlooms have a tendency to do that. For instance," he pulled away and stepped to one of the sheet covered bulks, tugging an edge to reveal an equally exquisitely sculpted rocking chair, "Was this what my dream-self sat on?"

Lizzy nodded an affirmative, relief washing over her countenance. She moved to his side, touching the fabulous chair. Darcy stroked her back. "Sit on it, love. I want to envision you there with our baby." He spoke huskily and Lizzy glanced up at his tender face, smiling as she did his bidding. The chair was sturdy, comfortably structured with armrests at the perfect level for holding a baby to one's breast, curved support for the lower back, and a seat worn smooth by generations of Darcy mothers. Lizzy rocked slowly, caressing palms over the wide armrests while gazing at the shining cradle, touched anew by the significance to being part of a lineage with such a wealth of history. Happiness and peace consumed her soul, enhanced by a sense of intense pride for the family she was now indelibly a part of.

Darcy knelt before her and placed one broad hand over her belly, the other grasping her hand, entwining her delicate fingers with his long, mildly calloused but elegant ones. It was then that Lizzy noticed the stains on Darcy's generally pristine fingers.

"You painted the cradle yourself?" she asked in surprise.

Darcy smiled and arched a brow. "Of course! Do you think I would allow anyone else to touch the bed my son shall lay on? Or perhaps you are merely amazed at how competent I am?" he teased, leaning in to kiss her soft lips. "You may be surprised, my dearest, at how diverse my talents." Lizzy laughed and hugged him tight.

L IZZY WOKE THE FOLLOWING day—the day before the Summer
Festival—earlier than she normally would have, although it was well
after the dawning sun had rose enough to blaze through the cracks in
the curtains. Darcy was soundly asleep, which was unusual at this late hour,
but he had been a busy man yesterday. Upon returning to the parlor from the
nursery, Lizzy and Darcy discovered Bingley returned from the Hasberry Estate
and clustered with the men around the liquor cabinet, all of them sipping slowly
on small tumblers of whiskey. Colonel Fitzwilliam suggested riding for a spell
before dinner and the idea was greeted with enthusiasm, the men simply waiting for Darcy's reappearance. Therefore, Darcy shortly found himself again
on Parsifal's back—not that he was in the least dismayed—and exercising for
another two hours, albeit not as vigorously as his morning horseback excursion.
Between his long day of riding, working on the cradle, managing Pemberley
affairs in his study, and the evening in the game room with the gents, he was
exhausted when finally crawling into bed beside his slumbering wife.

Now, he lay slightly curled next to Lizzy, clutching her arm and hand
with hot breath tickling her neck and shoulder. It was the combination of

his radiant warmth seeping into her skin and the fact that his head and shoulders were painfully trapping her hair that woke her. Darcy was a furnace while sleeping, a delight in the winter but rather annoying at times in the summer, especially lately as Lizzy noted her own internal temperature rising. The book said this was a common occurrence while pregnant, but it certainly made sleeping next to an inferno intent on snuggling difficult. Body dripping with sweat, Lizzy realized that she had been subconsciously attempting to pull away from her husband but could not due to the bulk of her long tresses being secured under the mass of muscular flesh comprising his torso.

As usual, he had thrown all the covers off his body, unknowingly landing them on top of his wife, adding to her burning distress. Lizzy rapidly discarded the coverlet, baring her flesh to the slightly cooler air of the room. It helped a little, and as long as she did not move away, her hair did not pull her scalp. With no real choice in the matter, Lizzy turned toward her comatose spouse, gently grabbed a shoulder, and shoved. He rolled onto his back with a grunt, mumbled something unintelligible, sighed deeply, and remained asleep. Finally free, Lizzy dashed to the windows and opened them wide.

She stood naked in front of the last window, allowing the cool breeze from the hills to wave over her skin, drying the perspiration, and lowering her temperature. The first few times she had seen her husband—who had not the slightest embarrassment about baring his flesh in the privacy of his quarters—positioned in front of the open window gazing at the landscape, Lizzy had blanched in shock. Darcy had laughed at her scolding, reminding her that, at three complete stories above the ground on this side and no other buildings in sight, a peeper would be in plain view on the field below and need binoculars to see into the window.

Long over her trepidation, Lizzy leaned against the edge and fingered the white chiffon curtain as her mind wandered. The Festival was tomorrow and all the plans were laid. Today the additional workers would be arriving to prepare the feast and begin setting up the pavilions, tables, and orchestra stand. Later today the musicians and other performers would be descending. In light of the chaos that would reign throughout the day, all of which would be handled skillfully by the Pemberley staff, Lizzy decided that it would be wise and fun to vacate the premises. Therefore, she had planned a picnic.

Lost to her musings, Lizzy did not mark Darcy rotating toward her side of the bed and reaching. His hands pressed into the hollow formed by her head and body, mumbling sleepily as he roused. Yawning and opening his eyes groggily, he spied his wife poised majestically by the near window. His breath caught and groin jerked at her sumptuous beauty.

"Elizabeth?" He rose onto one elbow as she turned her head with a ready smile. "Are you well?"

"I am fine, dearest. Merely soothing my scorching skin, thanks to my own personal heater."

He extended his arm, palm up "Come back to bed. I shall only heat you further in a pleasant manner."

Lizzy laughed, launching onto the bed as an exuberant child, Darcy instinctively adducting his limbs to protect sensitive regions. She attacked his ticklish sides briefly, but he need not worry overly as his wife was exceedingly cognizant of all his delicate areas and had no intention of harming him. Instead, she stretched next to him, kissing over his chest as she rolled him onto his back. Arms crossed above his nipple line, Lizzy rested her chin on his arms and happily stared into his face as he played with her hair.

"Mr. Darcy," she began, Darcy raising one brow at her form of address, "I hereby challenge you to a game of croquet during today's outing. Are you up to a beating?"

"It is my duty to inform you, Mrs. Darcy, that I am quite skilled at croquet. I would hate to humiliate my wife in front of all our guests, but I cannot back down from a challenge once extended."

"We shall see," she smugly rendered, directing her focus to the nearest nipple, Darcy sighing happily. She tantalized with lips and tongue all about his hard chest, croquet challenges rapidly forgotten by both. Rising eventually, she straddled his thighs, bending over to caress further along his muscles. Darcy stroked her smooth skin wherever he could reach, as aroused by the feel of her body under his hands as by her actions.

Lizzy stimulated him unhurriedly, always moved by the impression of his flesh touching hers. The pulsating power and raging heat of him pressed against the swell of her belly was a beautiful reminder of his strength and desire for her. Frequently their eyes met between their studied gazes that cherished the body of the other, his dark with passion and hers smoldering, both rimmed with unbridled love. She lightly fondled, Darcy groaning with eyes closing in sheer ecstasy, hands stroking her inner thighs.

"Elizabeth," he whispered with a throaty rumble. "Lord, that feels good. Please do not stop." She obeyed, rousing him further and further, Darcy reciprocating until they were both overcome.

He crazily seized her face, pulling roughly and engulfing her mouth in a penetrating kiss.

They held each other securely, stroking tenderly as they calmed. Darcy murmured sweet, loving endearments into her ears as he kissed over her face. In what was becoming a typical conclusion to their lovemaking, the baby expressed his thoughts on the subject by flipping about, easily sensed by his parents as their bodies were pressed harshly together. Lizzy giggled against his lips as the sensation felt mildly ticklish. Darcy's eyes were sparkling with mirth, the perception a bit ticklish to him as well, but primarily it was joy. Joy for this woman whom he loved so profoundly and with a greater depth each day, and joy for the healthy life created by their love and passion.

Darcy smoothed her hair, asking in a soft voice, "Is it at all uncomfortable having the child between us?"

"Not yet, although I imagine there will come a time when we will necessarily need to alter our positions. I will grow quite large in the midsection. Are you prepared, my heart, for how distended I shall become?"

He smiled and kissed her brow. "I am anxious. Then he will be readily felt and we will be closer to the moment when we can hold him. As for your midsection or any other part of your glorious body, I shall forever adore you and find you beautiful. Have no fear, precious wife, you excite me even if all I see are your toes!" Lizzy smiled with pleasure at his devotion, laughter bubbling over as he continued, "Allow me to amend that slightly. I become embarrassingly aroused merely at the thought of you. Be thankful you do not have the physical ramifications as I, since I know you are as lecherous!"

⌇

"Uncle George, may I disturb your peace for a spell?"

Dr. Darcy looked up from the enormous leather chair, where he was sprawled with one leg draped over an arm, into the earnest face of his nephew. George was reading in the library, escaping the picnic and festival clamoring that had invaded the hallways, reclining on Darcy's favorite chair primarily due to the fact that it was the one most accommodating for tall frames. Darcy was holding a rather large book clasped to his chest, the title hidden, although whether on purpose or accidentally George could not be sure.

"Of course, William. You are always welcome. How can I help you?"

Darcy dragged a chair close to his uncle, sitting and placing the book onto his lap, giving Dr. Darcy an opportunity to read the title. With a raised brow and crooked smile, he answered his own inquiry, "Ah, I see. Honestly, William, you are the married one not I, although I do have some limited experience and will happily assist if you need. Or is it pregnancy-related concerns you have?" His grin widened at Darcy's expression of amused disgust.

The book Darcy held was the medical text, boldly emblazoned with the title: *The Compleat Cyclopaedia of Midwifery and Reproduction.* "The latter, Uncle, thank you," Darcy replied sarcastically. "Elizabeth and I were talking after the whole skin-stretching scare," he paused for a brief shudder before continuing, "and we realized that this book, which has been our primary resource for pregnancy information, may be lacking. We do not want to be unprepared for any eventuality, especially those details which are apparently so common as to not warrant entry into the text. You are our best asset."

Dr. Darcy nodded seriously, all traces of humor receding. "This is wise. You know you can always count on me, son." He smiled. "You know, William, I must applaud your enthusiasm and interest. It is the rare man who deigns to partake in matters generally deemed totally female issues. It warms my heart."

Darcy waved his hand dismissively and flushed slightly, but he met his uncle's direct gaze with equal intensity. "Thank you, sir; it is not a tribute to my character, but rather to the rare woman I have been gifted. Someone as special as Elizabeth deserves a husband who will support her in all ways."

"I will not argue your wife's stellar attributes, as I wholeheartedly agree with you, but do not sell yourself short." He undraped his legs from the chair and sat up straight, leaning toward Darcy. "William, I have not been so fortunate as to find love to the degree as you have and James before you, but I do have a vast amount of experience with families and their interpersonal relationships. When one primarily encounters a family at their worst, suffering from disease or loss, one quickly notices what sets the successful, adjusted, and therefore capable of surviving trauma families apart from those who will fall to pieces. Always it is a deep devotion among the members, whether it parents or siblings or spouses.

This devotion translates into the realm of childbirth as well. Those women who have strong support will manage far more capably then those who are alone or unloved. Elizabeth is blessed to have you there for her."

"That is why it essential for me to know all I can about this process. I have seen hundreds of animal births and have a fairly firm knowledge base of human anatomy, but the books all seem vague regarding the details."

Dr. Darcy nodded. "Yes, most would, although I daresay I could acquire a newer text than the one you hold and more comprehensive. Unfortunately, birth, as I said, is considered a female issue relegated to midwives and therefore deemed unworthy of a physician's attention, hence the lack of textual information. Personally, I believe the tide is turning on all matters sexual, and a revolution of enlightenment is approaching, but that is for another discussion. As for me, I do have superior knowledge in the field, having delivered hundreds of babies. Indian women prefer their dais, their term for midwife, but often one is not about or trouble arises and a doctor is called for. Also, the English women will not allow an Indian dai to attend their birth, usually, so if I am around, I get summoned!"

"Is birth truly as horrible as one hears? Horses, for the most part, birth so easily with rare complications. Humans seem to suffer profoundly and frequently..." He looked at his uncle with undisguised fear. "If anything happened to Elizabeth, I..."

"She is young and healthy, William, so I am sure all will be well." He patted his nephew's trembling knee comfortingly. "Women in childbirth seem to fall into three basic categories. There are those who pass through the entire process with ease. This seems to be a combination of an innate control and an effortless, relatively pain free labor. They are the lucky ones. The worst are the women who fight the process, scream and thrash uncontrollably no matter what we do or say. Often the labors are not actually that horrible, but their lack of control and serenity create an atmosphere of intense stress, frequently leading to a negative outcome. Most fall into the middle category. Labor is so named because it is arduous and painful. There is no escaping the fact, but there are ways to control it and smooth the procedure."

Darcy leaned forward, listening avidly. "What ways?"

"Breathing techniques, focus, meditation, positions, and the like. However, the one essential is loving support. I cannot stress enough how vital it is for the mother to be surrounded by calming, strong, devoted presences."

Darcy sat back with a heavy sigh, mumbling sadly, "I wish I could be there with her."

"Why can you not? You are the one she loves the greatest. You have the premiere relationship with her so should be there if she needs you."

Darcy was staring at his uncle with stunned amazement. "You cannot be serious? Men are not allowed in birth rooms, Uncle!"

Dr. Darcy laughed, reaching into his coat pocket for a cigar. "I know you tend to be a stickler for the rules, William, but it is not a law from the Crown after all. You are the Master of the house and if your wife needs you, I judge you will rise to the occasion." He lit the cigar, inhaling leisurely while watching Darcy's contemplative mien. "In the meantime, let us open that book and see what wisdom is imparted. Just promise me you will not blush every time the word *vagina* or *penis* or *breast* appears, alright?" He grinned and Darcy blushed.

❧

It was close to noon before Lizzy was lovingly persuaded by her husband to relinquish the Festival management into the proficient hands of Mrs. Reynolds and the rest. Yesterday the thought of evacuating the house had appealed to Lizzy. Today, with workers arriving, wagons by the dozens rolling up to the side entrance, performers appearing, decorating and construction visibly transpiring, Lizzy experienced an internal sense of abandoning her duties. Only Darcy's gentle reminder that this is precisely the job of the commander, to delegate the responsibilities to his or her subordinates and trust that they will competently execute the tasks, finally swayed her. He certainly had no doubts regarding the adequacy of the Pemberley staff and his assurance in the end eased Lizzy.

Tightly packed into three open carriages with baskets, blankets, croquet and other game equipment, fishing poles, and a few miscellaneous necessities about their feet, the current inhabitants of Pemberley set off. Humor was high. Picnics always have a mysterious influence on folks, creating a carefree, childlike exuberance nearly impossible to resist. Lizzy was especially excited, as they were journeying along a thin track through the forest that led to a hidden lake and grassy knoll some three miles into Pemberley lands. She had never visited this part of the estate, as many of Darcy's planned excursions with his wife for spring having been postponed due to her accident.

The half-hour journey was delightful all by itself. Lizzy sat next to Darcy, who drove the open buggy, with Kitty and Georgiana seated in back. George Darcy commandeered the second vehicle with Anne de Bourgh and Dr. Penaflor. The last was steered by Richard with Jane, Charles, and Caroline Bingley. The narrow wagon trail was primarily utilized by the Pemberley huntsmen, so was rough, steep in places, and minimally maintained. Nonetheless, the terrain traversed was beautiful, counteracting the discomfort, at least as far as Lizzy was concerned. The vast forest looming to the east of the Manor covered miles upon miles, stretching far beyond the boundaries of Pemberley. Aside from the fringes, which formed the hidden grotto behind the Greek Temple, Lizzy had entered none of the wooded acreage.

The majority of the trees were species of oak with the random Scots pine, birch, rowan, and ash, many covered with a blanket of lichen and moss. Ground flora was thick in most places with a smattering of wildflowers, bluebells, rhododendrons, ivy, and ferns amongst the numerous shrubs. They halted at an extensive wild blackberry thicket, picking a bucket of dark berries for a later treat. The trees were dense in patches, impenetrable to the view beyond. Other stretches were sparse, allowing one to see for great distances, the grove extending for miles. The air was far cooler under the canopy of branches and leaves, smelling sweetly of fresh blooms, musky earth, and moldering wood. Twitters and warbles of varied birds were audible, mingled with the occasional scurry of small woodland creatures. At one point they stopped suddenly to allow a family of deer to cross the trail, and twice startled a fox. Darcy, the hawk-eyed hunter that he was, managed to efficiently drive and point to about two dozen game fowl and several rabbits, most of which the women did not see.

Passing by sundry divergent horse paths, the main track finally exited the edge of the wood, disappearing into a grass and clover carpeted meadow surrounding a generous sized, sandy-shored lake. Lizzy caught her breath, standing up without thinking and then grabbing her husband's arm to avoid tumbling onto the grass when he halted the carriage. Recovering instantly, she jumped out with a squeal of delight.

"William, it is so beautiful!"

Darcy previously told her the lake was named Rowan Lake, which she had rightfully assumed referred to the tree. What she had not understood was exactly why. There was a scattering of ash, birch, and oaks about the edges of the lake as the forest completely encompassed the area. Two enormous, ancient oaks dotted the meadow and provided essential shade. However, the rowan was preeminent. Furthermore, midway along the right hand shore an isthmus of pebbly sand connected to a small island roughly in the middle of the lake. The island boasted huge moss-covered boulders amid which grew a dozen rowan trees, currently bursting with white flowers and bright red berries. Beyond the isthmus, a score of tiny babbling creeks exited the rocky edges of the forest, forming a tributary that fed the lake.

The carriages were halted at the border, occupants disembarking with expressions of delight. Darcy, heart slowly returning to its regular rhythm after the near mishap of his childlike bride, felt a swell of pride. Naturally, he personally had nothing to do with the beauty around them, was simply lucky enough to be born into the Darcy family. Nonetheless, he adored sharing the wonders of their home with his wife. He lightly encircled her waist, leaning for a kiss to her temple.

"Dearest, it is breathtaking. Thank you for thinking of this spot for our picnic. Are there many more such areas in Pemberley?"

"Nothing quite like this. There are some unusual rock formations, small streams with fishing holes, terrain beautiful for its ruggedness or particular vegetation, and there are two areas with caves and caverns. One is within walking distance of this place, along that trail there," he said as he pointed to a barely discernible path to the right.

"Can we walk there later? I have never seen a true cavern before." Her eyes were shining; the consummate lover of nature and the outdoors inflamed at the idea of new adventures.

Darcy chuckled. "Perhaps, if you feel up to it. I am not sure the exploration of caverns is wise in your condition, my love, but we can look. I have not been to the cave in years."

Lizzy turned to her husband with a grin. "Let me guess. You and Richard, along with Mr. Vernor and Mr. Hughes, would play daring miners or Neanderthal cave dwellers?"

"Something like that, yes."

"Alright you two, quit dillydallying! There is work before pleasure, remember? I believe that is an English truism and virtue?" Uncle George, wearing a flowing outfit of beige linen with woven geometric waves of gold, scarlet, emerald green, and purple across the entire back and hem of the tunic, sauntered past with a canvas sack slung over his back.

"He rather resembles a gaudy, very thin Father Christmas, does he not?" Lizzy asked with a laugh, Darcy nodding.

They returned to the buggies while Dr. Darcy emptied his sack onto a level field of grass and proceeded to design a croquet course. The men carried the numerous baskets to the shady area, the women spreading the blankets and pillows. Colonel Fitzwilliam and Dr. Penaflor erected two broad umbrellas to expand the shade beyond that offered by the oaks. Lizzy had expressly ordered Mrs. Langton to expend no energy on the picnic victuals, her efforts monopolized by festival requirements. The cook had done as asked, merely stuffing the four baskets with remains from recent meals and fresh fruits, nuts, breads, and whatever else was at hand. It was not fancy, but it was more than adequate.

Lizzy and Jane placed the piles of food items onto a middle blanket, small plates and utensils nearby, allowing the picnickers to nibble as they wished. Kitty and Georgiana had immediately stripped their shoes and stockings, currently splashing along the edge of the cold water.

Soft conversation flowed, though most of the party was eagerly devoted to eating rather than idle chat. Lizzy leaned against her husband's bent leg, he reclining onto the oak's trunk. It was the last day of July, quite hot with the sun shining fiercely. Fortunately, there was a steady breeze, more warm than cool, but it eased the heat somewhat. All the women utilized their fans and were thankful to have worn light dresses and wide-brimmed hats. The men wore suits of finely woven kerseymere in pale shades of tan and grey; even Darcy wore a coat of ash grey over a grey waistcoat in an attempt to survive the heat. All of the men gazed in envy at Dr. Darcy, currently assisting Richard with the task of stringing kites, appearing cool and exceedingly comfortable in his loose Indian garb.

Caroline voiced all their thoughts when she turned to Raul Penaflor and said, "I daresay Dr. Darcy seems unperturbed by the balmy weather. Why do you not wear Indian outfits, Dr. Penaflor?"

He shrugged and smiled. "At the moment, I am wondering the exact thing, Miss Bingley! I do at times; however, Dr. Darcy has lived in India far longer than I and is greatly enmeshed into the culture. You may not believe it, but his appearance now is actually quite tame to how he is in Calcutta. He speaks numerous dialects fluently, naturally assumes the mannerisms of the locals, and dresses accordingly. I, however, am not as adaptable. I cling stubbornly to my familiar ways."

"How long have you worked for the East India Company, Dr. Penaflor?" Lizzy asked.

"Five years, Mrs. Darcy. George was my mentor when I first arrived. I was naïve, out of school just three years with so much to learn. He took a shine to me, a surprise to the fellow physicians, I later discovered, as George Darcy reputedly disdained the new arrivals. It may be hard to believe, observing his playfulness, but he is an astounding physician and tremendously serious about his craft. He is a gifted diagnostician with nearly magical skills. Therefore, he has little patience for foolish or inexperienced practitioners. Why he chose me is a mystery, but I am thankful."

Anne spoke in her muted voice, "He sensed that you share the same gift, Dr. Penaflor. He diagnosed you, so to speak." She smiled shyly and they all laughed.

"Perhaps, Miss de Bourgh, although I would be blessed to harbor a third his skill."

"Do you plan to return to India with him, Doctor?" Jane asked.

He glanced briefly toward Anne, who was gazing into her lap and did not note the unconscious gesture, answering after a slight hesitation, "I suppose so, Mrs. Bingley. At least that has been my intention. I have no desire to return to Spain; however, England is intriguing and has certain merits. A physician could earn a comfortable living in private practice or working in one of the hospitals."

Lizzy smiled, glancing to Darcy's calculating face. A girlish squeal diverted all their attention to the lakeshore where Kitty and Georgiana were flying their kites. Darcy laughed aloud at the sight of his baby sister nearly launched off her feet by a gusting updraft, Uncle George leaping to assist her. Richard called to the group, "Elizabeth, Mrs. Bingley, come get your kites."

Lizzy laughed, pivoting swiftly to plant a quick kiss to her husband's cheek, then grasped Jane's hand and pulled her to her feet. Charles looked to his sister from where he stood stringing fishing poles, Caroline's expression indecipherable as she watched the frivolity transpiring on the beach. "Caroline, join them. I believe we brought six kites, did we not Darcy?"

Darcy nodded affirmative, Jane speaking favorably, "Oh do come, Caroline! It is our duty to entertain the gentlemen." Caroline hesitated, clearly unsure if the activity was below her dignity, deciding positively upon glancing to Mr. Darcy's glowing face as he attended to his wife's pleasure, Lizzy already initiating her dash across the meadow to launch her kite.

"Dr. Penaflor," Charles inquired, "do you like to fish?"

"I have undertaken the endeavor only a handful of times in my life, but found it a pleasant diversion." He stood as he spoke, "You may have to assist me in the particulars of the craft, Mr. Bingley."

Darcy spoke, eyes yet focusing on Elizabeth, "The fish here are incredible, Doctor. The Lake is rarely disturbed, so the fish are allotted long seasons to grow to astounding proportions. Nor do they learn via the fish communication system to avoid strange dangling silver hooks."

Anne laughed. Charles chuckled as well, asking his friend, "Will you join us Darcy?"

"Later, Bingley. I believe I will relax and visit with my cousin." He gestured toward the island, "The best pools are on the far side of the island where the water is in shadow and very deep."

The men set off, Darcy and Anne happily easing into the calm silence. The kite-wielding women were laughing and cavorting in delight, George and Richard in the thick of it. Darcy observed his wife with serene peace, thrilled to note that the precious swell of their child could intermittently be noted when the breeze plastered her gown against her slim body.

"William, your wife is a delight. I truly cannot express how happy I am for you."

"Thank you, Anne. She is wonderful and I am beyond happy. Giddy, even, ridiculously so at times! Richard takes enormous pleasure in teasing me about my irrepressible joy." Darcy smiled and Anne laughed.

"Perhaps some day you can return the favor, although he does seem firmly entrenched into the world of bachelorhood."

Darcy peered at his cousin, who was serenely staring toward the lake. Her color remained paler than most, but with a pink tinge to her cheeks and lips the color of ripe strawberries. To one unacquainted with Anne de Bourgh, her frailty and faintly translucent skin would yet be obvious. To Darcy, who had watched her evolve from a vigorous child and adolescent to the pinched, tremulous young adult she had become, she now radiated health.

"Is the same true of you, dear Anne? Firmly entrenched or ready to climb out of your solitary hole?"

"You of all people know how painful it is for me, William. We share that trait. I think in a strange way I embraced my illness as an excuse to hide." She smiled, meeting his tender gaze. "It is somewhat of a shame our love was too strong to allow us to settle for each other, Wills. You would have been the safe choice for me. Now I have to contend with mother's arrangements." She laughed at his pained eyes, leaning to pat his hand. "Do not fret so, cousin. I may be a bit timid and inordinately complacent, but my backbone is not entirely comprised of jelly. I will refuse anyone too disgusting. Fortunately, I do not have to marry for money."

They were silent for a time, both dwelling on the past as well as the future. From their earliest remembrances, Lady Catherine had spoke of a union. When they were very young they had merely laughed, the concept of marriage to anyone being grotesque. As adolescents, the idea was met with mutual absurdity. The thought of marrying someone who was as close as a sibling was repellent. With the onset of adulthood, the reality that cousins did frequently marry prompted them to honestly deliberate the subject. By that time, Anne was ill with an unknown condition and Darcy was Master of Pemberley. As far as they were concerned, it was an untenable possibility on numerous levels. However, the main rationale was a genuine desire for the other to find what their hearts yearned for. Darcy needed a spirited, vibrant woman who he could truly love, his internal pain and emptiness intuitively understood by Anne. In contrast, Anne required a man with minimal demands who was tranquil and easygoing. Darcy and Anne loved each other, and that love would have, if pushed, bound them in mutual respect and care, but not true happiness or fulfillment.

Darcy broke the silence, speaking frankly as he would to few people in the world. "How run your feelings for Dr. Penaflor?" He expected Anne to blush and equivocate, so was surprised when her contemplative gaze traveled to the doctor where he sat upon a moss draped boulder as he fished.

"I am not sure, William." She spoke in a hushed tone, as if speaking more to herself than another. "Is my attraction to him because he has restored my health? Is it because he is exotic? Or am I merely lonely and he is the only available male in my immediate circle? Are those reasons acceptable? Unacceptable? And what does any of that matter if he is merely being polite and does not return my interest?" She smiled and turned to Darcy. "You see how terrible I am at this? Perhaps I should take lessons from Mrs. Darcy as to how one wins the hand of their soul mate."

Darcy snorted. "By all means, do not ask for my instruction! I succeeded by blind fortune and the grace of God. As for Dr. Penaflor, I judge he returns your interest, Anne, but must add the caveat that I am not intimate with him so cannot be certain. Keep yourself open to the possibility, would be my only counsel. He is a worthy man."

Anne had resumed her study of the fishing gentleman, her countenance sad. "Mother would never consent, so it is all moot speculation."

"I concur that it would require much persuasion; however, he is a proper match from an elite family, wealthy, and educated. I do not imagine it impossible."

Finally Anne blushed and lowered her head. "We should not be talking about him this way, William. He probably sees me as a patient and nothing more, yet here I am mentally shackling him not only to me but to mother as well! That is just plain evil!" They both laughed, recognizing the truth in her statement.

Elizabeth caught her husband's eye, blew a kiss, and then gestured for him to join her. Darcy smiled and waved, sitting up from his reclined pose. "Dearest Anne," he said, leaning close to his cousin and pressing her hand under his, "all I can assert with absolute confidence is the astounding joy to be found in a union with one whom you love and who loves you in return. Do not allow Lady Catherine or any other to convince you it does not matter. Do not settle for less than at the very least a mutual affection, promise me this!"

She intently studied his fierce, emotional eyes, surprisingly moved despite her recognition of the intensity of love in the Darcys' marriage. Seriously, she replied, "I promise, William. I will not settle."

The remainder of the afternoon passed pleasantly in frivolous pursuits. Capriciousness and jocosity reigned. Croquet was a triumph, although no one seriously attended to the actual rules of the game, fun prevailing over rivalry. Lizzy mischievously fixated on knocking Darcy's ball off course, vexing him initially, as his intrinsic disposition was a competitive one, but her glittering eyes and coy smile warmed his heart. In fact, as the nonsense escalated, the object of the contest rapidly became hitting another's ball rather than sending one's own through a hoop. Therefore, no one person could claim victory with any clarity.

Darcy and his uncle pitched a chessboard between them, settling in for a serious competition. Richard joined Dr. Penaflor and Charles on the island with pole in hand. The ladies sat quietly until Darcy nonchalantly mentioned that a thicket of wild strawberries grew along a casually indicated pathway, or at least had in years past. He glanced at Lizzy with an imperceptible nod toward Jane and she smiled. Darcy well knew how Lizzy longed for sisterly company with her eldest sibling, and that such solitude had been difficult to arrange even with the small number of visitors currently crowding them.

"Strawberries! How delightful. Jane, walk with me and let's see if we are in luck." Lizzy stood, leaning to kiss her husband's cheek. "Thank you," she whispered.

He snatched her hand, drawing it to his lips for a lingering kiss. "Enjoy yourselves. The path is easy and the thicket is not more than a hundred yards in."

Jane and Lizzy set out, buckets in hand and arms linked. Once they were beyond earshot and under the canopy of forest leaves, Lizzy sighed. "It is pleasant to walk with you, Jane. We have had so few opportunities to converse alone, although that shall change once you relocate here. Oh Jane, I am so thrilled you are moving close!"

"Yes, it will be wonderful. Derbyshire is so different than Hertfordshire. I do worry a bit about the winter. You know I abhor the cold."

"I cannot argue that point. Hasberry Hall is well constructed, though, with fireplaces aptly located. Besides, the excessive cold lends credence to long lazy days languishing in bed with your husband."

"Lizzy! Such things you say." Jane was blushing and Lizzy laughed.

"Oh Jane, you so amuse me. Surely you must be past your acute embarrassment of intimate matters by now? Is not nestling with your love a delightful activity?" Jane was silent and Lizzy noted her thoughtful expression. "Jane? What is it?"

"When Mr. Darcy holds you Lizzy, is it very tight?" Jane glanced at her sister, slightly reddened and stammering yet truly curious. "I mean, do you... touch completely?"

"It varies night to night. William prefers to be entwined, as do I. However, lately, between the warmth of summer and my internal body heat rising with pregnancy, I am discovering it preferable to merely hold hands or lay close. Why do you ask?"

"Charles wishes to hold me snug, which is very sweet, I know, and I do adore the intimacy and thank you, Lizzy, for encouraging me in that regard. It's just... I cannot sleep well. I keep telling myself I will grow accustomed to another body so... attached... to mine, but..." She sighed loudly and Lizzy could see tears shining in her eyes. "Oh, Lizzy, I am a terrible wife!"

"Jane, dear Jane, you are not terrible! You have always needed your freedom, that is all. Remember when we shared a bed? You would get so irritated if I invaded your side. We would snuggle for warmth, but you were always the first to push me away. It is simply how you are! You can share a bed with your husband without necessarily being in the same space. I am sure Charles would understand this."

Jane was shaking her head slowly. "No, Lizzy, I could never disappoint him so. Our relationship has blossomed since we began staying in the same room, as you said it would, and I truly do desire him there. He would be hurt if I altered it."

"You are merely seeking a compromise, Jane. Why should you be miserable? You are not suggesting he retreat totally. I am afraid I simply do not see the problem. Candidly explain how you feel. Talk to him."

They had reached the strawberries, Darcy's thicket having grown to a dense region of strawberry runners covering easily fifty feet of forest floor. Masses of ripe berries carpeted the ground in a speckled red and green pattern. Lizzy immediately knelt and began picking, but Jane stood still, staring into space.

"You sound just like Charles," she said vaguely.

Lizzy looked up into her sister's faraway eyes. "What sounds just like Charles?"

Jane jolted slightly, focusing on Lizzy with a faint flush "Oh nothing. He is forever inquiring as to my feelings. He does not seem satisfied with my answers." She shrugged. "Charles is ebullient and loquacious. I suppose he expects the same, yet it is not my nature to be effusive. It is frustrating, actually, to have him doubt my honesty."

"Yet you did not reveal the truth of your feelings regarding Netherfield nor leaving Hertfordshire," Lizzy said softly. Jane flushed and hung her head. Lizzy reached up and clasped her sister's hand, squeezing firmly. "Jane, I love you and appreciate your reticence; however, it can be hindering. You cannot deny your intrinsic nature, but you must learn to overcome to a degree. Charles deserves your whole heart and soul, as you do his."

"Lizzy, what if he thinks ill of me? Do you not fear this with Mr. Darcy? That if you tell all he will be wounded or falter in his love for you?"

"Jane! That is ridiculous! Mr. Bingley adores you. The man mourned for months without you in his life. I rather doubt he will be dismayed to discover you have a fault or two! Do you not trust his devotion?"

"Of course I do!"

"Then stop being so silly. You cast negative aspersions on his character by not having faith in his love and commitment."

Jane was pale, staring at Lizzy with dawning comprehension. "I never considered it that way," she whispered. "Oh Lizzy, I am such a fool. Charles is the best of men and I love him unconditionally, faults and all. Assuredly he loves me the same." Suddenly she giggled with an edge of hysteria, covering her mouth with one hand. "You see, I am a terrible wife!" She looked at Lizzy curiously, still giggling, "How do you know these pearls of wisdom, Lizzy?"

Lizzy laughed. "Wisdom bought with a tremendous price, Jane. You know what William and I suffered. I suppose the benefit to our tumultuous courtship was the trial-by-fire aspect of it all. We learned our lessons via grievous methods, but we did learn them."

CHAPTER TWENTY

The Cavern at Pemberley

FOR THE FINAL HOUR of the afternoon the picnickers broke up into three groups.

Charles and Dr. Penaflor caught a dozen impressive trout and carp, a couple perch, and even one yellow eel. Jane and Anne strolled leisurely about the lake edge, neither desirous of a strenuous trudge through the wood, eventually meandering to the island. Charles greeted his wife with effusive delight, proudly displaying his catch. Dr. Penaflor was more restrained but sincere in his happiness to see Anne. Before long, the ladies were sharing the rocks with the men, learning the fine art of catching fish. Jane had some childhood experience, but for Anne the activity was novel. She sat next to Raul, not touching but close enough to feel the heat of him, their hands brushing on occasion as he demonstrated the nuances of casting and baiting. Conversation flowed, and Anne would forever recall that lazy, hot afternoon as a turning point in her relationship with Raul.

Dr. Darcy, in the meantime, set off on his own exploring. He tramped far afield, past memories of rambles through these woods swathing him in peace. He returned long after the others were all back and reclining on the blankets, his arms loaded with a profusion of wildflowers utilized to grandly decorate and crown each lady with color.

A walk along the forest trail leading to the cave was embarked upon by Darcy, Lizzy, Richard, Georgiana, Caroline, and Kitty. The cave explorers set out with varying degrees of enthusiasm. Lizzy and Kitty were exuberant. Darcy was mildly concerned, as all of the ladies wore soft-soled slippers and areas of the path were rough with gravel or slick with decaying leaves and mud. Georgiana and Caroline seemed to have joined the excursion by default. Colonel Fitzwilliam was jolly as usual, happily lending an arm to whoever asked.

Darcy kept near Lizzy, attempting to secure a hand or arm; however, she was forever slithering away from his side to investigate a plant or colorful stone along the way. The trail to the cave and small cavern was only some quarter mile in length, easy for Lizzy and the girls. Caroline, in contrast, considered walking over anything coarser than cobblestones or longer than the distance between one shop and the next an utterly foolhardy undertaking. Yet, she had tagged along and was not grousing, at least not too inordinately!

Derbyshire boasted a number of truly astounding caverns, renowned throughout England and visited and explored by peoples from far away. Noted primarily were the Creswell Crags and Poole's Cavern, among others, but none of the famous or amazing caves were located on Pemberley lands. This modest subterranean grotto present at the base of a craggy hill amid the forest featured no glittering stalactites or bizarre formations.

The wood opened abruptly into a vague clearing with slender trees and shrubs interspersed amongst fallen stones. The cave entrance was approximately eight feet high and a rough triangle shape, with uneven edges of grey rock framing the yawning mouth chiseled into the face of the enormous stone cliff. They paused, gazing with vastly differing impressions, as Darcy explained that the morning sun illuminated the stony façade, rendering the grey limestone nearly white and piercing the shadows inside the cave. Now, in late afternoon, the gaping chasm was black as night.

Caroline immediately sat onto a flat rock at the edge of the clearing, rubbing her aching feet, and ignoring the cave. Georgiana paled at her first glance into the inky hole, instinctively stepping backwards and into the chest of her cousin Richard. He embraced her with a gentle pat and low chuckle. "Fear not, little mouse, you do not need to enter in." Georgiana visibly sagged into his arms with relief. Lizzy and Kitty slowed their pace but approached with awe and curiosity.

Darcy grabbed Lizzy's elbow. "Wait, love. Let us investigate first. In the past the cave has been safe and vacant, but we must be certain." He bent to light the Argand oil lamp he had brought along, Richard lighting his as well. The men disappeared into the black entrance, descending a short distance with the sporadic flash of their lamps visible as they moved about. It was only minutes until Darcy reappeared, beckoning to Lizzy and Kitty.

"Take my hand, Elizabeth, it is rocky here." He assisted her down the initial incline, lifting her bodily twice over the fallen boulders and calcified formations clogging the immediate entryway. Some five feet into the cave the floor flattened into a relatively level expanse of solid rock with patches of sandy dirt. The cave was irregular, approximately sixty feet at the widest, the asymmetrical ceiling ten to twelve feet at the most, and several narrow cracks and side passages fractured the walls. Richard stood with both lamps in his hands, casting wavering illumination about the room.

Darcy turned to help Kitty while Lizzy investigated. The cave itself was fairly unremarkable. The rock was the same grey limestone with grains of sparkling granite, smooth in places but mostly naturally rough. Lizzy was surprised at how cool it was inside the cavern, the rock almost cold to touch and slightly moist in spots with blotches of phosphorescent moss.

"Minute cracks allow water to seep through," Darcy spoke into her ear, startling her, "rendering the stone slick and very cold. It is too dim for vegetation to grow but certain mosses do not require light and, as you see, tend to glow." His arm was around her waist, pulling her slightly into his chest while he traced the ribbons of faint green with a finger. He planted several soft kisses by her ear, murmuring, "Are you afraid at all?"

She looked at him in surprise, his eyes black in the shadows. "Afraid? Why would I be afraid?"

He chuckled. "No offense intended, my brave love, it is just that some, Georgiana for instance, become unhinged at the closed atmosphere and sensation of vast weight surrounding them. I have always rather appreciated the damp air and tranquility that pervades."

"How far have you explored the passageways?"

"They do not extend any great distance and are all very narrow. Only one would allow my bulk to pass now. Even you, my svelte darling, would be hard pressed to wiggle through the others. I warned you it was not a particularly exciting example." They walked around the perimeter, Kitty and Richard meandering as well. "Nonetheless, as a boy it was an adventurous place and an opportune location to cool off on a hot summer day. Ah, here is the widest passage. Take my hand, love." He lifted the lamp and turned sideways, crouching a bit in order to squeeze through the constricted corridor. Lizzy managed easily, but thankfully the journey was only a few feet as Darcy was decidedly struggling.

The second chamber was some twenty feet in a vague triangle, the ceiling brushing the top of Darcy's head. At first glance, this room, as the previous, appeared unremarkable. Then Darcy led his wife to the far wall and shone his light upon a smoothly polished, flat expanse of rock.

"Look closely," he said, pointing with one long finger. Etched into the wall were several names: Richard Fitzwilliam, Gerald Vernor, Albert Hughes, George Wickham, Anne de Bourgh, and Fitzwilliam Darcy. Lizzy touched the names, smiling. Darcy then indicated another group of carved names: James Darcy, George Darcy, Alex Darcy, and Estella Darcy. On and on it went about the room, names extending back for generations.

"It is an initiation of sorts," he explained. "A Darcy tradition. Not just anyone could carve his or her name here. For instance, Georgiana's name is not listed. One had to camp here for the night. I was eleven the year we first stayed. Anne was visiting, although I have no doubt Lady Catherine would still attempt to thrash us all if she knew Anne had camped in a cave!" He laughed. "She was only ten and very brave. It is actually quite cozy. Here is the fire ring." He knelt before a niche cut into the stone; charred pieces of old wood a reminder of past adventures. "There is a natural flue here so the room remains smoke free. We, like countless other children before, would bring blankets and food, tell scary stories until late into the night when sheer exhaustion overcame the fear or will to welcome the dawn." He stood, laughing in memory. "Richard was always the best storyteller. I can be dramatic but I have little spontaneous imagination. Shocking, I know."

Lizzy slipped her arms around his neck. "I love when you talk of your boyhood. I imagine our sons, and probably daughters as well, playing here and at the lake and all the other marvelous places our home has to offer. They are very fortunate, in a myriad of ways."

Darcy bent to kiss her cool lips, warming her with his breath. "I am fortunate, as I will have a ready excuse to act the foolish child while showing them all these places." Lizzy chuckled, nodding at the vision as Darcy claimed her mouth for a deep kiss. His hand stroked her belly, their child apparently unimpressed as he slept on.

"Are we finished with the exploration then, Mr. and Mrs. Darcy?" Richard's voice drifted from the entrance to the chamber, Kitty's giggle echoing eerily.

～ひ～

Lizzy was drifting into a hazy doze against her spouse's shoulder by the time they pulled up to Pemberley's main entrance. Servants quickly approached, Darcy tossing the reins to a groom as he jumped to the ground, pivoting to assist his wife down. The women retreated to their chambers to freshen up while the men headed toward the refreshment of the liquor cabinet. Darcy escorted his weary love to their chambers, laying her onto the bed and kneeling to remove her slippers and stockings. Lizzy yawned with a deep moan, eyes sliding closed instantly.

"Forgive me dearest," she whispered, "I am not sure what has come over me."

"You need your rest, Elizabeth. The baby demands it. Are you hungry?"

"A little, but more tired. Would you be a dear and bring me a glass of water?"

"Of course," he said, already rising. He returned in seconds, aiding her to sit then caressing her hand as she drank. "Do you wish for me to stay with you?"

She shook her head, handing him the empty glass and laying back down. "It is not necessary, beloved. Go have fun with the boys. Kiss me first, though, and do not forget to wake me in time to prepare for dinner." He complied, drawing the coverlet over her and waiting until she was asleep, which was within minutes.

He returned two hours later, the chamber cast in early evening shadows, and his wife yet soundly asleep. He watched her for a spell, never tiring of simply observing her. She slept with parted lips and one hand resting on her growing womb. Darcy bent and gently spread one broad hand over hers, feeling the lazy undulations of their child. With a smile of profound contentment, he sat carefully onto the edge of the bed, reaching to sweep several loose tresses away from her eyes. The baby continued to roll about leisurely under his warm palm as Darcy leaned to brush his lips over Lizzy's brow. She stirred slightly, sighed, but remained asleep. Bestowing faint kisses across her brow to temple then to her ear, he whispered her name.

Turning instinctively toward him, she sighed again. "Fitzwilliam," she murmured softly as she sought his mouth. He happily reciprocated, kissing with gentle pressure initially, following her lead as she encompassed his neck and heightened the focus to his lips. Withdrawing after a blissful time, their eyes met, Lizzy now fully awake and well rested. "I love you, Mr. Darcy."

"I adore you and love you and yearn for you, Mrs. Darcy." He kissed her nose, pulling further away. "Marguerite is drawing a bath for you, beloved. Dinner is in an hour and a half. Do you feel well?"

"I am divine. Will you join me in my bath, William? I need someone to scrub my back."

"I suppose I could be persuaded. I would not wish my lovely wife's back to remain unwashed."

Fifteen minutes later he knocked upon her door, entering as she bid. Lizzy reclined in the water-filled tub, bubbles hiding some of her but not all. Darcy smiled instantly, eyes drinking in the sight. "Thank you, Marguerite, you may go. Mr. Darcy shall assist me further."

Marguerite bobbed and departed, Darcy's gaze not once leaving his wife. As his robe hastily fell to the floor, he swiftly entered the warm water and nestled Lizzy against his chest. He kissed along her neck, hands roaming freely over her front side. "We must install a larger tub at Darcy House," he declared huskily. "I so adore bathing with you, Elizabeth."

Lizzy wiggled over his lap. "Yes, I can deduce as much!"

"Minx! You invited me, remember."

"I merely wanted my back washed, husband."

"Your back shall be cleansed by rubbing deliciously over my chest as we love to euphoric completion."

He soaped his hands as he spoke, resonant voice sending shivers down her spine, then applied lubricated palms and fingers to her lush breasts. He caressed her, licking her ear and nibbling her neck all the while. Lizzy sighed happily and applied stimulating caresses of her own. Darcy groaned, vibrations saturating through her torso and giving her shivers.

Moaning and moving in rhythm, they stimulated leisurely. Warm water surrounded the intimate areas of their bodies, driving them mad and profoundly escalating the sensations. Darcy could barely think. He caressed incessantly, arousing her incredibly, but was hardly aware of his actions so agitated was his own excitement. Lizzy was curved into his torso, arms thrown backward to clutch his shoulders as she frenetically loved him.

They loved until utterly replete, collapsing further into the tub with water sloshing over the edge as they embraced tightly, holding on in lingering delight. Eventually Lizzy moved, turning about and soaping her own hands then proceeding to wash her husband, who reclined in absolute rapture. They talked, kissed, caressed, and laughed until the water was cooled. Darcy wrapped an enormous towel around her body, pulling her against him for a lusty kiss. In one graceful motion, he swept her into his arms and carried her to their bed.

"Time for your massage, little mother." He retrieved the jar of sweet-smelling cream that his uncle had given them, straddled her thighs, and scooped a fingertip sized amount. They had discovered that the greasy ointment spread far; the first time they had used it too liberally and Lizzy was caked with slime for two days.

"This is perhaps not the best idea, beloved. We are short on time and you know what inevitably transpires when we are in such a state." She smiled impishly, waving one hand in the general direction of their naked bodies.

Darcy did not answer, basically because there was no counter to her obser-vation. The fact is, there had not been a single time in eight months of marriage that Darcy did not become stimulated when he touched his wife's body. Furthermore, he was already sensing the renewed stirrings of his ardor merely by her close proximity and visual enticements. Beyond that, he welcomed his arousal, well cognizant of the extreme bliss to be found with her. Knowing all this added to the joy of serving her, he dutifully massaged the fragrant oil into the silky skin from thigh to navel, pausing to marvel at the fluttery movements of their child. He attended diligently to the beautifully swelling flesh of her abdomen and the far fuller breasts. As clinically as he approached the endeavor, they were both panting after fifteen minutes and his arousal was complete.

Lizzy grasped him, Darcy groaning and faltering in his task. "Lizzy, my love," he rasped, "I want you so profoundly." Massages forgotten, they made love again with strong hands grasping slender hips as he held her elevated to meet his kneeling body. Lizzy gazed dazedly at her astounding, gorgeous husband, his lean, muscular body displayed for her feasting eyes and fair skin damp from their bath with his dark, wet hair contrasting. His chin had fallen to his chest, respirations fitful, face flushed and gleaming with unspeakable passion. Lizzy was mesmerized, incitement rapidly escalating as she observed his joyous mien. For seconds only, he opened his eyes, meeting hers with teary brilliance and love before sliding them shut in raging rapture. Glorious bliss succumbed to with exquisite gratification yet again, the two lovers never tired in the expression of their love.

The host and hostess, beaming and nestled so closely it was nearly impossible to ascertain where their bodies separated, were the last to arrive for dinner. Richard glanced up with a knowing grin, Caroline with pursed lips and obvious disapproval, the others with standard and studied expressions of proper greeting. Dr. Darcy fell into step alongside Elizabeth as they filed into the dining room, leaning slightly and inhaling.

"Ah, lavender, naturally, Mrs. Darcy, although I detect a hint of lanolin. Delighted, I am, to know the unguent is being utilized so effectively."

To his surprise, Lizzy swiveled her head, capturing his eyes with a teasing gaze, and replied, "Yes, Dr. Darcy, we are unable to express how delighted we are at the results elicited from your ointment. I believe we shall need at least two more jars before you leave. Is that sufficient, William? Or should we order more?"

Darcy nodded seriously, lips twitching. "Perhaps three, my dear. Truly, Uncle, we cannot thank you enough for the satisfying consequences of your prescription."

George was nonplussed for the span of several heartbeats, then threw back his head and laughed uproariously.

CHAPTER TWENTY-ONE

Summer Festival

THE PEMBERLEY SUMMER FESTIVAL had been a traditional event for uncounted decades. Naturally, the specific entertainments had varied year to year, although feasting and dancing were always the main events. There had undoubtedly been years when the gala was canceled or subdued for various reasons; however, the custom by the Darcys to reward the hard-working tenants and employees whose labors ensured the survival of Pemberley had endured unwaveringly. Endured, that is, until the death of Lady Anne.

James Darcy had effectively, and nearly literally, ceased to live. He existed, moving through the rigors and demands of life with little joy. Celebrations of all kinds were forsaken, the house sunk in a state of perpetual mourning. Darcy, upon donning the title of Master, simply could not fathom how to reinstate the old traditions with his own crushing grief and discomfiture ruling him. In the present, after a twelve-year hiatus, the Master and Mistress of Pemberley embraced the restitution of all the old traditions. Furthermore, Elizabeth had determined that this Festival, as the mark of life restored, would surpass any other Festival in human memory.

She searched through the Pemberley archives for references to past events, both for ideas and to ensure this party was premiere. For hours, she met with Mrs. Reynolds and Mr. Taylor to innovate and form an agenda. Her accident interrupted the plotting for a spell, but she made up for lost time during her recuperation. Long weeks of lying abed afforded her the opportunity to attack the project zealously. All of the scheming she shared with Darcy. He, for the most part, listened, proffered the occasional opinion or insight, and happily helped when asked. Primarily, though, he allowed Lizzy to take the reins. This was her wish and aside from utilizing his knowledge base and extensive contacts, as well as digging deeply into the estate pockets, he was essentially a bystander.

At times, especially during her illness, he fretted that she was taking on too much. He had, only a couple of times, obliquely hinted that perhaps the event should be postponed one more year. Lizzy had erupted in anger, pregnancy playing a part no doubt, ordering him and his "negative attitude" from the room. So, he wisely relented, taking Mrs. Reynolds's advice to leave her be. The end result of all her careful contriving was now unfolding before his eyes and promised to be a perfect success.

Generally, the celebration was held in early June to avoid the oppressive heat of Derbyshire's summer and this had been Elizabeth's original plan. However, her accident and subsequent delay in joining the London season had forced them to postpone the Festival until August. As the schemes manifested, the decision to defer became fortuitous. Lizzy realized that the heat of August was of a degree that packing an enormous quantity of bodies into even the vast space of Pemberley's ballroom would be uncomfortable, to say the least. Therefore, she relegated the entire escapade to the outdoors.

The sweeping expanse of grassland surrounding the manor would serve as the primary locale. Five enormous white pavilions were erected: two for the lengthy, victual-laden tables, and three to provide a haven for an ample amount of dining tables and settees. A platform was situated beside the water for the orchestra, dancing to take place on the lawn. Hundreds of hanging lanterns were strung between tall poles dotting the entire field and casting illumination. Additional chairs were randomly dispersed along the edges of the main "dancing section." Separate zones were cordoned for specific entertainments, and the entire vicinity surrounding the Greek Temple above the Cascade Falls was taboo except for a select group of artisans who were preparing a special surprise.

The purpose of the Festival, as previously stated, was to reward the working members of the Pemberley family. As Lizzy had delved into exactly what this meant, she had been stunned at the incredible number of people who depended on Pemberley for their livelihood. Of course, she knew of the tenant farmers, having met all of them during her delivery of the Christmas packages. Additionally, she had become well acquainted with the household staff members and knew all of their names, with the exception of a few groundsmen and stable workers. What she had not realized were the quantity of folks from the neighboring communities who were employed at the fisheries, granaries, farms, and even the Manor itself, either continually or as seasonal help. All were invited.

Her first revolutionary idea was to not only provide entertainment for the laborers themselves but also for their entire family, children as well as adults. Therefore, another field was partitioned for children's games. The scheming Pemberley plotters had allowed their juvenile instincts to run amok, remembering favorite youthful sports and play. An array of activities were planned for the early hours of the evening, after which the children would retire to an additional pavilion where blankets were laid so they could fall asleep while their parents celebrated.

Lizzy's next idea was to hire helpers from the nearby towns to perform the necessary duties so that the entire household staff could partake in the festivities. Everyone, as Lizzy saw it, from Mrs. Reynolds and Mr. Taylor down to the last maid, should lay their burdens aside for an evening. Caroline had blanched at the news, questioning in shock who would assist them with undressing and dining. Lizzy, who had grown up with a modest number of servants, had difficulty resisting a sharp retort as to the shame of a grown woman not being able to remove her own clothing or pour a cup of tea! Instead, she placatingly assured Caroline that a handful of servants from the estates of their friends were being hired for the evening.

In point of fact, the Vernors, the Sitwells, and the Hugheses were happy to assist. Along with graciously allowing those maids and footmen who wished to augment their wage by serving the Darcys for an evening, they had also lent equipment such as tents, chairs, tables, and the like. In the end, the Darcy festival aided many throughout the local communities. Folks outside of Pemberley were engaged to implement most of the physical labor necessary to guarantee a successful event, the only exception being the kitchen staff. The simple truth was, Mrs. Langton would sooner walk over hot coals than have a stranger in her domain! Therefore, supplemental food was catered from the local inns and pubs, but the vast majority of the feast was miraculously furnished by the outstanding Pemberley cook and her unparalleled staff.

The resulting banquet would be simple but stupendous. Whole carcasses of sundry pigs, lambs, fowl, and one cow were roasted on spits or in deep pits over many days. There were vegetables, some the early reaping from Pemberley's crops, diverse breads, an inexhaustive amount of pies and cakes, which grew exponentially as most of the attendees brought offerings with them, and a multitude of nuts and fruits to nibble on. Smatterings of exotic or sophisticated cuisines were offered for those brave folk who wished for something exciting.

The new Mistress of Pemberley had perused the lists a hundred times. All was prepared, all arrangements confirmed, all essential items purchased and delivered, all staff assignments covered, all entertainers present. Barring a sudden freak rainstorm or equally cataclysmic event, all should transpire as planned. No one was worried; everyone from Darcy on down was quite used to handling such operations, albeit not on this scale, but the staff was imminently competent and would sooner die a painful death than disappoint their Master and Mistress.

Nonetheless, despite all logic to the contrary, Lizzy worried.

The day itself dawned bright, the sky cloud free, and promised to be as scorching as the one prior. The occupants of Pemberley observed the unfolding drama upon the grounds from the relative calm of the Manor. In the Master chambers, Lizzy had tossed restlessly for the bulk of the night. Her mind fretted and raced, preventing deep sleep, and what dreams she attained involved a Festival tragedy or dilemma of some kind. Darcy soothed her as best he could, finally unconsciously retreating to the far side of the bed to avoid her flipping body. Somewhere in the darkest hours of the morning, she fell into an exhaustive sleep so overwhelming that she did not note her husband departing for a morning ride or his return several hours later.

She woke from the faint breath of a cool breeze tickling her face, combined with the baby somersaulting on her bladder. The room was empty, windows open wide to encourage available airflow, and it was nearly ten o'clock. Lizzy jolted up in a panic, rushed through her toilette, and dashed toward the sitting room where she seriously prayed food of some sort was left lying about. Food was thankfully present, the sidebar laden and smelling delicious. Also present was her husband, dressed from riding sans his boots, slumped in a chair with long legs propped on the ottoman and newspaper open. He glanced up as she practically vaulted through the door, he the epitome of blithe serenity.

"Good morning, sleeping beauty," he greeted her with a debonair grin. "Hungry?" Of course, the query was unnecessary, as she was always hungry when she woke these days. He rose as he spoke, crossing to where she stood torn between delight at seeing him so devastatingly handsome and irrational vexation at his tranquility. He kissed her cheek, smoothing her wildly rumpled hair, smiling knowingly as he met her eyes. "Sit, love. What shall I get you?"

He turned toward the breakfast bar, Lizzy speaking but not answering his question, "You were out this morning. Is all well?"

He arched a brow in amusement. "All is according to your well-laid plans, Elizabeth. If they were not, heads would be rolling, I assure you. Marmalade or strawberry jam?"

"Very funny, William!" She retorted, again ignoring his inquiry, although she did flop into her chair with a heavy sigh.

"I was not attempting to be funny, although I suppose heads would not actually roll, but you get the picture. The staff knows what is required and will perform brilliantly. You, Mistress Darcy, are ordered to rest as much as possible today. No argument, Elizabeth," he said, this last spoken sharply and with a severe glower, Lizzy's mouth snapping shut. "My duty for the day will be to ensure your obedience. How I shall accomplish the feat, I have yet to decide." He grinned roguishly from the bar, where he was piling her plate high with everything since she seemed unwilling to inform him as to her craving. He returned to her slowly, speaking in a low tone as if perplexed, "Let me think. How can I make certain you lay about at perfect ease, expending minimal energy, engaged in activities delightful and requiring only fundamental cogitation? Hmmm… quite the pickle."

He handed her the plate, smiling broadly into her frowning face. "Now I am attempting to be funny. Humor is a chore for me, so you should laugh so as not to damage my fragile ego."

She took the proffered plate with a grunt. "Your ego, Mr. Darcy, is about as fragile as tempered steel, and you are still not funny!" He laughed boomingly and her frown deepened. Nonetheless, she attacked the food, Darcy returning moments later with a cup of tea, still chuckling.

He kissed her forehead then resettled into his chair, peering sidelong as he attended to the newspaper. Lizzy woke famished everyday, weak and shaky from hunger, yet in the end ate not much more than she ever had. Darcy was certainly far from an expert on matters relating to females and pregnancy, but it amazed him how essentially unchanged she was. Her breasts were fuller and darker, with fine veins visible as they had not been previously, her belly seemed daily to swell and she was slightly wider in the hips, yet her waist was as narrow, and viewed from behind, one could not tell she was with child. The remainder of her perfect body was unaltered, Lizzy as svelte as ever. However, she was only at the midpoint of her pregnancy and he knew the majority of their son's growth was yet to come.

Most of the symptoms of pregnancy as related by Dr. Darcy and the text had not affected Elizabeth. Occasionally fatigue would grip her, but generally her stamina was as inexhaustible as always. Her skin remained alabaster and supple, she did not experience the strange food cravings reported, she felt no pains or further muscle tingling in her back or hips, she slept very well, weight gain was minimal, and her sexual appetite was undiminished. George had stressed the importance of exercise, surprising Darcy, as he would have imagined laying about being preferential. Thankfully, this was not so, as Lizzy had no intention of being confined until, as she phrased it, she was too enormous to be evicted from their bed! Since Darcy simply could not fathom this, he rather expected she would be trudging the Pemberley gardens mere hours before their son arrived.

With visions of a waddling, rotund wife navigating the rose garden, Darcy chuckled lowly and seriously studied the paper. Lizzy finished her meal, about a third of what her husband had piled onto the plate, irritation vanishing along with her hunger. Naturally, Darcy was correct again. The staff would execute all details brilliantly, not only because they were loyal and stellar, but because their own entertainment depended on flawless implementation. In fact, her part to play was essentially complete. Even if a few minor snares or mishaps occurred, the entertainment planned was such that no one would be leaving having not enjoyed themselves fully.

She sighed, sipped her tea in peaceful silence for a spell, and then turned her musings to Darcy's jesting allusion to bedroom activities. Scrutinizing him unobtrusively, Lizzy smiled a slow and decidedly decadent grin. He sat once again with legs stretched onto the ottoman, crossed at the ankles, one hand holding a coffee cup with index finger tapping on the rim, the other hand gripping the paper while he read the finance page with intent examination. His beautiful lips were slightly pursed and those two little creases were fixed between his brows as he read. Lizzy's smile deepened. She loved watching him when he concentrated. The past hectic months had assigned them scant time to merely be together in placid pursuits. With a sudden and profound surge of sheer selfishness, she decided that she would take him at his threat. If he wished her to lie about and relax, then she would do so, but only if he was with her.

Relishing the moment, she candidly and adoringly studied him, allowing internal desires to rise as they invariably did whenever he was near. With a near jolt it occurred to her that he was growing more handsome each day. Perhaps it was just her personal prejudices, but she honestly believed it so. His face was mildly tanned from his daily rides, a faint scattering of tiny freckles across his nose and neck, and his hair was longer, having not been trimmed for several weeks, lending an air of barbarism to his normally cultured mien. Of course, his riding clothes always excited her and being half dressed meant his fine figure was readily visible.

As exemplary as was the masculine whole, equally aesthetic were the individual parts. She still adored his feet: strong and broad with long, straight toes and tiny dark hairs sprouting. His sturdy, elegant hands absolutely drove her insane. The hollow of his throat where a potent heartbeat could always be seen, his luscious neck, and his eyes. Oh God, his eyes! Lizzy continued to marvel at her previous blind stupidity for not at least noticing his eyes: a blue as vivid as the Derbyshire sky, blazing with intelligence and passion yet so sensitive and evocative. How could she not have recognized his beautiful soul as disclosed through his eyes?

Overcome with a flood of raging ardor and an intense need to express her devotion, she rose abruptly, Darcy starting at her sudden move. In seconds she was before him, nudging his legs off the ottoman so she could kneel in between. Darcy smiled, no need to ask her intent as it was clearly written on her face, and divested his hands of their encumbering items so he could twine fingers through her hair. She gazed into his eyes, those amazing eyes now clouding with immediate desire, while running her hands over his calves and feet.

"I love you, Fitzwilliam. Forgive my pique and for not laughing at your jokes. Allow me to offer contrition for my misdeeds." Smiling impishly, she rose on her knees and leaned in to kiss the throbbing pulse in the hollow of his neck. Darcy sighed happily, closing his eyes as she proceeded to deliver kisses down his chest and abdomen to his powerful thighs.

Lizzy proceeded to gently fondle him in all the ways which drove his passions wildly over the edge. She thrilled at the feminine power rushing through her as his excitement manifested. Now that Lizzy had read through the medical book and better understood the physiologic machinations of male arousal, it astonished her that the sudden rush of blood to his groin did not induce delirium from lack of oxygen to the brain! Of course, she chuckled as he groaned and dropped his head onto the chair; as evidenced by how dazed and befuddled he became, it apparently did nearly induce delirium.

Utilizing the firm and tender movements which she knew aroused him most profoundly, Lizzy adored her husband. The power and manliness of him, all hers to enjoy, titillated her to unbearable levels. Shoving her own excitement to the side for the present, she focused on his pleasure. Darcy was in a haze of passion, overwhelmed with love and adoration for his wife. "Elizabeth," he whispered roughly, "I love you, God how I love you! Please, please do not stop my love."

Lizzy did not stop. No initial planned intent of how she ultimately wished to please her husband, she now knew she wanted to concentrate on his satisfaction rather than her own. She knew him well: every gasp, shudder, muscle clench, writhe, wiggle, moan, or murmured word spoke clear volumes as to how he was feeling and where the level of his ardor was. She knew precisely how to bring him the greatest joy, and she did so.

After blissfully bringing him to completion, she nestled onto his lap, nuzzling his sweaty neck. Darcy was yet shivering and gasping. "My love, my husband. How I adore you. Do you have any idea how perfect you are?" She kissed over his face, caressing inside his shirt, Darcy unable to speak. Reaching his lips, she suckled the lower, murmuring, "Is my poor attitude forgiven, beloved?"

Darcy laughed with a harsh bark. "Lord, Lizzy! After what you have done for me I would likely forgive you anything. However, there is nothing to repent for." He cupped her cheek, smiling with utter contentment and happiness. "Will you stay with me here all day? I know you fret about the Festival but truly all is well, and I find I desperately need you all to myself. I cannot bear another day of sharing you!"

Lizzy encircled his waist, hugging fiercely. "You have read my thoughts, love, as you always do. And you are correct, as annoying as it is to admit!" She giggled and pinched a nipple, Darcy chuckling. "The Festival is beyond my control. I am confident all has been planned well and the guests will have a marvelous time."

Darcy hugged her tighter. "Elizabeth, I am so proud of you. Have I told you this?" He gently clasped her chin and peered into her bright eyes. "I am completely serious. You have stunned me in your enthusiasm and competence in this endeavor." She blushed and attempted to lower her gaze but he held firm. "You must understand how amazing you are. I mean no offense, but I must confess that I had my doubts, as you have no experience in running a household, let alone organizing a major fête. I never doubted your eventual capabilities or intelligence, but frankly, I did not expect you to grasp it all so quickly. Elizabeth, I married you because I love you. I fell in love with you because of your passion, humor, quick wit, and intelligence, not to mention your luscious body." He grinned and she tickled him briefly.

He continued, "In all seriousness though, I knew you would evolve into a wonderful Mistress of Pemberley. I told you so many times when you questioned yourself, remember?" She nodded, staring into his intense eyes. "However, in truth, I honestly thought it would take a couple of years. When you declared, upon your first day at Pemberley, that you wished to reinstate the Summer Festival, I confess I laughed. Again, not because I dispute your energy or heart, but because I figured it too much to undertake in so short a time. I wanted you to ease into being Mistress, afraid that the duties might overwhelm you and that you may become unhappy as my wife."

"Never!" she interrupted firmly, kissing him with fierce urgency.

"Well, see," he finally stammered breathlessly, "we both harbored residual anxieties in those early days. Elizabeth, despite my incredible love for you and faith in your potential, you have astonished me at every turn. What you have accomplished, my love, is truly unparalleled. Pregnant, ill, and wounded, so young, inexperienced, and naïve, none of those handicaps have hindered you. I want you to comprehend how extraordinary you are as a person, as my wife, and as Mistress of Pemberley, and to believe how bursting my pride in you. I do love you immeasurably, Mrs. Darcy."

Sending word via a maid, the Darcys stayed together in their chambers all day. Resuming a pattern they had grown accustomed to during the timeless winter months, they lounged about in their robes talking, snuggling, reading to each other, making love as the yearning arose, playing games, and whatever else seemed pleasurable at the given moment.

Lizzy brought out the interlocking puzzle, which had remained unmolested since her birthday. Clearing a table, they began to work on the odd recreation, experiencing a blissful oneness as they linked the pieces together. Sitting close, they managed to form almost the entire circumference of the picture before the frequent brushing of their bodies ignited passion. It began with an innocent caress to her knee, Lizzy rapidly distracted by his scent and firm muscles, especially since she had not slaked her amorous appetite that morning. Having no doubt whatsoever that he would readily rise to the task, Lizzy's caresses became quite focused and were not the least bit innocent. Darcy glanced at her with a raised brow and crooked grin, Lizzy clarifying her demands by the simple expedience of grasping the front of his robe and pulling him onto the floor.

She was unmistaken in her assumption. He did rise to the task, quite speedily as a matter of fact. Clothes were discarded in haste with frantic fondling and kissing ensuing. Lizzy flipped him onto his back with incredible force, straddling and loving him leisurely. Darcy, as always when she blissfully assumed control of their lovemaking, was as enraptured by her actions as he was by the joy exhibited in every inch of her flushed flesh. She was wholly perfect. The swell of their child between them, the baby occasionally felt when their bodies were squeezed, her bounteous breasts swaying as she moved, were all glorious reminders of their abounding love. Naturally, the end result of their lovemaking was satisfying and wondrous.

They transferred to the comfort of their enormous bed for a long, satiated interlude of cuddling and communication transpired in the aftermath of their loving. Bared bodies entwined as they lazily caressed and spoke of anything and everything, neither ever tiring of the simple pleasure found in a mere touch or sound of the other's voice. They read for a spell. The baby chose to become quite active, allotting Darcy the opportunity to speak to him and kiss the burgeoning bulge.

A late luncheon was sent on a tray and taken in bed between giggles and kisses. As they had discovered long ago, food could be deliciously utilized as an aphrodisiac. Honey, chunks of apple, thick custard, and wine were all used to enhance and arouse. The sheets were ruined and their flesh a sticky mess, but neither cared. Driven mad with desire, he loved his wife again, her body pressed under his. Lingering tastes of honey and fruit mingled with their unique flavors as they kissed, starved for the breath of the other.

The need to connect on every plane of their bodies kept them harshly glued together, Darcy only rising slightly on his elbows to avoid completely crushing her. Darcy incessantly murmured words of love into her ear between tender kisses and nibbles. Lizzy clutched him greedily, limbs wrapped tenaciously about his body, not at all feeling crushed.

They slept for a time, necessary for them both to regain their strength. Darcy could not readily recall the last lovemaking session they had shared of such intensity. He was utterly depleted, blissfully so. Lizzy woke long before he did, gazing at his relaxed face with a nearly overpowering sensation of adulation. They had needed this day to purely devote to the other, to cherish their union for the special one that it was. No one had disturbed them, as surely they would have if there were any serious problems. Lizzy realized that for two months now she had been so consumed with the obligations inherent as Mrs. Darcy that, although she had always placed her husband first, her mind was often distracted. With a sudden rush blinding in its acuteness, she wanted this evening to be over and all their guests to depart so she could rededicate every waking moment to him.

So earnest was her emotion that tears sprang to her eyes and she involuntarily squeezed, causing him to sluggishly rouse. "Elizabeth?" he asked in a hoarse whisper. "Are you alright?"

She nodded. "I am wonderful. I love you, William, so very, very much!"

He smiled and drew her close. "I love you too, my Lizzy. Forever." He yawned hugely, lifting to glance at the clock then sighing heavily. "I suppose we should rise. Bathing is essential," he said as he laughed, capturing a tress of her hair gummed with honey.

"Will you join me?" she asked. "I do not yet wish to part from you."

"I will always happily bathe with you, my love, as long as we both fit, that is." He chuckled and rubbed her belly. "However, do not expect more than actual washing. I honestly do believe I have attained my daily quota of arousals. Can a man be totally drained? I shall have to investigate the subject."

Lizzy laughed. "I have difficulty imagining your virility ever exhausted, beloved, but considering my unearthly satisfaction from this afternoon, I shall have no grand expectations."

In the end, they were both pleasantly surprised. Once again, Darcy's response to the touch of his wife's flesh, especially in a soapy tub, was automatic, maintaining his record of never being able to touch her without becoming profoundly aroused.

❧

The invitees began arriving around five that evening. Mr. and Mrs. Darcy greeted each one under a flower-laden pergola erected beyond the terrace on the southern side of the Manor. Designated as the reception area, the wide arbor opened onto the vast grasses surrounding the trout lake with shooting fountains. In keeping with the informal, fun atmosphere, Darcy and Lizzy wore understated outfits carefully chosen to not intimidate yet maintain their status as Master and Mistress. Marguerite dressed Elizabeth's hair in a simple chignon and Samuel insisted on trimming Darcy's hair so he did not look so disreputable.

Between the two, they remembered nearly every person's name. Mrs. Reynolds and Mr. Taylor, as the senior staff members, stood nearby to assist with the greetings, aiding Darcy and Lizzy with those folks they did not know. The enormous quantity of people employed in some capacity or another overwhelmed even Darcy's extreme mental faculty.

The children were immediately directed to the play zones, games of all sorts in progress. Dr. Darcy, dressed in a truly marvelous khalat of vivid fuchsia silk with the edges detailed in silver, had voluntarily stationed himself at the children's area. One glance at the tall, lanky man in the bright flowing dress with beaming smile, and the children squealed in delight. He joined right in, leading groups in competitions of blind man's bluff and Mother, may I.

"He is the biggest child among them," Darcy whispered to his wife.

Lizzy giggled, turning to the next person in line. It was a tall man, vaguely familiar, but Lizzy could not immediately place him until she noted the adolescent at his side. "Caleb!" she declared, turning then to the handsome man beside his son. "Phillips, forgive me. I did not recognize you without your livery and wig. Welcome to the Festival. This must be your wife?"

Phillips bowed regally, his lack of his dress uniform not inhibiting his proper manners or stateliness. "Mrs. Darcy, allow me to introduce my wife, Doris Phillips."

Phillips was not the first footman Lizzy had difficulty recognizing, although now that she expected it, she knew to mentally erase the powdered wig to form a picture. It was interesting to view the familiar staff in their casual garb, laughing and conversing with ease. Samuel and Marguerite appeared arm in arm, proper and reticent although eventually they did relax enough for Samuel to overcome his numbing bashfulness to dance with his fiancée.

For over an hour the wagons and carriages rambled along the drive. The harsh August sun was low on the horizon, yet still delivering scorching beams of heat. Children, of course, seem impervious to the heat so embraced the entertainment with all the enthusiasm of youth. The adults were not as resilient, retreating to the relative cool offered by the shady tents located near the water, fans fluttering crazily. Nonetheless, they ate and drank, communing with friends, laughing and flirting. Steady streams of heaping platters of food were forthcoming from the kitchens to replenish the emptied ones. Jugs of lemonade and cold tea were continually refilled.

Reverend and Mrs. Bertram arrived with the orphans. Clustered in hand-holding groups as they walked down the drive, the children stared at the massive house in wide-eyed awe. The enthusiastic welcome of Mrs. Darcy, their cheerful patroness who always displayed affection and brought lovely treats, eased their nervousness. Within minutes, they too were scampering with George Darcy and the other children, playing games and winning prizes just like all the fortunate ones with families.

Perceptive to the fact that the tenants and employees would likely better enjoy themselves if the Master and Mistress were not uncomfortably close, Lizzy had set up a shady secluded area on the terrace for the inhabitants of Pemberley. Aside from Dr. Darcy, the others reclined in comfort. Darcy and Lizzy joined them, taking their seats with sighs of relief. Lizzy poured lemonade for herself and her husband while Darcy motioned to a waiting maid to serve dinner.

"I never realized there were so many people working at Pemberley," Georgiana said in awe, observing the mingling crowds on the grass. "When we visited the tenant cottages before Christmas, Elizabeth, it did not seem like so many."

Darcy smiled. "There are many more besides the tenants, Georgie."

Anne suddenly laughed aloud, interrupting Darcy's explanation. "Dr. Darcy is playing hopscotch!" All eyes pivoted to the far field where George could easily be seen in his bright robe, hopping through the grid with a score of clapping children cheering him on.

Dr. Penaflor rose to stand next to Anne, laughing at the spectacle. "Children love George. Even when horribly ill he cheers them, finding ways to make them laugh. It seems a shame that he has none of his own, but then, perhaps God knew he was needed to love them all." He turned and smiled at Anne, eyes meeting for a time before Anne blushed and lowered her gaze.

"Well, it is cute I suppose, but he should remember he is uncle to the Master of Pemberley," Caroline said primly. "A whit of decorum is expected, after all."

Raul laughed. "I am afraid, Miss Bingley, that Dr. Darcy does not take such things very seriously."

"All those years amongst the savages, I suspect," she continued. "What a shame."

Charles looked at his sister with slight anger. "I rather think he would disagree in your assessment of them being savages, Caroline, or that it is a shame to have dwelt among them. Having never met an Indian, you should defer your hastily rendered judgment."

"Besides," Darcy spoke quietly, serenely cutting his meat and not looking at Caroline, "the Master of Pemberley takes no issue with his uncle's antics and is actually planning on joining the fun once dinner is finished. Will you accompany me, Mrs. Darcy, for the egg race?"

Lizzy smiled. "I would be honored, Mr. Darcy."

"I am anticipating the dancing," Kitty chimed in. "When will the orchestra play, Lizzy?"

"After dark."

"You will dance, will you not Georgiana?" Kitty begged. "Please?"

Georgiana blushed, glancing to her brother. "I do not think so, Kitty. I have not had my coming out and have never danced formally."

"Why, Georgie! You wound me," Richard declared dramatically. "Miss Bennet has agreed to dance with me as has Cousin Anne, so you must as well. The night will not be complete!" Georgiana paled, mutely pleading with her brother.

Darcy chuckled. "Do not turn to me for saving, baby sister. Colonel Fitzwilliam is an equal guardian, thus if he wishes to dance with you, I have no say in the matter. You can refuse, of course, but he will be devastated. He may cry."

"You see, Georgiana! I told you it would be all right. With all the available gentlemen about, we can dance every set, all night long!" Kitty clapped her hands in glee.

"I regret that I must exert my authority at this point, Miss Kitty," Darcy said softly. "It would not be appropriate for Miss Darcy or you to dance with any beyond the immediate members of the household. Do not fear," he said, smiling gently to ease the blow, "there are plenty of us to go around."

As the dinner hour drew to its completion, dusk was approaching and the groundsmen initiated the time consuming task of lighting the numerous lanterns dispersed about the lawns. Darcy lent his arm to Lizzy, leading the Pemberley residents into the crowd and toward the roped off sections of the yard. It was now nearly time for the scheduled performances to begin.

First, however, Lizzy led her husband to the children's arena. Darcy faltered a bit, in truth having blurted the whole "egg race" comment just to irritate Caroline Bingley. His wife, on the other hand, took him at his word. All thirty-three of the orphans released squeals of delight when she entered the cordoned play zone. They adored their patroness, rushing her en masse to cluster about her legs and clamor for attention. Darcy kept a grip on her elbow, fearful that she would topple over in their enthusiasm. Naturally, his close proximity meant that they also bustled about his legs, not sure what to make of the gigantic, silent man, but in the typical innocence of youth deciding that if he was with Mrs. Darcy then he must be tolerable.

Lizzy laughed, bending and attempting to hug all of them while bestowing kisses and hair tousles. Darcy watched her obvious delight with rising pleasure, beginning to relax into the unusual situation when suddenly his attention was captured by a firm tug on his trousers. He glanced down into the tiny, serious face of a boy of perhaps three. He was staring at Darcy with great intensity, his sandy hair combed into a perfect slick bowl except for a swirl to the crown which stuck straight up. His eyes were huge, colored a lovely green with gold flecks, and he solemnly studied Darcy for several minutes, apparently eventually deciding the big fellow was safe enough as he abruptly lifted his chubby arms and reached toward the stunned man. Without thinking, Darcy bent and picked the little boy into his arms, resting him naturally on his hip.

"Hello, lad," Darcy said, deep voice causing the boy's eyes to widen and thumb to implant between sucking lips. Still, he did not squirm and bravely examined his captor, reaching the other plump fingers to poke Darcy's nose then the cleft in his chin with avid curiosity. "Do you have a name, little one?"

"His name is Francis." It was Elizabeth, watching the drama with misty eyes and a broad smile. "He is the newest arrival. His mother died not two weeks ago and his father before he was born. We hope to settle him with an aunt who lives in Exeter."

"He is adorable," Darcy said, Francis continuing his study with pokes and soft pinches. "Does the aunt want him?"

"She is willing, yes, but the orphanage needs to arrange the funds for her to travel so far. I have given some of my pin money. I hope you do not mind, love…"

Darcy was shaking his head, gazing at the boy who yawned and then laid his head onto Darcy's shoulder, entire soft body relaxing as a warm rag into his chest. Darcy's breath caught, an intense surge of what could only be paternal emotion lancing his heart. He looked to Elizabeth, gruffly clearing his throat. "Whatever is needed I will provide. Tell them so, Elizabeth."

Darcy held the boy until he was soundly asleep, one of the orphanage staff women then taking him away. His arms felt strangely bereft, the need to touch his wife and their child overwhelming him. Lizzy was on the far side of the field, preparing the equipment for the egg race when Darcy snuck behind her, snaking one arm about her waist for a tender but brief hug and caress to her bulging belly. She twisted in his arms, planting a kiss to his chin with a smile. "Soon, my love," she whispered, patting his cheek. "Very soon we shall have him to hold. You will be an amazing father."

They did join the egg race, both Darcy and his uncle quite excellent, their natural grace and elegance evidenced in precise balance. Darcy drew the line at jumping rope himself, but he did twirl one end while the children, and Drs. Penaflor and Darcy took turns performing elaborate steps over the fast-spinning rope. Leaving George, Raul, and Anne to entertain the children, Darcy and Lizzy finally escaped.

Lizzy and her cohorts had conjured all kinds of ideas for entertainment, so enraptured with the various concepts that they attempted to do it all. Darcy had been frankly skeptical but had written to a number of people he knew, sending out requests for the skilled professionals required. To his amazement, most of what Lizzy dreamt up had been realized. Three unique offerings were scheduled for the bedazzlement of the assembly, each to be performed several times throughout the evening so all could watch in divided groupings.

Darcy was personally most thrilled by the equestrians to perform at the corral so steered his wife in that direction next. The success of Philip Astley's circus in London over the past thirty years had sparked a swarm of duplicators in traveling shows throughout England. Darcy hired a troupe with a stellar reputation that specialized in trick horseback riding. He had been to Astley's Amphitheatre dozens of times and had taken Elizabeth once while in London, never tiring of the astounding equestrian feats the riders executed. While he did not actually expect this group to be as proficient, he was praying for at least a moderate mastery.

Lizzy climbed the bottom rung of the fence, Darcy supporting her at the small of her back. They had missed the first performance. The riders and mounts needed time to rest in between sets, but Darcy had arranged for three sets to be played, allowing all guests time to view the other entertainments and not miss what he considered the highlight. With eyes shining, Lizzy laughing at his childlike exuberance, the act began.

Galloping wildly, a grey horse burst out the stable doors, a man dressed in flowing rags clutching frantically to the reins. His face was a study in absolute terror as he yelled and wailed, body bouncing crazily on the animal's bare back. Round and round the ring they flew, all the while the seemingly hysterical man clung to the horse and his hat. As they raced about, the rider began to flip and twist, always acting as if he was in a frenzy of terror and barely holding on. In time, the humor of it all hit the crowd as the man's actions turned from random and desperate to elegant and masterful. He flipped his body backwards, clinging to the horse's rump, hat flying off, and then proceeded to lift his legs straight into the air. With another abrupt swivel, he again faced forward, holding the reins with his feet while he casually removed the frayed jacket. Little by little, always while racing in circles and sitting sideways or steering with his teeth, articles of his threadbare clothing were discarded. Underneath, he wore a tight fitting garment of white with gold and silver sparkles interwoven.

The crowd cheered, clapping furiously. Finally, completely transformed into a stunningly fit vision of masculine athleticism, the barefoot man stood on the back of the galloping horse. He held the rein loosely in one hand, the other gallantly waving to the applauding spectators. The stable doors opened then and three more horse and rider teams emerged, all dressed in similar scandalous outfits and all standing on their mounts. Together, the four proceeded to run around the ring in dazzling arrays of antics. They leapt from horse to horse, straddled two animals at once, somersaulted, stood on one leg while bent completely forward, balanced upside down, lay flat over the horse's rear, and so many more tricks that it became a blur.

The only difference Lizzy could readily detect from Astley's program was the length, quantity of artists, and wealth of props and costumes. The riders themselves were amazing and the simple country folk of Derbyshire, quite likely none of whom had ever witnessed such an exhibit, were spellbound. Darcy was gazing with what could only be described as extreme infatuation and yearning, eyes glittering and bedazzled.

Lizzy leaned toward his ear and said, "Do not even think about it, William! The way you ride Parsifal is challenging enough. I do not wish to see the father of our child attempting to stand on a running horse's back!"

Darcy flushed, averting his eyes. "It never crossed my mind, Elizabeth."

She laughed, kissing his earlobe. "Of course not."

The crowd broke up as the horses and their riders retreated into the stable for a relaxing intermission. Darcy and Lizzy meandered, pausing for occasional chats, although most of the people were far too nervous to attempt conversation with their stoic Master. A number of blankets had been spread over the extensive yard, upon which sat feasting families or flirting couples. Encountering all three of the Bingleys, they together headed to the middle enclosure where another performance had just started. Colonel Fitzwilliam was already there with Kitty and Georgiana.

This roughly rectangular grid of lawn was intersected with ropes stretched taut and narrow beams positioned anywhere from one to six feet off the ground. An Italian family of acrobats, five male and one female, were displaying their skills of balance, flexibility, and agility. Dressed in skin tight clothing similar to the trick riders, tinted in vivid shades of red and blue with flowing gauze scarves attached to the arms, legs, and waists, they resembled human butterflies. In a truly impressive exposition, they walked along the ropes, the thinnest no thicker than a man's thumb, sometimes using long poles or umbrellas to balance. They flawlessly traversed all the ropes, stopping frequently to raise one leg in all directions, bending over both forward and backward, twirling about, hand standing, tumbling, swinging, and more. Usually, they performed individually, but on the wider beam they worked in teams. They leapfrogged over each other, climbed onto shoulders or feet as high as all six of them, and contorted their bodies over each other in truly grotesque ways.

The stronger men grasped the lithe woman and completely tossed her high into the air, always catching her after she spun and twisted while flying. The people gasped and screamed, clapping enthusiastically at each demonstration of incredible aerodynamics. Lizzy was sure they were going to fall at least a dozen times but they never did. The spectators went crazy, applauding loudly with whistles and shouted praise, the acrobats bowing deeply in all directions, at the last toward the Darcys.

The sun was nearly set, the fading rays casting long shadows over the landscape. All the torches and lanterns had been lit so the area was well illuminated. The younger children were asleep in the pavilion, the orphans being rounded up to return to their home, and the older children were finishing the games or chasing each other about the grounds amongst the roaming adults. Young singles fortuitously grasped the social situation to claim dances or, if very lucky, a stolen kiss. Adults reveled in the rare delight of large quantities of food, relaxation, and fun. The wine was brought out as the sun slipped lower on the horizon, stars appearing as the air cooled dramatically. The orchestra took their places on the platform and began the process of tuning their instruments.

The Darcys visited the refreshment tent for a cool drink and a snack, Lizzy unable to pass too many hours without ingesting something. To their incredible surprise, Mrs. Langton was lounging on a chair, large body barely fitting amid the armrests, glass of wine in her hand, laughing boisterously at something Mr. Taylor had said. Darcy humorously raised one brow, waving the cook back down as she ungainly attempted to rise.

"Stay seated, Mrs. Langton. I am delighted to see you enjoying yourself. You deserve to reap the bounty of your labors. The food is marvelous and I do believe you and your staff have eclipsed all prior feasts. Mrs. Darcy and I are forever in your debt."

Lizzy bit her lip to forestall a case of the giggles as the hefty woman blushed and stammered at her Master's praise. Darcy smiled slightly and bowed, clasping Lizzy's elbow and steering her out of the pavilion to leave the servants at their unencumbered amusements.

All the Pemberley Manor residents converged at the last designated area, taking seats in the front rows to await the final show. A sudden hush fell over the audience as the tent flap opened to reveal a small man sedately walking onto the arena. He was costumed in a loose, garish patchwork suit of every shade in the spectrum, enormous blue shoes, face painted with colorful stripes, and head bald. If all that was not enough to awe the crowd, the little clown was walking on his hands! He advanced across the field unhurriedly, gigantic feet flapping and florid face grinning, until he reached the very end whereupon he abruptly crumpled into a heap, lying still as death. The audience collectively gasped, some even rising or taking involuntary steps forward, only to halt mid-stride when the tent flap exploded open and out blasted two more clowns. One was dressed as outrageously as the hand-walker, a fluttering ball of color with hundreds of brightly patterned strips of fabric apparently glued onto every inch of his body, a scarlet wig, oar-sized boots of green, and red circles about his eyes and mouth. He was running pell-mell and steering a rickety wooden wagon, inside of which sat the third clown. He was costumed as a proper English gentleman, only highly exaggerated. The collar of his waistcoat extended way past his ears, the cravat knotted at least three dozen times and some eight inches beyond his chin, jacket tails touching the ground, baggy breeches with three-inch wide knee buckles, and, of course, huge shoes. All this topped off with a ridiculously high beaver hat.

The audience was roaring as the wagon-driving clown raced haphazardly about the arena, finally skidding to a halt near the "unconscious" clown, tipping the wagon and unceremoniously dumping the English clown onto the grass. Acting in pantomime, the outraged Englishman righted himself, scolding the contrite clown who rushed to assist him in dusting off and fixing his clothing and retrieving his spilled accessories, wreaking havoc with every move while the Englishman grew further comically incensed. Gathering his belongings, a mammoth black leather physician's bag and cracked monocle, also ridiculously large, the English clown was unveiled as a doctor arriving to revive the fallen clown. Opening his bag and randomly extracting a number of strange metal devices, including decidedly non-medical items like a quill, spoon, shoehorn, toothbrush, and more, the doctor attempted to examine his clown patient. Naturally, he was hindered by the fumbling assistance of the other clown, who constantly tripped, handed him the wrong instrument, punched and poked, stabbed with the quill, and on and on.

It was absolutely hysterical, not a soul in the audience without tears from laughing. The stricken clown was eventually cured by the good doctor, so ecstatic to be alive that he tumbled and jumped and vaulted about the arena, launching into the seats to delightedly pat and hug and tease the audience. More clowns joined the fray, capering through the people and playing tricks. For another half an hour, they interacted with the onlookers in various humorous ways: tweaking noses, discovering hidden coins behind ears and in pockets, tickling, pulling endless ribbons of scarves from sleeves, and so on. The entire ring was a multihued plethora of other clowns falling over each other, running on spinning barrels, juggling balls and clubs and even knives, dazzling with magical sleights-of-hand, and performing daring acrobatics. It was an astounding pageant, the perfect crescendo to the trio of stunning entertainments. Not a soul was left wanting as full darkness descended and the guests laughingly wandered toward the food pavilion for sustenance before dancing.

People were randomly weaving their way to the grassy flatland alongside the lake where the orchestra platform was stationed. Kitty began bouncing on her toes while Georgiana grew paler by the second, Richard laughing at both the girls who tightly clutched his arms for very different reasons. Leaving the others on the edges of the assembling dancers, Darcy escorted his wife to the platform, stepped upon the raised dais, and walked to the middle. He stood quietly; the Master of Pemberley poised domineeringly and aristocratically with his exquisitely genteel wife at his side, linked arm in arm. Darcy had no need to say a word, the crowd respectfully quieting instantly under the gaze of their Master.

"Mrs. Darcy and I are delighted to see you all enjoying yourselves. If I may be granted a moment to interrupt the festivities," he paused and smiled slightly, "and I do promise it shall only be a moment." Hushed laughter spread through the company. Darcy continued in his resonant voice, lifted loudly to reach the press of people, "The majority of you have served the Darcy family for long years, decades in many instances. Your faithful employment and devotion has persevered unwaveringly and undeterred. Those of you who remember the Festivals of the past know that it was an essential part of Pemberley life. A sincere offering by the Darcy family to express our appreciation for your dedicated and arduous labor. For too many years, grief has ruled the Manor and these communications of our thanks have been suspended. I am thrilled beyond measure to stand before you as Master and proclaim that grief is unequivocally an emotion of the past. Therefore, it is with tremendous joy that I and Mrs. Darcy," he glanced to Elizabeth with a beaming smile, "the Mistress of Pemberley, welcome you formally to the first of many years of celebrations. With that declaration, let the party resume!"

The congregation cheered, clapping enthusiastically. Darcy turned to the orchestra, signaling them to begin, then bowed deeply to his wife and extended his hand formally. Elizabeth curtseyed, clasping his hand as he led her onto the dance floor, assuming the first place in the line. The orchestra launched into a lively gavotte, couples rapidly filling the space. Charles escorted his wife, Kitty was with Colonel Fitzwilliam, Dr. Penaflor partnered Anne de Bourgh, and Dr. Darcy dragged Georgiana. Unfortunately, the odd number of men to women in their company meant that Caroline was left alone. Luckily, she did not particularly care, the idea of dancing on the grass with a mass of commoners not overly appealing to her.

When the music ended on an upbeat note and blaring crescendo from the orchestra, the crowd erupted again into hurrahs and applause primarily directed toward the Darcys. Darcy bowed, offering his arm once again to his wife, and together they regally departed the scene. Strolling casually toward the Manor, they halted frequently to nod or converse briefly with a guest. Darcy sought out the head groundskeeper, Mr. Clark, and shared a whispered conversation with a couple of gestures toward the distant inky outline of the Greek Temple. Darcy nodded in satisfaction, reacquiring his wife's hand to resume their slow ramble, and they finally reached the sanctuary of the terrace.

Darcy had made it very clear to Lizzy that it would be highly improper for the Master and Mistress to invade the festivities or mingle overly with the attendees. She had been skeptical at first, but as he explained it, her understanding grew.

"First of all," he had told her, "they will not be able to fully relax and enjoy themselves if I am hovering nearby. Since the purpose of the Festival is to extend our thankfulness in the form of their complete gratification, it would be remiss of us to deter said gratification by creating an atmosphere of unease by our presence. I want them to forget, for a time, that they are servants or employees. Secondly, at the risk of being branded haughty and arrogant, it is unsuitable for us to mingle socially with our servants." Lizzy had frowned slightly and Darcy had taken her hand. "I know you abhor such distinctions, Elizabeth, and a part of me agrees with you. Nonetheless, it is the world we live in and for all that it may seem unkind or pompous, these class divisions have served our country well for hundreds of years. Even if I wished to alter it, and I in truth cannot say I do, few would follow my lead. Most importantly, our servants and tenants would be the loudest protesters! They are comfortable and well cared for, therefore having no wish to deviate from the status quo."

Lizzy had assented to his decision, although not wholly agreeing with his assessment of their reception. Tonight, however, as they ambled amongst the people, she had noted clearly the immediate stiffening and mask of formality that fell over each face as they approached. Gazing out over the boisterous, clusters of folk and comparing that with the instantaneous decorum and tenseness that ensued upon the presence of the Darcys, Lizzy finally comprehended. In a strange way, it was the last turn of the key, the final stroke of the axe which severed her old way of thinking and completed her transition into the Mistress of Pemberley.

Now, she happily flopped onto the sofa, suddenly tired and desirous of the solitude found in the shadows. Few lights had been lit, mostly those glowing from inside the parlor, yet the location of the raised terrace offered a panoramic view of the grounds. Darcy dragged a chair over and lifted her feet onto it.

"There," he said. "Are you comfortable, love?"

"Yes," she answered with a laugh, "but why the chair?"

"You have been on your feet for hours and the book states that pregnant women's feet can swell." Lizzy glanced to her perfectly slender and tiny feet but chose not to point the fact out. Darcy continued, "I am going to pour myself a brandy. Do you wish for anything?"

"A small glass of wine would be lovely, thank you, dear." He kissed her forehead and disappeared into the house. Lizzy sighed contentedly, rising to retrieve several remaining meat rolls and a croissant from the dinner table. Darcy returned shortly and they sat quietly, nibbling and sipping as the revelry persisted.

From their hidden vantage point, they could espy most of what transpired on the dance area. Richard was occupied for each dance, the man apparently tireless. Lizzy had delighted to see him lately in attire other than his military uniform. She adored Richard and thought him a handsome man—naturally not as much as her husband, but a fine figure in any suit. Today, as yesterday, he had dressed casually but nonetheless regally, in snug pantaloons of beige and a jacket of russet and gold. Dr. Penaflor had worn shades of grey with a waistcoat of forest green, all designed to accentuate his exotic darkness. He primarily squired Anne, although careful to accompany every other woman as well. Anne was beautiful in a gown of blue and white, modestly cut but not as severe as the majority of her gowns. Naturally, George drew the most attention in his vibrant fuchsia, dancing with feline grace and refinement. Georgiana appeared to relax with each subsequent turn on the floor, none of the gentlemen allowing her to evade.

Even Caroline had apparently relinquished her disdain, as Darcy noted her frequently partnered with each man.

For three hours, Darcy and Lizzy reclined in isolation, happily observing the fun. They talked softly, kissed frequently, and cuddled. On occasion, they were visited by someone from the party, usually seeking brief respite and refreshment, only to be snatched away forthwith by a seeking dance partner. There were enough interruptions for Darcy and Lizzy to curb their improper urges, maintaining a regulated decorum in their mild intimacy.

As the midnight hour approached and the orchestra announced the last two sets, anticipation for the final crescendo to the Festival began to rise. Upon entrance to the party, the Darcys had informed each guest to, if possible, remain until after the dancing as they had a special treat planned. None knew what to expect, but based on the grand exhibitions and entertainments offered thus far, the fever pitch of expectation was high.

The last dance ended to extended applause for the outstanding musicians. Folks wandered about in small groupings, not sure what to expect or where to look. Darcy rose to stand prominently at the terrace railing, Lizzy embraced tightly to his chest, both gazing toward the dark knoll above the Cascade Falls, the intermittent flicker of light visible if one attended to the area. Within fifteen minutes word had spread, folks noting the direction the Darcys were staring and turning to peer curiously upward. A hush fell, everyone holding their breath without consciously realizing it, breaths released in a collective gasp of stunned awe mere seconds later.

With a thunderous boom piercing the calm, a rocket was launched far into the starry black sky, exploding loudly into a brilliant shower of gold sparkles. The crowd erupted into claps of joy, the sound instantly lost amid the next rocket blast, this with a rain of white. For twenty minutes, the combined noise of rocket detonations and cheering ruled as the sky above Pemberley lit up with dazzling shimmers of red, gold, blue, white, orange, and green in dozens of shapes and sizes.

Interspersed with the enchanting aerial displays, the firework technicians hired by the Darcys lit a profusion of ground level pyrotechnics. Dense showers of brightly colored sparks resembled water spewing from fountains; fireworks set on small floats drifted down the Falls as the light reflected off the water; and elaborate sculptured shapes were set aflame with a profusion of color. The shapes were myriad: a rose of red, a horse of gold, the flag of England in red and blue and white, "PEMBERLEY" spelled in orange, a dog in white, and—the masterpiece—an enormous detailed replica of Pemberley Manor in gold.

This last was lit simultaneously with the discharge of a dozen rockets; the resulting illumination was brilliant and bathed the entire grounds in nearly broad-daylight radiance. It was stunning; the assembly was momentarily dumbfounded as silence descended in a crashing wave only to be replaced seconds later by a deafening barrage of clapping and yelling. Reports later received indicated that the colorful lights were seen in Lambton to the east, Baslow to the north, and Rowsley to the south. The satisfying finale was stupendous and would be remembered for decades hence.

Darcy hugged his wife, drawing her again into the shadows and turning her about in his arms. He pressed her into his chest, embracing with intense emotion. Speaking huskily to the top of her head, he said, "Elizabeth, you accomplished all this. You! I am so very proud of you. I am… overwhelmed." He finished in a whisper, caressing her back as he held tight.

Lizzy melted into his embrace, happy and relieved. Withdrawing only enough to grasp her chin with his palm, Darcy bent to kiss her lips tenderly. Meeting her glittering eyes and smiling, he softly said, "Come, beloved, let us retire. The others can fend for themselves. I want to hold you in my arms and whisper into your beautiful ears my abounding adoration."

With his arms firmly about her, they ascended the stairs to their chamber where Darcy did precisely as he promised… and more.

CHAPTER TWENTY-TWO

Solitude

WITHIN A WEEK OF the Festival, the secret wish of both Darcys was granted even beyond their wildest dreams. That is, all of their beloved friends and family members vacated the Manor to adventures of their own throughout England, and Darcy and Lizzy were completely and blissfully alone.

On the day following the Festival, an extremely lazy day for all the inhabitants of Pemberley, Charles was the only one who expressed any desire to move beyond the parlor. Everyone was in a particularly mellow mood, the party aftermath ruling with aching feet from dancing, aching heads from drink, and aching stomachs from nonstop eating. While everyone was lying about on comfortable chairs and sofas with needlepoint, books, or letters in hand, Charles spoke into the relative silence.

"Darcy, I believe we shall depart tomorrow if this is agreeable with you. Now that the decision has been made, my Jane and I are anxious to speak with the Bennets and then begin our preparations for relocating."

Kitty and Georgiana were the only persons in the room whose faces fell in dismay. Darcy laid aside his book with an understanding nod. "Of course,

Charles. I understand your eagerness and you know you have my blessing. However, if I may remind you, the Matlocks are joining us for dinner tomorrow and I was imagining that being our last engagement prior to our being parted from the delightful company of you and your lovely wife for several months. Is one additional day at Pemberley too daunting to imagine?" Darcy smiled at his friend, Bingley rapidly assuring him that one day was agreeable.

"Mr. Bingley," Colonel Fitzwilliam spoke from his relaxing pose near the window, "if you would be willing, I believe Miss de Bourgh and I will accompany you on the road. It is always wiser to travel in groups if possible."

"Naturally, Colonel, you are welcome. Netherfield is open as well if you or Miss de Bourgh desire a brief respite ere traveling on to Kent."

"Well, since a caravan is forming, I shall chime in and rudely insinuate myself and Raja to the party," George declared. His spindly, yellow and corn-flower blue garbed frame stretched flat on the rug before the fireplace hearth. "I know Dr. Penaflor wants to keep an eye on his patient and I am sensing the urge to visit my sister." He sat up, crossing his long legs. "William, I was going to ask permission to stay at Darcy House for a spell before traveling on to Devon. I should warn Estella I am heading her way, at the very least. Perhaps I will even give her more than one day's notice." He grinned at his nephew, recalling his abrupt appearance in London.

Darcy laughed. "I rather doubt Aunt Estella's consternation would be too severe, Uncle, warning or no, but naturally you may stay at Darcy House as long as you wish, and Dr. Penaflor as well, of course."

"You will return to Pemberley before you leave England, George?" Lizzy asked, truly concerned.

"Not weary of me yet, Elizabeth?" He smiled fondly, Lizzy emphatically shaking her head. "I am touched!" He stretched his arms above his head with a deep sigh, still gazing at his niece speculatively, "No, I think I shall stick around for a while. I am rather enjoying being decadent and useless, at least for now. Perhaps in a few months I will feel the urge to work for a change, maybe volunteer my services at the hospital in Derby, deliver a baby or two," he said shrugging and grinning at Lizzy's blush and Darcy's arched brow. "Besides, I deem wild horses could not drag Raja away."

Dr. Penaflor merely smiled, Anne hastily averting her eyes.

"Then it is settled," Charles declared with a slap to his knee, "all shall ride to Netherfield, whereupon the final separation will occur. Two days hence."

Kitty was silently crying. "Oh Lizzy, please can I stay? Please?"

"I am sorry, dear. Mama and Papa need you, too. The quiet in the house is likely driving them mad. Think of poor Papa who only has Mama to keep him company! Besides, you will all visit after the baby is born, perhaps at Christmas." Darcy winced involuntarily at that thought, but luckily Lizzy did not notice.

With this decision made, the usual bustle of pre-departure activity ensued. The dinner party planned was a simple affair, the Darcys aware that the staff would yet be busy with restoration. They had scheduled the event a week before, knowing it would likely be the last soiree preceding the scattering of their guests. Aside from the imminent exodus of the Pemberley visitors, the Matlocks were also embarking on a month-long tour of Wales with their eldest son, Jonathon, and his wife, Priscilla. Therein came the final surprise.

"William, if I may have a moment of your time?" Lord Matlock lightly clasped his nephew's elbow, indicating the emptiness of the hall. Once alone, he continued, "I know this is rather short notice, but your aunt and I were discussing our trip and Georgiana came to mind. We would very much like to take her with us if this meets your approval?"

Darcy frowned slightly, to be replaced instantly with a smile as it abruptly occurred to him that Georgiana's absence would provide complete privacy for him and Elizabeth. Attempting to not appear the utter lovesick fool, he gruffly cleared his throat and stroked his chin as if deep in serious contemplation. Naturally, Lord Matlock was not the least bit duped, but he played along.

"I know you fret, especially after Ramsgate, but rest assured she will be well chaperoned. Mrs. Annesley can accompany her if you wish, and we will not let her out of our sight. It would be good for her to travel a bit, and she has never been to Wales. Besides, you and Elizabeth have earned some solitude. You shall have precious little once the child arrives. Consider it a belated wedding present or early baby gift to you both."

Darcy laughed. "Very well, Uncle! The truth is, I need no persuading as it sounds delightful to be alone with my wife. Perhaps it would be wisest to postpone Georgiana's enlightenment until after Miss Kitty departs. It may be too much of a blow to her heart to see Georgie ecstatic when she is so depressed at leaving."

Therefore, exactly seven days after the Festival, Darcy and Lizzy stood on the Pemberley entryway and waved adieu to a smiling Georgiana. It was very early in the morning, Lizzy rising far earlier than she was becoming accustomed to. Darcy was dressed for riding, in truth having assumed that his wife would not wake to kiss Georgiana goodbye, having said her farewells prior to retiring last night. Now, however, with the house essentially empty and his desirable wife still with a sleepy face and hair hastily pulled back, the thought of walking away from her side even for the thrill of a morning race was unappealing.

The carriage turned the final corner, Lizzy sighing deeply and leaning against Darcy's side with a yawn. "You know, I have all my life considered myself an early riser. Meet the dawn with a smile and all that." She lifted her eyes to meet Darcy's brilliant ones. "Perhaps my early rising became habit out of a necessity to escape the craziness of Longbourn before it began each day! Here, with you, I find life so peaceful that I do not wish to leave the comfort of our bed and chamber. It is all your fault, you know. Your charms are magnetic, my love. I am not only a hopeless wanton but slothful as well!"

Darcy was smiling happily. "If you are anticipating an apology, I fear I shall disappoint you, beloved. I am perfectly content to wake preceding you and stare at your beauty as you sleep. Furthermore, I live for the opportunity to rouse you with kisses and caresses. As for being wanton, well, I need not address my opinion on that subject surely?"

"No, you do not. In fact," she glanced about but they were alone, and then reached up to toy with his open collar as she continued, "if you think Parsifal would not be too terribly annoyed with me or heartbroken, perhaps I could induce you to forego your morning excursion for the time being? My wicked mind is suddenly conjuring all sorts of alternate ways for you to work up a healthy sweat."

Darcy nodded sagely, glittering eyes belying his calm pose. "Do you think the servants would gossip overly if we sprinted up the stairs?"

Lizzy pivoted with a giggle, leading him sedately inside. "Maybe we should maintain proper decorum until the second floor landing, at the least."

Thus began a lazy pattern that would be embraced for the next several months with few exceptions. It was akin to their first weeks at Pemberley after their marriage, only now they were incredibly bonded and all the shades of newness or discomfort were wholly dissipated. They did, in fact, laze about quite a bit. Naturally, Darcy had a fair amount of work to do, letters to write, and the occasional trip about the estate but nothing terribly time consuming or critical. Aside from his study and the informal dining room, they rarely visited any of the other rooms, and the majority of their time was spent in their chambers.

Darcy, as always, rose with the sun. There was absolutely no doubt that his immediate preference was to wake his wife and make love with the sunrise. On occasion, his hunger was such that he did just that, Lizzy responding with only mild pique before passion flared. However, Darcy was a gentleman and recognized his wife's need to sleep, so usually he kissed her gently, cautiously detaching her body from his as he slipped away. Either a ride followed or quiet paperwork of some sort at the desk in their sitting room. On occasion, he scheduled morning sessions with Mr. Keith to attend to estate affairs. Whatever the case, the bulk of the morning hours were delightfully and rewardingly lapsed in the company of his love.

Despite Lizzy's jesting, she did tend to rise fairly early compared to most women of leisure. Generally she was up and freshened, nibbling on toast or fruit to curb the worst of her stomach pangs, awaiting Darcy's return from whatever endeavor he was tending to that morning. Whether he was sitting at the desk when she rose, or entering the room to discover her placidly reclining in her chair, they greeted each other with eager enthusiasm and bright smiles. Neither desired to part for the remaining hours of the morn and rarely were they forced to.

All appearances to the contrary, they actually accomplished much in the way of real work during those morning hours. Lizzy reapplied herself to learning more of the household management as well as general estate business. As Darcy conducted the ceaseless enterprises that comprised Pemberley's wealth, Lizzy aided him and increased her awareness of the overall organization. She would forever stand in awe of the vast interests and responsibilities that Darcy managed flawlessly and easily. Never would she fully comprehend it all, especially since he was forever shifting their money into other ventures or companies. Always he sought new projects or improved ways to handle an established area. It was mind boggling to Lizzy for the most part, but over time she learned to grasp much of it.

For the present, they planned primarily for the first of Duke Grafton's brood mares, which would be arriving soon, and for their child. Since Lizzy knew basically nothing about the entire world contained within the stables, their morning talks were an enormous education. Darcy explained it all in minute detail. Lizzy, frankly, grasped less than half of what he said, but she loved how he glowed and enthused whenever he spoke of his horses, so she happily allowed him to ramble. She did a tremendous amount of head nodding and mumbled vocalizations of assent, Darcy usually pacing with coiled energy as he spoke and therefore utterly unaware of whether she was understanding or not. A fly on the wall would die of hysterics at the typical scene: Darcy marching with long treads, robe fluttering wildly about his shins, fingers flickering or running through his hair while he prattled jauntily, eyes gleaming and unfocused, while Lizzy sat with a gentle smile on her lips and an expression of intense adoration mingled with dazed incomprehension.

As pertained to their baby, they discussed a number of topics. Lizzy was to be seen by a local midwife, Mrs. Henderson, who had delivered at least half of the babies in the immediate vicinity. Darcy talked to probably every person he knew and all recommended Mrs. Henderson. Despite Uncle George's vague allusion to delivering their baby, neither felt they could depend upon his presence with complete certainty. Either way, he was currently absent, so Darcy insisted she be examined by an expert. Her pregnancy was proceeding without apparent complications, but Darcy, not surprisingly, refused to assume anything.

Mrs. Henderson was a woman in her late fifties, a mother of six and grand-mother of seven. She had delivered Harriet Vernor's and Marilyn Hughes's babies as well as Georgiana Darcy seventeen years ago. She was a large, very serious woman, and Lizzy was a bit intimidated by her, but her reputation was impeccable, which was all that truly mattered.

Mrs. Henderson was greatly taken aback when Darcy accompanied Lizzy into the bedchamber. "Mr. Darcy, I plan to examine Mrs. Darcy. You should wait in the sitting room. We will rejoin you when all is complete."

Darcy, however, was shaking his head. "Thank you for your concern, Mrs. Henderson, but I have seen it before and wish to stay with my wife." He was blushing mildly but the penetrating Darcy stare and commanding posture was in full effect. Mrs. Henderson, for all her authority, could not muster the strength to countermand, but she was clearly distressed.

Lizzy eased the tension by softly touching her arm and saying, "I assure you, Mrs. Henderson, I want my husband with me. How about a compromise? He will stand by the window while you perform the examination, but speak freely. We have no secrets."

The midwife's professionalism overcame her nervousness eventually.

Darcy frowned at Lizzy's compromise but obeyed, standing by the far window with back to the room, keen hearing missing nothing. Mrs. Henderson was thorough. Her examination concurred with the physician's assessment that the baby would arrive in early December. This meant that Lizzy was beginning her sixth month of pregnancy. She spoke at length as to the immediate expectations as Lizzy entered her last few months. She imparted nothing that they had not already gleaned from the book or Dr. Darcy, easing both their minds. Darcy spoke frequently and bluntly from his pose in the corner, startling Mrs. Henderson initially, but by the end of the interview, she was rather used to his presence and unusual interest in the subject. This, of course, had been Darcy's plan all along.

He had thought long and hard on his uncle's statement regarding being with Lizzy when the baby was born. As shocked as he was at first, the more he ruminated, it became clear that he truthfully could not fathom *not* being there. He discussed it with his wife, who blanched at first, the same standard protocols and habits rising to the fore.

Darcy grinned and repeated his uncle's words to him verbatim, "I know you tend to be a stickler for the rules"—Lizzy snorted at this fallacious assertion—"but it is not a law from the Crown, after all." Lizzy had laughed, realizing as Darcy had, that neither could she imagine him not being with her. No one alive could comfort her as he could, and no one else should see their son before him.

So, although the decision had been made, Darcy certain that nothing or no one except Lizzy herself would drag him from the birth chamber, they agreed that springing the idea on the midwife at this point in time would be unkind at the least.

Darcy had not knowingly recognized any anxieties regarding Lizzy and the baby, yet hearing the midwife confirm all was well was a tremendous relief. With each passing day, as she swelled with the baby's maturing, he floated further and further off the ground. Darcy had long since given up rationalizing his devotion and ardor for his wife, accepting it fully, so was therefore blissfully unaware of how strange he was compared to most husbands in his circumstance. If he had desired his wife prior to pregnancy, and he most assuredly had nearly every second of every day, he now became obsessed. Not only was his sexual appetite as vigorous as always, but his yearning to merely gaze upon her body, to touch their child and feel him move, to talk to the burgeoning bulge, to massage the ointment over her skin, and to plan for their infant's arrival consumed him.

Thankfully, Lizzy did not mind his devotion. It was also seriously fortunate that Mr. Keith was an excellent steward, as much of the necessary estate business fell unwittingly onto his shoulders. Darcy was frequently unfocused during their discussions or business excursions about the farms. If the issue was critical or required intense concentration, Mr. Keith knew how to phrase his words and tone his voice to crack through Darcy's haze, at which point the commanding Darcy snapped into place and assumed control, his mental faculties not the tiniest bit diminished. However, generally, Mr. Keith smiled and handled matters himself. He may not completely understand his Master's relationship with Mrs. Darcy, his own marriage being of a typical nature; however, long association with Mr. Darcy had given him great insight into the younger man's character. Although he may not have couched it in exactly the same words as the late Mrs. Darcy, he had long ago identified the passionate nature of Mr. Darcy as seen in all areas of his life but had been clarified most profoundly in the grief exhibited when he lost Elizabeth Bennet and the utter joy when he found her.

The question of a nanny was answered before either of them had asked it. Darcy returned one afternoon from an excursion to several farms with mournful news. One of his tenants, Mr. Hanford, who had managed a plot of land for over thirty-five years, was found dead in a far field having apparently been felled by an abrupt heart seizure. Lizzy was terribly distressed, having grown fond of Mr. Hanford's gracious and motherly wife during her various visitations.

The next day, Lizzy commandeered her new curricle for the first time to pay a call to Mrs. Hanford. She brought a basket hastily gathered with enough food for the entire family to subsist on for a week, a huge bouquet of flowers from the Pemberley gardens, and an envelope from Mr. Darcy. Darcy, per standard practice in these situations, paid for the burial expenses and allotted a sum to the widow adequate enough for her to survive for a couple of months until able to establish subsequent employment and residence. He was fortunate in this particular circumstance in that Mr. Hanford's eldest son already worked the farm with his father and was more than willing to assume the tenancy.

Mrs. Hanford met Lizzy on the stoop when she drove up. Alighting quickly, Lizzy approached the widow with sympathy evident. "Mrs. Hanford, I am so very sorry for your loss. Mr. Hanford was a good man, decent and kind. He will be sorely missed by all."

Mrs. Hanford nodded, wiping at swollen red eyes. "Thank you, Mrs. Darcy. Please come inside. I have tea brewing."

Lizzy readily joined the grieving woman for tea. Mrs. Hanford scurried about the kitchen, Lizzy sitting quietly as the older woman spoke of her husband in tones of affectionate remembrance. The Hanfords, like many of the tenant farmers, were generational, meaning that Mr. Hanford's father had managed this particular plot of land as his son would now do. Altogether the Hanfords birthed six children who lived. All were married and settled in the region except for the youngest, a daughter now seventeen, who currently aided her mother in serving the Mistress of Pemberley tea and cakes.

"What are your plans, Mrs. Hanford? Will you stay here or relocate with family elsewhere?" Lizzy asked quietly, sipping the excellently steeped tea.

Mrs. Hanford sat at the table, fidgeting with a moist, wrinkled handkerchief. "My son and his wife have asked me to continue dwelling with them." She smiled as she said, "For a time, I suppose this arrangement will work, but they are expecting their third child soon and the house is getting crowded. We had been talking lately of asking Mr. Darcy if another house was available or could be built, as my boy Roger did not want to leave Pemberley." She paused to dab at her eyes, voice catching as she continued, "I guess his papa passing solved that problem, at least."

Lizzy patted her hand sympathetically, not knowing what to say. Mrs. Hanford gained control finally, looking at Lizzy with a brave smile. "Forgive my horrible manners, Mrs. Darcy. I understand you and Mr. Darcy are expecting and I have yet to congratulate. This is wonderful news, for all involved."

"Thank you, Mrs. Hanford. We are very excited and pleased."

The widow nodded. "Babies are God's greatest gift, Mrs. Darcy. So soft and innocent. Then they grow to be the delight of their parent's heart. Naturally, those of us who depend on the Darcy family wish to see the line continue, but it is more than that. It is a tremendous blessing. I have ten grandchildren already," she declared with pride. "Ten! I love them all so dearly and am doubly blessed to have them nearby." Then, as if her last statement added to her grief, she hung her head and continued with a sob, "It will be hard to leave them, but I cannot intrude forever. Roger and Millie need their own home. My sister and her husband run an inn in Birmingham, so perhaps she could use my help."

As an epiphany, the solution dawned on Lizzy. Naturally, the reality of hiring a nanny was a concept she and Darcy understood, but it simply had not yet been discussed. Lizzy planned to nurse her baby, so a wet nurse was unnecessary, and she intended to personally attend to the bulk of his other needs. However, as her new status required a certain amount of social obligations and duties, a competent nanny was indispensable. Besides, Lizzy knew little about the rearing of a baby, which was all the more reason why the flash of inspiration regarding Mrs. Hanford was brilliant.

"Mrs. Hanford," Lizzy leaned forward saying seriously, eyes sparkling, "I have a proposition for you. I do not desire an answer forthwith, as I judge you need time to grieve and rationally decide the course best for you. However, I see that we both have a need that may best be fulfilled by the other. I will, come December, need a nanny. I want someone who has vast experience, as I have none, who loves babies, and who is faithful and respective of the Darcy family. You are such a woman, Mrs. Hanford. Of course, I would need to attain Mr. Darcy's approval, but I do not imagine he would disagree with my assessment."

Mrs. Hanford was clearly overcome, tears rushing anew down her cheeks. Even her daughter was crying. "Oh, Mrs. Darcy! Bless my stars! I do not need time to consider. I am honored, so honored... Oh my!" She blew her nose loudly, breathless and weeping.

Lizzy laughed, standing to hug the poor woman where she sat. "Mrs. Hanford, calm yourself! Please, let us leave the offer on the table for now. I cannot promise until I speak with Mr. Darcy, and you are too overwrought, rightfully so, to render a clear decision. There, there." The remaining time dissolving in tears of grief and joy, Lizzy finally left drained yet jubilant in spite of the sadness.

Darcy thought Mrs. Hanford a capital choice as a nanny, knowing the family to be a strong one with all the children raised to be upstanding Derbyshire citizens. He spoke with Roger Hanford, extending the formal request of the Darcys for his mother's services but clarifying that they did not want an answer, affirmative or negative, for at least two weeks in order to allow Mrs. Hanford time to mourn and meditate on her options. Secretly, they estimated it a surety and were correct in their appraisal. Mrs. Hanford waited exactly two weeks, and then wrote a formal letter of acceptance to the post of nanny to the Darcy firstborn.

Six days after the house had been emptied, Darcy woke to the joyous sensation of a cooling breeze and his wife nestled in his arms, back plastered against his chest. He had a lingering impression of a particularly vivid dream of him and Elizabeth under the copse of willows near Pemberley. They were making love as they occasionally did in the moonlight, only she was as thin as a reed, naturally beautiful with hair a mass of curls about her head, eyes luminous in the half-light, but her breasts were full and round, even more so than they were now in pregnancy. His dream-self nuzzled her bosom, delighting in her warmth in the crisp nighttime air, realizing suddenly that it was spring with fragrant buds of dandelions near his face. As he moved deliciously within her, he glanced over and noted a large basket sitting close by. It was swaying slightly, soft gurgles and mewls issuing forth. He reached one hand out and rocked the basket gently, murmuring, "Patience, my son, you can have your mother all to yourself in a few more minutes." In the dream, Lizzy chuckled, grasping his face with a firm palm, drawing his lips to hers, and whispering before she kissed, "Perhaps more than a few minutes."

He smiled into her hair, inhaling deeply of her fragrance as he nuzzled into her neck. "Elizabeth, my eternal love," he whispered, Lizzy stirring slightly. He cupped both breasts with his large palms, rolling partially onto his back and pulling her with him. She sighed and stretched, pressing her bottom into his groin with a wiggle. Darcy leisurely stroked over her front side as she woke further, in no haste whatsoever, his arousal increasing sweetly as he caressed all her succulent curves. He nibbled her earlobe, kissed along her neck, and tickled with the tip of his tongue.

"I want you, my Lizzy. I need you and cannot wait. Please forgive my urgency. I dreamt of you loving me so beautifully, giving yourself gloriously to me, and I woke with desire and yearning. Oh, my love! How you arouse me! How I love you, Elizabeth, forever, my wife."

She turned in his arms, halting his murmured professions with a hearty kiss. She pressed firmly against him and he could feel the insistent prods of their son into his abdomen. Lizzy withdrew slightly, smile radiant as she stroked his face and lips. "Fitzwilliam. My husband, my soul, you do not need to ever apologize. However, I must ask you to hold this thought," she said as she reached to his groin, stroking with a lusty smirk. "I must visit the water closet first!" He chuckled and nodded, Lizzy bestowing a quick peck as she left the bed.

Darcy watched her walk across the room with studied devotion, eyes kept riveted to the door so as to observe her returning. He adored how she swayed so gracefully, flesh glowing in the dawn's light, and the beautiful bump of their child especially prominent when she stood. She sat beside him, Darcy instantly rising to encircle her waist, burying his face into a heavy breast.

She held his head, fingers running through his thick hair as she sighed in contentment. "You had a dream?" He nodded, moving to the other breast, taking his sweet time before addressing her inquiry.

Holding her tightly, he nuzzled up her chest to her neck while pulling her onto the bed. In between licks and kisses he responded, "We were at the willows making love and our son was in a basket with us." He lifted to gaze into her eyes, caressing over her plump lips with one finger. "He began to wake but we both told him he would need to wait. Neither of us had any intention of halting our passion." He smiled and Lizzy laughed with a shake of her head. "Anyway, you were transcendent in the moonlight and I was loving you with all my body and soul."

Lizzy smiled, reaching down to caress him, Darcy groaning hoarsely as he claimed her lips in an ardent kiss. Morning loving was generally of an extremely ravenous nature, Darcy usually waking in a state of near complete excitement. Lizzy was thankful, for selfish reasons, that he did not wake her each morning as he surely wanted to; yet knowing how difficult it was for him to calm once aroused, she was surprised he was so thoughtful. She felt a bit guilty about her increased need for sleep—not that it was entirely her fault—so she readily acquiesced when he did rouse her early. Of course, loving her husband was never a chore, her own passion for him as voracious as his for her.

With equal yearning, they reached for each other, stroking and caressing until necessity demanded their merging. They kissed passionately, loving with consuming desire and unity. Lizzy withdrew from his mouth mere inches, gazing into his brilliant eyes while lightly fondling each beloved feature of his face.

"Is your dream being fulfilled?" she whispered.

"No dream ever has lived up to the reality of you, Elizabeth. The feel of you, your scent, your voice, how you hold me and touch me and kiss me… it is impossible to capture this in a dream."

She smiled, tenderly biting his lower lip. "Yet it must be somewhat reminiscent for you to wake so aroused, my potent husband!"

"Lord, Elizabeth! I do not need to dream of you vividly… you are in my heart always. The question is not why I am so easily excited when near you but how to prevent the reaction! I cannot look at you nor think of you without desire rising." He kissed her consumingly as he rolled her onto her back, loving continuously as he fondled her breasts.

Lizzy was mad with passion, legs roaming frantically from hip to calves and hands squeezing the taut muscles of his shoulders and back. The weight of his body crushed her deliciously and his raging heat burned her flesh divinely. "William, oh God, William! I love you so!"

He slowed, rising over her with arms extended. His face was flushed, skin gleaming with sweat, and eyes vivid with reverential love and fervent hunger. Lizzy caressed his solid chest, their gazes shifting from the other's face to their bodies. Darcy spoke, voice muted and grating, "You tease, best beloved, at being a hopeless wanton, and I am overjoyed that you are! Yet, it is I who am truly wanton. Insatiable, ravenous for you, awestruck by how you move me." He gulped, inhaling vigorously for control, arching his neck and closing his eyes in ecstasy.

Lizzy studied his perfection, teetering on the edge in her rapture yet spellbound by the vision of his masculinity coupled with his poignant words. Eventually, he opened his eyes and resumed, "In the wildest of my imaginings, both before meeting you and since, I have never remotely evoked the actuality of touching your essence while making love to you. The pleasure I derive from your body and soul melding with mine is indescribable. I cannot… have enough… of you, my wife!"

"Fitzwilliam, hold me!" Lizzy clutched his shoulders, pulling his body onto hers, Darcy succumbing with a prolonged moan. Shouts of love burst forth as they clung with limbs nearly strangling. Gasping and shivering, Darcy assaulted her mouth, plundering deeply with throaty rumbles. Broad hands secured her head, fingers laced into her hair as he rolled onto his back, Lizzy anchored against him. She withdrew from his lips with effort, needing air, but remained a scant hairbreadth away. "William," she whispered, brushing his jaw then chin, "I love you." Eyes met for a second, and then with a ragged breath, she dropped her head to his shoulder.

They embraced for a long while, Darcy expecting her to fall into a sated asleep as she usually did. He, too, experienced a vague guilt at waking her so early and did attempt to control his morning lust as often as possible. Fortunately, the worst of his remorse was allayed by the fact that she easily resumed her slumber. Lying in his arms, body flushed and as pliant as dough in her satiation, he patiently and blissfully awaited the rhythmic respirations indicative of sleep. Then he would kiss her gently, disentangling himself gingerly to attend to his morning routine, invigorated and abounding with love.

Today, however, they were both too excited to sleep or embark on any other activity but being together and preparing for the day's planned excursion. Lizzy moved her head enough to see his profile, tracing one finger over his straight nose. Darcy turned toward her, avidly and adoringly looking upon her sunny visage as she commenced a delicate inspection of each perfect facial feature.

"Are you no longer sleepy, beloved?" He asked, kissing the finger resting on his lips.

"Too excited about our trip, I suppose. You know, I honestly will not be hurt if you wish to pursue some sort of manly occupation rather than trudging through fabric and ribbon stores with me. Phillips will ensure my safety and carry my burdens."

Darcy frowned slightly. "Normally I would concur; however, I wish to be a part of all aspects of our child's needs, Elizabeth."

Lizzy laughed, interrupting him with a kiss to the shoulder. "William, you truly are too good for this earth! You already refinished the cradle and dresser, met with the decorator offering more opinions on the subject than I deem he wanted, and now you want to pick out endless yards of muslin, yarn, and lace? Are you next going to take up knitting needles to create little sweaters and blankets?" She tickled his ribs, Darcy chuckling as he grasped her hands.

"Very well. Point taken. Not that I would be unwilling to attempt knitting if necessary; however, I do not think you would desire to garb our son in anything constructed by me! You understand I only want to help?"

"Yes, and I love you even more for your enthusiasm." She placed her palm flat onto one of his broad hands, long fingers extending more than an inch beyond hers, entire dainty hand engulfed. "I will utilize your larger hands to spin the yarn though. Also, you can read to me in your resonant voice while I sew, thrilling me, and keeping my mind stimulated." She played with his fingers, caressing and lacing hers between as she spoke. "Will I shock you, husband, if I confess to not being overly fond of sewing?" Darcy chuckled and shook his head. "Knitting even less. Of course, these womanly tasks I previously have balked at are for our baby, so I am motivated as never before." She drew his fingertips to her lips, kissing and nibbling each one. "So, you see, William, your help is necessary not in picking fabrics but in preventing my insanity and boredom!"

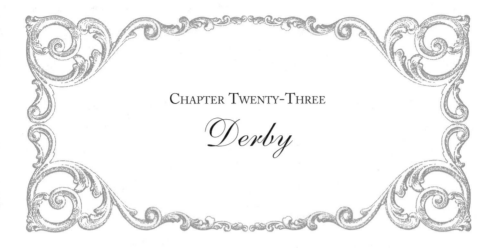

CHAPTER TWENTY-THREE

Derby

TWO HOURS LATER, THE Darcys entered their carriage and began the twenty mile trek to Derby. As they had previously mutually decided, they wished to purchase the baby's clothing and other requirements from the local communities. Derby, as the county seat and largest town in Derbyshire, would offer the greatest variety of goods. Also, Darcy felt it was high time the wife of Darcy of Pemberley ventured beyond the immediate vicinity and familiarized herself with the broader county she was now indelibly a member of. Therefore, he planned a three- or four-day excursion to a few of the local sights of interest as well as the shopping. Lizzy was very excited, despite hating leaving Pemberley so soon after returning from Town. As always, the joy of being exclusively with her husband was the primary delight. Additionally, there was the thrill of purchasing the material fundamentals for their son, each step of preparation authenticating his existence. A further perk was the pleasure of exploring the environs.

The Georgian Inn in Derby was a very old establishment, but premiere and swank. Lizzy was extremely impressed with the coaching inn, the massive building constructed of sturdy red bricks with a white colonnaded entryway the width of two carriages. Servants dressed in fine livery dashed to retrieve baggage from the Darcy carriage while others genuflected and escorted the Darcys to their reserved suite of chambers. Their rooms were generous and well appointed, flowers in vases scattered about, and had a breathtaking view of the River Derwent below with Darley Park beyond. Samuel and Marguerite immediately attended to the necessary tasks that would provide additional homey comforts for their Master and Mistress. Luncheon was taken in the common room, the food nearly as excellent as anything prepared by Mrs. Langton.

Lizzy was initially astonished at the number of people Darcy was acquainted with in Derby, the introduction of his wife made with pride as they strolled along the streets. Lizzy expressed her surprise, and Darcy smiled as he explained.

"Well, aside from growing up in the area, Derbyshire is not as vast as you might think, my love, especially if one is a Darcy. I do a great deal of business in Derby. I always stay at The George, which is why Mr. Harris knew me immediately. Of course, the room I usually stay in is a single room on the other side of the building." He paused, glancing sidelong at his wife with a smirk, continuing dreamily, "I always wanted to stay in one of the large rooms with a view of the river, so it is fortunate I am now married, for that reason if for none other."

Lizzy squeezed his arm and pinched him unobtrusively, harrumphing under her breath. Darcy chuckled and continued, "All our wool is brought here to the mill, as well as the grains and other harvests. Derby is the center for commerce in the region, and the way to London and beyond. You know I am part owner of a cotton mill here where baled cotton is processed. Also, I have a financial interest in the silk mill. Therefore, I travel here frequently for one reason or another, although I do usually return the same day. Actually, being married to you, beloved, has another advantage, as I can extend my stay beyond business to visit many of the sights I have not enjoyed for years." He smiled down at Lizzy, who smiled in return.

"How pleased I am, dear husband, that marriage to me has afforded you so many joys. I feared your disappointment most acutely." Darcy merely laughed.

The shop they entered, tiny bells tinkling at the door, was a store recommended by Harriet Vernor that specialized in infant and child accouterments, furnishings, and clothing. Meryton had a similar establishment—although substantially smaller—that Lizzy had frequented on occasion for friends, so she was not completely unfamiliar with the merchandise and atmosphere.

Darcy, however, had never in all his life stepped foot into such a place. The instant inundation with paraphernalia exclusively infantine was overwhelming. His heart constricted at the plethora of miniature garments and accessories. The air even smelled like a baby, or at least it seemed so to Darcy, although in truth he had only a vague seventeen-year-old memory of what a baby smelled like—except for foals, which had a freshness about them that was reminiscent to what he scented now. Tears sprang to his eyes and he cleared his throat gruffly, turning aside to finger the first item nearby: a spun-cotton-stuffed toy hound dog.

Lizzy had begun speaking to the proprietress, a Mrs. Higgins, explaining that she was expecting her first child and essentially needed everything.

"William?" she called to her husband. "Mrs. Higgins will assist us with our requirements. We are certainly not the first new parents to enter her shoppe!"

Darcy stepped forward as she spoke. He had taken control of his emotions, the Darcy mask of rigid calm and aloofness firmly in place. He bowed, and said haltingly with studied restraint, "Mrs. Higgins. We thank you for your time and patience. We will need everything, as Mrs. Darcy revealed. Cost is not an issue, and I insist on the best."

"Mr. Darcy?" the store owner asked with awe. "I did not realize... well, naturally I will do all to help. Allow me a moment to call my assistant." She bobbed and departed to a back room hastily.

Lizzy was frowning at him, crossing to where he stood with a concerned gaze. Laying a hand on his arm, she asked, "William, are you well? You seem so... uncomfortable. If you do not wish to be here, you need only say so. I will understand." Her voice caught, but she tried to assure him with a weak smile.

Darcy's face fell, the mask instantly slipping as he grasped her hand. "No, beloved! There is nowhere else on earth I would rather be than here. I was merely... overcome for a moment. Please forgive me." He kissed her forehead and she smiled brilliantly in relief.

He straightened stiffly when Mrs. Higgins returned, accompanied by a young woman introduced as Christina. For the next three hours, they closely examined every square inch of the store and many items pulled from the storage rooms. Darcy was not at all jesting when he said cost was not an issue, refusing several products that did not appear adequately constructed or were too plain. Gradually, Mrs. Higgins came to understand the truth of his assertions, and cognizant of the reputed Darcy wealth, she retrieved certain articles of extreme elegance and extravagance kept stashed away for just such special customers.

Therefore, they eventually exited having spent, to Lizzy's way of thinking, an obscene amount of money. Any attempts on her part to insert rationality or frugalness into the discussions garnered the infamous Darcy glare with brow creases deep and eyes flashing, so she relented. Along with the fundamentals, such as thick diapering cloths, pins, linens, towels, bathing essentials, and the like, they also purchased a few clothes and blankets. Most of their son's garments Lizzy wished to make herself, as well as the cradle blankets and cushions, fabrics to be obtained at the drapers.

Darcy was intently interested in each item, especially those things unique or revolutionary. Lizzy smiled at this, remembering with clarity all the remarkable gadgets he had acquired for her birthday. He was spellbound by the colorful mobile and purchased three of them, "for variety and to stimulate our son's intellect," he said.

Equally amazing to him were the perambulators. He examined them thoroughly, pressing on them and driving them about the room. He frowned with a look of deep concentration, fingers flicking in a manner Lizzy was very familiar with. "It is like a miniature carriage," he mused to himself. "If springs were placed here and here, it would have more bounce and ride smoother. The wheels could be sturdier to withstand the gravel paths around Pemberley. Hmmm..." He rubbed his chin. Lizzy watched him with admiration, Mrs. Higgins clearly confused.

Darcy continued, peering at his wife with a grin, "I think I, with Mr. Clark's assistance, could fashion improvements, Elizabeth, so the ride would be comfortable for him and you could walk far afield as you desire without safety concerns. Or better yet, the groom Stan! You remember him?" Lizzy nodded, smiling at the enthusiasm which led to him relaxing his formal pose. "He is a wizard with mechanical devices, always fixing the carriages and fountain pumps and anything else, usually ameliorating them in the process. Do you have one of these with natural tan leather for the canopy?" He asked suddenly of Mrs. Higgins, startling her.

"Y-Yes, Mr. Darcy, we do, although the black is in style now."

He waved his hand, interrupting her. "That is inconsequential. Lighter colors block the sun."

Next were the baby slings, new contraptions that carried a baby close to one's body while leaving the hands free. Both Lizzy and Darcy saw the advantage of this, although it was Lizzy who remembered the yards of Indian fabrics Dr. Darcy had gifted and instantly deduced how she could fashion her own slings. Darcy laughed at the mental vision of his wife and son draped with garish Indian silks.

Completing the infant wares were a tightly woven basket carrier, a tiny brush of silver and fine horsehair, two oil paintings of pastel-hued floral arrangements, and the stuffed hound. All were to be bundled and shipped to Pemberley.

Darcy and Lizzy strolled arm in arm, content at the day's accomplishments. It was late in the afternoon and the sun was shining brightly, but a gentle breeze eased the heat. The plan was to visit the drapers, but Lizzy felt drained after so many hours of shopping and the heat sapping her strength. "Dearest, can we postpone the fabric store until tomorrow? Suddenly a walk through the park sounds appealing."

When they returned to the inn after a leisurely hour under the old oaks of Darley Park, an invitation was waiting for dinner that evening with Sir Allen Griffin of Alveston Hall. An odd expression crossed Darcy's face, but before Lizzy could inquire, it had disappeared and he sighed.

"I was hoping to avoid any social engagements; however, we should accept this, beloved, if you feel up to it. Sir Griffin was a friend to my father and his brother was married to my Aunt Muriel, who, I am sure you recall, died when I was six. They had no children and he remarried years ago, but there remains a vague familial relationship."

In truth, Lizzy much preferred to stay alone with her husband, but such social requirements were expected, and she would not shirk her responsibilities. Therefore, by seven that evening, the Darcy carriage had halted before the massive front doors of Alveston Hall. The butler greeted them formally, leading them to the parlor. Neither knew exactly what to anticipate as far as the guest list was concerned, although they both prayed it was not an elaborate social affair. Nonetheless, they were both taken aback to note only Sir Griffin, his wife Lady Griffin, the eldest son, Mr. Lawrence Griffin, and his wife Annabella, another son, Maurice with his wife, Sarah Beth, and his daughters, Edith and Amy Griffin.

Lizzy realized that she had indeed met Sir Griffin, his wife, and the eldest son and wife at the Cole's Masque. Frankly, many of the names and faces from that night had blurred over time, and she could not recall being introduced to the second son or either daughter. Sir Griffin greeted them both with a ready smile and honest delight.

"Mr. Darcy, thank you for accepting our sudden invitation. Please forgive the abruptness, but you have a terrible habit, my boy, of quitting town ere anyone knows you are here! Mrs. Darcy, how are you finding our quaint community?"

"What I have viewed thus far is lovely, Sir Griffin. Mr. Darcy and I strolled the park today and along the river after a bit of shopping; however, most of the region I have yet to survey."

"Darcy, you must take your wife to the Cathedral and Allestree Park. A trip to Derby is not complete unless you do."

Darcy nodded. "I planned as much, Sir Griffin. We intend to tarry for three days at the least, affording enough time."

The remainder of the introductions commenced. Lady Griffin was pleasant if quiet. The sons were around Darcy's age, agreeable, and talkative like their father. Edith was the eldest daughter, perhaps two or three years younger than Darcy, and recently engaged to a Lord Ryan of Oxfordshire. The Darcys congratulated her as was appropriate, Edith obviously a Caroline Bingley type who was quite proud of herself for her conquest.

Amy was a year or so older than Lizzy, vivacious and incredibly beautiful. She eyed Lizzy with intense interest, an undercurrent of distaste in her greeting that Lizzy could not fathom initially. Darcy's greeting was stilted even for him, and Lizzy, who knew him so well, instantly sensed his discomfiture. It was confusing, but the mass of voices and activity allotted her no time to puzzle it out.

Dinner advanced without unusual incidence, amusing in fact, Lizzy entertained especially by Sir Griffin and his sons. They were animated and humorous, even the usual business discussions entertaining. Lizzy had culled a fair knowledge of animal husbandry and agriculture via the numerous, in-depth conversations with Darcy, startling all three gentlemen at her contribution to their exchange. Darcy, as typical, was sedate. He added the occasional commentary but generally ate in silence and delighted in his wife's effervescence.

The women, with the exception of the cheery and somewhat flirty Amy, said practically nothing. Amy, to Lizzy's annoyance and Darcy's disquiet, continually attempted to draw him into conversation. She sat diagonal to him, frequently asking him questions he was obliged to answer and referring to past events they apparently had mutually attended. Eventually, a stern glower from her father ended the worst of her inappropriate attention, Lizzy relieved for both herself and her husband, but also curious.

When the groups parted as propriety deemed mandatory, Lizzy rolled her eyes toward her husband, who hid his laugh with a kiss to her fingers. "Have fun, love," he whispered wryly with a slight smile and arch of one brow.

The women settled on sofas, sipping tea and entering into the standard women's chat of local gossip, fashion, gardening, and other idle topics.

"Mrs. Darcy, I understand congratulations are in order," Lady Griffin said politely, "you and Mr. Darcy are expecting, I believe?"

Lizzy smiled, nodding as she agreed. "Yes, Lady Griffin, this is true and thank you. We are overjoyed."

Annabella spoke dreamily, "I remember my first confinement. I have two children, Mrs. Darcy, the youngest only six months. It can be difficult at times, but the rewards are quite worth the sacrifice."

"That is comforting. Thank you, Mrs. Griffin. I have been fortunate thus far so am hopeful it will continue."

"Yes, you have been most fortunate, Mrs. Darcy," Amy said with a faint sneer, "ensnaring the most eligible bachelor in Derbyshire, of cert. What was your secret? Do tell, so we can know how we failed."

Lizzy was stunned and extremely uncomfortable, not sure if Miss Amy was jesting or alluding to something in particular.

Miss Griffin laughed and patted her sister's hand. "Still a sore loser, Amy? Forgive my sister, Mrs. Darcy. She, like many other young women, plotted to no avail. Mr. Darcy was a singularly tough nut to crack, until he found what he was searching for, obviously." She smiled kindly and nodded toward Lizzy.

With a giddy, vapid laugh, Mrs. Griffin the younger chimed in, "Then he apparently proceeded with due haste! Quite the surprise, it was. One month he is courting our Amy and seemingly the next he is engaged to you!" She giggled, casting a pointed glance to Lizzy's midsection. "Apparently, he works quite fast in every way!"

Lizzy paled, suddenly feeling quite ill. With a triumphant smirk, Amy shrugged as if unconcerned. "Well, men too can be fickle. Who really knows what they are thinking, especially the quiet ones? Is that not true, Mrs. Darcy?"

Lizzy collected herself with effort, responding as firmly as possible with a sudden flare of jealousy. "I do not believe I can concur to such a generality,

Miss Amy. Perhaps some men do not reveal themselves to those they are only mildly interested in."

"This may be the case. However, a woman should be able to take a man at his word when he expresses interest and asks to call. After all, we poor females are completely at the mercy of a man's pleasure, so can only assume he is serious if he states his intent."

"Enough, Amy," Lady Griffin interjected with a laugh, as if the subject were highly amusing, "Let the past fade and look only to the future, I always say! I heard that the Prince Regent plans to hold a major fête next spring for his birthday. Now there is a discussion worth engaging in!"

For Lizzy, the remaining hour, despite the innocent banter, was torture. She managed to push her pain and jealousy aside for the most part, but was subdued, and when the men reentered the room, Darcy instantly knew something was amiss. Lizzy avoided his gaze, was pale, and her hands trembled. Falsely deducing she was fatigued and perhaps ill, he extended their thanks to Sir Griffin and escorted his wife to their carriage as quickly as decorum allowed.

The carriage had barely begun moving and he was facing his wife, clasping her cool hands in his warm ones. "Elizabeth? Are you ill? You should have called for me, beloved. Elizabeth?" Her face was averted, cast into the shadows of the inky carriage interior. She did not answer and his alarm escalated. Cupping her cheek, he attempted to pull her toward him, but she resisted and he felt wetness on his fingers. Truly terrified, he pulled harder. "Elizabeth! You are worrying me! Are you in pain?"

She was facing him now, lips trembling and tears shining in the pale moonlight. It was difficult to see her in the gloom, but he noted pain in her eyes, and her voice, when she spoke, was anguished. "When did you court Amy Griffin? Mere months before our marriage, so I was informed. While you were reportedly prostrate in your grief over me?"

Darcy staggered backward onto the seat, mouth open in shock. "What...?"

"She told me. Took great delight in telling me, in fact, of your *intent* and *interest* and *seriousness*. Why, William, would you take me to meet a woman you courted without at least warning me?"

Darcy pressed his lips together tightly and clenched his jaw, directing his gaze toward the far window. "I will not discuss this here, Elizabeth. It can wait until we are in our room." His voice was flat and low, brooking no argument.

Once alit from the carriage, a rigid Darcy escorted Lizzy to their room, dropping her arm and crossing immediately to pour himself a brandy. He stood with his back to her, drinking, while Lizzy suffered waves of intense nausea.

Knees weak, she sat down feeling seriously ill, willing him to speak. When he finally did, his tone was icy and he kept his back to her.

"Elizabeth, I never claimed that I did not consider other women before I met you. From the time I was eighteen, I had every acceptable lady shoved into my face with friends and family incessantly harping on me to make a match, not to mention Lady Catherine badgering me about Anne every time I turned around. I was eight and twenty when I fell in love with you. Ten long years of potentials with their pedigrees and necessary standards listed ad nauseam, the qualifications drummed into me. Believe me, my family was frantic at my persistent single status, anxious about the Darcy line, and beginning to seriously fret that I was becoming too particular and set in my ways. Ten years of pressure. In those latter years, I began to agree with their assessment. I was tired of being lonely, tired of searching, tired of the parade of unsavory options, tired of relieving my sexual desires myself, tired of wanting."

He finished the brandy with a large swallow, setting the glass down with a loud crash, and then turned around. His eyes were black with anger and old pain. "The stupidest thing I ever did in all my life was leave Hertfordshire. Maybe, just maybe, if I had stayed I could have proven my love for you and learned to accept it myself. Instead, I idiotically tried to forget you. Amy Griffin was at the Masque that winter. She flirted; we danced twice, and talked a bit. Do you know what my first thought was when she spoke?" Lizzy shook her head slightly, staring into his eyes. "That she reminded me of Elizabeth Bennet." He smiled wryly. "She was witty, vivacious, pretty, proper, and acceptable. I wondered if she could fill the void in my heart that I keenly felt was only touched when I was with you. We encountered each other that winter at a few social engagements, and I called on her twice after Twelfth Night: all proper, in her home, with family present. I do not even know why I bothered the second time, except I had to be sure. Not sure that she was *not* the one for me, but sure that you were. Miss Amy is the only woman I had ever met who was nearest to what I had sought, yet she was not the one. That place was already taken by you, Elizabeth. After that second visit, I was convinced and decided to somehow find you again and win your hand."

He sighed, hanging his head wearily and running a palm down his face.

"Only now I see she is nothing like you. You do not have a cruel or vindictive bone in your body, Elizabeth." He swore, meeting her eyes with guilt. "I have failed you again, my love. As with Lady Catherine, I trusted and had no foresight that Miss Amy deemed my meager interest serious, nor that she would seek to hurt you in spite."

"No! William, stop," she replied, as she jumped up and rushed to him, placing her hands on his chest. "You do not need to apologize for her! I am the stupid one. I was ragingly jealous that anyone may have garnered your affection, however minutely, and I took it out on you. In my juvenile suspicion, I forgot your age and searching and loneliness. Naturally you would have courted others! I am a fool. Please forgive me?"

He shook his head curtly, declaring resolutely, "I never courted anyone, my Lizzy. Not even you actually. I was very inept at the game. A call for tea upon occasion, a dance at the appropriate places, dinner, and such, but never anything official. Nonetheless, there was a handful that I seriously considered. They never materialized, obviously, but I was looking very hard. This is all further proof of my incompetence in that I brainlessly walked away from you. I am flattered at your jealousy, but it is unwarranted." He clasped her face passionately. "How many times must I tell you that you are the only woman I have ever wanted? Anyone I remotely considered pales in comparison to you."

Lizzy responded by throwing her arms about his neck and claiming his lips in a possessive, aggressive kiss. When she released him, withdrawing scantly, he was panting and parted lips were swollen. "You must tell me and show me often, Fitzwilliam Darcy, because I will not share you. You are mine, exclusively mine, for all eternity and I will not let you forget it nor have cause to want another!"

"Elizabeth, I will never…" but she stopped his words with another equally covetous kiss, attacking his coat with rapid enthusiasm, tossing it violently away and then assaulting the cravat. Darcy was momentarily confounded by her onslaught but quickly reciprocated with his own raging need to prove his faithfulness and ownership. At the precise instant that she reached the lowest button of his waistcoat, yanking in frustration at the time consuming process and sending the button flying, he grasped her dress where the endless row of tiny buttons began and ripped. The dress gave way, hastily falling to the floor alongside his vest, the tinkling of a dozen pearl buttons hitting the wooden floor unnoticed by either.

Darcy clutched her harshly, her feet lifted off the ground as he crushed her to his chest, Lizzy kneading his shoulders with steely hands. The kiss continued unrelentingly, both probing and claiming custody rights. Slithering as an eel, Lizzy escaped his grip, loosening his shirt tail from his waistband, and crouching to plant moist kisses to his belly.

"Only mine," she murmured against his exposed abdomen.

Lizzy traveled voraciously up his torso as the shirt was peeled away, eventually tossed haphazardly as she interspersed hungry kisses with numerous firmly declared *only mine* statements. She was everywhere on him, kissing and touching. Not an inch of his flesh escaped her conquest; her demand to once again affirm her title to him ruled.

Darcy was dizzy, swaying on his feet with passionate flame. Neither fully realized they were stepping incrementally toward the bed until the edge was felt behind his knees. With a combined shove and pull, they fell onto the mattress, Lizzy on top of his body. Their eyes met for a second, insane lust and absorbing protectiveness visible.

Lizzy reached to free him, holding his gaze. Untying her chemise to expose her breasts for firm caresses, Darcy watched her, panting stridently as she shifted. She paused, the moment stretching as eyes locked. "All for me, Fitzwilliam, and I only for you." He nodded, unable to speak, and they merged, Darcy hungrily pulling her in for a savage kiss.

Forever, it seemed, they danced. Always needing more, wanting the sensations to cascade higher and endure eternally. There is a limit; however, they consistently managed to transcend the previously attained boundaries over and over again. Lizzy dug her nails into his shoulder, whimpers passing ruddy, occupied lips as they crashed and flew joyously over the pinnacle of bliss.

They both collapsed, lying entwined and dazed for long minutes. Lizzy caressed over his fair skin, a feeling of intense relief rendering her again breath-less. Despite it all, the reality of how close they came to losing each other yet reared up and terrified them. Tears sprang to her eyes and she squeezed him tight, Darcy lifting to brush her tears away.

"Hush, beloved," he whispered tenderly, bottomless amounts of love conveyed in his husky voice. "We were meant to be, fated by God, I believe. Nothing would have kept us apart, and nothing ever will." He kissed her softly, brushing warm lips over hers, no longer possessively but with belonging and unity.

The Darcy's sojourn in Derby lasted five days total. It had, in fact, been seven years since Darcy tarried in Derby for more than a day or two, many of the local curiosities and attractions unseen. For Lizzy, having only passed through the Midland area on her way to and from Pemberley, it was an adventure and a delight.

They rose early on their second day in town, breakfasting light in the common room, and then set out to tour the township itself. They walked first to the Derby Cathedral, an ancient church built in the tenth century originally, although much of the early stones of those far gone days no longer remain. The truly impressive part of the church, and where it attained its fame, was in the two-hundred-foot, Gothic tower built in the sixteenth century during the reign of Henry VIII. The church proper and attached building for clerics and attendants had undergone numerous renovations over the centuries, the final product a mélange of varied styles. However, one glance at the tower and all else faded. It was stupendous.

Lizzy and Darcy arrived early, only a few other folks about. The grounds were beautiful with blooming flowers and tall shady trees. Like all churches everywhere, a serene hush existed in the arched interior. Long rows of wooden benches with a handful of supplicants in meditation and prayer graced the inner sanctum of curved white and gold columns. An elaborate and truly breathtaking, lacy, wrought-iron screen separated the nave from the chancel, two clerics actively offering prayers as Lizzy and Darcy entered. They wandered quietly, admiring the beauty visible in every inch of the environs. Darcy sat for a spell, gazing up at the altar, visage peaceful as he said silent prayers.

The nearly two hundred steps ascending to the topmost landing of the tower were steep and narrow, but the view from above was exhilarating. A faint breeze blew over the treetops, brushing soothingly over their perspiring brows, the air fresh as they inhaled deeply to recover from the strenuous climb. One could see all of Derby stretched below, as well as much of the valley extending beyond. They stood together, winded but admiring the view in quiet solitude, no one else energetic enough to tackle the stairs as yet. The rivers Derwent and Wye could easily be seen as they wound through the valley until they merged, wending to the horizon where they disappeared into a blue glint.

"I have never in my life been in a building so tall," Lizzy said in awe.

"Amazing that man can build such a structure and have it last these three hundred years." She leaned against his arm, breathing heavily.

"Are you alright, my love?"

"Yes, although I do not think I should venture the climb when nine months pregnant!" Darcy chuckled, hugging her close. Once she felt adequately rested they descended, the downward climb far easier.

Leaving the cathedral, they meandered leisurely through the streets. Darcy pointed to the occasional oddity or old building, impressing Lizzy with his knowledge of the area. She expressed her pride, but he laughed. "Thank you, dearest, for your faith in my ready recollection and intellect, but I assure you that for each fact imparted, I have likely passed by a dozen others unremembered or unknown. I truthfully have spent little time learning the region this far south. Now, when we tour the highlands and Peaks, I will dazzle you with my brilliance!"

Despite his words, Lizzy had a fair familiarity with the town by the time they rested for luncheon. The highlights as far as she was concerned were the Cathedral, naturally, as well as Exeter House where Bonnie Prince Charlie plotted his failed reclamation of the throne in 1745, and the silk mill, one of a dozen mills utilizing the power of the River Derwent, but the oldest such mill in all of England and the one Darcy was financially invested in.

He took her to the cotton mill that he owned as part of a three-way partnership. She met Mr. Shultz, one of the partners, and received a full tour. Once again, she was astounded by the breadth of her husband's expertise. Peripheral awareness that he owned a mill had not translated to comprehensive appreciation of his proficiency on the subject. Mr. Shultz interjected upon occasion, but primarily Darcy explained in detail the function of each machine throughout the massive four-story building. Lizzy found it all immensely fascinating, having previously devoted minimal time to learning about machinery and technology. Marriage to a man like Darcy prevented ignorance, although she would never boast the intense comprehension he possessed. It was an enlightening morning, deepening their communion as they shared another facet of the complex Master of Pemberley.

They ate lunch at the Dolphin, the oldest pub in town dating from the mid-1500s. The food was not fancy, but the atmosphere of the tiny, intimate pub was fun. Lizzy felt as if she had stepped back in time with the dark wood bar and paneling, the stone fireplace massive, and windows of crackled glass. Darcy explained that, after dark, the pub would not be an appropriate place to take a lady, but the rowdy customers who retreated to such places for a pint or two were currently still working.

After dining, Darcy escorted Lizzy to the drapers. After much persuasion, Lizzy had finally convinced Darcy that, not only would he be bored out of his skull in such an establishment, but also his lurking presence would irritate her and likely prevent full concentration on necessary purchases for the baby. Therefore, he had agreed to pursue "manly" occupations while she shopped. In truth, he was relieved and rather excited about his planned amusement. Derby boasted the premiere fencing academy in Derbyshire, an establishment Darcy did attempt to visit whenever in the area. The combination of strenuous exercise in a pastime he so enjoyed while honing his skills with some of the best swordsmen in the region was too magnetic a draw to resist.

Of course, Lizzy did have to tease when he revealed his plan for the afternoon. "Oh yes, William, by all means strengthen your swordsmanship skills. One never knows when one will need to call upon such proficiency!" He did have the good grace to blush slightly.

So, with Phillips sent to play bodyguard on the dangerous streets of the Derby merchant shops, as Lizzy jokingly stated, an appeased Darcy embarked on his afternoon activity. Lizzy had a wonderful time. One of the shop clerks had recently delivered her third baby and the two women bonded instantly over the joys of maternity. The clerk's expertise was extremely beneficial. Lizzy purchased enough fabrics, ribbons, lace, quilt battings, patterns, yarns, needles, and notions to not only keep her fingers occupied for the remaining months of her pregnancy but also to outfit baby Darcy for the first several months. Feeling very satisfied with the afternoon's accomplishments, Lizzy and Phillips returned to the inn. It was far too early for Darcy to have completed his drills, so Lizzy grabbed a book and walked to one of the benches by the riverbank.

"Mrs. Darcy?" Lizzy glanced up as one of the inn's maids approached. "Pardon me, madam, but this missive just arrived for you."

"Thank you." Lizzy opened the note with a smile, having recognized the seal. The only people in the immediate vicinity that Lizzy and Darcy wished to visit were the Drurys. Their estate, Locknell Hall, was only a few miles outside of Derby. Lizzy had not been to their home as of yet, the Drurys instead traveling to Pemberley or seen while in London. Lizzy had written to Chloe when they arrived yesterday, hoping that they would be able to visit. Chloe's reply was enthusiastic, her friendship with Lizzy a deeply felt one. Darcy and

Clifton were not as close, but they had enough in common to spend a pleasant evening together, in truth extending the courtesy for the sake of their wives.

Lizzy smiled. It had not been but three weeks since visiting with Chloe, but she missed her. Suddenly, Lizzy experienced the yearning to gather all her women friends together for a lengthy afternoon of tea and gossip, deciding on the spot that as soon as she was back at Pemberley she would arrange it. Hastening to the inn, Lizzy scribbled a quick note to Chloe, confirming that she and Darcy would dine with them for dinner tomorrow. Normally, Lizzy would not be so presumptuous, such invitations necessarily being discussed with her husband, but she was too excited.

It was nearly six o'clock before Darcy finally materialized. Lizzy was passing the time catching up on correspondences to Charlotte Collins, whose baby was due shortly before her own, and her sister Lydia, who rarely responded but Lizzy continued to write as often as possible. Darcy entered briskly, energized from his training and smiling broadly as he bellowed his wife's name.

"Elizabeth! Look what I found!" His arms were laden with a mass of packages, bags dangling on both sides and bumping his knees. He looked utterly ridiculous, barely managing the knob and peeking through a small gap between two boxes. Lizzy started at his abrupt entrance, momentarily paralyzed at the small desk where she sat. Darcy swung around, searching for her through his narrow peephole, finally spying her as she rose to assist him. "Ah, there you are! Dressed too, that is good. Mr. Howe! Enter." He pivoted toward the open door, the tower of parcels swaying dangerously as Lizzy jumped to the rescue.

"William! What in the world…?"

"Elizabeth, you will not believe my luck… Oh thank you, Mr. Howe. Place it there." Entering cautiously was one of the inn's manservants carrying an enormous rocking horse. Lizzy retrieved three of the boxes as they tumbled from Darcy's arms, nearly dropping them herself in her astonished amazement at the horse. Darcy bent and deposited the mass of bags and packages onto the sofa, straightening with a stretch. "What a relief," he declared, "some of those are heavy." He turned to his wife with a grin, planting a hearty kiss as the door closed behind Mr. Howe.

"Are you going to explain all this or must I remain in suspense?"

"Yes! So, I am departing the Academy, walking down the street as I have a dozen times in the past, when I glance over, not two doors down, and there is a toy store! Can you believe I never noticed it before? This," he patted the horses head, sending it gliding, "was in the window, calling to me as it were."

"I see. You entered and left some time later, having bought *all* the merchandise the store had to offer?" She swept her arm toward the pile on the sofa with a laugh.

"Do not be ridiculous, Elizabeth. I can show some restraint when necessary." He was beaming, Lizzy laughing harder.

"Oh really? We have a rocking horse, as you are well aware, William, as it was yours."

"Yes, but it is quite old and used roughly. I yet need to refinish and repair it. Besides, this is the newer model set on gliders rather than large bowed rockers, and now we can station one upstairs in the playroom and the other downstairs."

"Well, since you have apparently given this a tremendous amount of forethought, I shall not argue the matter. He really is beautiful," she said as she gave the horse a push, stroking the polished wood, "although I am surprised he is dappled grey rather than coal black."

She smiled at her husband, who answered absently, "They did not carry a black one." Lizzy laughed anew. The hobbyhorse was pearly grey with a long flowing white mane and tail of genuine horsehair. The saddle was pliable leather, thick, cushioned, and tanned a rich brown. A leather detailed wool blanket lay underneath, stirrups of sturdy steel attached with durable leather straps. The horse itself sat on a raised wooden base, also polished to a gleam, metal hinges and bars through the legs providing the gentle rocking motion upon the simple sway of a child's body. It was a masterpiece of craftsmanship and detail, easily imaginable as enduring for generations to come.

Darcy cleared a place on the sofa. "Here, Elizabeth, have a seat." He dragged a chair over, sitting on the edge and reaching for the largest box. Ripping apart the strings, he explained, "The shop was amazing. Every kind of toy you could imagine, my love. Many familiar from my own youth. In fact, I am sure there are boxes in storage I have yet to uncover containing old toys of mine and Georgie's. However, there were many that were unusual to me. Of course, you will recognize these." Inside was a collection of building blocks, at least fifty, of all shapes, sizes, and colors.

Lizzy laughed. "I always wanted blocks, but it was not considered a girl's toy. These are wonderful, William." With sudden stunned amazement she stared at her husband. "You carried these all the way from Oak Street?"

Darcy flushed slightly. "Well, no. They piled the parcels into a wheelbarrow and a clerk followed me with them. I only carried them from downstairs. I did carry the horse all the way, if that impresses you sufficiently." He grinned and flexed his right arm, Lizzy laughing and leaning in for a kiss.

One by one, the packages and bags were opened, disclosing a vast array of child's playthings: three spinning tops, colorful and of varied sizes; a Chinese yo-yo; a spectacular army of minutely detailed tin soldiers, American Colonials and His Majesty's Regimentals; a Jack-in-the-Box; a replica of Admiral Nelson's flagship *HMS Victory* inside a glass bottle; four stuffed animals consisting of another dog, an elephant, a bull, and a lamb; and four dolls.

"Dolls?" Lizzy asked with arched brows.

"I know you are certain the baby is a male, but just in case you are wrong, or for our daughter, whenever she is created." He smiled and caressed Lizzy's face.

Lizzy turned and kissed his palm, chuckling as she said, "Very sweet, my love, but since I am the one blessed with all the aches associated, let us take this process one baby at a time." Three of the dolls were fairly standard, with porcelain heads and beautifully painted faces, garbed in frilly dresses over softly stuffed bodies. The last was simply the strangest doll Lizzy had ever seen. "Is it a little Indian doll?" she asked.

Darcy explained, with the enthusiasm he customarily showed whenever confronted with something strange or unique, "Exactly! It is designed after the dolls the natives of the Americas play with. It makes sense, does it not? All girls play with dolls based on what they are familiar with. You have seen the drawings. They wear their hair long and braided, with beaded leather dresses and shoes. Is she not lovely?" In fact, she was exactly as he described and as Lizzy had seen in the papers. Browned cloth skin and black bead eyes, black yarn braided on each side of the head, the dress and moccasins sewn with tiny multihued beads, all constructed over a cushiony body.

A smaller bag contained two carefully wrapped baby rattles. One was of silver with many tiny silver bells attached to the outside and a knob of coral on the end for sucking on. The second was a gourd painted with a tropical scene of palm trees, foam cresting waves on the seashore, and brilliant blue sky, attached to a handle of burnished ivory.

The remaining packages contained a half a dozen odd puzzles. Puzzles of entangled wires looped about into shapes, others of wood carved into knots, one with string and metal balls threaded into an intricate shape, and the last two were wooden Burr interlocking puzzles shaped as a pyramid and a horse. All were brainteasers, the idea to figure out the mystery of how they were formed. "I had many of these when a boy," Darcy proclaimed. "By far my favorite pastime. I love trying to figure out how they are constructed. I know for a fact I have several of these yet hidden in a storage box, but these are different."

Lizzy was overwhelmed, Darcy grinning like a cat after swallowing a canary. He grasped her hands and pulled her onto his lap, cuddling her into his arms. "William, you are too wonderful. You do too much…"

He halted her with a kiss. "Hush, Elizabeth. I can never do enough to express my love and appreciation for what you have given me, my beloved wife." He flattened a hand over the swell of their child, smoothing her gown taut to better visualize the bulge. "This," he smiled, caressing tenderly, "and you are the greatest gifts I have ever received in all my life. I *will* take care of you as I deem appropriate."

Lizzy frowned nonetheless, "I understand this, dearest, but are you sure of the expense? You have been so extravagant."

He nodded, kissing her forehead. "Elizabeth, you have seen my ledgers and know the financial burden is not a hardship. Besides, I have been saving and planning for my family for years. There is no concern. Now, let me hold you and feel our son for a spell before I freshen up for dinner."

Dinner was delicious. Afterward, the Darcys tarried in the common room to listen to a traveling minstrel sing and play a lute. He was excellent, and the room filled to capacity with cheering listeners. It was entertainment of a sort Lizzy had never partaken of; she and Darcy sat snuggly together at a corner table sipping wine as the troubadour displayed his talent with an eclectic mix of mournful ballads, folk hymns, and lively dance tunes.

Upon later reentering their temporary bedchamber, Lizzy spied her husband in his robe sitting on a chair and examining one of the string and metal puzzles with deep intensity. She observed him unawares for a few moments, desire allayed with wondering if he would solve the mystery. He was leaning with elbows on knees, brows knitted with those precious creases visible, fingers traveling purposefully over the pieces. He turned, wiggled, and pressed in concentration. Suddenly grasping two of the steel rings with an expression of abrupt perception, his hands blurred as he twisted a piece. The pieces separated and Darcy released a satisfied shout.

Lizzy smiled, applauding in pride. "Bravo! My brilliant spouse."

Darcy glanced up with a smile of smugness, rapidly replaced with stunned awe and raging ardor as the pieces fell from slack hands. "My god, Elizabeth! You are… ravishing! Where did you buy that gown?"

Raising her arms, Lizzy performed a swaying dance as she twirled about. "Oh, this old thing? Do you like it, my lover?"

The gown in question was black satin and clinging to every curve. The bodice gathered under barely concealed breasts and split open between to reveal her cleavage; string thin straps crossing over creamy shoulders and down her back. The back of the gown was essentially nonexistent, the fabric covering her bottom just barely. The long skirt was slit in four places all the way to mid-thigh, flashes of leg tantalizing as she danced.

Darcy was instantly aroused, the vision of his wife in swaying satin nearly more than he could tolerate. It was not only the visual stimulation but also the joy in these constant gifts she sprung on him, all for the express purpose of pleasing him. Of course, she most assuredly reaped the benefit of his intense delight. With a sultry smile he rose, slowly traversing the space separating them, Lizzy watching with bright eyes.

Reaching tender fingertips to caress over her cheeks, jaw, neck, and then to her shoulders, he slipped a finger under each slim strap. He huskily spoke, holding her gaze, "The gown is stunning. However, the true magnificence is found sheathed inside the satin." He traced over her collarbone, trailing fire downward to brush fleetingly over each hard nipple. "It is always you, best loved wife, who completes any outfit, rendering it supreme and me your slave."

Continuing the fiery assault over her flesh, Darcy augmented the torrential sparks flowing through her by applying lips to the tender skin behind her ear. Lizzy shivered, moaning faintly as he maintained a steady, leisurely devotion to every inch of her. Murmuring love and adulation as he kissed her, his hands traveled from her hair to upper thighs as he moved over and around her body. Standing behind her now, pulling the lush mass of hair aside, he administered the same dedication to her back. Kissing and licking the nape of her neck, down the entirety of her spine to sumptuous buttocks, his hands stroked her lovingly.

Lizzy arched backward, sighing with pleasure. "I love you, Mrs. Darcy, immeasurably," he whispered into her ear, nibbling the lobe. "So beautiful, desirable, and sensual. Mmmmm… you smell delicious enough to feast on and I believe I shall do just that." He cupped her breasts, pulling her against his chest, sucking delectably over her neck and shoulders. "Thank you, my beloved luscious lover, for striving to thrill me further. Although you need nothing to heighten your beauty and power over me, I do appreciate your enthusiasm and effort." He pressed into her body, groaning hoarsely. "Love, my precious love. You provoke me to astounding reaches of desire. Never have I imagined such raging passion as with you, my Lizzy. I so love you!"

"Fitzwilliam, take me to bed."

Darcy smiled, lips tickling her shoulder blades. "I have a better plan." He kissed her neck, grasping shoulders and turning her about. "Go stand by the window, sweet wife, whilst I douse the lights."

She did as he asked, waiting and watching as he glided about the chamber extinguishing each lamp. He approached with sinewy grace, eyes indigo, and desire proudly evident. Darcy untied his robe, exposing his multitude of masculine attributes to his wife's thirsty stare. "So powerful and virile you are, my heart. All of you alluring and sublimely male."

Darcy smiled. "It is you, Elizabeth. You move me and arouse my potency as never previously attained. I confess I am still frequently shocked at how I respond to your love. I never reacted so grandly until I began loving you." He cupped both hands around her slender neck, his thumbs caressing over her jaw and his fingers laced into her hair. Leaning in, he licked lightly over her full lips before claiming her entire mouth, inner and outer, in an all-encompassing kiss.

Lizzy encircled his waist, hugging tight and arching into his body with a sibilant moan. For long moments they embraced, kissing and caressing with ever increasing passion. Darcy finally broke away with a raspy growl, panting heavily. "Turn around. Let me show you how desperately I yearn for you."

Obeying with a nod, Lizzy faced the window. Moonlight shone faintly on the rippling surface of the river, millions of stars twinkling, the pale light bathing Lizzy's skin with a bluish glow. Darcy fondled warm hands over the curves of her hips, down firm thighs and around to the sensitive inner flesh, satin sliding sensuously. Gliding hands over the precious prominence created by their child, upward to cherish each breast, again drawing her securely onto his body.

"I shall love you here in the moonlight with your succulent body merged with mine. Moving, always moving as our passion rises to heavenly heights. I shall possess you with my body as you possess my soul. You, Elizabeth Darcy, my wife and eternal love." As he finished speaking, voice low and vibrant, he ran one hand up her spine while bending her body slightly and initiated the delicious process of wholly loving his wife.

Slowly, leisurely they loved, caressing as passion rose. They were lost to increasing sensations, sighing and moaning in need. Darcy kept his eyes open, marveling at her beauty in the reflective light and her roaring response to him, overjoyed at her blatant pleasure, and always with love spiraling unimaginably as his own ardor escalated until he felt the intense bliss gathering to a point of uncontrollability.

Passion cresting until neither wished to hold back, tumbling over as souls melded in the process. Immediately, Darcy pulled her upward and onto his burning chest, enveloping her with trembling arms and delivering moist kisses along her glistening neck as he panted with gradually declining rapture.

"Elizabeth, my beautiful love, my soul, my delight and life. How amazing you love me! My joy is fulfilled with you, so perfect you are." Lizzy tarried in a place of heavenly stupefaction, allowing his words of veneration to wash over her consciousness as his hands tenderly caressed her arms.

"Fitzwilliam," she whispered, "I love you." Darcy smiled with supreme happiness, brushing her lips and then sweeping her into his arms, carrying her to the bed.

They nestled close, face to face with hands entwined and fingers lightly caressing. Darcy played with her lush curls, a favorite pastime, while Lizzy feathered through the downy hairs on his chest. All the while eyes mere inches apart were locked in a loving gaze, one or the other frequently leaning for a kiss. Oddly, considering their busy day and recent strenuous activity, neither felt overly tired.

Darcy brushed over the satin of her gown. "You never told me where you bought this scandalous gown."

Lizzy giggled. "Scandalous? Madame du Loire is French and you know the reputation they have! Apparently, it is well founded as she creates an entire line of such decadent garments for clients so inclined. I must have an invisible sign stamped on me for those able to discern that shouts, 'Her husband is insatiable and she is licentious.' The third time I visited her shop for a fitting, she brought out the short chemise from Christmas Eve that you so love." Darcy smiled salaciously in remembrance. Lizzy continued with a laugh, "Yes, I think I must have had a similar expression on my face, beloved, for when she asked me how I 'enjoyed' the chemise, suddenly a dozen scanty bedroom garments appeared, each more scandalous than the last. So now I have a collection and don a new one every so often for the humorous cast of your face when you see me, not to mention the sexual delights as a result." She kissed his chuckling lips.

"I shall have to extend my appreciation to Madame du Loire," he said, stroking enticingly down her waist and hip.

"You shall do no such thing, William! I would die of embarrassment. I still blush scarlet when she shows me her latest creation."

"Yet, you purchase it," Darcy interjected with a grin.

"Well, of course! Mortified speechless I may be, but not stupid. I am abundantly thankful she knows my size and I need not have them fit. Again, it is all your fault, but the sensations rushing through my body when I wear one of these filmy lingerie, as the French call them, are most inappropriate for a public house!"

"I wonder if Marguerite knows of such French delicacies. I do hope so, for my valet's sake." Darcy ran the back of two fingers along the swell of her breast under the bodice.

Lizzy laughed. "Well, if she did not before, she does now, as she helps me dress and launders my undergarments. I deem Samuel will be quite satisfied, especially if his shy nature harbors great passion as it does with you, my heart."

Darcy blushed faintly, hiding his humility within her bosoms for a spell of nuzzling and kissing. Lizzy released a sigh of pleasure, kissing the top of his head. His muffled voice rose from where his lips were planted firmly on one nipple, "How many of these *lingerie* did you bring on this trip, my wife? Perhaps we should forego our plans for the morrow and stay inside." He rose with a hopeful, questioning look to his wife, but Lizzy giggled and shook her head.

"Forgive me, lover, for disappointing, but I only brought this one." She laced her fingers through his hair, smiling happily and tickling her lips over his. "However," she whispered breathily, "I do not judge the positive effects of this particular gown have yet been utterly exhausted." With a last nip to his full lower lip, she twisted from his grasp and stood on the bed.

Darcy smiled lasciviously, eyes brazenly grazing every inch of her head to toe. Lizzy flushed, boldly inventorying his physique as he was hers. Then she laughed, tossing her hair with a flip of her head and sweep of her hands. Arms raised over her head, she stretched, breasts jutting perkily and the bulge of the baby clearly defined by the clinging satin. Darcy continued to grin, groin already responding to all the marvelous attributes of his bride.

"You see," Lizzy spoke softly, fingers skimming airily down her neck toward her chest, "this is fine satin. A silk woven fabric that clings yet also glides and flows. Black as the night to contrast with ivory skin"—she brushed along her cleavage—"thin to display a hint of what hides underneath"—she lightly circled each visible nipple with one finger and Darcy licked his suddenly dry lips—"yet covering much of the skin to spark the imagination and tantalize."

She stroked over her hips and thighs, continuing huskily while Darcy's excitement manifested before her eyes. She undulated her hips, the long tails of the gown fluttering about her legs. "Note how it moves? So soft, cool to the touch, erotic in how it caresses the skin. Very, very, very stimulating," she whispered, eyes open a mere slit as she observed her husband's avid passion.

Darcy groaned audibly. "Elizabeth," he murmured.

Lizzy smiled naughtily. "I watch you, my handsome husband, in all your masculine glory. The memory of how you incite me coupled with the sensation of smooth satin encasing and caressing my body, and I am immeasurably aroused. I imagine you touching me, kissing me, loving me, and I lose all sense of anything but you." Lizzy was truly growing highly excited, but no more so than Darcy, who was unable to speak in his hunger for her.

With a thirsty glance, she wheezed, "Does this spur your ardor, my lover? Do you want to take me now, hard and fast?"

Darcy snapped, sitting up and grasping her legs as Lizzy fell onto the bed. Within seconds he was over her, skirt rapidly moved aside, and he claimed her with a hoarse growl. It was over in seconds, yet still rapturous and intense. It was rushed, manic, dynamic, glorious, and wholly fulfilling.

Collapsing in consummate bliss, Darcy rolled to the side with her encased in his arms. "Elizabeth Darcy, you take my breath away, literally." He inhaled deep and shuddering, laughing shakily. "No sooner do I think I have reached the boundary of how far I can be aroused by you then you push me beyond. How will I survive this continual physical exertion?" He kissed her head and she laughed tremulously.

"Your heart is strong, beloved. I trust you will survive brilliantly. Of course, if you deem it too much for you, I can desist." She kissed his chest, lifting to gaze at his smiling, joyous face. He twisted a tress of her hair around his fingers, profound love emanating from every pore and beaming through his eyes.

"No, my Lizzy, do not desist. I shall take my chances." He clasped her face, drawing her to his mouth. "I love you, Elizabeth, forever."

"I love you, William, beyond forever." They kissed languidly, tenderly, faithfully. Endlessly kissing and embracing, gentle caresses of devotion continued until sleep overtook them.

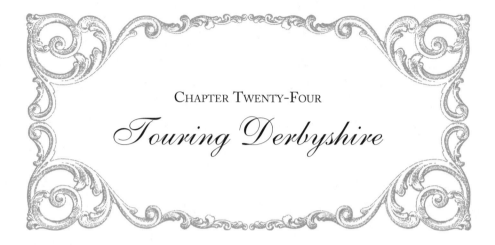

CHAPTER TWENTY-FOUR

Touring Derbyshire

THE FOLLOWING THREE DAYS were passed exclusively in sightseeing. Each day would begin with breakfast at the inn after which they would set out upon a new adventure abroad. Darcy rented a cabriolet, the newest carriage model from France, similar to a barouche but much lighter and swifter with a folding canvas calash hood and rear window. This particular cabriolet was designed to accommodate a separate driver mounted on the back, but Darcy preferred solitude and control, so operated the vehicle himself.

The first day, they headed east toward Nottinghamshire. The country, once beyond Derby town limits, was exclusively devoted to agriculture. The plethora of rivers and streams created a lush land of vegetation, ample water supply, and numerous fisheries. Darcy confessed he had only twice traveled through the region to the east of Derby, once to travel to Nottingham itself on business, whereupon he grasped the opportunity to tour Sherwood Forest. Alas, the forest and numerous Robin Hood museums scattered throughout the area were too far north for them to comfortably reach on this trip.

"Something to anticipate for another excursion, my love," he placated, kissing her pouting lips.

As they set out, Darcy began his narrative of the vicinity. Both Darcys had discovered to their immense delight that they were lovers of history. Darcy, as a fortunate result of his birth, had the means to quench his thirst for ancient history, architecture, and ruins. He confessed to Lizzy that he often believed that, if he had been the second son, he would likely have become an explorer or archeologist, such was his love of old buildings and stories. It was not an exaggeration when he told her about tramping through old ruins in France to the dismay of Bingley.

Lizzy, sadly, had not been blessed from birth with the resources to travel beyond the confines of Hertfordshire. Instead, she embraced what history was found in her familial environs, frequented the various old houses, churches, and ruins nearby, and immersed herself in every book she could find. She surprised Darcy in possessing a fair knowledge of obscure English history, including Derbyshire. The truth is, she confessed, she had researched the area prior to her trip with the Gardiners and more extensively once they were engaged. This information pleased Darcy tremendously, and now he was fulfilling a dream of sharing such treasures with his wife. Of course, for Darcy it was also another positive entry on the long list indelibly etched on his heart of why Elizabeth Bennet was the only woman in the entire world meant for him.

So, with no fear whatsoever that she would grow bored or annoyed, he launched into his tale. "This entire region was once the Saxon kingdom of Mercia from the fifth to sixth centuries. To this day, buried artifacts and old foundations from that era are unearthed. It was in the seventh century when the Saxons were introduced to Christianity, with a subsequent slow infusion of Biblical teaching and ways supplanting the old. In Spondon, there is an ancient church with both Celtic and Christian markings. In fact, religion was so important to the superstitious common folk that churches sprang up everywhere. Most of the remaining buildings from those times are churches."

Their first stop only a few miles outside of Derby was, not surprisingly, a church. The focal point of the small village of Chaddesden was the church dedicated to St. Mary the Virgin. The building was certainly not the grandest example of the genre, but many of the stones were ancient beyond dating, the foundations laid in a time so distant as to be forgotten. The main architecture dated from the 1300s and, aside from necessary restorations, was unaltered. Again, Lizzy and Darcy strolled through the hushed interior and then onto the grounds, leisurely admiring and absorbing the peace that infused such places before resuming their journey.

They traveled through the village of Spondon, where another ancient church resided. The current building was rebuilt in 1390 to replace a far older one destroyed by fire. This one named after Saint Werburgh, the seventh century daughter of King Wulfhere of Mercia who became the senior Abbess of Mercia. So famous was she that some seventeen churches were dedicated to her throughout England. The little village sat on a hill offering a beautiful view of the encompassing Trent valley, including Derby itself a mere four miles away. Darcy and Lizzy paused to enjoy the panorama, sipping fruit juice contentedly in the relative silence of the sleepy town before continuing their quest.

They passed through Ockbrook, not pausing to inspect the church there, turning vaguely south until reaching Long Eaton on the northern banks of the River Trent. They halted here for a brief stretch of their legs and light repast on the banks of the river. Reclining on a blanket, watching the ducks paddling and fish leaping, they talked and ate. Although Lizzy seemed completely unaffected by her pregnancy, stamina and bodily functions all within normal limits, Darcy fretted. The book and Dr. Darcy clearly listed muscle strain, backaches, fatigue, and benign uterine contractions as frequently occurring during the latter months of confinement, even to the degree of causing early labor or bleeding. For this reason, as well as the delight of a leisurely pace to better inspect the countryside, Darcy did not want to move too fast or venture a prolonged excursion abroad.

The capstone of the day's expedition was Wollaton Hall near Radford in Nottinghamshire. This sixteenth-century masterpiece was reputed to be one of the most amazing manors in all of England. Darcy had long wanted to view it, but during his previous trips into Nottinghamshire he had taken a northeasterly route, which had precluded a visitation.

"Is Wollaton Hall grander than Pemberley?" Lizzy inquired with a teasing smile.

Darcy glanced at her face with a laugh. "Despite Miss Bingley's assertion that Pemberley is the grandest manor in all of England, and my own prejudice and pride regarding my ancestral home notwithstanding, I cannot in truth proclaim that it is the largest, most ornate, architecturally unique, or historically interesting specimen. Certainly not in all of the extensive kingdom, although I will affirm it the finest in all of Derbyshire. Or perhaps that is merely my arrogance shining through!"

Lizzy lifted her brows in mock shock. "You arrogant? How absurd."

Darcy elbowed her side with a chuckle, continuing undeterred, "Be that as it may, we are now officially in Nottinghamshire, so I feel no sense of disloyalty if I am awestruck by another house."

The crossing into the bordering shire was unremarkable. There were no road signs or change in scenery to indicate the passage. They drove on through several small hamlets, most no larger than a pub, and three or four shops, and crossed two small rivers before finally entering the deer park surrounding Wollaton Hall. The massive house was easily visible from far away, a truly impressive example of Tudor structural design with spires, towers, gables, carvings, and niches. Lizzy's breath caught and Darcy's regulated mien of complacency slipped slightly. The house truly was magnificent.

"Do you know the owner?" Lizzy asked in a stunned whisper.

Darcy nodded. "We are not intimates, but I have socialized with Lord Middleton on a handful of occasions. His wife delivered an heir this spring, which is why they were not in London for the season; otherwise, I am sure you would have met him yourself. He is a pleasant man, a few years older than me I am guessing."

They alit some distance from the house, planning to merely walk about the grounds and admire. However, in one of those odd twists of fate which occur from time to time, one of the groundsmen spied them and recognized Darcy of Pemberley because the groundsman's sister happened to be a maid at Pemberley. Word traveled and within fifteen minutes of arriving, the house-keeper approached Darcy and Lizzy where they stood amid some shady trees.

"Mr. Darcy of Pemberley, I believe?" She asked with a curtsey. Darcy was surprised but hid it well with a formal bow and confirmation. "My Lord Middleton requests the honor of your presence, sir, and Mrs. Darcy as well, if it is not too inconvenient?" Naturally, they could not refuse, in truth the idea of seeing the inside of the manor quite appealing.

The Baron of Middleton greeted Darcy like an old and dear friend. "Mr. Darcy! What a delightful surprise. You must explain what business or pleasure brings you so far from Pemberley. But first, please introduce me to your wife."

What followed was an unplanned but in all ways pleasant noontime visit with Lord and Lady Middleton of Wollaton Hall. Luncheon of a substantially improved cuisine than the snacks packed in their carriage was shared by the four, and conversation was gay. Lizzy had little in common with the rather mousy Lady Middleton except for motherhood, a topic her ladyship delighted in sharing. They did embark on a thorough tour of the manor, Lord Middleton intricately familiar with the array of structural oddities, art, and history, a subject riveting to Darcy, so the two men had an endless host of discussion pieces.

Finally pulling themselves away from their impromptu hosts, the Darcys resumed their journey. They were a bit behind schedule, but neither regretted the delay at Wollaton. Turning northwest, extending the loop toward Derby, they sedately traveled the five miles to Ilkeston. The moderate sized mining town naturally sported an old church, another dedicated to the Virgin Mary, built in 1150 with a noteworthy clock tower and effigy to the most powerful ancient Lord of Ilkeston, Nicholas de Cantelupe from the fourteenth century.

Again, they paused to wander about the prosperous town. Several shops interested Lizzy, the weaving of fine hosiery being an Ilkeston specialty. However, by four o'clock they were weary and ready to finalize their journey. The seven miles to Locknell Hall passed easily, the Darcys arriving to joyous enthusiasm from Chloe Drury and a more sedate greeting from her husband, Clifton. Thereafter followed another block of time spent in engaging company, even Darcy and Clifton enjoying themselves with billiards and chess.

Chloe could hardly wait to finagle privacy with Lizzy, grasping her hand the moment her parlor door was closed and pulling her to the settee. "Elizabeth, I was thrilled beyond words to receive your note. How fortuitous that you chose this time to visit. I have wonderful news." She paused a moment before gushing with happiness, "Clifton and I are expecting!"

Lizzy squealed and hugged her tight. "Oh Chloe! That is marvelous news. When is your date of confinement? How are you feeling? Have you told anyone else?"

"Slow down, Elizabeth!" Chloe laughed. "One question at a time, please. The baby should arrive in late January, I am feeling as well as can be expected, and other than immediate family, we have told no others. There. Any other queries, Mrs. Curious?" They both laughed, Lizzy bending to pour tea.

"Well, I am overjoyed. Our children will be months apart. In fact, we all seem to be procreating at an alarming rate, rather like rabbits! Filling Derbyshire with the next generation of citizens in one fell swoop." Lizzy handed Chloe a cup. "Mr. Drury must be ecstatic. Tell me, is he as ridiculous as my husband? If he is, be warned, as the nursery will be decorated lavishly, and there may be no toys remaining in the little shop on Oak Street!"

Chloe smiled sweetly. "Clifton is yet refusing to allow himself to anticipate fully." She glanced at Lizzy's puzzled face and sighed. "I have told few this, Elizabeth, but I lost a child four years ago."

Lizzy squeezed her hand in sympathy, instinctively resting the other on her own baby, safe and secure in her womb. Chloe continued, "We had been married but a few months when I conceived. All seemed well until the third month." She swallowed in remembered grief, shaking her head briefly and then smiling weakly. "Since then we have tried but to no avail. The physicians all said there was no reason why I should not conceive, but it simply did not happen until now. We waited to be sure, but quickening has occurred and I am feeling well. Clifton is yet afraid to hope and would rather I maintain the secrecy, but I am too happy."

"Oh Chloe, I am certain all will be well! It must be! You appear hale enough, better than I did at your stage as a matter of fact." Chloe laughed, confirming that she had hardly been ill a day, Lizzy declaring that horribly unfair, and the two pregnant friends embarked on a long discourse of all things baby.

⁕

Day three, they headed south, halting first at Chellaston. This tiny suburb of Derby was famous for the alabaster quarried there and, not shockingly, was home to a thirteenth-century church. After a brief tour, they rambled on, meandering in no discernible pattern as far as Lizzy could ascertain. They passed through Swarkestone and over the famous thirteenth-century stone bridge spanning the River Trent. They paused on the far side, remaining in the cabriolet while Darcy explained that it was this bridge where the army of Prince Charles Stuart the Pretender was repulsed in its march on London. Local lore, he further informed her, maintained that the bridge and small, attached chapel was built by two sisters who lost their loves in the waters of the Trent during a flood. Whatever the truth, the bridge was a marvel of construction and art.

Continuing on due south, they headed toward Calke Abbey. Calke Abbey was in fact not an abbey at all, but was built over the ancient site of an Augustinian abbey in the early 1700s and was given the illustrious name by one of its early residents. The Harpur family, Darcy told Lizzy, were known for their extremely strange eccentricities, rarely leaving the manor and constantly renovating the essentially baroque style mansion with rumored bizarre enhancements. Reclusive in the extreme, their brief appearance at the Cole's Masque was a shocking surprise. Darcy was unacquainted with the current occupants—few were—and presumed that the peculiar suppositions were probably exaggerated. Nonetheless, he thought it would be fun to view the manor and walk through the gardens, which were reputedly some of the grandest in all of England.

Lizzy immediately noted the similarity between Calke Abbey and Pemberley. Both country manors were of the baroque style with extensive, cultivated grounds surrounding. Where Pemberley boasted fountains, a river, and ponds as a focal point, Calke Abbey centered on exotic vegetation and garden buildings. The notoriety of the sculptured and varied landscaping was not unfounded. Lizzy and Darcy could have easily passed all day strolling about the grounds so incredible were they. Apparently, other tourists agreed, as the area was busy with gaping pedestrians.

They toured the small church, the psychic garden, one of the greenhouses, and the recently constructed domed orangery. Darcy gazed with longing at the fantastic stables, but they were near the house proper and restricted to visitors. The expression on his face was so pathetic that Lizzy squeezed his arm tightly to her side and kissed his cheek.

"In two days we shall be home, beloved, and you can salve your aching heart in your own stables." He smiled and returned her kiss, causing two elderly ladies to gasp in shock, and causing Lizzy to giggle as they ducked quickly around a corner.

After two hours and a snack necessary for the woman feeding two, Darcy and Lizzy recommenced the trek, heading due west through Bretby to Burton-upon-Trent just over the border in Staffordshire. They halted here, as Darcy worded it, "Out of necessity, as Burton-upon-Trent produces the finest ales in all of England." This particular claim to fame held little weight to Lizzy, as she detested ale, but Darcy was of a differing opinion altogether. The village itself was quite small, the fame of Burton's breweries having not spread too far beyond the immediately surrounding shires, although Darcy was of the mindset that this would change in time. For the present, they located a pub that seemed decent for luncheon and, therefore, Darcy's requisite pint or two.

With sudden inspiration, Darcy settled his wife in the carriage and commanded her to stay put, walking briskly back into the pub. Lizzy obeyed, watching the front door with bafflement. Hence her extreme surprise when Darcy appeared on the other side with two pub workers in tow, each of them carrying a heavy cask of ale.

He was grinning, obviously quite proud of himself. "What brilliant maneuver have you dreamed up now, my heart? You are positively glowing with self-satisfaction."

"It occurred to me that the rear driver's bench is empty, saddened by fulfilling no purpose in life. Therefore, in an effort to appease its grief, I am loading it with a burden."

Lizzy laughed, Darcy swinging up beside her, embracing her quickly and bestowing a tender kiss. A mile north, Darcy veered off the main road onto a nearly invisible trail between trees that made it barely wide enough for the carriage. "Where are we headed now?" Lizzy asked, Darcy demurring, only telling her it was a surprise.

The trail twisted amongst the thick trees, the main road long since vanished, as the carriage bumped along the rugged trail. Lizzy held on securely, clutching Darcy's arm and the side rail. Just about the time she was prepared to beg him to halt—the jerking sending vague twinges through the stretched muscles and ligaments of her lower abdomen—the path opened into a narrow glade, grassy with a minute pond to the left. Not dissimilar to Darcy's grotto, although far smaller and less lush, it nonetheless presented a serene atmosphere.

Lizzy turned to her husband's smiling face. "It is lovely, William, but how did you know this was here?"

He shrugged. "A friend of mine from Cambridge, Mr. Harold Kensington, resides near here. In fact, we are on his lands, but I do not think he will mind, especially since he is abroad right now." Darcy reached up and cupped Lizzy's face, bending until brushing her lips. "I experienced an overwhelming urge to be alone with you, to kiss you without old-fashioned biddies gasping in shock." Lizzy giggled, but he interrupted her with a consuming kiss, leaving her breathless. "Also, I want you to rest. You overexerted yesterday—do not deny it, my love—and were falling asleep in the carriage." He trailed one finger along the tops of her breasts. "Additionally, my selfishness is unmasked in that I desire my wife alert tonight so I can ravish her body, bringing her joy unlimited as well as my own profound satisfaction."

They spread a blanket along the shady tree edge, reclining contentedly. Darcy removed his jacket, stretching long legs and laying back with one arm folded under his head and the other around his wife's waist, stroking her arm gently. "Are you enjoying yourself, dearest?"

Lizzy gazed at her husband with undisguised love. "I am having a marvelous time." She stretched beside him, chin resting on his chest, fingering his cravat. "The scenery is sublime. The history and buildings fascinating. The tour guide is handsome and extraordinarily intelligent. I honestly cannot fathom how the outing could be improved upon."

Darcy was smiling happily, playing with loosened strands of her hair and her ear. Lizzy nibbled the corner of her lip, dexterously untying a knot of his cravat. "Hmmm… Perhaps, I can fathom an improvement after all." After she had another knot unraveled, she continued, "Such a gorgeous and talented tour guide should be rewarded. Let me think… What could a man of such dazzling capabilities want from a simple girl like me? A kiss? Would that please my handsome guide?" The cravat was completely undone, Lizzy working her way down the buttons of his waistcoat when she bestowed her kiss.

The kiss was thorough, encompassing, teasing with tongues and lips altering between soft and demanding. Darcy loosened more strands of her hair, otherwise allowing Lizzy to lead the kiss in whichever direction she chose and becoming rapidly intoxicated by the taste of her. Lizzy completed the task of unbuttoning the vest, next removing his shirt from breeches waistband and running a hand over his abdomen. She lifted her face then, Darcy's eyes hazy with desire.

Fingering over his lips to chin, then along solid jaw line, she whispered, "William, my husband. I love you immensely. I do not wish to wait until tonight to love you. I intend to ravish your body right now. I trust this meets with your approval?" She smiled impishly, allowing no opportunity for more than a slight nod before capturing his mouth with hungry urgency. Darcy reciprocated equally, moaning deep in his chest and clutching her shoulders. With a final rough suck to his lower lip and sharp nip, she withdrew, delivering wet kisses over his jaw to exposed neck. Darcy arched with a delighted sigh, shifting to relieve the sudden tightness in his groin.

"Elizabeth," he murmured, "you are astounding and amazing. How did I live without you?"

Lizzy rose from the vicinity of his sternum with a grin, hands peeling the shirt hem upwards. "I do not know, William, but you have me now and I assure your absolute gratification." With a hike of skirts, she straddled his thighs and lustily attacked the flesh of his abdomen with her mouth.

Darcy closed his eyes with a heady sigh, relaxing into the waves of pleasure washing through every cell. *Never*, he mused, *will I not be rendered a helpless puddle of arousal when she touches me.* He remembered every moment they had touched, from that day so long ago at Netherfield until today, and always, each and every time, he received an electric shock of profound magnitude. Love, that elusive emotion, was now the cornerstone of his existence. As thrilling as her touch was in a purely sexual aspect, the ruling stimulus was their infinite love and devotion. She reached the soul encased within his flesh, arousing the very fiber of his being to a level that eclipsed the physical.

Passion, faithfulness, and veneration raged through both of them, the giving and taking of kisses and caresses a potent impulse. Lizzy continued to ravage his torso, her hands roamed under him to squeeze his derriere, continued on down clenched thighs, and traveled, with brushing glances, over to his groin. Darcy was moaning, uttering unintelligible words, hands flattened on the ground as he rocked into her body.

"Elizabeth! Please… I beg you… I need you!" He lurched to a sitting position, grasping Lizzy about the waist desperately. She responded with alacrity, clutching his shoulders and rising while he frantically swept her skirts aside. In a swift second they were joined.

Darcy released a reverberant growl, gripping her body to his chest intently and kissing greedily. Lizzy wrapped arms tightly over his shoulders and neck. They raged on, eager and consumed, precipitously attaining their peak. As if by telepathy, they slowed at the same time, mutually sensing the demand to prolong the loving.

Retreating an inch, breath mixing as they panted opened mouth with gazes locking. Lizzy fingered airily over his face while Darcy caressed her back.

"Fitzwilliam," she whispered, "my love. So perfect… all mine… always." She kissed his nose and then returned to his mouth, nibbling. "Oh, my lover, the feel of you! Oh God, William! I love you so! How can I describe the joy of your body buried in me?" Uncontainable passion whirled and radiated, bonding them together in unity. Lizzy cupped his face and rested her forehead against his, submitting to the power of his love.

"Elizabeth," he moaned, "my love… let go… come with me… now!" Pressing his mouth blissfully against hers they allowed the rush of acute pleasure to overtake them.

They held each other tightly, kissing and fondling, neither desiring to leave the other, relishing the intimacy of where their naked flesh connected. Inexplicably, an upsurge of emotion brought tears to Lizzy's eyes and she released a shuddering sob. Darcy withdrew to see her face, frowning as he brushed her tears with his thumbs. "Elizabeth, what is wrong?"

She was shaking her head, squeezing him tight. "Nothing, forgive me, William, I just... love you so much... sometimes it... overwhelms me." He kissed her tenderly, shushing and soothing. Laying back onto the blanket with her firm in his embrace and pressed over his body, he murmured adoration until she quieted. Finally, with a tremulous laugh and while lodging one arm possessively against the hot skin of his chest, she spoke, "Pregnancy emotions running amok, I suppose." She nestled closer, more than half her body lying on his.

Silently they enveloped each other, feeling each respiration and heartbeat. Lizzy delighted in the sensation of her husband's warmth. Darcy reveled in the softness of her form under his hands, even clothed, and the occasional movement of their baby against his lower right abdomen. Darcy, cognizant of the change in her breathing signaling that she was moments away from sleep, drew her closer to his body and held her thus for over an hour, ignoring the cramping muscles and sharp rock under his left shoulder blade.

⚜

Their final destination for the day was the village of Repton. Darcy thoroughly detailed the history of the pivotal town as they drove, Lizzy in a fever of excitement by the time they crested the small rise and viewed the town spread before them on the sloping hillside.

"Essentially, in the present," Darcy explained, "Repton is no more than the typical farming and fishing village. Except for the school. Repton School is the oldest independent school for boys in all of England, functioning unbroken since 1557 if you can imagine. My grandfather attended here for three years and my father considered sending me, but the headmasters following my grandfather's day had allowed the school to decline. I honestly do not know the reputation currently. I remember I was disappointed, as the idea of formal education appealed to me. I begged for Eton or Winchester or Harrow instead, but mother was ill, and I think father could not bear wounding her heart by sending me away." He paused in memory, Lizzy squeezing his knee.

With a smile, he resumed his narrative, "We will tour the school, as it sits on the same campus as Saint Wystan's Church, which is the real draw of the area. Repton, my love, unassuming as it is, was the capital of Mercia in the sixth century. All the kings and princes resided here and were buried in the church. The crypt and mausoleum are mostly intact and the remains of several kings can be viewed. It is very exciting! In fact, these artifacts are some of the oldest and best-preserved Saxon relics in England. Additionally, Repton is the first village where Christianity was preached in the Midlands. Priests were sent from Northumbria, as northern England then was, to convert the pagan Mercian kings. Amazingly, they were successful. The church was built over the mausoleum in the eighth century and has remained relatively unchanged to this day. A priory was founded here as well, but no longer remains, except as the foundation stones for the school."

"Who was Saint Wystan?"

Darcy pursed his lips in thought. "A prince, if I recall correctly, the son of one of the Kings of Mercia. He was murdered, and miracles apparently ensued as an aftermath. The history is vague, as it often is with legends and superstitions. Eventually, he was sanctified and the church was named for him as its patron saint."

Lizzy was very impressed, thrilled to touch the ancient stones and imagine medieval men carving and building. Of all the marvels seen on their short jaunt into the past, these ruins were the most ancient. The press of age and history, life lived to the fullest if utterly divergent from the modern familiar, was palpable as they descended the archaic, worn stone steps to the crypt. It was easy to sense trapped emotions and memories, the ethereal whisper of forgotten voices echoing. It was eerie yet oddly comforting to know that time marched on but the indelible stamp of the past endured.

They roved about the grounds, sat in serene contemplation inside the church itself, and then strolled through the town. Like all country hamlets, the buildings were primarily stone and thatch, most old with the random, newer construction interposed. Children dashed about the streets, dogs yapping at their feet as they laughed and skipped and teased. It was very relaxing, and neither Darcy nor Lizzy were in any hurry to return to Derby. The numerous evidences of the past at each turn delighted them and further astounded. It was the perfect end to a perfect day.

The final day of the Darcy journey through the lower Midlands of

Derbyshire dawned cloudy with rain threatening. Darcy was tempted to cancel the outing, but Lizzy refused. "You will not melt, William." She declared firmly. "This is England, after all. If rain halted us, we would never accomplish anything."

He assumed a disapproving frown, lips twitching. "Very well, Elizabeth, but if you catch a cold do not expect me to nurse you!"

The day's excursion would be interrupted somewhat by intermittent showers, but as luck would have it, they were light and occurred primarily while driving. Elizabeth inhaled deeply of the clean air, lifting her face to the sprinkles, and despite Darcy's dire prediction, did not become ill.

The first stop was Tutbury, a village technically in Staffordshire although it hugged the border so closely that many Tutbury residents lived on the Derbyshire side of the River Dove. The reason Darcy wished his wife to visit the sleepy village was for the thirteenth-century castle. The ruins of the once vast fortress strategically located on a promontory above Tutbury was notable for its aesthetic value and crowning Norman architectural significance; however, it was the history that interested Darcy.

"The fortress city was initially built by the Kings of Mercia long ago," he told Lizzy, who actually already knew the history, but she loved to hear his voice so did not interrupt. "The natural butte was a perfect location for tactical reasons, and there is archeological evidence that the Romans built a settlement here. The main road we traveled on is a Roman road constructed before the turn of the millennium, a trade route between the south and north. Unfortunately, other than a few coins and similar artifacts, little is known of what the structure here might have been. It may have been no more than a campsite as soldiers moved from one battlefield to the next."

He paused as they reached the northern edge of the cliff, both captivated by the panoramic view of the Dove valley far below, odiferous bog clearly visible.

Darcy resumed his tale in a hushed voice, "You can imagine why this place was ideal. A fortress was built and some of the kings resided here. Along with Repton, Tutbury was the prime seat of power. However, from the eighth to the eleventh century, between Saxons, Vikings, and the Normans, war raged. Tutbury changed hands numerous times, was ravaged and rebuilt, abandoned and reoccupied. I venture it is nearly impossible to ascertain now which stones were laid when or what the fortress may have actually looked like. In fact, the early Mercian castle was undoubtedly more wood than stone." They strolled about the fallen piles of rock and half erect walls, catching vague glimpses of rooms and symmetry, only to have the emerging shape lost abruptly in open grassy spaces.

"Over the centuries, various inhabitants renovated the castle, but never to full potency. The constant civil wars of our Norman ancestors, and later the English rulers, prevailed well into the 1300s, love, as you know. As a fortress and city of authority, Tutbury was inhabited and besieged over and over again. One would barely manage to bolster the defenses when another would come along and break holes." He shook his head at the stupidity of it all. Taking Lizzy's hand, they descended the slick steps leading into the dungeon and remains of the castle, heading toward the south tower. They paused inside the dungeon, not nearly as ominous as it probably once was now that the roof and one wall were collapsed.

"The following three hundred years were peaceful and attempts were made to rebuild with fair success. It was never entirely completed, long years of disuse and delayed restoration preventing full restitution. Nonetheless, the South Tower was considered impenetrable and served as one of the many prisons for Mary, Queen of Scots in the late 1500s. Of all the places she was confined in during those eighteen years, she wrote that she hated Tutbury the most. The castle was largely falling down and poorly constructed, the area surrounding extraordinarily damp and marshy with foul odors frequently arising, and the distance from London detained the delivery of necessary goods. The legends say she became very ill here from the harsh winters."

One look at the moldy damp stones of the ruined keep and Lizzy felt a surge of sympathy for the long dead Mary, despite her English prejudice toward the treasonous Queen. Lizzy shivered the entire time they rambled about the place, actually thankful to depart.

They turned north from Tutbury, planning a relatively short circle back to Derby. The journey home would be long, as Darcy intended to visit a few places of interest along the way, so he did not wish to travel too far afield today. Therefore, they snaked leisurely through the farmlands and tiny towns dotting the plain. They traveled north through Church Broughton to Longford, onward to Shirley then veering east to Brailsford. Along the way, they stopped as the mood arose to sightsee another church or ruin, nibble a snack, or simply stretch their legs.

After luncheon at a pub in Brailsford, they turned southeast toward Derby. The last stop of significance was Mackworth Castle—or rather, the finely detailed gatehouse of what may have been a castle. Here was a location of true mystery. Why would the arch and façade of a two-story structure be all that remained of a manor house? Was the house destroyed utterly without leaving a trace except for the untouched gatehouse? Or was it some unknown man's folly and never completed? Why was there no history surrounding the structure? Apparently the questions would never be answered.

It was a humorous, puzzling end to a glorious sojourn in lower Derbyshire. The goal of acquainting Elizabeth Darcy with her new home was flourishing. Darcy was supremely satisfied in all ways, and Lizzy did sense a greater kinship and connection to the land that would be her home for many years to come and her children's home. She knew that Darcy now itched to drag her to the wealth of attractions the Peak District boasted. Englishmen were by nature territorial, especially the gentry. For a man of Darcy's station and lineage, Derbyshire was more than merely the place he resided. It was in his blood. His very identity was first as a man of Derbyshire then as an Englishman. Lizzy did not know if she would ever attain his level of affinity for the region, but she understood his passion and felt it touch her through him. It affected her most profoundly when their child moved inside her. The reality that she carried the heir to Pemberley, and all that it meant not only to her husband but also to the future of Derbyshire, was a staggering, but also a joyous honor.

CHAPTER TWENTY-FIVE

North and East

LIZZY WOKE THE FOLLOWING morning at eight-thirty to an empty bed. There was nothing at all unusual about that, although she was surprised Darcy had allowed her to sleep so late. His agenda for the journey home was a secret, but the distance to Pemberley was a nearly two-hour carriage ride without halting. She had assumed he would want to depart early.

Donning a robe, she entered the small sitting room to discover her husband busily scribbling at the desk. He jumped up when she entered, Lizzy laughing and waving him down. She was forever telling him not to do that, but long years of gentlemanly manners could not be erased. He ignored her gesture, approaching with a smile.

"Good morning, my love! Did you sleep well?" He kissed her forehead, smoothing through her hair.

"I always sleep well, dearest, except for when your hot body smothers me completely!"

Darcy grinned. "Forgive me. Even subconsciously I must be near you. I have no control over the matter. Tea and a scone?"

"Yes, please." She sat, tucking her feet under her. "No need to apologize, William. I simply elbow you hard and you roll away, temporarily at least. Come winter you can repay the treatment when I slip my frozen feet between your thighs." She lifted her face for a kiss, which he happily bestowed. "What are you so diligently working on this morning?"

He resumed his seat, taking a long gulp of coffee before answering. "A letter to Mr. Keith." He turned to her, face animated. "I had a thought, if you are amenable and physically tolerant. Our miniature holiday prior to our main one in September has thus far proceeded so enjoyably that I am considering extending it for a few more days. Does this appeal to you?"

Lizzy was already nodding positively. "It definitely appeals to me! I am having a marvelous time, darling, and love sightseeing. Physically I am wonderful, although I would request traversing well maintained roads." She rubbed her lower abdomen with a grimace, Darcy instantly frowning.

"Why do you say that?"

"The bumpy road to the glade day before yesterday was uncomfortable on my stretching muscles." She smiled and smoothed the robe fabric tight over a remarkably protruding belly.

Darcy, however, was pale and scowling. "You did not tell me you were in pain, Elizabeth." His voice was low and stern, eyes steely.

Lizzy sighed, rolling her eyes. "I never *will* tell you, Mr. Darcy, if you display that face each time! You worry too much, William. It is perfectly normal but uncomfortable nonetheless. I was fine the second we stopped, as you are well aware by how I attacked you not ten minutes later! All I am requesting is we avoid rugged terrain, otherwise I am right as rain and eager for more adventures with you." She smiled placidly and sipped her tea.

Darcy was yet frowning and thinking frantically. The fear of her not confiding in him due to his overbearing anxiety was a threat he could readily imagine his stubborn Elizabeth implementing. However, he could not pretend he did not fret nor could he allow her stubbornness to push her into overextending herself or ignoring a negative symptom. With consideration of her one request, he resumed.

"Very well then. I have been giving this some thought for the past two days, assuming you would be agreeable to prolonging our journey." He leaned forward, gazing at her seriously. "My preference, in truth my greatest desire, is to travel through Dovedale and tour the High Peak. Not only is the region majestic and the supreme attraction in all Derbyshire, but," he paused and shifted uncomfortably, holding her eyes, "Elizabeth, I am keenly cognizant that your trip was prematurely cancelled last year. Since that time, I have deeply yearned to be the one to show you my country, be your tour guide as it were." He smiled faintly, Lizzy gazing with love in return. "I had a trip planned for early May, but that too was interrupted."

A cloud of pain crossed his face and Lizzy hastily rose and nestled onto his lap, Darcy hugging tightly. He rested his head against her shoulder, Lizzy kissing the top. "I never knew, William," she said softly. "Why did you not tell me?"

He shrugged. "It slipped my mind at first and then seemed irrelevant. My joy was having you alive. Adventures and prideful boasting of landscapes paled in significance. Anyway, I imagined that we could tour this fall, but I fear I still judge it unwise." He glanced up at his wife with a slight grin. "At the risk of incurring your irritation at my worrying overly and being presumptuous and domineering, I will remind you of your own request to avoid rugged roads."

She arched a brow, gazing questioningly, "You are confusing me, beloved. Are we touring the High Peak or not?"

"I fear not. It is my desire, but perhaps we can finagle a trip there in the spring or next fall. I do worry about you and our child, Elizabeth. Forgive me, but I cannot deny it. Also, I am needed back at Pemberley in five days at the latest for the arrival of Duke Grafton's mares. We could not do justice to the region if rushed, but that does not mean we cannot prolong our trip other places. Please tell me you understand, love?"

Lizzy chuckled, cupping his cheek and leaning in for a long kiss. "My dearest love, you do worry far too much! I will be residing in Derbyshire for the remainder of my life. I am quite certain this will accord us a multitude of opportunities to travel. I do not believe the Peaks will be disappearing anytime soon. Wherever we go will be wonderful because I am with you, not due to the landscape or artifacts."

Darcy sighed in relief. "I love you, Mrs. Darcy, so very much."

"Yes, I know," she answered pertly with a peck to his nose.

She rose, but he grasped her hand, halting her leaving. Placing both broad hands over the daily-burgeoning swell of their son, he held her, waiting and smiling happily when a faint nudge was felt. "I can no longer completely secure him under my hands," he noted. "In four months we shall see his face, my heart, perhaps less." He nuzzled his face against the soft mound, kissing tenderly and murmuring nonsense.

Lizzy ran her fingers through his hair, delighting in these moments which were fast becoming a ritual. Darcy's need to connect on some level with his child was instinctual and so incredibly endearing. Additionally, his devotion to and adoration for her "bump," as she teasingly named it, allayed her sporadic private feelings of dismay at her changing form. Already, though with so much baby growth yet to occur, Lizzy experienced moments of awkwardness and unattractiveness. Her husband, however, seemed unaffected, unless it was to be increasingly amorous and worshipful of her body.

Two hours later they were on the road. Now traveling in the Darcy coach, comfortably nestled on the plushly padded seats with windows open and shades up, Lizzy said a silent adieu to Derby. Their purchases were to be delivered to Pemberley, Darcy having hired a transport wagon yesterday. Today he had sent letters to Mr. Keith and Mrs. Reynolds by express courier warning of the wagon's arrival and of their plans. As for the plans themselves, Lizzy remained uninformed.

Darcy relished these little surprises and Lizzy trusted him, so had no issue with sitting back and watching the scenery go by. They exited town, heading north on the main thoroughfare, which they had entered on, slicing down the middle of Derbyshire. Assuming they had adequately covered the southern and immediate east and west of the lower Midland of Derbyshire, and aware that they were foregoing the northwest and far north for this trek, Lizzy figured they would veer northeast. She was correct.

Only a mile or two up the road, they did diverge. At this point, Darcy decided to enlighten his wife. "I realized we would not have the time to traverse the entire Peak, beloved; however, I figured we could see a remnant of it. Since you relish caverns, the least we can do on this trip is explore one or two." Lizzy's eyes brightened with excitement and Darcy laughed, squeezing her hand. "Before you leap for joy and rap your head on the ceiling, allow me to explain. I have plotted a circuitous route through the Ilkeston district to Chesterfield today. The town is second to Derby in size, so we can shop if you are not yet weary of the activity." He paused with a grin, halting her sharp retort with a kiss.

"We can tarry there for a couple of days, shop, see the local attractions, and visit the Sitwells, if you wish it, as Reniswahl Manor is nearby. Then we can travel to Castleton to view Peak Cavern before returning to Pemberley. It is merely the lower edge of the Peak, but it will provide a taste of what to expect at a later date."

Lizzy was practically bouncing in her seat with enthusiasm. "William, you are brilliant! This is a perfect end to our holiday!" She threw her arms about his neck, hugging his shoulders and kissing his face.

Laughingly, he grabbed her rapidly moving face, pulling in for a centered kiss, and then withdrew to meet her shining eyes. "Thank you for your enthusiasm, love. I fear I must warn you that the terrain between here and Castleton is rather dull. No rugged roads, as you requested, but, alas, the countryside is tame and relatively devoid of interesting peculiarities."

Lizzy shook her head. "I shall be with you. That is all that truly matters. Besides, I adore pastoral countryside and do not deem it dull in the least. You shall make it exciting, William. My own wonderful, personal tour guide."

He stroked her cheek with a smile. "A challenge, then, for me to dazzle you. Ah," he glanced out the window as the carriage slowed, "our first destination. The village of Horsley." They stood before another church, this one stunning and remarkably different in style then all the ones visited thus far. The entire structure of beautiful grey stone, ornate with a strongly buttressed, spire-topped tower nestled on a grassy, flower laden rise. An ancient cemetery graced the immediate surrounds, dating back to the thirteenth century. A fifteenth century addition of a high clerestory with a dramatic array of windows under a handsome parapet of battlements and pinnacles gave the church a castle-like appearance. The multitude of windows lit the wide interior to nearly full daylight intensity. It was wholly spectacular.

Lizzy and Darcy wandered about, once again filled with the peace which inevitably saturated such places. The moderate hill yielded a stupendous view of the immediate environs to the north. Despite Darcy's dismal prediction of monotony, Lizzy found the landscape breathtaking. The endless rolling hills stretched to the horizon, hazy grey mist merging the sky with the land. Glittering little streams and patchwork-quilt fields of crops and orchards with simple country homes were all that was readily seen, but it was serene and earthy. The air was teeming with freshly tilled soil, sweet flowers, cut grass, the songs of birds and bleats of sheep, and a host of other natural sensations.

Lizzy inhaled deeply, squeezing her husband's arm in contentment. "It reminds me of our home. Growing things, organic and wild, and the workaday life of unpretentious folk. I have always adored simplicity and raw nature. I am thankful that, for all the opulence of Pemberley even with its cultured gardens, at its heart, it is a farm and a home." She glanced up at Darcy, who was looking at her in astonishment. "You see, my love, we never were that different, you and I. I may have more easily dressed the part of a country girl, but your soul is of the land."

It was with tremendous effort that Darcy resisted embracing his wife where they stood in public. He cleared his throat gruffly, blinked several times, and silently squeezed her hand in return.

The eight miles to Alfreton were entirely rural, the villages passed tiny in the extreme. Twice they were forced to halt for herding sheep crossing the road and once to lend a ride to an elderly man whose wagon wheel had broken. They entered Alfreton, a community predominately reliant on coal mining, nestled in the Amber River Valley, on their Friday market day. Farmers from miles around converged to sell their wares every Friday since 1251. Neither Darcy nor Lizzy were aware of this fact, it being a local event, but were thrilled nonetheless. The narrow streets were jammed, forcing the Darcys to disembark on the edge of town, Darcy commanding Mr. Anders to circle around to the north where they would meet him later. The Darcys set out to explore, a blushing Samuel escorting his betrothed in the opposite direction through the press of people and stalls.

The festive atmosphere was enchanting. Stall upon ceaseless stall of fresh vegetables and fruits, cured meats and sausages, homemade ales and wines, arts and crafts, and so forth. Vendors sold delicious smelling meat pies and tarts, whole roasted turkey legs, corn on the cob, stews, freshly baked breads and pastries, and so much more. Deciding on which culinary delight to devour was agony! Lizzy ate until she almost felt ill, and Darcy was apparently a bottomless pit.

A stall selling lovely bracelets of polished stones intrigued Lizzy and she purchased one for each girl child and caretaker at the orphanage. For the boys, she purchased small, hand-whittled whistles, sure to delight the boys and irritate the adults. For Georgiana, who incessantly complained of the cold, she found slippers fashioned of sheepskin. They were unadorned but sturdy, with thick soles and excellent stitching.

They wandered leisurely through the crowded streets, listened to the varied minstrels playing, watched a puppet show and a crude enactment of *Henry V* on the grassy village square, and were charmed at the overheard conversations of the locals, which universally centered on romance and agriculture. The press of people thinned as they reached the northern boundary of the village, meeting up with the carriage and Samuel and Marguerite. They resumed their journey, after providing Mr. Anders and Phillips with fresh food and small mugs of ale.

Pausing briefly in Tibshelf, mainly for Darcy to show Lizzy one of the shallow coal mines the area has been famous for since the 1500s, when Bess of Hardwick had opened the first one. Darcy stood with his wife on a low rise near the edge of the village; across a narrow gorge sat a hulking monstrosity in grey and black with smoke billowing from tall stacks. It was one of the new deep mines recently opened to delve hundreds of feet into the ground for hidden caches of coal. With expressions of disgust, they watched the blackened workers attending to their duties while Darcy explained the fundamentals as best as he knew them.

"Do you invest in coal mining?" Lizzy asked nervously, fearing a positive response.

Darcy shook his head. "No. I have looked into the prospect and it is tempting, as the industry is profitable and I fear the wave of the energy future. However, I could not bring myself to be a part of such a filthy and dangerous production. Cotton milling and the various occupations necessary to keep Pemberley solvent are hazardous enough. Besides, I have a sufficient number of ventures to keep me busy."

He smiled at the relief written on her face, taking her elbow and steering her along the pathway until the ugly mine had disappeared from view. In stark contrast to the dismal vision of scarred landscape to the south was the majestic mansion Hardwick Hall. Standing again on the edge of a shallow vale, Lizzy and Darcy could clearly see the stupendous house and magnificent grounds. In fact, Hardwick Hall, the breathtaking mansion home of the wealthy Elizabeth Hardwick, could readily be seen from nearly all points of the little hamlet.

"As you know, my love, versed in English history as thoroughly as you are, the Countess of Shrewsbury was a powerful and rich woman, second only to Queen Elizabeth herself. I must confess that if any Derbyshire mansion rivals Pemberley, it would be Hardwick."

"I will concur that it is impressive, dearest. I do not think I have ever encountered a house with such enormous windows. Perhaps I too am merely prejudiced, but I think I prefer the baroque style of Pemberley to the Tudor. In the end, I suppose it depends on one's taste without there being a definitive winner. Pemberley seems homier and not so ostentatious. I could never imagine a Darcy wanting their initials boldly emblazoned from each pinnacle!"

Darcy laughed, glancing at her impishly. "Are you certain? I was just envisaging how it would look to have E. D. in scrolling steel or marble on all four corners of the manor."

Lizzy seriously shook her head, but her lips were twitching with humor. "Too bold, William. Perchance a niche in the parlor for a carved idol and candles? Or possibly a blooming hedge shaped like my face?"

Darcy shook his head, lips pursed. "No to the idol. I prefer to offer my worship upon your physical body. As for the hedge," he said, nodding, "I shall give it some thought."

"Ha!" Lizzy pinched his side. "Good luck on that one. I am positive Mr. Clark would flatly refuse if you requested such an atrocity on his grounds."

"His grounds?" Darcy said with lifted brow.

Lizzy laughed. "Make no mistake, William. You own the estate and pay the bills, but when it comes to the landscaping, Mr. Clark is king."

Chesterfield, although the second largest town in Derbyshire, was a third the size and population of Derby. Initially this disparity was not evident, the bustling activity along the streets fairly intense. Chesterfield's central location on the northeastern region of the county, coupled with lying on the northern road to Sheffield, ensured a steady traffic.

"Why do you never travel here, William? Chesterfield is closer to Pemberley than Derby."

Darcy shrugged. "I have no business ventures here, and Derby has more to offer in both commerce and entertainment. Frankly, I tend not to travel there all that much. In the past, prior to marrying you"—he bent for a kiss to her brow—"I passed so much time in London that I had little need to venture afield once at Pemberley. You are correct that Chesterfield is nearer to us. One can be here in an hour by carriage, far less on a fast horse. We should keep this in mind as we wander about. It may be a more reasonable alternative, my love, if you need wares not attainable in Lambton or Matlock."

The carriage pulled into a long drive before a substantial sized inn entirely constructed of multihued river stones. Numerous singular stone cottages and moderate two-story buildings were scattered about the extensive, park-like property. The whole campus bordered the River Hipper.

Lizzy was gazing out the carriage window in awe. "This is a lovely inn for such a modest town. Are they expecting us?" She turned to her husband with questioning eyes.

"No, but that is immaterial. We are the Darcys. They will have a room for us." He said it bluntly and absently, Lizzy taken aback momentarily; then she remembered with a start the truth of his words, especially as the carriage halted and five livery garbed servants leapt forward to assist with their luggage while Phillips hopped down and opened the door. They were greeted formally by the hotel's superintendent, the man fawning as if welcoming the Prince Regent himself. Darcy assumed his full Master of Pemberley pose, the semblance natural and anticipated in these sorts of situations.

Lizzy, after months in London, was quite familiar with this presentation of her privately boyish, casual spouse. Therefore, it no longer shocked her and, in fact, sent little shivers of excitement up her spine. She adored both aspects of Darcy's personality: the charming, teasing, passionate man that he was when relaxed as well as the commanding, forceful, aristocratic man of means who was every inch a Darcy.

Within minutes, they were escorted to a secluded cottage on the edge of the river. Samuel and Marguerite instantly set about unpacking Lizzy's and Darcy's personal effects; a maid arrived with freshly cut flowers and to open the windows; a servant with a tray of wine, cheeses, and bread appeared; and a last materialized to provide an orientation to the cottage's facilities. It was a whirlwind, and Lizzy was exhausted by the time they all departed.

As soon as the door closed behind the last maid, Lizzy slumped onto the sofa with a heavy sigh. "My, my! What an ordeal. The rooms are delightful though. Have you stayed here before?"

Darcy was at the sidebar pouring a whiskey. He shook his head, taking a large swallow. "No. I asked the manager at the Georgian in Derby for the best lodging Chesterfield had to offer, and he recommended this: the Royal

Cottages. I shall have to send a note of thanks. The grounds alone are worth the expense." He gazed out the window as he sipped his drink.

"Well, I like the privacy of a separate dwelling with our own patio and river view." Lizzy rose, approaching her daydreaming husband, slipping both arms about his waist, and nestling her head between his shoulder blades. "Lost in thought, my love?"

"Forgive me, dearest. I was merely trying to decide what to do next. Stroll about the grounds? Walk into town and see the sights? Or remove all your clothes and make love?"

"What a dilemma, Mr. Darcy. What shall you do?"

He laughed, pulling her around and clasping her face. "First, I shall kiss you, my wife, as I have yearned to do all day." He did, Lizzy rapidly growing weak in the knees from the power of his allure and love as poured was evident from his kiss. Such a simple thing a kiss is, yet potent to a degree unmatched by any other force on earth. Darcy encircled her waist, pressing her tightly to his body. Both allowed the magic of the kiss to course through their beings, the indescribable intimacy of this fundamental act of devotion bonding them.

Darcy broke away with a contented sigh, resting his forehead on hers. "My Elizabeth, how tremendously I love you. So much so that I do not wish to rush loving you." He brushed her lips tenderly with a feathering tickle of his tongue. "Let us walk a bit, my heart, explore, and enjoy each other's company. Tonight I shall make love to you slowly, no haste whatsoever, followed by endless hours of bliss in your arms." He withdrew, meeting her eyes with a smile; Lizzy's expression suffused with passion and clearly undecided regarding waiting. Darcy chuckled softly, bestowed a brief buss to her nose. "Anticipation is sweet, lover. Now, write a note to the Sitwells, and then we shall survey the land."

They stopped at the lobby to obtain a general map of the town and information from the manager as to the main attractions. Darcy called for the coachman to deliver the missive to Reniswahl Hall, and then he and Lizzy set out. They walked through the immediate surrounds, highly impressed by the finely landscaped gardens so perfectly merged with the natural vegetation by the river. Enormous trees grew haphazardly, offering shade and providing the beginning carpet of autumn leaves of red and gold that padded the cobblestone pathways. An arched stone bridge spanned the narrow, placid river, Chesterfield proper looming on the far side. Ducks and swans paddled serenely across the still water.

Like all English towns of ancient ancestry, there are always the occasional stories to tell. Chesterfield was no exception, although the vast majority of the town was fairly modern and the region relatively devoid of any truly exciting history. A narrow street known as The Shambles held the claim as the oldest part of town, dating from the twelfth century. It was an area of tea houses, small exclusive shops, and a pub called the Royal Oak, which was reputedly once a resting place for the medieval Knights Templar.

The shopping district was inclusive, even boasting a small toy store that Lizzy forbid Darcy to enter. They did a bit of shopping, purchasing four baby outfits which were simply too adorable to resist. Darcy noticed the rare bookstore on the far side of the street prior to Lizzy, grasping her arm and propelling her onto the road, narrowly avoiding a pile of horse droppings in his enthusiasm. No doubt the highlight of that leg of their trip was finding a Chaucer, Thomas Paine's *Rights of Man*, and Molière's *Le Misanthrope* in the original French that he promised to read to Lizzy, who had read the English translation but nonetheless delighted in hearing his melodious voice speaking French.

Late afternoon found them before another church. Here was the one true oddity and tourist attraction of Chesterfield. The thirteenth century church, dedicated to Saint Mary and all Saints, was beautifully constructed of grey and gold bricks in the typical cruciform formation, with tall arched windows gracing the sides and above the main entrance. Both the interior and exterior was a marvel of ornate craftsmanship at its finest. However, it was the spire atop the clock tower which lent the church its uniqueness and countrywide fame. Apparently, the architects erred in their engineering and erection. The two-hundred-foot spire of wood was built perfectly and then covered with over thirty tons of stunning lead tiles in a herringbone style, a massive cross at the pinnacle. It was brilliant and surely struck awe in all who beheld it. Unfortunately, the error was in utilizing unseasoned wood, which, as it gradually dried over the centuries, had been twisted by the sheer weight of the tiles. Now, the once reportedly spectacular but standard spire, was yearly changing as it continued to spiral incrementally, creating a wonder both strange and extraordinary.

They returned to the inn as dusk was descending. Deciding to dine early so they could spend the remainder of the evening in quiet, casual solitude was Darcy's idea and was met with his wife's smiling approval. Therefore, by eight, they were reclining in their sitting room in robes, Molière imparted in flawless resonant French to a rapt Lizzy. She sat propped against the sofa arm, her feet on her husband's lap being softly massaged while she knit a blue baby blanket. Lizzy did not understand a word, but this was inconsequential as far as she was concerned. The joy was in hearing Darcy's voice and the placid companionship engendered in these relaxed enterprises.

"I finished!" she announced with pride and relief. "How does it look?"

She held the small blanket up, Darcy reaching over to touch the edge. "It is so soft. Is this special yarn for infants?"

She nodded. "Yes. It is woven to be pliable and tender to their delicate skin. Harsh wool would be scratchy and leave a rash."

"Oh. I did not remember that their skin was so sensitive. It makes sense, I suppose. Foals have fine hair and delicate hides initially."

Lizzy laughed. "Well, I do not expect our child will be covered with hair nor have a hide necessarily, but his skin will be fair and very soft, like velvet." She cocked her head. "Have you truly not seen or touched a baby, William?"

He shrugged. "I remember Georgie when she was small. Her skin was nearly translucent it was so fair. Minute veins visible and she had little hair. I recall mother bemoaning in jest how bald she was." He smiled in memory. "Mother said I was born with a mass of dark hair, so perhaps our son will be as well." He paused, still stroking the blanket with faraway eyes. "The blanket is beautiful, my love. You knit masterfully despite your disdain for the activity. As for the answer to your question, I have seen infants in perambulators about the park, held by parents as they stroll, that sort of thing. However, I have not, since Georgiana, actually touched nor really examined one. I confess this with trepidation as you will likely decide I am unfit to hold our child, and you would be wise to do so." He smiled, laying one hand on her belly.

Lizzy shook her head. "You are mistaken, love. I have no fears whatsoever as to your competence as a father." Darcy beamed, leaning forward to initiate his ritualistic conversation with his child, but was interrupted by a knock at the door.

He rose with a frown, tightening his robe as he walked to the door. Lizzy observed him, always delighting in his fine figure so perfectly displayed when robed. It was a servant delivering an envelope. "It is from the Sitwells," he declared, handing the letter to Lizzy and promptly resuming his interrupted task.

Darcy spoke French endearments, Lizzy reading Julia Sitwell's letter with a giggle. "Julia insists we visit tomorrow afternoon and stay for dinner. She even enclosed a sketch map with noted interesting sights between here and there. She says Mr. Sitwell is already chalking his cue, determined to triumph over you."

Darcy snorted. "Highly unlikely that. Rory has never been proficient at billiards. I taught him when we were at Cambridge, but he never readily grasped the game. His hand to eye coordination is horrendous. Now, give the man a deck of cards or dice and a genius emerges. His tactic is to mellow me by gracefully losing several billiard sets then roping me into faro and emptying my money clip." He kissed above her navel, resting his cheek on her mound. "I shall ensure I have adequate funds on hand so our host will feel vindicated. Ah, there you are my son! He was being very sedate tonight."

"Perhaps he did not recognize your voice in French. You confused his fragile mind." Lizzy ran her fingers through Darcy's hair, smiling at the sweet vision of her husband's head lying on her abdomen, one hand gently stroking her belly.

"Pardonnez-moi, mon petit fils, mon enfant précieux. English hereafter, until you are older. Then, alas, you must learn French, and more." He lifted slightly, peeling Lizzy's gown upward until bare flesh was revealed. He kissed her belly again, stroking and talking quietly. "How big do you think he is? Do you recall what the book said for the sixth month?" He glanced up at Lizzy, who shook her head.

"I believe it said a little over a pound. Still so small to cause me to swell so," she finished with a frown.

Darcy raised a brow. "Are you concerned, beloved? You should not be, as you are beautiful. This"—he kissed her belly once more—"is beautiful. It is only for a short span of time, my heart, and then you shall be thin again."

"How can you be so certain of that, William? Women's bodies do alter dramatically after childbirth, or so I am told."

He rose, threading his way up her body until fully over her and caressing her face. "Not always, Elizabeth. My mother birthed three children and was as tiny as when a maiden. You have seen the portraits. Aunt Madeline is comely and she has birthed four. I imagine there are alterations. Subtle changes a husband would notice such as those stretches Uncle George spoke of. In the end, these marks are a part of aging and a God-given reminder of human travails and, in the case of childbirth, the miracles of motherhood and life." He smiled into his wife's eyes and kissed her softly.

"All that being said," he continued, "my love and desire for you is not based on the appearance of your body. That is not to say I do not adore your shape, your perfect breasts and lush bottom, and all points head to toe. However, it is your heart I love, my wife. Whatever the flesh encasing the soul, it is you I yearn for and need to survive. This will never diminish."

He kissed her deeply, hand stroking down her side and pulling one leg over his waist. Breathlessly, lips near her ear, he resumed, "When I become aroused by you, my precious love, I am not thinking of your flesh, but of you. Who you are, how you love me and touch my soul. How your gorgeous eyes caress me and gaze with love upon me. How I am fulfilled by your presence in my life. How you have gifted me with your devotion and promises and commitment."

He withdrew, fingering over her parted lips. "Elizabeth, my eternal love. Your body is rapturous to me not because it is perfection, but because it is yours. I fell in love with you ere I began imagining what figure hid under your clothing. Your luscious shape has exceeded my imaginings, but I know my love and passion for you would be as strong if you had eleven toes or a big birthmark or hairs on your chest or…"

Lizzy chuckled softly, halting him with a kiss. "Fitzwilliam," she purred, delving deeply into his blue eyes that shone with pure love, "I love you."

He smiled. "There is to what I refer. No one on this earth says my name so that I melt as heated wax while becoming hard as iron simultaneously. Only you, my Lizzy, now and forever." He claimed her mouth with fervid passion yet caressed gently, robe opened as he joined with his wife in blissful harmony.

Lizzy sighed in happiness, his adoring professions coupled with the feel of him loving her bathing her in joy and reassurance. He moved slowly, caressing—always caressing—as he kissed her. Lizzy pulled the robe off his shoulder, gliding a hand over his back and hugging him closer. Traveling lips along his jaw to ear and shifting to encompass his body with all her limbs, Darcy moaned faintly as Lizzy whispered, "Fitzwilliam, how do you know precisely what to say to fill my heart and restore my confidence?"

He lifted his upper body so he could see her face, halting all movement momentarily, fingers fondling each feature and kissing tenderly. "I only speak the truth in my heart, Elizabeth. You have no reason to suffer negative emotions regarding my love for you and undying devotion, but I shall offer comfort and assurance every waking second if necessary." He resumed his steady rhythm with a breathy growl. "Additionally, I shall make love to you endlessly and adoringly. My wife, my own love. So beautiful you are to me. Elizabeth," he finished in a reverent whisper.

Grasping his face with a sudden burst of passionate enthusiasm, Lizzy pressed into his mouth, Darcy responding immediately. Never relenting in her kiss, Lizzy next attacked his robe, struggling to free his arms to her touch. Darcy attempted to assist yet refused to cease kissing or moving, the conjoint endeavor on the narrow sofa humorously spiraling.

They both began to giggle, the robe catching on his elbows so that when he tried to rise he began to sway off the couch. Desperately seeking a grip on something to correct his precarious perch and imbalance, he clutched the only thing at hand: her thigh. As a result, they both tumbled onto the floor in a heap, laughing hysterically.

His laughter, combined with the breath being knocked from his lungs as a result of hitting the hardwood floor and Lizzy's legs squashing his chest, had Darcy gasping. Laughing, Lizzy strived to right herself, silken robe and gown tangled about her legs.

At length she knelt beside her teary-eyed, wheezing spouse. "William? Are you all right? Oh my goodness, you look so ridiculous!" She dissolved in further giggles, bending to kiss his cheeks and reaching to disencumber him. His arms were trapped at odd angles under his body, robe askew and bunched bizarrely about his nakedness. She sat him up; his robe finally slipped from arms that he instantly threw about her waist with hands flattened on her back, pressing in for a thorough kiss. Still snickering, she captured his lower lip between her teeth and fondled his groin.

Darcy groaned, hands sliding to her bottom but Lizzy jumped up and stepped back. The puzzled pout crossing his features escalated her humor. "Elizabeth?" She shushed him, flouncing as she removed her robe with a twirl, trailing the ends over his face before releasing the silk to fall as a cloud onto his head.

"Come, lover. Catch me if you can." The gown followed the robe in a pile on his head, Darcy sweeping blindly for her legs but she was gone. Moments later, entering the modest bedchamber Darcy found his lovely bride stretched languidly and deliciously in the middle of the bed. "What took you so long?" she teased, opening her arms with hands reaching.

Smiling broadly with indescribable happiness, he joined her, body pressing beautifully over hers with mutual heat seeping through every pore. Not uttering a word, he kissed her consumingly as his hands stroked through her tousled hair. Lizzy clutched him tight, legs over legs and arms about chest, rubbing and fondling flaming skin in ecstasy.

Darcy kissed softly over her face, ending on her nose. Meeting her blazing eyes with a smile, still smoothing through her hair and brushing thumbs over her cheeks, he said, "I love you, Mrs. Darcy. I love how you make me feel like a giddy child and a virile man at the same time." He nibbled her ruddy lips. "I love how you tease me and cherish me. You are my breath and life, Elizabeth, best beloved." Another deep kiss was followed by a trailing firestorm of sweet kisses and suckles down her neck to shoulders.

Winding his way downward, Darcy aroused his wife to insane heights. Lizzy still, after nearly nine months of marriage, could not understand how his hands and lips were everywhere at once. Every inch of her skin was scorched and begging for more of his masterful, provocative touch. Each nerve throbbed, every cell ached in yearning, and all her muscles trembled. Blood rushed with the pounding of her passion infused heart. Lungs cried for air. It was divine agony and she beseeched him to persist, her very existence dependant on his touch.

Ardor raged. Lizzy was incoherent with desire. Darcy loved his wife, kissing and caressing, the giving of pleasure transcendent until she arched and shouted his name in glory. Tremors wracked her as he bestowed brushing kisses over her thighs and abdomen. Ceaseless delicate kisses imparted as he worked his way back up to her bosom, eventually rolling to his side with Lizzy in his firm embrace. "William," she murmured faintly, "I love you."

He lifted himself, gazing with bottomless depths of love, smiling as he pulled her shivering body against his chest. "Elizabeth, you have no idea how I enjoy pleasuring you."

They embraced in silence for a time, Lizzy's wits gradually returning to normal. Well aware that he remained aroused and unfulfilled, Lizzy commenced the succulent exploration of his body. She kissed the hollow of his throat, pulse warm and strong. Hands traveled over his chest and belly to all other masculine parts, Darcy groaning from the sensation. As lazily and competently as he had rocketed her passion, she did the same.

It was a magical night of interminable lovemaking. They had found on occasion that their mutual desire was insatiable, both seemingly inexhaustible in their need for each other. Tonight was such a night. Not two hours of deep sleep later, it was Lizzy who first roused her husband with caresses and kisses.

Darcy's response was instant, even if he remained more asleep than awake when she loved him. Several hours of limb-entangled slumber passed before they sleepily reached for each other, Darcy moving onto his welcoming wife.

"Lizzy, my beautiful Lizzy." He murmured gravelly, holding tightly while nuzzling her neck. Lizzy wrapped about him, relaxing pliantly under his crushing weight as he moved so beautifully. It was a prolonged flowing interlude, lapping and waving bliss warming and intensely satisfying. Darcy collapsed with a throaty groan, pulling her to his chest as he rolled to the side. Promptly, they returned to refreshing slumber.

Many hours later, sunlight streaming through the parted curtains, Lizzy roused to discover her husband lying beside her and staring. She smiled groggily, reaching to caress his neck. "I still deem it horribly unfair," she whispered.

"What is unfair?"

"How you can actually be more handsome with mussed hair and unshaven face. Even your grating voice is sexy and irresistible. Horribly unfair as I, thanks to you my lover, look a fright."

Darcy smiled, elegant fingers tracing circles on her breasts. "Thank you for the compliment. However, you are grossly mistaken regarding looking a fright. You are ravishing. Never more lovely than in the morning sun with hair loose and the flush of our lovemaking yet apparent on your skin." He leaned in for a kiss, staying near her mouth. "I have watched you for the past twenty minutes, love abounding and desire rising. I need you my wife, always."

He finished with a sigh, tenderly encompassing her mouth as he merged with her, two bodies now one. They made love again, the end to a perfect night and beginning of an eventful day.

※

"Will you please see this reaches Reniswahl Hall as soon as feasible?" Darcy asked the desk clerk, handing a folded parchment with the Darcy seal melted securely over the edge.

"Certainly, Mr. Darcy." He motioned toward a page who rushed over.

Darcy waited patiently while instructions were given and then continued, "Mrs. Darcy and I will be away all day. Please ensure a tray of fresh fruit and drinking water is available in our room."

"Of course, sir. If I may inquire, are you planning to enter the Sherwood Forest region? I only intrude as a warning. There have lately been reports of bandits in Nottinghamshire. That ilk always seems to believe the foolishness of the Robin Hood legends lend a credence to their nefarious activities."

Darcy scowled. "Romantic ideals of thievery, although I doubt they share their spoils with the average citizens. Thank you for the warning; however, we will not be traveling that far east. Nonetheless, we shall be cautious. Good day."

He joined his wife by the carriage, setting off for another excursion abroad. Samuel and Marguerite were freed for the day to ramble through the town and seek their own adventures. The weather was lovely, the sun shining brightly with the promise of sweltering heat in the late afternoon. Currently, though, there was a brisk, cooling breeze. The terrain due east of Chesterfield was identical to the landscape passed all the previous day. Endless rolling hills of green, generally crop covered with the scattered copse of trees and small stone farmhouses. Dotting the beauty were the increasingly frequent black-scarred rubbles of stone indicative of a coal mine.

"How far under the ground do the rails extend?" Lizzy asked curiously.

"Miles in some cases, I suppose. I confess to not being well educated on the inner workings of coal mining. The east Midlands is replete with coal. A wonderful blessing for England's economy but depressing for the locals. I envision this area gradually diverting from farms to mines as the years unfold." He shook his head sadly. "The waves of industry and progress march on, Elizabeth."

The eight miles to Bolsover displayed this odd mixture of lush scenery with interspersed mutilated holes. However, the closer they drew to the modest town on the hill, all else faded except the looming vision of Bolsover Castle. The massive keep, a true remnant of a long gone day of medieval knights and chivalry, sat on a prominent bluff as expected, and dominated the entire horizon. They drove up the curving incline to the castle, Darcy launching into his usual narrative.

"Another claim of the Cavendish family, love. The original medieval castle built during the Norman Conquest is essentially gone, but Lord Cavendish, who acquired the property in the seventeenth century, built his fanciful keep with the original in mind. Therefore, the walls have never withstood a siege, but it certainly looks as if it could!"

"Do any of the Cavendish family members dwell here?"

"Not any longer. All the furniture has been removed to Welbeck Abbey and a token staff inhabits to maintain, although the lack of constant upkeep is beginning to show. Lord Cavendish and the bulk of the family remain in Devonshire. The castle is more of a tourist attraction than a home, which is fortunate for us." He smiled at his wife, leaning for a kiss before they disembarked on the wide lawn before the main entrance to the vast house.

Thereafter followed a three-hour, leisurely stroll about the estate grounds and tour of the castle public rooms. The recognition by the staff of the Darcy crest afforded them greater access than the general visiting public. They walked along the battlement walls, the views, across ostensibly the entire width and length of Derbyshire, absolutely breathtaking. It may not have been a functional castle as in the ancient stories, but the atmosphere was authentic. Lizzy honestly expected to see a shining steel encased knight gallop into the courtyard with lance and broadsword at the ready.

The interior was as all fine English manors: lavish and well apportioned. Richly painted murals famous for their depiction of romanticism and English Renaissance chivalry graced nearly every wall and ceiling. It was stupendous, if slightly overwhelming. The cavernous feel of the ostentatious rooms was especially noticeable without furnishings.

Lizzy and Darcy picnicked in solitude in one of the immense courtyards with a bubbling fountain of Venus centrally located. Resuming their journey, Darcy explained the next planned adventure. "I know how you love trees, so thought you would appreciate visiting Whitwell Wood. It is far and away the finest and most sweeping woodland in England, with some four hundred acres of ash, oak, beech, sycamore, and hazel trees predominantly. We can easily swing through the fringes as we veer west toward Eckington and Reniswahl Hall."

The roughly six-mile drive was delightful. Leaving the coal mines mostly behind, they passed through areas rich in vegetation mingled with limestone buttes. The cool breeze of earlier in the day had long since dissipated, leaving a rising heat. Darcy opened the windows, aiding his wife with fanning as they left the tiny hamlet of Elmton and casually meandered through the barren countryside.

The carriage halted unexpectedly, a sharp rap on the roof indicating the driver's wish to converse with the occupant. Darcy frowned, leaning forward to the open window.

"Yes, Mr. Anders?"

"Sir, pardon the intrusion, but there appears to be an overturned wagon ahead. Should we stop to check it out?"

"Are there any people about?"

"Not that I can see from here, sir."

Darcy thought for a moment, peering out the window at the empty landscape. "Approach slowly and be cautious. Halt if anyone is visibly hurt. Phillips, be alert and prepared."

"Yes sir," they echoed, the carriage moving forward slowly.

"Elizabeth, pull the shades on your side and stay back," he commanded tensely, reaching to assure the doors were securely latched and to shut the window.

"Do you suspect something amiss, William?" she asked, voice strained.

He glanced over his shoulder with a quick smile. "I am sure it is nothing, love, but wisdom begs for caution." He resumed his watchfulness to the outside, running a hand under the seat briefly. Eventually he glimpsed the aforementioned wagon lying upside down and partially in the road. Immediate bells rang in his head as there were neither horses nearby nor the expected cargo strewn about the ground. The region surrounding was rocky, with numerous trees thinly spaced on either side of the road, but relatively flat with narrow depressions and hollows. Nonetheless, the road was a well maintained one without ruts or ditches, no loose boulders on tall cliffs or other ready causes to overturn a wagon.

He sensed Lizzy closely behind him before she spoke. "Sit back!" he snapped, Lizzy obeying reflexively to his terse demand. Darcy patted her knee to ease his rudeness precisely as all hell broke loose outside.

CHAPTER TWENTY-SIX

Death Interrupts

A LOUD SHOUT SOUNDED from above and a gunshot crack rang out. The carriage stopped precipitously with a lurch as several voices erupted with yells. Lizzy released a startled squeal as Darcy's hand flashed under the seat. She gasped and eyes widened at the sight of the pistol he retrieved and hastily tucked into the waistband of his breeches at the small of his back. Eyes yet riveted to the window, he reached behind to squeeze her leg, jerking backward in reflex when a grizzled face abruptly appeared at the window.

Lizzy clutched frantically onto Darcy's arm, heart pounding crazily. The man outside brandished a pistol, gesturing for Darcy to exit the carriage. "Elizabeth," Darcy's deceptively calm and icy voice commanded, "stay inside if you are allowed; otherwise, keep close and to my left side. Do not argue or resist and keep your eyes on me."

She nodded, not that he could see her as his focus was on the angry man outside, who was now banging on the locked door. Darcy unlocked and opened the carriage door, holding his hands up so the man could see he was unarmed.

"Get out! Now!"

Darcy complied with a quick glance at his wife. Lizzy could see the towering fury in the steeliness of his eyes and clenched jaw, but she also saw the intense fear that she knew was all for her. She kept her seat in hopes that it would be over quickly, the bandits surely wanting money which Darcy could provide, and then they could be on their way. Terror paralyzed her, rising further as the burly man grabbed her husband's arm as he descended and yanked hard, Darcy stumbling on the steps. He righted himself, straightening to his full and impressive height, broad shoulders blocking the doorway.

"I have money," Darcy offered in a tone of cold authority and command, "take it and be on your way."

"Not so fast, guv'ner," a voice answered. "We are in charge here. I reckon a smart lookin' fella like you has got more than just a money belt."

"Check inside, Clyde," another voice spoke. "He ain't alone. And you, up there, throw us the luggage and get down."

"There is no luggage," Lizzy heard Mr. Anders reply.

Darcy interrupted, "My wife and I are on a pleasure ride. We have nothing but the clothing on our backs. Allow me to give you…"

"Enough!" shouted the first voice. "You two, down! Clyde, move rich boy out of the way and get the wife! She probably weighs a ton with jewels."

Darcy pivoted quickly, leaning in for Lizzy before Clyde could obey his boss. "Elizabeth, come. Stay close."

"Out of the way!" Clyde yelled, grabbing Darcy's arm. "I am in charge here!"

Darcy's face was livid, Lizzy panic stricken as he turned to the highwayman with a gleam of pure murder evident. "My wife is with child. I *will* assist her from the carriage…"

Suddenly the pistol was pointed square at Darcy's forehead, a mere inch away. "You will step away, hero, and do as I say." The moment seemed to stretch, although in truth it was only a fraction of a second, as Darcy glared into the eyes of the thief.

Lizzy leapt forward. "William, it is alright. I can exit myself. Please step back as he said!" Darcy looked at her, absolute terror warring with supreme fury. He nodded brusquely and stepped away, but only a foot, his eyes never leaving Lizzy. She carefully disembarked, Clyde near with pistol waving between her and Darcy. Darcy instantly and painfully gripped her right elbow, pulling her to his left and predominantly behind his body.

This is the scene as Lizzy now beheld it: She and Darcy stood near the rear of the coach with the identified Clyde now pointing the gun straight at Darcy's chest. Mr. Anders and Phillips were positioned by the lead set of horses, another scruffy, dirty bandit covering them with a pistol. The remaining two highwaymen were some ten feet to the side of the road, mounted on horses with muskets loaded and aimed, pistols on each hip. Compared to the two mangy-looking characters on the ground, these two men were fierce and hardened. One appeared to be in his thirties, commanding and calm, a faint smile playing about his lips as if this sort of behavior was of tremendous amusement. The second man was quite young and handsome in a rugged way, probably about Lizzy's age, but there was an edge of menace in his flat, grey eyes that was altogether frightening. He was staring at Lizzy in a manner far too bold and extremely discomforting.

Darcy was rigid, the tension radiating in nearly visible waves. Lizzy could hear him taking deep breaths in an effort to regain control of his emotions and anger. For her part, Lizzy had never experienced such fear, even when facing Orman. The sensation of being utterly at the whimsical mercy of men with obvious low morals and disdain for the law was petrifying for her, but to a man of generally supreme dominance like Darcy, it was torture. The internal struggle to overcome formidable rage and equally daunting anxiety for his wife was enough to buckle him, but he fought the emotions and gradually mastered.

Mere seconds had passed; the older mounted man finally speaking, his voice identifying him as the first man Lizzy had heard and undoubtedly the leader. "Lou, check the pockets of those two," he waved to Mr. Anders and Phillips. "They are servants, so likely have nothing, but we may get lucky. Victor," he said as he nudged his fellow horseman, "get the jack-a-dandy's money clip and check the woman. Clyde, keep our hero in your sights. I don't trust 'im."

Victor dismounted, drawing his pistol and pulling a canvas sack out of his saddlebag. He approached with a swagger, grinning evilly. "Hand it over and don't fuss. Doubt the loss will hurt you any."

Darcy moved warily, removing his money clip, which was quite thick due to his planned evening of gaming with Rory Sitwell, and retrieved his pocket watch, placing both in the sack. Lizzy bit her lip to prevent a whine escaping. The pocket watch she knew had been a gift from his father when Darcy graduated Cambridge and was therefore dear to him.

"That's it?" Victor asked in doubt. "Thought you dandies carried all kinds of useless baubles." He patted the pockets of Darcy's jacket and waistcoat, Lizzy nerveless with the certainty that he would discover the hidden pistol, but he did not. His search apparently focused on hidden treasures without suspecting a "dandy" would have a weapon.

"There is nearly three hundred pounds there and the watch is valuable. You have no complaints." Darcy's voice was quiet and placid. Lizzy, however, saw the clenching jaw and thin-set lips, as well as detecting the muted iron in his tone. Victor stared into Darcy's eyes, clearly noting the same and considering it a challenge of sorts.

Peering unblinking at Darcy, he addressed Lizzy, "How's about you, pretty? Got something for me?" His tone was lecherous and not lost on Darcy, who stiffened even further and gripped Lizzy's arm so firmly she nearly yelped from the pain. Victor's leer broadened as he suddenly shot a hand out and grabbed Lizzy's left arm, yanking her forward.

She did emit a sharp cry as a tug-of-war ensued, Darcy refusing to relinquish his grip even when Victor cocked the pistol and dug the barrel end into the flesh of Darcy's forehead. "Let go or I'll kill ya and then what good would ya do her?"

"William, please! Do as he says!" Lizzy shouted, her fear for her husband outweighing her own for the moment. The sight of a gun yet again aimed at him was more than she could take. She was trembling violently, tears cascading down her face and eyes pleading. Darcy hesitated another second then reluctantly released her arm. Lizzy let lose a sob of relief and terror.

Victor smiled smugly, meeting Darcy's murderous gaze boldly. "Don't worry about the little wife. I'll take *very* good care of her."

"You lay one hand on her and I promise I will kill you," Darcy replied in a tone of pure venom and conviction. Lizzy noted a glimmer of uncertainty in Victor's eyes and then it was gone, to be replaced with arrogance. He led her away a dozen paces with pistol trained on Darcy. The hold on her arm was surprisingly tender and almost caressing. Lizzy shivered in revulsion; Darcy's countenance grim and eyes anguished.

"Okay, pretty, give me those earrings and the necklace. Not particularly fine specimens, are they? Rich boy don't share his wealth with the missus, huh? Want you for only one thing, does he, and no compensation for the job? Maybe you need a real man who will appreciate your charms." He ran the back of one hand down her cheek, Lizzy shuddering and jerking away.

Darcy released a growl of pure animal intensity and lunged forward, only to be brought up short by Clyde's pistol in his gut. Lizzy vaguely heard a sound to her left from the direction of Phillips, but her eyes were tightly closed with tears streaming.

"Enough playing!" shouted the leader from his horse. "Get the rings, Victor. Clyde, check the carriage for anything else. This is taking too long."

Victor scowled but obeyed. "Give me the rings, pretty. Hurry up!"

Lizzy's eyes flew open in shock, hands instinctively enfolding to her chest. "My... my rings? No, please, they are my wedding rings! You cannot..."

"I can and I will. Now hand them over!"

Lizzy cried in silence, hands shaking so badly that she barely managed to remove the rings, neither of which had ever left her finger since Darcy placed them there. With incredible difficulty she dropped them into the bag, hands instantly covering her face as she dissolved into sobs.

Glancing to Darcy's stony face and smiling insolently, Victor slid one arm around Lizzy shoulders and stroked her neck while murmuring placatingly and smirking at Darcy, "Don't fret, pretty lady. Victor knows how to make you feel good. I'll bring you with me and we can have some fun." As he spoke, he moved his gun-toting hand upward and brushed his fingers over one breast.

At that precise moment, several things happened at once.

Lizzy, in an impetuous explosion of rage and abhorrence, screamed hysterically while pitching her entire upper body into Victor's. He was taken completely by surprise, flailing wildly as he vaulted backward from the force of her shove, pistol flying through the air.

Darcy was already moving toward Lizzy in manic wrath, Victor's pointing firearm inconsequential at that point, but reacted instantaneously and proficiently to her unwitting diversion. He yelled to Phillips while simultaneously drawing the hidden pistol with his right hand and lunging toward his wife. He was sidetracked, however, by the reemergence of a startled Clyde, who was just exiting from the carriage with his pistol and Lizzy's reticule in one hand and their lunch basket in the other. Darcy latched onto his neck with a strangle hold and viciously smashed the back of his head against the carriage railing, Clyde crumpling in a heap.

Meanwhile, Phillips and Mr. Anders drew their concealed weapons. Lou was distracted by the antics of Victor and Lizzy, completely unaware of the fist heading his way until Phillips, who was a big and remarkably strong man, connected with an echoing crunch to his jaw. It was an impressive hit and a weaker man would have succumbed easily. Lou, however, was hired for his brawn and not brains. He staggered but rallied quickly, rounding on the amazed Phillips with pistol ready. The tall footman had no time to bring his own gun to bear, instead choosing to rush the smaller man and grab the pistol-wielding right hand. Thus ensued a dramatic, if at times strangely humorous, wrestling match between the two mismatched men.

The leader responded with the same cold efficiency as Darcy. Immediately, he lifted his rifle and focused on Darcy, deciding he was the greater threat. The shot was well targeted and fired rapidly. Darcy was missed by mere inches, saved when he attacked Clyde. The ball hit the corner of the carriage, wood splintering and showering fragments onto Darcy. Undeterred, the leader pulled one of his two hip pistols and reacquired his target, Darcy rapidly pivoting toward him with gun raised and lethally aimed, the two men in a sudden stand-off dependant on who would pull the trigger first.

Lizzy was feral, panting and yelling as she unremittingly kicked the fallen Victor—in the ribs, head, back, or wherever else he was exposed—as he flipped about on the ground screaming. Her sturdy walking boots coupled with robust legs and deranged ire inflicted a substantial amount of damage.

Mr. Anders, a coachman and groom by profession and not well accomplished in the art of marksmanship, nonetheless proved his worth by readily identifying the greatest immediate threat as the mounted leader. He stepped away from the grappling Phillips and Lou, calmly sighted his quarry, who was centered on Mr. Darcy, and fired. The bullet hit and shattered the left shoulder, not where Mr. Anders had aimed but effective. The leader flew off his horse, Darcy's shot missing him completely which was a shame, as it was well centered and would have been fatal. Still, it was providential as the shot fired in Darcy's direction was also precise and it was only the impact of Mr. Anders's ball which lifted the bandit's gun at the last second, his shot erratic and harming no one.

Lizzy continued to pummel Victor, the man seriously hurting from two broken ribs, a split lip, broken nose, and numerous bruises. Darcy glanced at his raging wife with a mixture of awe and fright, striding briskly to retrieve Victor's gun off the ground and rushing toward the leader who was already rising.

So far the entire spectacle had consumed barely a minute.

Once again, Darcy leveled his newly acquired pistol at the leader, who was on his knees with blood soaking the left side of his body but right arm rising with his other pistol steady as a rock. Darcy hesitated nary a millisecond, cleanly dispatching the man with a perfect blast to the heart. Bending to ensure the man was no longer a threat, Darcy claimed the last functioning gun and swung about to assist his wife, the blood rage still coursing through his body.

Mr. Anders, in the meantime, was torn between aiding Phillips or helping Mrs. Darcy, who was clearly at risk of harming herself in her frenzy. As he had no time to reload, his pistol was useless except—enlightenment dawned on him—as a blunt object. Deciding that Mrs. Darcy was well enough for the moment, he turned toward Phillips just as Lou's gun discharged.

The shot was random and entered Phillips's left thigh. He screamed, hands instinctively clutching at the area that was promptly slick with gushing blood as he fell to the ground. Mr. Anders swiftly raised the pistol and bashed the wooden grip forcefully onto the top of Lou's head, the man slowly sagging like a sack of grain.

Darcy rushed toward his wife, the next moments eerily dragging as if time slowed. Every second was as a minute and the clarity of the scene between Lizzy and Victor was bizarrely crisp and all-inclusive.

A frantic and agonized Victor finally managed to capture one of her flashing ankles. He wrenched harshly with a grunt of satisfaction. Lizzy was unbalanced, legs flying up as she landed on her bottom with a sharp exhale and crunch of her teeth. The impact onto the rocky ground was hard on her tailbone and felt through the stretched muscles of her lower abdomen, Lizzy clutching her belly with a groan. Victor, blood streaming from nose and lip, was no longer smirking but grimacing in pain and anger. He twisted her ankle, hauling his injured body partially onto hers. His free hand encircled her throat and with a snarl he began to squeeze, Lizzy's screams of terror and pain abruptly cut off. His other hand roughly groped under her skirts, pinching and kneading up her inner thigh.

Darcy saw it all and his thus far controlled rage boiled over into a blinding, destructive fury bordering on madness. He roared a vile expletive and latched onto the robber's hair, tossing him off Lizzy with astounding force, clumps of hair and scalp ripping painfully. "I warned you not to touch her," he bleakly intoned to a suddenly white-faced Victor. Without blinking, Darcy fired, Victor not feeling a twinge of pain as the ball penetrated his brain.

Abrupt calm fell. Clyde and Lou were unconscious; Victor and the nameless leader were dead. Phillips moaned in torment, Mr. Anders at his side attempting to halt the bleeding.

Darcy was breathing heavily but dropped the pistol and knelt next to his sobbing wife, gathering her into his arms. Neither spoke, words simply unthinkable at this juncture. They only wanted to hold each other. Darcy's hands began roaming all over her body, testing for injury and assuring her existence. He began to tremble, clutching her face and possessively kissing with a soft sob. Both sensed their control slipping, Lizzy's hysteria rising again and Darcy's chest constricting as he was overcome with weakness.

A cry from the injured Phillips penetrated their fogged minds, Lizzy's head snapping his direction. "Phillips!" she exclaimed, struggling from Darcy's embrace. He helped her up, moving together to the fallen footman. Action was necessary for both of them to regain mastery over their shattered emotions.

Lizzy dropped to her knees beside Mr. Anders by Phillips's left leg. "William, give me your cravat. Hurry!" The wound was gaping, blackened about the edges from the gunpowder. She examined it quickly, discerning no exit wound, which meant the ball was lodged in his leg, probably in the bone. She grabbed the hole in his breeches and ripped, exposing the entire thigh. Phillips's screams were turning to weak moans and his hands were now loose by his side and face dreadfully pale. The wound continually spurt blood through Mr. Anders's pressing hands. Darcy handed the cravat to Lizzy who immediately and with surprising efficiency tied it tightly around Phillips's upper thigh above the seeping hole.

Darcy was observing her with deep curiosity and amazement. "How do you know what to do, Elizabeth?"

"That medical book in your library has a section on emergency treatments. I thought it interesting, although I never imagined having to utilize the knowledge! This is called a tourniquet and halts the bleeding by restricting the circulation. See?"

She was correct, as the bleeding had fallen to a slow trickle. "Think, Lizzy, think!" she murmured to herself. Phillips was bordering on unconsciousness, a faint bluish tint circling his lips. "Mr. Anders," Lizzy said, "there are napkins in the picnic basket, as well as water and wine. Bring them to me and give me your cravat as well." The coachman jumped to the task, Lizzy turning to her husband and whispering, "William, I only know to halt the bleeding and a little about shock. He must get to a physician immediately!"

Darcy nodded, standing and surveying the mess around them as the mantle of command and decision making fell over his shoulders as a warm, familiar covering. Mr. Anders returned with the entire basket and his cravat. Lizzy formed a wad with the napkins and used it as a bandage over the wound, tying snuggly with the neckcloth.

"Mr. Anders, find something to place under his feet. The legs should be elevated, I think." She frowned, mind frantically trying to remember what she had read. She moved to Phillips's head, his glazed eyes open and blurrily focusing on his Mistress.

"Mrs. Darcy?" he murmured, "Are you... unharmed?"

"I am fine. Now hush, Phillips. Save your strength." She lifted his head onto her lap, placing the wineskin at his lips. "Drink slowly, as much as you can. That's it, very good..."

While Lizzy continued in her gentle ministrations to the stricken man, Darcy pulled Mr. Anders aside. "We need to leave this place as soon as possible, Mr. Anders. Phillips requires a physician. Are we closer to Clowne or Whitwell?"

"Clowne is nearest and not as remote, sir. If they do not have a doctor there, Staveley and Eckington are both within a few miles."

Darcy nodded, thinking. "It is likely unwise to move him, but I do not wish to stay here." He scanned the area with piercing eyes. "Obviously they were alone, as no others have come to the scene, but I would rather not risk it. Mrs. Darcy must be away from this place." He paused. "Do you have any rope?"

"Of course, sir."

"Restrain these two firmly, hog tied and secured to the wagon." he gestured toward the still unconscious Lou and Clyde. "I will gather the firearms and reload just to be prepared. I will require your assistance placing Phillips into the carriage. Then I want you to take one of the robber's horses and run fast into Clowne. Summon a physician and alert the local constable. We will follow slowly so as not to enhance his injuries." Mr. Anders jumped to obey his Master.

He glanced at his wife, softly crooning to the servant while daubing his forehead with a water-soaked napkin. He frowned. As thankful as he was at her calm focus, it seemed odd under the circumstances. His heart was yet racing with the frayed edges of panic barely mastered due to years of dealing with tragedy and stressful situations. A large part of him wanted to collapse with her in his arms, and the effort not to do so was enormous. How could she maintain her composure? He paused to observe her, realizing that nursing Phillips was as much a result of primordial instinct and concern as it was a diversion necessary to forestall crushing shock. He would need to carefully watch her. No stranger to the effects of shock, having seen it dozens of times in wives and families of men killed or injured, as well as experiencing it himself, he knew that it would consume her eventually.

Mentally adding it to his list, he turned to the urgent demands. Retrieving and loading the weapons was speedily done, Darcy tossing all but one of them onto the driver's bench alongside the sack containing their stolen property. The extra pistol was given to Mr. Anders so that he now carried two. Darcy glanced to the gruesome sight of Victor's body lying near the coach, but there was no time to shield the scene from his wife. A barely controlled sense of panic and fear impelled him to step quickly and vacate this locale as rapidly as possible.

Moving Phillips was not an easy task. Bodily, he was only two or three inches shorter than Darcy and nearly as broad in the shoulders. Darcy and Mr. Anders together struggled carrying his bulk, not to mention getting him into the carriage. Phillips screamed once when lifted and then abruptly fainted.

Lizzy discovered that her legs had lost all feeling, moving them a quandary. Couple that with the aching bruise to her backside and the intermittent, sharp pains to her lower abdomen which she continued to ignore, and Lizzy was in misery. With tears of pain stinging her eyes, she sluggishly battled to rise. Darcy, fortunately considering the current crisis, did not see her striving to move. By the time she joined him at the carriage, her legs were functioning and the other numerous aches and pains were tightly controlled and hidden.

Darcy sent Mr. Anders on his way. Lizzy climbed into the carriage to check on Phillips, who remained unconscious but whose wound was no longer bleeding even when she loosened the tourniquet.

"Elizabeth?" Darcy was at the doorway, love and desperate concern allowed to nakedly wash over his face. He reached for her bloodstained hands, enfolding them with his warm ones. "Are you well, beloved? You are very pale and trembling still."

"I am fine. Just worried about Phillips. We must hurry, William."

He searched her face, greatly discomfited by what he saw there but unable to delve into the cause at the present time. "Very well. I will drive as speedily as feasible. Keep the window open and call for me if you need." He cupped one cheek, drawing her in for a brief kiss. "I love you."

She smiled wanly, lips quivering and eyes blinking, and shakily whispered, "I love you, too."

"I managed to remove the bullet from his leg," the physician said to Darcy and Lizzy while washing bloody hands in a basin. "It hit the bone but does not appear to have broken it. He is most fortunate in that regard. Unfortunately, he has lost a tremendous amount of blood and the risk of infection is severe. On the plus side, he is healthy and very strong, so should mend well with careful nursing. Your intervention, Mrs. Darcy, was fortuitous. I have no doubt he would have bled to death without the tourniquet." He smiled at Lizzy, and Darcy squeezed her hand in pride.

Turning to Darcy, the surgeon resumed, "Your servant will need to stay here for a while, Mr. Darcy. A week or two at the very least, depending on the course of the infection."

"Of course," Darcy said. "We want him to receive the best care possible. However, whenever you deem it safe, we would like him transported to Pemberley. His family is there and it is home."

The physician nodded, glancing at a silent Lizzy. "Naturally, Mr. Darcy. If I may have a word in private?" The two men drew apart, Lizzy barely noticing.

They were in Staveley. Clowne's lone physician was attending to another emergency involving a young boy, so they had been informed, forcing them to drive five miles further. Dr. Welles in Staveley dwelt in a modest home with an attached miniature hospital of sorts. He seemed highly competent with a staff of three nurses. A discriminating Darcy had carefully peered about the place and instantly recognized an efficient facility. For an hour, he and Lizzy had waited inside the small antechamber while the doctor tended to Phillips, cries intermittently erupting from behind the closed door.

Darcy's concern for Phillips was negligible compared to the growing panic regarding his wife. Lizzy had said few words since arriving, refused to meet his eyes, frequently quivered and clenched her fists in her lap, and avoided physical contact as much as possible. Darcy sat close, watching and worrying, but any attempt to engage her in conversation was met with monosyllables or silence. He must have asked her if she was well a hundred times but she kept repeating she was "fine." This alone was proof that she most assuredly was not fine because his Lizzy would have snapped at him long ago for his persistent questioning.

She shivered and felt cold despite the heat of the late afternoon. He placed his jacket about her shoulders, but she did not seem to notice and continued to tremble.

His fear for her mental state was threatening to overwhelm him, but he did not know how to deal with her withdrawal. Now, the physician was questioning him about Mrs. Darcy's obvious shock, but Darcy had no answer. Dr. Welles suggested he take her someplace calm and comforting. "She most probably needs sleep more than anything," he advised.

Lizzy was in a daze. As long as she had Phillips to fixate on, the horror nipping at her consciousness was kept at bay. She was truly concerned for the footman, Phillips being a frequent companion since Darcy insisted the burliest footman in his employ guarded her whenever she ventured beyond Pemberley Manor. Nonetheless, honest solicitude notwithstanding, a small portion of her brain recognized what she was doing. She absolutely forbade her thoughts to stray beyond the man hurting behind the door. This willful regulation had carried her through the agonizing carriage ride and for the first thirty minutes at the hospital, but the discipline was slipping rapidly.

The periodic pains to her abdomen, which she knew on some level were ominous, continued. Her tailbone ached, feet throbbed, and legs hurt. The vision of her heart's existence with a gun pointed at his body repeatedly danced before her eyes. The images of sightless eyes staring in violent death with blood pooling refused to go away.

Primarily, though, it was him.

Victor.

His leering face. His insinuating words. His touch.

She hung her head, eyes closing in misery. She could still feel him, smell him, hear him. His blood and some other unmentionable bodily fluids stained her dress. Filthy, that is how she felt, but not from the mess all over her body.

She stared at her hands. Darcy had cleaned them thoroughly and tenderly, displaying his love through even that simple task. She had watched him in silence, the emptiness of her finger glaring at her accusingly. Then he had kissed her palms and started to say something, but she jerked away, leaving him standing by the basin in anxious perplexity.

She knew it was wrong. Foolish even. Yet she was plagued with the revolting sensations. She felt violated. *He* had touched her. Her skin crawled and goose pimples rose. The memory was repulsive and she bit her lip to prevent a whine from escaping. For the thousandth time, she shuddered, breathing deeply to avoid bursting into sobs, and wrenched her thoughts to Phillips.

Coherency was no longer an option. She walked in a cloud of pain and misery. Vaguely she heard voices: something about Phillips sleeping now and then about departing for the Sitwell mansion where she could bathe and rest. Darcy was there, naturally, lovingly guiding her to the carriage, but it was all a blur. Strangely, she noted that the carriage was immaculate. No evidence of Phillips's blood or the dirt from the ground. She remembered sitting here on the interminable ride into Staveley and staring with rapt interest at several leaves and pebbles which had fallen onto the seat and floor. Now they were gone and her mind experienced a leap of panic wondering what she would now focus her attention on.

She looked through a long tunnel with no light at the end. Weariness and physical discomfort ruled her, with perception distorted and sounds muted. Meaning was skewed, rationality altered. Someone was talking to her, but she could not recognize the voice. It was a man and now he held her hands, caressing gently with soft fingers and warm strength. It was pleasant but faintly disturbing as images flashed in her mind of hands touching her. Hands very different from these, rough and dirty with blunt fingers. Hands that took instead of giving. Hands that demanded and caressed with false intent. Hands that robbed her of something precious and vital to her heart and soul. Hands that stole her rings.

Her rings! She needed her rings! They were important to her, although she could not readily grasp why. And now here they were; golden glints of metal and sparkles of diamond and blue sapphire slipping over her knuckles. Large boned fingers that fluctuated from long and elegant to stubby and grimy touching her slender fingers and assaulting her precious rings.

"No!" she screamed, jerking away from the clawing hands of the thief and clutching her rings, the cool metal and hard gems digging into her palms. "You cannot take them! They are mine and I need them! No! No! No!"

"Elizabeth! Stop! Listen to me!" Darcy grabbed at her flailing arms but she screamed louder. Words now tumbled disjointedly from raving lips, her body nearly convulsing in a combined attempt to attack him and withdraw as far as possible. He had read somewhere that the cure for hysteria was to slap the person very hard, but he could not slap his wife. Instead, he fell to his knees before her thrashing body, moving in, heedless to the scratches she bestowed, and clamped her face firmly between his palms, wrenching her glazed eyes to his.

"Elizabeth, look at me," he commanded in the coldest, most authoritative tone he could muster. She whined, fighting to withdraw but was no match for his strength. "Elizabeth Darcy, open your eyes and look at me!"

Tears were streaming down her face; the fight abruptly halting as all energy drained and she slumped, as if boneless, with a whimper. "Please," she moaned and sobbed, "Please do not take my rings. Please do not touch me. Please do not hurt him, you cannot... hurt him... I need him, please. I... need... William, my... husband... I... need..."

"Elizabeth, look! It is me: William. I am here, my love. Focus! Hear my voice. I am here."

Again and again, patiently and firmly he pleaded for her attention through her incoherent ramblings. Struggling had ceased, but her eyes remained dazed for several terrifying minutes. Darcy felt his panic rising, almost ready to instruct Mr. Anders to return to Staveley and Dr. Welles when she finally spoke the first lucid word.

"William?"

"Yes, Elizabeth, it is me! I am here, beloved. All is well, shhhh, hush now, my love," he sobbed in relief.

Lizzy's hazy vision cleared and she saw finally that it *was* him. Her William. His loving gaze full of tenderness and profound distress for her, his face so near, his grip powerful, and his radiant heat all real and alive. She collapsed into his embrace, weeping and clutching his body with an iron grip. Now it was her who roved all over him with seeking and pressing hands and fingers.

He held her tightly, rocking and swaying with the movement of the carriage, smoothing her hair as she cried and clasped him. Slowly, very slowly, she began to calm and he felt his anxiety waning. He moved back onto the seat with her in his arms, still crying but more controlled, her trembling lessening slightly.

"It is over, beloved. We are safe now. You are with me and we are safe. Hush now." Continually he reassured, murmuring endearments and love as she gradually quieted.

Releasing a massive shudder, she stiffened briefly then wilted against his shoulder with a prolonged groan. "He... touched me, William. I cannot erase it and I feel so, so... filthy!"

"We will be at the Sitwell's soon, love. You can bathe and sleep. I will not leave you and will hold you until you forget." He bent to look into her eyes, finding that she still evaded his gaze. "Elizabeth, I love you. Will you please look at me?"

Haltingly, she lifted her eyes to his. Darcy with monumental devotion and care, smiling tenderly; Elizabeth with torment and shame. He cupped her cheek, caressing away her tears. "It is over, my heart. No need to fear. I love you." He bent and brushed her lips fleetingly.

"He hurt me, William. I... hurt," she whispered against his lips, Darcy withdrawing an inch to see her anguished eyes.

He frowned. "What? Where? Your bottom?"

She nodded, staring at him with intent fear. "Yes, a little. My legs and feet, too. And..." She swallowed, Darcy's alarm rising. "William," she squeaked, tears filling her eyes yet again, "I am having pains, sometimes, in my belly."

Darcy paled, heart constricting as if outwardly squeezed. "Oh God!" His hand instantly reached to cradle the small bulge of their son, so warm and soft. Elizabeth was trembling anew, lips quivering as silent tears rolled down her cheeks. His mind raced without coherent thought aside from the murderous wish to run back to Victor's corpse and fill it with a dozen more pistol holes.

The carriage halted at that moment, forestalling any further words. Darcy glanced up, realizing they were at Reniswahl Hall. As quickly as the panic rose with her words, he shoved it down, command naturally falling over his shoulders. Pressing his lips tight, he kissed her forehead and then fiercely stared into her troubled eyes.

"It will be fine, Elizabeth. I promise. Our son is fine."

Briskly and with cool capability, he leapt from the carriage, scanning the front of the Hall. Rory and Julia Sitwell were descending the stairs with concern written all over their features. Darcy spared no time with pleasantries.

"Rory, Elizabeth needs a physician, now. She is having abdominal pains. Julia, I need a comfortable bed, hot water for bathing, and a clean nightgown." He did not wait for an answer, turning to the carriage while Rory barked orders to a servant. Carrying Elizabeth in his arms, Darcy followed Julia to a large, airy bedchamber. A flurry of activity ensued, all the required items provided in record time while Darcy stood aside holding his numb wife, eyes never leaving her face.

"Mr. Darcy, the bath is ready and the physician should be on his way soon," Julia said. "Can I help?"

"No, thank you, Julia. I will care for her and ring if I need assistance. Send the doctor the moment he arrives."

Lizzy murmured a weary thank you, Julia squeezing her arm then hastily departing. Finally Darcy relinquished her onto a sofa and began removing her filthy clothing, tossing the garments in a far corner to be disposed of later.

"Beloved, tell me about the pains."

"They started after I fell, when… he…" She closed her eyes and inhaled deeply before resuming, "They are not overly painful and intermittent, but it scares me, William. The book said pains are not right until closer to the end."

"It also said stress can bring on labor pains, Elizabeth. I remember that. Today assuredly qualifies." He had most of her clothing off, only her chemise remaining. He held her gaze, speaking calmly as he untied the ribbons to her undergarment, "Do you feel any bleeding? Has the baby been moving?"

"No bleeding, I do not think, and he has been active. He is now."

Darcy placed his hand over her bared belly, their child lazily flipping under his palm. Despite his fears and anxiety, he could not resist smiling. He bent for a kiss, caressing her gently. "He is strong, my love, and feels healthy and unperturbed." He lifted his eyes with a smile, meeting Elizabeth's. She was watching him with a strange expression, pale and haunted. He frowned, rising hastily to clasp her chin with his fingers, studying her disturbed countenance. "What is it? Are you in pain now?"

She shook her head, staring. "I… William, do you still want… Are you repulsed by what he… his hands touching me? I feel so dirty and ashamed! I was so afraid he would kill you that I willingly went with him and then he… if I disgust you, I understand." Her words were halted by a crushing and thorough kiss, Darcy's hands firm about her neck with thumbs stroking her cheeks. It only lasted a few seconds, ending with tender nibbles to her lower lip, Darcy breathing heavily.

His voice was husky with emotion when he spoke, eyes blazing with ardent love. "Elizabeth, I love you! Nothing that happened today was your fault. Nothing! As soon as you are well, I shall obliterate any memory of another's touch. I will remind you of my devotion on every inch of your skin, burning away any trace of him. I promise you this! In the meantime, let me wash away all evidence of today."

Darcy bathed his wife head to toe with a touch gentle and loving, for the first time ever not becoming aroused by her nakedness. His only desire was to comfort. Stripped to the waist, he sat on a stool by the tub, soaping and scrubbing while she relaxed, nearly falling into a doze. They spoke little, although she did tell him the pains had ceased and there was clearly no bleeding.

The physician arrived just as Darcy placed his damp wife onto the bed. Allowing a maid to dress Lizzy in a nightgown of Julia's, Darcy explained the events of the day to the doctor and described her complaints. A complete exam showed all to be normal. The doctor's recommendation was for her to rest, staying immobile for a couple days at the least. Her bottom was bruised, which may cause some discomfort, but otherwise, he concluded, she was in remarkable health, all things considered.

"Mr. Darcy, I am fairly confident the pains were a result of the stress and shock, augmented by her reported frenzied activity and the fall probably irritating weakened muscles. She needs quiet and rest. The episode has emotionally disturbed her and she needs comforting. However, no activity for two days if the pains remain absent, longer if they resume. No activity, is this clear?" His penetrating gaze left no question as to his meaning.

Darcy flushed slightly, for the first time consciously aware of his improper state of dress. He stiffened, not sure he appreciated the insinuations, but nodded. "I understand."

Peace

THEY TARRIED FOR THREE days in the company of the Sitwells. After a refreshing night's sleep in her husband's arms, Lizzy was nearly her old self. The pains did not return, although her rear end sported an amazingly colorful bruise that was exceedingly tender. She had sporadic nightmares, waking screaming or crying with Victor's face floating in her mind. Darcy was always there, soothing with caresses and kisses until she calmed and returned to sleep.

Julia Sitwell was a constant companion during the daylight hours. She and Lizzy actually delighted in their extended visit, spending hours reclining on comfortable chaises placed under shady trees alongside gently lapping ponds. Darcy hesitantly succumbed to the persuasion of his wife and joined Rory in a fox hunt, horseback riding, and numerous games of faro and billiards, the outcomes of the latter as he had anticipated. The planned excursion to Castleton, Peveril Castle, and Peak Cavern was cancelled, obviously, Darcy beginning to privately suspect a conspiracy to prevent his wife ever seeing the Peak District! Lizzy merely laughed at his theory, restating the fact that the Peaks were going nowhere. Her joy was in the security of their child, who continued to dance on her bladder and demand sustenance on a frequent basis, utterly unaware of the worry inflicted on his poor parents.

Phillips's fever raged uncontrollably for two days. The physician offered meager hope, the ability to counteract infections of this magnitude minimal. Darcy sent Mr. Anders to retrieve Mrs. Phillips and the children from Pemberley. Whether it was the excellent medical care, the love of family, or Phillips's own intestinal fortitude and sturdiness they would never know, but on the morning of the third day, his fever broke. Lizzy, who was forbidden to leave the confines of her bed and visit, cried with heartfelt relief. It was a slow recovery thereafter, but Phillips was fortunate. No bones were broken and the tissue healed without defect. In three weeks, he would be home and partially resuming his duties.

Darcy dealt with all the legal issues regarding the surviving bandits and the two dead ones. It was a routine process involving numerous questions but little else, the case being clear cut. Darcy flatly refused to allow Lizzy to be questioned and there was no need. The Darcy name alone was enough for the magistrate to inquire minimally and render harsh judgment, but the added testimony of Mr. Anders and Phillips left no doubt.

Faced with the doctor's proscription, Darcy was unable to make love to his wife until they returned to Pemberley, a decision Lizzy was none too happy about. She could not argue the logic in being cautious, but she was not pleased. Darcy feared her fragile emotional state far more than curbing his own desires. As in April, the thought of harming his wife or their unborn child was so horrendous that his personal lust was easily cooled. However, remembering Lizzy's verbalized assumption that he would be repulsed by her after Victor's disgusting caresses, he desperately longed to show her how wholly unfounded her apprehension. The balance allotted him the ability to embrace her, caress her body tenderly, kiss possessively, and whisper words of adoration without becoming unduly aroused. In the end, these minor liberties probably allayed any residual horrors from her ordeal more proficiently than actually making love. Darcy's ceaseless fondling and devotion without physical gratification on his part was entirely selfless and effectively erased all residual memory of the thief's touch.

They were greeted on Pemberley's long avenue with a line of horse wagons, Duke Grafton's breeding mares having arrived an hour prior. Darcy hastily kissed Lizzy's cheek, abdicating her care into the steady competence of Mrs.

Reynolds, and disappeared to the stables. Lizzy would not see him until dinner that evening.

The warm familiarity and comfort of Pemberley surrounded and penetrated her very essence. They had only been gone a little over a week and Lizzy had not realized how much she missed the house. All afternoon, she simply walked from room to room, garden to garden, pausing for frequent respites at all her favorite places: Darcy's enormous leather chair in the library, the conservatory, the rose garden, the lily pond, Darcy's study, the terrace corner where they met almost a year ago and where he loved to kiss her as he said he should have done then, the nursery, and finally their bedchamber. She stood gazing out the window at the mountains, tranquility settling into her being, and she finally felt completely cleansed. All she needed now was for her husband to make love to her and all would be right.

Lizzy waited for Darcy in the parlor. She had bathed in jasmine, dressed in a new gown created by Madame Millicent which spectacularly accented her newly acquired curves while hiding her pregnancy. Her hair was lavishly coiffed and bejeweled, and she purposefully stood by the large window with the soft rays of sunset illuminating. The effect was as she anticipated. A freshly washed and elegantly dressed Darcy entered and stopped dead on the threshold, mouth dropping in awe and evidence of desire instantly apparent.

"Elizabeth," he croaked, "my God, you are stunning!" He crossed in quick strides, enfolding her outstretched hands and unabashedly admiring. He shook his head slowly, raising his gaze with difficulty to her beaming face. "You cannot truthfully expect me to calmly consume a full course meal with you sitting next to me like this?"

Lizzy laughed, stepping closer until brushing lightly against his chest. "I seem to recall wise words uttered that anticipation is sweet. Sound familiar, lover mine?"

Darcy groaned, feathering fingers over the generously displayed tops of her breasts. "This may well be my undoing, Elizabeth. I so want you!" His eyes were pleading.

"I have cut the courses in half, William. No dessert, as that shall be served in our chamber. I want you as much, beloved, as you shall see. All night long." She kissed him lightly, Darcy bending to prolong the enjoyment but she pulled away. "Come, my heart. I am starved and I know you have not eaten all day. You *will* need your strength," she finished with an impish grin.

It was a struggle for them both. Lizzy distracted her husband by inquiring as to the horses, and Darcy finally wrenched his gaze from her bosom to his plate as he spoke animatedly about the mares. Gradually, they calmed enough to dine, both of them quite hungry—Darcy especially, who ate a massive quantity as he talked. The meal passed pleasantly, passion quenched for a time in the joy of companionship and fine cuisine. Lizzy finished well before her husband, sitting back as she sipped her wine and observed him in happy serenity.

She was captivated by his face. She knew now why he presented to the world such a severe, regulated countenance. It was because without that rigid control, every thought and emotion was communicated on his face as clearly as a lighthouse beacon on a cloudless night. His eyes sparkled and flashed, lips lifted and twisted revealingly with each word spoken, brows arched and knitted affectively, and his skin glowed. Even his voice betrayed his sentiments. Lizzy had been amazed to discover the range of tones to his voice, how the timbre of his speech altered within the naturally resonant and dulcet tonality.

He laid the utensils aside, picking up his wine glass and relaxing into the chair as he drank, and turned his gaze upon his smiling wife. "You seem amused by something, Mrs. Darcy. Have I entertained you in some manner?"

"Your presence entertains me, my love. I find tremendous pleasure in merely staring at you."

Darcy held her gaze, smiling salaciously as he curtly ordered the lurking servants to leave. Reaching, he captured her hand, bringing the palm to his lips for a soft kiss. Never looking away from her eyes, he lightly licked her inner wrist, traveling leisurely over the creases to each fingertip for gentle sucks. Lizzy already felt dizzy, swaying as he rose and simultaneously pulled her onto her feet.

"Fitzwilliam," she began, but he shushed her with a fingertip to her lips, gliding airily over the ruddy fullness to her chin then down her neck, throat, breastbone, until dipping into her cleavage, smoldering eyes trailing. Dark, impassioned eyes briefly encountering her equally feverish ones, Darcy smiled then lowered his head to her bosom, moist mouth pressing firmly onto the crevice created by the swell of each mound. He moaned faintly, as did Lizzy, abruptly sweeping her into his arms and marching from the room.

His strides were powerful and hasty down what seemed like endless hallways and up the extensive flight of stairs, both of them restrained until the third floor landing whereupon Lizzy began working the knots of his cravat while licking his ear, and fingers of her other hand entwining in his hair. Darcy stopped suddenly, eyes closed and breathing deeply but not from exertion, the burden of his wife minimal.

"Lord, Elizabeth! Please desist or I will walk us into a wall!"

"Only if you hurry, William. I cannot resist for long." He looked at her blazing eyes, leaning his head down with a groan to kiss her ardently. Seconds later, they were stretched onto their bed, fully clothed with hands frantically reaching to remove encumbering fabric. Mere seconds more and they were merged, entangled, and propelling with pent up passion, but also with the necessity on both their parts to blot out the final remnants of the horrible recent events and ensure their possessive bond.

"I love you, Elizabeth! Sweet, beautiful wife, how I love you!" It was sheer rapture, unifying and cleansing. They lay for a spell, breathing heavily as they recovered, stroking and kissing. Endless minutes of studied devotion and placid communion followed. No words; only eyes locked with silent messages speaking volumes.

Lizzy rose first, fingering over his face and leaning for a brushing kiss. "I absolutely must feel all your skin, my heart, and feast on your flesh. I will not be utterly satisfied until I have seduced you several more times at the least." Darcy chuckled lowly, offering no argument. Instead, he reached to twine a loose tress of hair around his finger while Lizzy completely removed his cravat, promptly leaning for a lingering kiss to the pulsing hollow of his throat.

She sat, discarding their shoes and stockings, and then pulled him to his feet, Darcy happy to follow her lead. The process of undressing each other was a familiar one, but it never failed to arouse them both profoundly. He liked to tease her about the multiple layers of women's clothing, but the truth was he relished the joy of incrementally peeling each garment off her alabaster skin. The delight of slowly revealing the other's body to hungry eyes while stimulating tactile nerves was tremendously exciting. The layers covering his flesh were as numerous as hers, and she too savored the revelation as he disrobed.

Never, ever would Lizzy tire of seeing her husband's body. Lean and muscular, fair skin with scattered freckles across the shoulders, hard with rigid planes, round and tight on the rear, all of him so incredibly male. She fluttered and became astoundingly inflamed simply by the appearance of him. Of course, her arousal was heightened by the touch of his warm, firm hands all over her body. Nor would she ever not thrill to the obvious incitement he felt to her ministrations. The relaxed Darcy was a man transparent with his emotions. Not only in his face, as noted earlier, but in all ways. He gasped and shivered every time her hands encountered his skin. Running her hands up his bare chest, feathering over puckered nipples, around to shoulder blades, and then down the spine to taut buttocks; all this was met with moans, wheezing respirations, and quivers of rushing desire. It was the one place—the only place—where Darcy lost all restraint.

They kissed everywhere. Darcy moved around to her backside, kissing from the delicious nape of her neck down to the bruise on her tailbone, his hands caressing her trembling muscles. Lizzy moaned, Darcy unrelenting in his attention to her skin. Not once did the memory of the thief's rough fingers invade her mind. Her husband's delicate touch of fine-boned, graceful hands transcended all else and effectively annihilated anything else. He stood, hands flattening on her thighs as he pressed her against him.

"Elizabeth, my Elizabeth, how I hunger for you. I love you so consumingly I do believe I shall burst from the emotion! Let me please you, my soul. Know what it is to be touched by one who lives for your presence, for your voice, for your kiss, for your shining eyes, for your smile…" On and on he spoke huskily as he pleased her, Lizzy writhing onto his naked chest until sagging in repletion. Darcy held her securely and bestowed hot kisses to her neck. Picking her up into his arms they relocated to the bed, Darcy ceaselessly kissing her.

He stretched beside her, propped on an elbow while lazily fondling. He gently cradled their baby, waiting, but the precious bundle of joy was asleep. "How do you feel? Any pains?"

Lizzy shook her head, resting over his hand with her own, and the other brushing over his chest. "No pains, only heavenly shivers of pleasure. Fitzwilliam?" He looked into her eyes, blue depths brimming with happiness. "You do know how wholeheartedly I love you? How perfect you are and how thoroughly you fulfill me?"

He smiled, bending for a soft kiss. "I have no doubts, my Lizzy. I know I do not deserve you, but I accept your love as a gift." He ran his hand along her inner thigh, Lizzy shivering involuntarily and releasing a muted moan. Darcy chuckled, kissing her nose. "Only one who loves me profoundly could respond as you do, lover. I do not think you that fine an actress." He snared her lower lip, sucking, his hand stroking her masterfully.

Lizzy arched against him, ardor renewing instantly with his touch.

"William! Unfair." She rolled to face him fully, reaching to caress him. "I want to pleasure you as well, my husband. Give equally, fulfilling you until you do burst, my love." She kissed over his heart, stroking gently. "Bursting deep inside me, my perfect lover, gloriously linked so intimately."

Darcy's eyes closed in rising delirium, face buried in her hair as she electrified each nerve with her touch and kisses. As graceful and flawless as the finest dancer, she maneuvered all over his body, spurring his yearning to celestial heights. She paused, poised beautifully above him. They stared, enraptured by sensations and the face of their heart's survival gazing in return.

"William, I love you. Forever."

Sliding, swaying, caressing, and watching. Entering a timeless realm of sheer pleasure and connection. Marriage as it should be... two individuals loving the other more than they cared for themselves. Giving and giving until theoretically they should be empty, yet always invigorated with more to give. There was physical ecstasy to be sure, beyond the imaginings either had ever entertained. Yet it was the soul relationship that drove them on. There were no words in the human language to adequately describe this nexus and the sensations educed. Perhaps a heavenly, angelic voice could convey the depth. Darcy and Lizzy could only feel. Raw passion and intrinsic lust merged so blissfully with supernatural affinity and intimacy.

About the Author

Sharon Lathan is a native Californian currently residing amid corn, cotton, and cows in the sunny San Joaquin Valley. She divides her time between being a homemaker, nurturing her own Mr. Darcy and two teenaged children, and working as a registered nurse in a Neonatal ICU. Throw in the cat, dog, and a ton of fish to complete the picture. When not at the hospital or attending to the often dreary tasks of homemaking, she is generally found reposing in her comfy recliner with her faithful laptop. For more information about Sharon and her Darcy Saga serial, visit her website at: http://www.darcysaga.net.

Mr. and Mrs. Fitzwilliam Darcy: Two Shall Become One
SHARON LATHAN

"Highly entertaining... I felt fully immersed in the time period. Well done!" —*Romance Reader at Heart*

A fascinating portrait of a timeless, consuming love

It's Darcy and Elizabeth's wedding day, and the journey is just beginning as Jane Austen's beloved *Pride and Prejudice* characters embark on the greatest adventure of all: marriage and a life together filled with surprising passion, tender self-discovery, and the simple joys of every day.

As their love story unfolds in this most romantic of Jane Austen sequels, Darcy and Elizabeth each reveal to the other how their relationship blossomed from misunderstanding to perfect understanding and harmony, and a marriage filled with romance, sensuality and the beauty of a deep, abiding love.

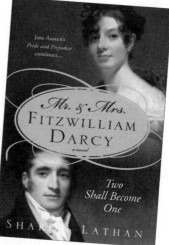

What readers are saying:

"This journey is truly amazing."

"What a wonderful beginning to this truly beautiful marriage."

"Could not stop reading."

"So beautifully written...making me feel as though I was in the room with Lizzy and Darcy...and sharing in all of the touching moments between."

978-1-4022-1523-0 • $14.99 US/ $15.99 CAN/ £7.99 UK

Mrs. Darcy's Dilemma
DIANA BIRCHALL

"Fascinating, and such wonderful use of language."
—JOAN AUSTEN-LEIGH

It seemed a harmless invitation, after all...

When Mrs. Darcy invited her sister Lydia's daughters to come for a visit, she felt it was a small kindness she could do for her poor nieces. Little did she imagine the upheaval that would ensue. But with her elder son, the Darcys' heir, in danger of losing his heart, a theatrical scandal threatening to engulf them all, and daughter Jane on the verge of her come-out, the Mistress of Pemberley must make some difficult decisions…

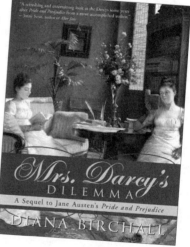

"Birchall's witty, elegant visit to the middle-aged Darcys is a delight." —PROFESSOR JANET TODD, UNIVERSITY OF GLASGOW

"A refreshing and entertaining look at the Darcys some years after *Pride and Prejudice* from a most accomplished author." —JENNY SCOTT, AUTHOR OF *After Jane*

978-1-4022-1156-0 • $14.95

The Darcys Give a Ball
ELIZABETH NEWARK

"A tour de force." —MARILYN SACHS, AUTHOR OF *First Impressions*

Whatever will Mr. Darcy say...

...with his son falling in love, his daughter almost lured into an elopement, and his niece the new target of Miss Caroline Bingley's meddling, Mr. Darcy has his hands full keeping the next generation away from scandal.

Sons and daughters share the physical and personality traits of their parents, but of course have minds of their own—and as Mrs. Darcy says to her beloved sister Jane Bingley: "The romantic attachments of one's children are a constant distraction."

Amidst all this distraction and excitement, Jane and Elizabeth plan a lavish ball at Pemberley, where all the young people come together for a surprising and altogether satisfying ending.

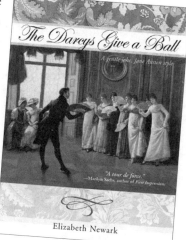

What readers are saying:

"A light-hearted visit to Austen country."

"A wonderful look into what could have happened!"

"The characters ring true, the situation is perfect, the conclusion is everything you hope for."

"A wonder of character and action... an unmixed pleasure!"

978-1-4022-1131-7 • $12.95 US/ $15.50 CAN/ £6.99 UK

Mr. Darcy's Diary
AMANDA GRANGE

"A gift to a new generation of Darcy fans
and a treat for existing fans as well." —AUSTENBLOG

The only place Darcy could share his innermost feelings...

...was in the private pages of his diary. Torn between his sense of duty to his family name and his growing passion for Elizabeth Bennet, all he can do is struggle not to fall in love. A skillful and graceful imagining of the hero's point of view in one of the most beloved and enduring love stories of all time.

What readers are saying:

"A delicious treat for all Austen addicts."

"Amanda Grange knows her subject... I ended up reading the entire book in one sitting."

"Brilliant, you could almost hear Darcy's voice... I was so sad when it came to an end. I loved the visions she gave us of their married life."

"Amanda Grange has perfectly captured all of Jane Austen's clever wit and social observations to make *Mr. Darcy's Diary* a must read for any fan."

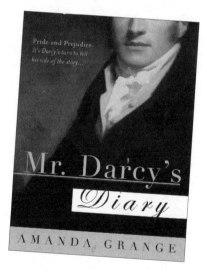

978-1-4022-0876-8 • $14.95 US/ $19.95 CAN/ £7.99 UK

The Pemberley Chronicles

A Companion Volume to Jane Austen's Pride and Prejudice

The Pemberley Chronicles: Book 1

REBECCA ANN COLLINS

"A lovely complementary novel to Jane Austen's *Pride and Prejudice*.
Austen would surely give her smile of approval."
—BEVERLY WONG, AUTHOR OF *Pride & Prejudice Prudence*

The weddings are over, the saga begins

The guests (including millions of readers and viewers) wish the two happy couples health and happiness. As the music swells and the credits roll, two things are certain: Jane and Bingley will want for nothing, while Elizabeth and Darcy are to be the happiest couple in the world!

Elizabeth and Darcy's personal stories of love, marriage, money, and children are woven together with the threads of social and political history of England in the nineteenth century. As changes in industry and agriculture affect the people of Pemberley and the surrounding countryside, the Darcys strive to be progressive and forward-looking while upholding beloved traditions.

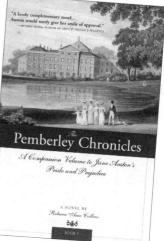

"Those with a taste for the balance and humour of Austen will find a worthy companion volume."
—*Book News*

978-1-4022-1153-9 • $14.96 US/ $17.95 CAN/ £7.99 UK

The Women of Pemberley

The acclaimed **Pride and Prejudice** *sequel series*

The Pemberley Chronicles: Book 2

REBECCA ANN COLLINS

"Yet another wonderful work by Ms. Collins."
—BEVERLY WONG, AUTHOR OF *Pride & Prejudice Prudence*

A new age is dawning

Five women—strong, intelligent, independent of mind, and in the tradition of many Jane Austen heroines—continue the legacy of Pemberley into a dynamic new era at the start of the Victorian Age. Events unfold as the real and fictional worlds intertwine, linked by the relationship of the characters to each other and to the great estate of Pemberley, the heart of their community.

With some characters from the beloved works of Jane Austen, and some new from the author's imagination, the central themes of love, friendship, marriage, and a sense of social obligation remain, showcased in the context of the sweeping political and social changes of the age.

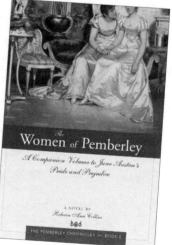

"The stories are so well told one would enjoy them even if they were not sequels to any other novel."
—*Book News*

978-1-4022-1154-6 • $14.96 US/ $17.95 CAN/ £7.99 UK

Netherfield Park Revisited

The acclaimed **Pride and Prejudice** *sequel series*

The Pemberley Chronicles: Book 3

REBECCA ANN COLLINS

"A very readable and believable tale for readers
who like their romance with a historical flavor." —*Book News*

Love, betrayal, and changing times for the Darcys and the Bingleys

Three generations of the Darcy and the Bingley families evolve against a backdrop of the political ideals and social reforms of the mid-Victorian era.

Jonathan Bingley, the handsome, distinguished son of Charles and Jane Bingley, takes center stage, returning to Hertfordshire as master of Netherfield Park. A deeply passionate and committed man, Jonathan is immersed in the joys and heartbreaks of his friends and family and his own challenging marriage. At the same time, he is swept up in the changes of the world around him.

Netherfield Park Revisited combines captivating details of life in mid-Victorian England with the ongoing saga of Jane Austen's beloved *Pride and Prejudice* characters.

"Ms. Collins has done it again!" —BEVERLY WONG,
AUTHOR OF *Pride & Prejudice Prudence*

978-1-4022-1155-3 • $14.95 US/ $15.99 CAN/ £7.99 UK

The Ladies of Longbourn

The acclaimed **Pride and Prejudice** *sequel series*

The Pemberley Chronicles: Book 4

REBECCA ANN COLLINS

"Interesting stories, enduring themes, gentle humour, and lively dialogue." —*Book News*

A complex and charming young woman of the Victorian age, tested to the limits of her endurance

The bestselling *Pemberley Chronicles* series continues the saga of the Darcys and Bingleys from Jane Austen's *Pride and Prejudice* and introduces imaginative new characters.

Anne-Marie Bradshaw is the granddaughter of Charles and Jane Bingley. Her father now owns Longbourn, the Bennet's estate in Hertfordshire. A young widow after a loveless marriage, Anne-Marie and her stepmother Anna, together with Charlotte Collins, widow of the unctuous Mr. Collins, are the Ladies of Longbourn. These smart, independent women challenge the conventional roles of women in the Victorian era, while they search for ways to build their own lasting legacies in an ever-changing world.

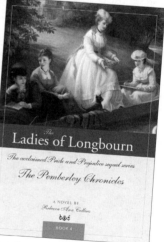

Jane Austen's original characters—Darcy, Elizabeth, Bingley, and Jane—anchor a dramatic story full of wit and compassion.

"A masterpiece that reaches the heart."
—BEVERLEY WONG, AUTHOR OF *Pride & Prejudice Prudence*

978-1-4022-1219-2 • $14.95 US/ $15.99 CAN/ £7.99 UK

Eliza's Daughter

A Sequel to Jane Austen's Sense and Sensibility

JOAN AIKEN

"Others may try, but nobody comes close to Aiken in writing sequels to Jane Austen." —*Publishers Weekly*

A young woman longing for adventure and an artistic life...

Because she's an illegitimate child, Eliza is raised in the rural backwater with very little supervision. An intelligent, creative, and free-spirited heroine, unfettered by the strictures of her time, she makes friends with poets William Wordsworth and Samuel Coleridge, finds her way to London, and eventually travels the world, all the while seeking to solve the mystery of her parentage. With fierce determination and irrepressible spirits, Eliza carves out a life full of adventure and artistic endeavor.

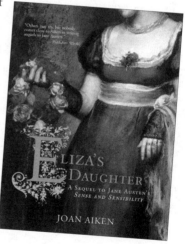

"Aiken's story is rich with humor, and her language is compelling. Readers captivated with Elinor and Marianne Dashwood in *Sense and Sensibility* will thoroughly enjoy Aiken's crystal gazing, but so will those unacquainted with Austen." —*Booklist*

"...innovative storyteller Aiken again pays tribute to Jane Austen in a cheerful spin-off of *Sense and Sensibility*." —*Kirkus Reviews*

978-1-4022-1288-8 • $14.95 US/ $15.99 CAN

Mansfield Park Revisited

A Jane Austen Entertainment

JOAN AIKEN

"A lovely read—and you don't have to have read
Mansfield Park to enjoy it." —*Woman's Own*

It's not so easy to keep scandal at bay...

After Fanny Price marries Edmund Bertram, they depart for the Caribbean, and
Fanny's younger sister Susan moves to Mansfield Park as Lady Bertram's new
companion. Surrounded by the familiar cast of characters from Jane Austen's original,
and joined by a few charming new characters introduced by the author, Susan finds
herself entangled in romance, surprise, scandal, and redemption.

Joan Aiken's diverting tale vividly imagines how
the Crawfords might have turned out, and Jane
Austen's moral tale takes new directions—with an
unexpected and somewhat controversial ending.

"Her sense of time and place is impeccable."
—*Publishers Weekly*

"An excellent sequel...remarkably effective and
very funny." —*Evening Standard*

978-1-4022-1289-5 • $14.95 US/ $15.99 CAN